PERSEPHONE

PERSEPHONE

First Contact

WILLIAM ROLSTON

ARPress
45 Dan Road Suite 5
Canton MA 02021

Hotline: 1(888) 821-0229
Fax: 1(508) 545-7580

Ordering Information:
Quantity sales. Special discounts are available on quantity purchases by corporations, associations, and others. For details, contact the publisher at the address above.

Printed in the United States of America.

ISBN-13:   Paperback   979-8-89330-897-6
                eBook   979-8-89330-899-0
                Hardcover   979-8-89330-898-3

Library of Congress Control Number: 2024902461

TABLE OF CONTENTS

Stories should start at the beginning. But opinions differ as to what "the beginning" of any story really is. Some would claim that the nature of the God who created all things is really the beginning of any story. Others would say The Beginning was the creation of the Universe. A third set would claim that our stories begin with the Fall of the First Person, and the subsequent introduction of evil across the galaxy. A narrower view would say that any story about space travel should begin with L'Terr's first discovery of the Intersections that allowed for movement between solar systems. Since Terrans are involved, many would move "The Beginning" all the way out to the first Terran travel from the system of the Alpha world of Terra to a new planetary system. The most restrictive beginning, the one specific to only this story, would be the third day Stephen Hunter had failed to fix the recurring software bug in the detection computer aboard the starship *Persephone*.

For the last three days, Hunter had been unable to track down the software failure that was causing false warnings to be displayed on the search computer. The long range scans were being ruined by occasional bursts of light that would appear and disappear on the screen. There was no pattern to the behavior, and all the diagnostic software kept reporting that the software was running fine. Hunter would have written the whole thing off as a one- time glitch, but it had occurred four times in the last four days. He verified that the problems couldn't be reproduced in the test program, and wrote up his report that the whole thing should be ignored until the ship went back for its 6-month refit on-planet. His captain, a bitter woman who found Stephen to be a useless waste of space, refused the report, and told him to fix the bug before his next sleep shift.

Stephen had had the usual physics and astrodynamics classes, and like everyone else, had forgotten almost everything within a year or so. His job dealt with software development, and software repair. If asked, he could probably recite the usual description of how it had been postulated that incomplete dimensional expansion could form joint regions of space. He could describe in rough terms how a chunk of space therefore existed in multiple places simultaneously, and how a ship small enough to fit completely inside the "Intersection" could fly into the joint space from one place and exit in another. Although he could recite the words, he didn't really remember the details or their importance. He didn't need to worry about dimensions for his job; he needed to be able to write and run software, and find out why on-board systems like the detection computer had problems.

His three days of work had not gone unnoticed by his friends. Stephen had been part of the group request for a "retro" movie week, but had now missed both *It Came to Mars* and *Space Serves Death Cold*. His failed attempts to find the problem were interrupted by a call from a fellow retro fanatic from the Search team. The wall screen was filled with Darron Mason. After a long description of how he was working on something that couldn't be solved, because there was no problem, and the captain wouldn't listen, Stephen started talking about all the things he had been trying in the past three days. Darron listened to all the software jargon he didn't understand, and threw in a comment about the one thing he recognized in the displays behind Stephen.

"So you think the software glitches are connected with the Intersections?" he asked.

"No, the flashes look random. We aren't going through any holes or anything." As soon as he had said the sentence, Stephen recognized his dreadful mistake. Experienced crewmen knew to never say "Hole" to one of the Physicists. If the entire "Intersections not Holes" speech was triggered, the real experts could listen to the entire ten minute talk, nod at all the right times, look very serious and interested, and spend the entire time deciding whether Waffles or Pancakes were the better breakfast food. If he had to get another lecture about Intersections, or rather the same lecture yet again, he would have preferred to have the lecture from *It Came to Mars* when the station captain told the new recruit how the alien had reached Mars – 'The holes are different spots that are in two places at the same time. The Hole is here, and it is also in a different solar system, or galaxy. It is sort of like how an elevator shaft is on every floor of the building at the same time. If you can fit in the elevator and the doors will shut, you can walk in on one level and walk out on a completely different floor.'

"They aren't "Holes", they are Intersections." Darron said automatically. "There is no such thing as a "hole" in space. An Intersection is the set of points which simultaneously exists in multiple sets of points in disassociated regions of space. It is called an Intersection, of course, because of the terminology of basic set definitions. These joint regions are the opposite of holes – they are where two sections of space, often light-years apart, are actually the same location …" Stephen set his face to 'serious and listening', and nodded. "It was once believed that the dimensional expansion after the Big Bang was uniform and linear. But it is now known that the expansion was irregular, nonlinear, and incomplete. Points, even small regions of space, are connected to the locations around them as the locations expand apart, and are at the same time, still unseparated from other Points that are connected to locations expanding in a completely different direction… " A long time later, Stephen tried to come back to the present when the last sentence was off-script. He asked Darron to repeat the question.

"So, why do you have the chart with the Intersections if it isn't connected to the bug?" repeated Darron.

Stephen looked back to the chart on a screen behind him. "Those aren't Intersections, those are the four failures – I plotted the time and location of the bright spots to see if they were connected to specific times, like operator shift changes, or specific directions, maybe from a faulty sensor. But they aren't. There isn't any pattern at all." Darron's face on the display looked a bit confused, then suspicious, then confused again. He asked again what the original problem had been.

"The detection computer keeps showing a big e-m spike that flashes up and then disappears. Messages show up all over about changes in light intensity, and it drives the operators nuts. They have to clear everything out and reset the registers for the light pulse detectors. But there isn't anything there, and the bright spot appears and is gone. Like I was saying, none of the diagnostics shows anything wrong with the computer, or the detectors. And I can't… " Stephen trailed off as he saw Darron's face had gone completely blank; he was staring at the chart behind Stephen. Stephen waited a few minutes, then slowly waved his hand back and forth in front of the chart until he saw Darron refocus. Darron looked at Stephen, and turned off the monitor.

Stephen decided that it was once again time to disobey the Captain's orders and go to bed. Maybe he could understand the problem, and his friends, better after some sleep. He was just shutting things down when Darron walked into the lab. Darron didn't even say hello. He just asked Stephen to repeat everything about the failure. Stephen was a little worried at how focused Darron seemed on the entire description. Darron then demanded Stephen bring up every piece of information about the flashes – recorded frequencies, intensities, durations, variability, times – everything.

Stephen started to call up all the data and looked back at his bizarre friend. Darron was flying through the data, checking off information. He looked up at Stephen, and his face had gone white.

"That is your chart of the failures, not a chart of the Intersections?" Darron demanded. Stephen assured him that the chart, and the failures, had nothing to do with Intersections.

Darron turned to the monitor with the failure chart displayed. "Computer, access current local Intersection map, authority Darron Mason. Display identified Intersections on current graph, same axis definition." The monitor flashed and a second display overlaid Stephen's chart. It showed 17 identified Intersections – the local Intersection field *Persephone* was currently mapping. Four of the discovered Intersections fell exactly on the four locations from which the light pulses had been displayed.

Darron turned back to Stephen. "You know that the Intersections have different gravity profiles than normal space. They are close to the mass in both regions, not just the mass on one side. That's how we find them – we send out swathes of light, and have detectors all the way out beyond the Intersection field. The detectors send back the received light to the ship. The detection computer looks for any slight variation in the path of the signal, indicating a gravity disturbance, or a slight variation in the strength of the signal, indicating that some of the light has gone through the Intersection to the other side. If you were on the other side, looking at the same Intersection, you would see a brief flash of light as part of our pulse came through, then nothing."

Stephen looked at Darron for a moment, then said slowly, "So these aren't software bugs. We are seeing the same thing someone would see if they were on the other side watching us search for Intersections."

Darron pointed at the records of the light pulses. "Someone is on the other side, looking for the field just like we are. But the frequencies used are different from ours, and different from any survey ship I have ever heard of.

And that pulse is much larger than anything we could use for scanning. And either there are more than one of them, or they had to accelerate at 6-g for a day to send out the third pulse you recorded, and the fourth just nine hours later. The best *Persephone* can manage is 3.2-g, and we can only do that for a few hours. We are here looking for ways to get further out into space.

Someone, or some-*thing*, is out there, looking for ways to get further in."

Persephone ran on the usual 24-hour, 3-shift schedule maintained by almost all starships. It was easiest to set schedules similar to the familiar 24-hour schedules and shift changes from Earth. "Night" was determined by when the crew decided to power down and sleep, and "Day" was determined by when the crew powered things back up again, and showed up for the first shift. The equipment ran continuously; most analysis was performed on the first shift, when the majority of the crew was awake and able to coordinate as needed. Third shift had the fewest alert crewmen – mainly operators watching the equipment as it ran along on its own – so the captain and almost the entire crew were asleep when Stephen and Darron requested entrance to the captain's quarters at two in the morning, local *Persephone* time. After a minute, they heard the captain's voice telling them to come inside.

Stephen couldn't help looking around a bit as they entered. He hadn't been inside the captain's quarters since he was assigned to the ship two years previously. When Stephen had first joined, Acting Captain Adams had invited all of the new crewmembers to dinner in her quarters to welcome them aboard. He hadn't been invited back since. The room looked normal before, and looked almost empty now. The viewscreen used to display two people he had assumed were her husband and son; now the viewscreen was blank. There had been the usual scattering of pictures and trinkets; now the room had printouts, several mobile displays, and nothing else but some clothes on the floor. The captain looked much older and grayer than the not- yet-promoted woman from two years ago. Captain Adams was fully dressed – she had learned long ago that the fastest way to cause a problem on board was to go to bed relaxed and comfortable. Captain Adams had the pained and disgusted look of someone who has just been woken from a deep sleep. She squinted at the two annoyances, and said simply, "Well?"

Stephen and Darron looked at each other for a second, then Stephen answered, "It isn't a software bug."

The Captain looked at Stephen with resignation and disgust. "At least that is a straight answer – something I rarely get from you. Two-thirds of all the problems you are assigned you never fix – you claim they aren't really problems, or they can't be solved. So you now you have to wake me up in the middle of the night to tell me so?"

Darron said, "The recorded light bursts are real. Coming out of the Intersections."

Captain Adams was coming awake enough to look carefully at the faces of her two crewmen. "Come in and tell me what's up." She motioned to the table, and sank into a chair on the other side. Darron summarized the original problem, the locations of the lights, and the probable cause. Captain Adams listened to the entire story in silence. When he finished the report, Captain Adams yawned, lowered her head, and was silent for several minutes. Stephen and Darron looked awkwardly at each other and waited, each wondering if the Captain had fallen asleep. After what seemed to them like an eternity, Captain Adams looked up, wide-awake. "Is it possible that we have found a sort of circle of Intersections? That the other side of the Intersection field is actually back at our home system itself? If there were established stations on the other side, they might use different frequencies, and be able to utilize much greater light intensity than we do."

"I don't believe so, sir. If there was a system on the other side, we would have detected the gravity much faster. The other side is almost certainly a region of empty space, just like this side. And the Earth system is pretty well mapped. It is possible that someone is still looking for Intersections, but it is doubtful. The light also wouldn't be coming and going. This looks like someone, or many someones, moving across the field."

Captain Adams nodded in agreement. "The three colony systems have some capability to produce their own vessels, and they aren't as fully cooperative with the Earth Space Command as many of us would like. Could one of the independent fleets be searching the same place we are?"

"I don't believe so, sir. The light intensity would require a bigger ship than I have ever heard of an independent being able to build. And every ship we have uses the same frequency to search with. To use something different, they would have to build all new equipment, instead of just using something off-the-shelf."

Captain Adams nodded in agreement. "So if these readings are correct, there is something, probably alien, probably far more advanced than us, right on the other side of those holes."

Darron's mouth automatically opened at the word "holes". Darron's brain, uncharacteristically connected to reality and common sense at the moment, realized he was about to lecture his commanding officer and snapped his mouth back shut.

Captain Adams looked seriously at Stephen. "If we start reporting about aliens, we have to be right. If we send out a false alarm, the end of all our careers will be the least of the Fleet's worries. Are you Absolutely Sure the readings are real? That there really is no failure of any type with the software?"

Stephen met her gaze for a moment, then answered, "The software is working properly. The data can be trusted."

Captain Adams kept focused on Stephen. "We are betting everything on this data, and once we start taking action, there is no going back. I ask again, are you Absolutely Sure?"

"Yes."

The ghost of a smile, and a brief look of respect crossed the captain's face. She was silent again for several minutes, then continued. "Well done, the both of you. If they have been there for a long time already, I don't think they will attack in the next few hours. Get some sleep. This stays between us. Tomorrow, I want you both to go back over every piece of data we have captured from the field, and see if there is any indication of similar readings in the past. Dismissed." Stephen and Darron saluted, and stepped out of the cabin. They looked at each other, muttered some random observations about the cabin, about the interview, about movies Stephen had missed, and about how late it was, and then separated to their cabins.

Darron's scream woke him; he found himself sitting half-up on his bunk, with the visions of the alien attack still in his mind. He shook his head, and rubbed his eyes, partly because he was still exhausted, and partly because that assured him that his eyes were still there — they really hadn't been ripped out by the alien's tentacles. Sitting up in bed, Darron solemnly promised himself that he would never, ever again watch *Space Serves Death Cold* the night before probably discovering the first alien species ever detected by Mankind.

He started touched the wall as he laid back down, and sat back up again with a jerk. The wall had been vibrating. Built into the wall of the ship were the angular-to-linear converters, "angulins", that pushed the ship through space, and that powered all of the onboard ship systems.

The angulin was a converter attached to a huge, spinning slab of material so dense it weighed about as much as a 10-story building. When the ship had left Loren Station, all of the angulins had been charged up so that they were spinning as fast as possible. Anchors held the angulins in place inside the hull of the vehicle.

When the converter was activated, the spinning angulin slowed down slightly, and started moving straight forward. Because it was anchored into the hull of the ship, the entire ship was pulled forward with it. This caused the ship hull to be stressed; the *Persephone* had to spend a full 6 months having the hull repaired after her 6-month survey. If the anchors came loose, an unbalanced angulin could start tearing the ship apart. Darron had a brief moment of panic before realizing that the wall had not been rocking back and forth, his hand had been. Darron hadn't been able to sleep until about four o'clock, and it was only seven o'clock when he had woken. He decided it was hopeless to try and get back to sleep, and got ready for the day. After a few minutes, he headed out to the mess hall for breakfast.

The trip to the mess hall was only about 40 feet – since a starship had to fit completely inside an Intersection to be able to emerge in a different location than the one from which it entered, space was always the greatest restriction on any ship design. When crossing through an Intersection, *Persephone* was folded into a ball only 200 foot across. Once through, wings extended out which held communications equipment and detection devices. The "front" of the ship would pull out from the ball, and the "rear" launching bay would extend back. The center of the ship would unfold into the living quarters and extra storage for the crew. During jumps, most ship systems were disabled; whenever possible, equipment would be broken down and carefully arranged in close-packed storage. The human crew could not be broken down, but they could be stored in rows of bunks 15 inches tall, 4 foot wide, and 7 foot long. Properly stacked, rows of bunks could contain the entire 120 person crew in two storage compartments. The crew was the last thing to be stored away before the jump, but stacking everyone up took time, and crossing the Intersection itself took time. The ship had to be entirely contained within the Intersection to have a chance of exiting into a different region of space. Once inside and moving back out, it was random whether the ship would exit back into the region from which it came or into the new region of space it was trying to reach. If the Intersection was exited back into the region of space you started from, there was no choice but to come back around and try the whole process over again. Each time, the exact alignment of the ship with the Intersection had to be performed, and if the ship and the Intersection were very close to the same size, this itself could be a long process. Depending on how many times the ship had to enter and exit the Intersection to happen to come out on the other side, the crew might spend several hours in storage. The lowest-ranking personnel were the unfortunate ones packed first and unpacked last. Emergency personnel packed themselves in last in case they had to respond during a crossing; the lucky few actually involved in the crossing itself got to sit in real chairs at their workstations on the uncompressed bridge.

Claustrophobia could take hold rapidly with everyone packed in tight. Many crewmen attached earphones and tried to pretend to sleep the entire time. Some responded by going completely quiet and trying to wish the whole situation over, and many responded to the compression by talking to everyone in the compartment. Being packed in for crossing had other dangers as well. Before the first crossing of the trip out to their current survey, Susan Underwood – a normally-rational crewman - had been so thoughtless as to make the double mistakes of drinking coffee and then forgetting to use the restroom before Crossing. It had been a very tight fit for the ship, so aligning the ship in the Intersection took significant time. The first try failed – the ship exited back where it started in the solar system containing Loren Station. As the bridge crew were lining things up for a second try, Susan's muttered curses on the slow bridge crew and pleas that this crossing would succeed were audible to the crewmen packed around her. As successive crossings failed, her louder and louder comments about the bridge crew were drowned out by the louder and louder snickering. By the fourth attempt, the entire compartment was laughing, with the loud prayers of the crewman beneath her leading the rest on. It was believed to be the only time that people had actually wanted to have a crossing fail, just so they could listen to Susan's complaints go even higher. Most of the time nothing much happened on a starship, so Susan's distress was told and retold to the crewmen who had been packed in the other compartment, and Susan received endless ribbing for months.

Darron walked the 40 feet, and everything around him seemed like a dream. The people passing by looked like aliens themselves – it was as if he had never really focused on his shipmates before, and was seeing them now for the first time, through an alien's eyes. The characteristics of the ship stood out as if floodlights were shining on every piece of equipment. He was still exhausted, and all the sounds seemed unfamiliar and filled with meaning he didn't understand. He took out a prepared tray of "breakfast", heated it up, and found a seat. Instead of eating, he just sat and looked at the food.

Everything seemed so *improbable*, almost ridiculous. "Corn" was a plant you stuck in the ground. It grew up like magic, then you tore parts off, ground them down, stuck the pieces back together, stuck it in a heat source, and then ate it. He had never really thought about food – it was just there. He imagined trying to describe the process to something that had never eaten a plant before. He wondered if the aliens even had plants. He wondered if the aliens were plants. He wondered if "plant" really had any meaning, or made any difference. Yesterday, corn and humans seemed very different – parts of completely different kingdoms of biology. Tomorrow corn and humans might seem more closely related than nearly anything in the universe – both were from Earth, and whatever they might meet probably was not. The crewman sitting across from him was named Jones. Maybe. He had never taken much time to really get to know most of the people on board. They were just sort of there. Jones was pretty amazing. He had hands and feet that worked. Fingers, and fingernails that were stuck in them somehow, and didn't fall out. Would the aliens have fingernails? If they didn't and asked what kept the fingernails in the fingers, Darron couldn't tell them.

Eyes were amazing. They took an entire outside world of e-m radiation and processed it into *sight*. Then Jones' brain took all those inputs from hands, and eyes, and ears, and other stuff, and built it into a coherent world – the same coherent world everyone else individually built. If Darron thought about it, Jones was so amazing and improbable, he wouldn't have believed such a device could exist – but Darron never really had thought about it, he had just sat down and ate each day and took the miracle that was Jones for granted. The crewman who might be Jones thought for a second that he had something on his face as he saw Darron stop staring at his food and start staring at him, but then decided that Darron was just weird. He asked if something was wrong, and Darron snapped back to breakfast and said everything was fine, sorry, said something else he didn't remember, even as he said it. Darron started to eat as the crewman who might be Jones watched him cautiously.

After breakfast Darron headed back out to go over the recorded data Stephen was retrieving. He found Stephen up and already in the lab. Darron started reviewing the records as Stephen continued the retrieval. From the nose down Stephen looked as tired as Darron. His eyes were alert, almost wide. He was working fast, writing small retrieval routines on the spot to pull out any combination of data Darron wanted. As he looked through more than four months of data, Darron started talking to the only person he could confide in. "Things looked different to me today – like I was seeing everything for the first time."

Stephen kept fiddling with the retrieval software. "Different? Everything looked the same to me. Of course I have only been in my quarters and in here. What changed?"

"I just sort of noticed things. Things I see every day, and sort of take for granted. People are amazing, if you think about it." Seeing no response at all from Stephen, Darron felt a little self-conscious and backed off with the statement, "Maybe I'm a little tired. It was hard to get to sleep last night."

Stephen laughed. "I was so wired I couldn't sleep at all. Finally I just watched a movie. I had missed *Space Serves Death Cold*, so I called it up. What a movie. I laughed through the whole thing. Did you see the scene where the alien had a gun in each of his 8 tentacles? It only had 6 in the other scenes. And all those eyeballs. Why would an alien attack a whole ship just to eat eyeballs? And why do evil aliens always have tentacles?" Stephen started laughing again as Darron resisted the urge to clutch at his eyes.

"After the movie I came back in here and started looking through stuff. I didn't see any other report of anomalies."

"So far, I don't see anything that looks like what we saw these last four days. I think this really is a new phenomena. And I don't see anything suggesting there is a natural source on the other side."

Stephen stopped and turned to face Darron. "So you think it's real? That there really is some alien ship on the other side?"

"I don't see any other explanation." After Darron spoke, he saw something in Stephen relax. Stephen turned back to his workstation, but he wasn't coding anymore, he was just looking at the records they were reviewing.

"I guess that's it then. I guess we know all we need to know." After speaking, Stephen sat looking at the piles of data and then fell sound asleep.

Darron looked at the unconscious programmer and wished he could do the same – just lie down and sleep. He started another review of the data, again failing to find anything to challenge his hypothesis.

Two hours later, the messenger sent by Captain Adams found them still in the room – Stephen passed out leaning back, mouth open, and Darron sound asleep leaning face-forward on the table.

Stephen and Darron stood at attention with 16 others in front of Captain Adams. The Captain was handing out summaries of the observed light pulses. The captain had arranged six teams of three, and set five teams to examine the recorded bursts without any consultation with each other, or with anyone else on the ship. For Team Six, Stephen and Darron were joined by, of all people, the crewman who might be Jones except for the fact that he was actually named Jonathon Sykes. Jon worked with the sensor equipment that measured the light emitted from the *Persephone's* search antennae across the potential Intersections. When opened, their sealed orders were to estimate what information anyone on the other side of the holes would have received from the *Persephone's* search signals.

The three moved back into the room Stephen had been working in at first. It was a bit awkward at first, with Jon wondering what was up, and trying to stay a little ways away from Darron, just in case. As Darron and Stephen filled in the details for Jon they could see him tense up as he realized the implications of the light pulses. Jon started calling up records of the survey pulses sent out over the last few weeks, and started listing out each successful transmission through an Intersection. Sixteen bursts were found which could have possibly been detected by someone on the other side. They couldn't say if any burst would have been seen, because the observer would have to be close to the Intersection and caught within or near the widening light pulse. A list was started of what information could be guessed if one pulse was recorded, if two or few were recorded, or if many were recorded.

The team decided that if one had been received, the listener could guess that the signal had a non-natural source, and could know what frequency was used by the emitting ship. The strength of the signal would be hard to settle on, because the receiver would not know if they were just seeing the very edge of the sweep, or if the ship had been unusually far away from the Intersection. Several records would allow the observer to guess the intensity of the pulse used, and from that, guess at the power capabilities of the emitter. Some guess at direction and speed might be made. If most had been detected, the observer could estimate the speed of the *Persephone's* search, the available strength of the signals, and probably, how good her sensors were. If most had been detected, the aliens would have a good guess at the *Persephone's* abilities and limitations.

The team reported back just after the start of Third Shift. The captain took their report in her office. In addition to the captain, the ship's chaplain was present. Captain Adams did not ask him to leave; he had apparently been brought in on the secret. Captain Adams listened to the report in silence. After the three had given their report, the Captain informed them that two other teams had already reported in. They also had guessed that the bursts were coming from a ship on the other side of the Intersections. The independent estimates seemed to have decided the issue. The Captain thanked them again for their efforts and dismissed them. The Chaplain asked if he could accompany them when they left. The Chaplain was the oldest person on the ship by decades. He was generally popular, and a few dozen of the crew were regular attenders at service.

"Our Captain believes that a little counseling may be needed in the near future", he said with a smile. "Also, this is about the only opportunity we will ever have to examine the response of humans to discovering a new race for the first time."

There was some nervous laughter, and each of the three looked warily at the Chaplain, wondering if "counseling" was about to break out. None of the team were close friends of the Chaplain. Like most people on the ship, they attended the "weekly" services from time to time. For one thing, the services were a break from the mind-numbing routine that could easily take hold after months locked in a little ball with the same people all the time.

The Chaplain smiled at the nervous response, and continued. "Since I heard about this, I don't think I have slept more than about an hour. There have been a lot of questions about the existence of other life in the galaxy. It is really strange to think we may be the first to find out. When do you think one side or the other will go ahead and make contact?"

All three stopped and looked at each other to see if the others were going to answer. Jon waited for the others; Darron's mind had always been jumping to the encounter itself, without thinking about the time in between; Steve waited for someone else to respond, then said, "They will probably be here pretty soon", and started walking on. The others looked at him, caught up, and asked why he thought so. "Their first flashes were spaced out, like they were moving at a normal speed through the Intersection field. The last two were close in time – they had to really move to get to the last Intersection for the fourth pulse. And that was just after about 5 of our flashes might have been seen by them. So they probably have been intentionally looking for Intersections in the direction we are going. Why would they do that if they didn't intend to come across?"

Everyone stopped and thought about Steve's statement. The Chaplain finally said, "You didn't point that out in your report."

"Why? It's obvious. I assumed everybody would think so. And you didn't ask when they would get here, just what they knew." Steve yawned, said goodnight and headed off to his quarters. Jon excused himself as well and headed back to his quarters and a sleepless night. Darron and the Chaplain headed back to the Captain. The two reported the additional comment from Steve and headed back out. The Chaplain turned to Darron, and asked him if he had any other comments that he had assumed everybody else probably knew. Darron laughed, and said he hadn't discovered anything else. Then he paused and seemed to be trying to decide whether to add any other comment. The Chaplain cocked an eyebrow and waited. Darron thought about the Chaplain and the odd thoughts at breakfast, and finally said, "Breakfast was a little strange".

The Chaplain led him to his room, and opened the door. Darron stood at the entrance for a second, and then looked around the room and stared.

The walls had pictures, a large cross hung across from the door, and there were multiple sets of clothes. The desk was littered with pictures in frames that must have taken a big chunk of the tiny personal space allotment given to each crewman. A blanket lay across the bed. As Darron stepped in and stared, the Chaplain motioned for him to close the door. When the door was shut, he indicated a seat for Darron, and took out from the bottom of the closet an actual coffee machine. Darron leaned away from the illegal device in shock. All water used on board was recycled. The humidity in the air was carefully monitored and excess amounts were recycled. Water could not be effectively compressed, and took up a painfully large amount of the ship's space, even with constant recycling. There was always some waste, and lack of water could force the early cancellation of an entire mission. For a crewman to use water in something so likely to cause loss as a stand-alone personal coffee machine could mean dismissal from the Fleet.

The Chaplain started to rummage through the bottom of the clothes pile, pulling out a hardened block of coffee grounds. As Darron watched in horrified silence, he scraped some of the grounds off into the top of the coffee maker, and poured in a full pot of water from an inflatable container that was filled with the precious fluid. Darron finally asked "Is that authorized?"

The Chaplain motioned to the coffee maker. "This? Of course not." He looked at Darron's shocked face and added, "With the new recyclers, there hasn't been a mission cut short due to water loss in 35 years. Unless there's a major failure of the recyclers or a tank collapse, we could lose water at a much higher rate than we do and still stay out for 15 months or so. The mechanical stress from the Angulins forces a refit long before that."

Darron turned away from the coffee maker and looked at all the decorations on the walls, the pictures, and the clothes and asked, "How did you get all this stuff on board?"

"I get the usual 2 cubic feet, plus one more for being an officer, and the formal clothes count as ship gear. It all packs in if you are careful. Plus, all the clothes you can wear and still fit in your bunk when packed are effectively free."

Darron looked at the ancient Chaplain with suspicion and watched carefully as he pulled out two real coffee mugs and started pouring out the coffee. Darron wasn't sure if just drinking the coffee would be grounds for dismissal. The cups didn't even have a lid – the steam was rising in swirls above the dark fluid. All of the cups on the ship and even on Loren Station were closed, expandable cylinders. He hadn't had coffee from a regular cup since leaving the Earth system nearly two years before. He took the offered cup and asked, "Couldn't you get fired for this?"

The Chaplain laughed. "They would have to be quick about it. I passed retirement age about the time you were born, and mandatory retirement age 12 years ago. I am only here by special authorization. If someone starts to say 'You're fired', I just have to say 'I quit' before they finish the sentence to retire with full pension."

The Chaplain sat down facing Darron and both took a drink of coffee.

Darron looked at the Chaplain, shook his head and glanced down at the photos. "So", said the Chaplain. "Aliens."

Darron tensed up, muttered, "Hopefully without tentacles", and seemed lost in thought.

"Don't tell me you watched *Space Serves Death Cold* a few nights ago."

"Yes. I am starting to regret it now." Darron laughed nervously. "You were there for the show too. You like old movies?"

The Chaplain smiled and leaned back. "I have a dark confession to make." The Chaplain lowered his head in mock shame. "I not only saw the movie, I am in it."

Darron almost spilled the steaming coffee he was now carefully savoring. "What? But that movie is so old!"

"And I am even older." The Chaplain saw Darron's questioning glance and added, "I am 127. They got permission to film on a Fleet ship. All of us in the crew were in the background at one time or another. I was the guy in the back praying over his food in the first dining room scene."

"How long have you been in space?"

"About 90 years. My first tour was on *StarFinder*."

"Wasn't that one of the first?"

"We were the third ship to cross over. Things were a lot different. The Angulins were a lot more primitive back then. The first ones had been invented not long before the discovery of the Intersections. They still took up over half the volume of the ship, and hardly stored enough momentum to provide artificial gravity, or compensate for ship thrusting. We still called them "Dean Machines" after the physicist back in the 1900's who first claimed angular momentum could be translated into linear momentum. We had to use entirely propellant-based thrust. The personal space for the crew was anything you could fit with you in your storage bunk."

"Were you the Chaplain then too?"

"The crews were a lot smaller then. On the *Persephone*, I am the Chaplain and one of the Assistant Medical Officers. On *StarFinder*, I was the Chaplain, the Medical Officer (the only medical officer we had), on the engineering crew for the Angulins, a reserve navigator, and a reserve communications crewman."

"I never knew that – you never talk about your past assignments."

"You really want to encourage an old geezer to go on and on about the old days? Careful what you ask for. 'Back in my day, we had to squeeze in! Back in my day we didn't need a full g for gravity. We felt the full ship acceleration, and We Liked It!'"

Darron laughed. "You must have seen a lot."

"I have. But I am not sure what I will see next. Soon, if your friend is right." The Chaplain leaned forward and refilled Darron's cup.

"The strange thing about breakfast was that everything on the ship seemed new – like I had never seen it before. " Darron continued on, and described his morning.

"So after hearing about the possible presence of other people and worlds you recognized the wonder of the people and world you come from yourself." The Chaplain thought for a second. "Maybe we should meet aliens more often. " Both laughed, and Darron reached out for another cup of coffee.

"So are you going to report me to the Captain as insane?" Darron queried.

"Only if I report myself as well. I think you are more sane today than yesterday. If you aren't careful you will end up as my replacement.

Sometimes the first step in recognizing the value of the Creator is recognizing the value of the creation."

Darron smiled and considered his coffee. Then he looked at the coffee maker, and back up to the Chaplain. "I thought you ship counselors were supposed to give people harder drinks to get them relaxed and talking."

The Chaplain laughed for a brief second, then his smile disappeared. "Not since the *Icarus*. Most of us who responded didn't drink at all after that. Not exactly a rational response, since we aren't always on starships, but there it is. It was an illegal still that caused the whole thing."

"The *Icarus* lost confinement on an Angulin, didn't she?"

"Yes. I was on the *Daedalus*. We had to operate in pairs back then.

One ship would be on each side of the projected Intersection field. Angulins put an enormous stress on the frame of a ship – all that stored velocity. Back then things wore out even faster, and the confinement anchors took constant maintenance and review. Everything was triple-checked, to make sure no one missed the first signs of breakdown. The problem with the procedure was that all three checks were performed by personnel from the same maintenance group. They had worked together to smuggle on the parts for a still, and started making their own drinks on the sly. Nobody ever got drunk, just a little buzzed, to make sure no one noticed. But one bad day they had a birthday celebration for the team lead, and managed to have too much. The first man to check 231, the main Angulin over the drive compartment, missed the signs of stress. The second man to check never did. He slept through his shift. The control programs were going crazy, putting up all sorts of warnings that containment of the Angulin was failing, but the warnings were being displayed to man number three, the team lead, who wasn't paying any attention – he hadn't had any alcohol in so long before his birthday celebration he had spent half the off-shift throwing up, and was just sitting blankly in front of the screen in misery. He had turned all the audible warnings off.

"The first warning the rest of the ship had was when the Angulin came free, converted half its angular momentum to linear all at once, and tore the *Icarus* in half. Our first warning was that all communication from the *Icarus* suddenly stopped. The Captain immediately made for her last known location at every g we could pull. Some parts of the ship were still intact, and there were a few people who had managed to survive – if the compartment they had happened to be in was sealed, and had functioning life support.

There were 86 on board, and 67 died during the initial explosion or afterward, in cold, dark, airless tombs. One more died after we got there. The team lead had happened to survive the catastrophe, and wrote out a long letter describing everything that had happened, and his own role in the failure.

Then he walked into an airlock without an exo-suit and blew himself out into space.

"Most everyone on the *Daedalus* never touched alcohol again – as much out of superstition as reasoning. And it took us a long time to re-learn to forget that every second on a starship we are surrounded by huge pools of energy and momentum that could kill us in an instant if we are not careful, or maybe just really unlucky."

Darron glanced at the walls for a second, then back to the Chaplain. "Are all your stories of the old days this disturbing?" he asked.

"No, most are boring. You got one of the exciting ones."

"So why are you still here? You could have gotten away from all this energy and momentum, and be retired somewhere safe, with a lot more room, and a real window."

"Well, I think this is my vocation – what I am called to do. And I have to admit, I like it. We live in a little shell, with a job that nearly kills with repetition and boredom. We are out here with no chance of assistance when things go wrong. We are about to meet aliens for the first time, and so we have a pretty good chance of ending up dead. Is there anywhere in the galaxy you would rather be?"

Darron thought for a moment, smiled, laughed, and admitted, "No – I guess if I could pick anywhere to be, I would be right here."

Darron won his bet with Chaplain Eisen. Eisen insisted that he would have won except for the flashes that occurred about 20 hours after their conversation. Until then, it still looked like the secret might hold for another 16 hours, and Eisen would win the right to trade his "concentrated pea soup" Day 6 dinner for Darron's prized "constructed chopped steak" Day 7 dinner. But after the multiple light bursts, too many people were passing in the hall visibly trying not to talk in public. Captain Adams had to make a formal statement 4 hours later. As this was almost exactly Darron's 1-day prediction, Eisen accessed his food log and transferred his Day 7 "chocolate cake" dessert to Darron, receiving the despised Day 4 "dehydrated fruit compote" in return.

Darron spent a lot of time watching how people took the news. It was a lot like the responses to being packed for crossing. The talkers talked, the withdrawers withdrew, and some just used the restroom a lot. Over time, the realization began to sink in that this crossing would never end – that the fact of the existence of aliens was not going to be a phase that ended, but the way the world would be from now on. The Captain had lots of new tasks for the crew, thinking that that a busy crew wouldn't be a worried crew. But as the light bursts continued over the next days, the Captain's prediction was right that the Chaplain would be busy.

Six days after the announcement, the Captain herself paid a visit to the Chaplain. She walked in, shut the door, sat down, and demanded coffee. She said nothing while the coffee was made and served, and drank down an entire cup in silence. Eisen waited, watching Adams, and noticing the ways in which the Captain had aged in the last few days.

"I think Stephen Hunter is right", Captain Adams finally said. "I don't think it will be long now."

"I agree. They must be finishing up this Intersection field, and everything is concentrated around us."

"What do you give for our chances?"

"If they are anything like us – not much." Both laughed, but the Captain's face quickly returned to the tired and sad expression she had worn on coming in the room. After a few more moments of silence, she came to the point.

"So what is your view on suicide. Is it a moral action? Or always wrong?"

The Chaplain was silent for a few minutes, watching the Captain carefully. Then he looked down at the pictures he kept on his desk. "Opinions vary. According to the Catholics, suicide is never morally acceptable. A number of the Protestant denominations are not so explicit."

"I asked you, not a bunch of Catholics or Protestants."

"I think it might depend on why you are committing suicide. Is this an act of despair? If so, it is wrong, because it implies that God can't save you. Is it an act of self-loathing? If so, it is wrong, because you are a creation of God, and worthy of respect, just like His other creations. Is this an act to punish others? If so, it is wrong, because it is an attempt to hurt your neighbors, not love them. Is this an act to save others? Maybe then it is the right thing to do – if you are acting in the only way you can to give others a chance to survive."

The Captain was silent for a long time, and reached out for a third cup of coffee. Then she looked up at the walls of the room, and said, "She's been a good ship."

"Pretty good crew, too."

"I have been pleased with most of them. Funny thing – one of the few I wanted to get rid of was Stephen Hunter. But since this all started, he's been one of the best men on board. Not only has he learned to stick to his guns, but he has been working fast – I have used him for a lot of the simulations we've started, and he gets things up and running, correctly, every time.

Finding aliens has been the best thing for him."

"It's been good for his friend Darron as well."

The Captain smiled for a second, with a real smile, not just a tired attempt. Then she got up, looked at the walls again, the cross on the wall, and then back down to Eisen. "It has been a pleasure serving with you, Fredrick."

Fredrick Eisen stood up, and shook Captain Adams' hand. "A pleasure for me as well. And an honor." He held on to the Captain's hand, and laid his other hand on her shoulder. "Go with God." He stepped back and watched as the Captain left the room.

After two more days, the crew was given a little more time to relax. The *Persephone* had no weapons, and didn't have any trained diplomats on board, so there wasn't that much that could be done to prepare for war, or for peaceful negotiations. The Captain authorized enough water use to actually wash the clothes the crew would be wearing when and if contact was made, and a series of relay transponders had been launched, to relay signals back to the Intersection field that joined back to Loren Station. The transponders were small enough and used a low enough level of power to be very hard to detect, and the laser communication was next to impossible to detect from any distance. The furthest relay transponders had already been commanded to cross back to Loren station with the news, and then automatically return to this side to ferry back a constant stream of information if alien ships were encountered. Captain Adams had strict orders that should any contact be made, no information was to be given as to the location of the Intersection field leading back to Loren Station, the location of Earth, or the location of any of the three colonies.

With the extra time, Stephen and Darron actually had time to get together for *It Came to Mars*. Darron had been kept busy tracing back the light flashes, and sorting through the gravity distortions found by the *Persephone* before the present chaos. Using the latest alien flashes as a guide, Darron had been able to add another four Intersections to the field. He had also been able to convince himself, and the Captain, that the latest flashes were too close together in time to have come from a single ship. His current guess was that there were at least three ships on the other side. After the movie, he and Stephen talked for a while about the probable alien technology, appearance, and intentions. It was hard to really nail anything down when there was no real data – any theory or statement could be true, with nothing to disprove it. So, like everyone else onboard, they pretty much described to each other all the possibilities, and expected whichever one they felt like at the moment. They had known about the aliens for longer than anyone else, and so had run out of things to say pretty soon. They had moved on to how Earth would respond to the news of alien life. They had no real data to go on there either. They gave up on this topic pretty quick. Despite the deep knowledge of human behavior and customs so often held by programmers and physicists, neither really had a clue how normal well-adjusted people responded to anything, much less aliens. This brought them to the activity that occupied the rest of their time together. *Space Serves Death Cold* was called up again, and after careful viewing, the dining room scene was called up and enhanced. The praying crewman in the back was isolated, cut out, and added to an email to the entire crew with the title DARK SECRET REVEALED and text about the presence on board of an actual movie star. The picture was accompanied by Stephen's animation of the old picture blending into a current picture of Chaplain Eisen. The email was flagged as an urgent message, arriving half an hour before Eisen's weekly service. It was read by nearly every crewman except Eisen, who was busy preparing for a crowd –this was the first service since the alien presence had been recognized.

Half an hour after the email, over 100 of the crew had jammed into the dining area – it was literally standing room only, almost as close-packed as for a crossing. A few people had stayed away because they were convinced atheists, and a few others stayed away to show that they weren't nervous.

Eisen had expected the crowd, but had not expected the laughing, the tablets held up for him to press his thumb to, or the exaggerated flirting from several of the women. While *Space Serves Death Cold* was not the most comforting movie to consider at the moment, the revelation of the Chaplain's thespian history became the release for a lot of the pent-up tension among the crew.

After some semblance of order was attained, the Chaplain began the service. When he reached the sermon, Eisen looked at the mob and said that he had expected the service would have quite a few people, but since he had a captive audience, he would talk about aliens last, and more important things first. He continued with a sermon focused on God's love as shown by Jesus, God's forgiveness, and our duty to forgive. He ended his talk with his first comment on the probable alien presence. "Just as we need forgiveness from God and others, so others need forgiveness from us. It doesn't matter who the "others" are. It could be your neighbor on the ship, or someone on Loren Station, or it could be the alien life you will meet in the future. One God made each of us, whatever race or species we might be. Each of us, whatever race and species, has the same God-given rights and value before Him. Who or whatever comes through those Intersections, however they treat you or me, they are God's creations as well, and deserve from us the same fair play we know we ought to be showing each other. Unless they are angels, which I seriously doubt, if there is ever to be peaceful cooperation there is going to have to be a lot of forgiveness. You will have to offer the same forgiveness you would want given to yourself. Looking out today, I have a feeling that the world is changed forever. My time has already become the past, and a new day is soon coming – your time, the time when humanity takes its place among God's wider creation. Be strong and courageous. Love your God, the neighbor you already know, and the neighbor who is a stranger. Forgive." Eisen led the crew in a final prayer, and looked out over the faces before him, feeling that this was likely the last time everyone present would be gathered together. He lifted his hand and gave his final blessing on the crew, and the service was dismissed.

The crew had been given the second half of Sunday off, and most of the personnel from all three shifts were awake when four ships appeared at Intersection sites half an hour after Eisen's benediction. All four began moving towards the *Persephone* at 5 g, not waiting for the other three ships that came through over the next fifteen minutes. Within an hour it was clear that the seven ships were not all moving directly towards the ship, but were moving to enclose it. The *Persephone* had started with a higher velocity than the incoming ships – they had been going very slow to move through the Intersections, so they could more quickly circle around and go through again if the Crossing failed. But the difference in acceleration was so great the *Persephone* would be surrounded long before she had any hope of moving all the way back to an Intersection leading back towards Loren Station. Captain Adams instead dropped in speed, and changed course to move directly into the middle of the oncoming ships. Seeing the course change, the incoming ships cut their accelerations down to a steady flight towards positions on all sides of the humans. At this point, the ships existed only as radar returns on *Persephone*'s sensors. As the humans continued their slow drift into the middle of the oncoming formation, the seven alien ships began a slow deceleration; all eight ships would come together in about one day. A constant record of everything was being sent back through the communication line towards Loren Station. The signals were expected to be impossible to identify, and the first relay had been sent off at an angle from the others to ensure that the line of relays couldn't be used to get an estimate of the Intersection field's location behind the *Persephone*.

After the humans turned towards the unidentified craft, the center ship began a broadcast consisting at first of a series of pulses with brief pauses in between. After the frequency of the Persephone's communication links had been updated, the signals were immediately recognized as the digits of Pi, and the numbers were broadcast back in response. The approaching ship then began a long sequence of signals, using atomic numbers and other universal constants to start a series of responses between the two vessels. The communication continued through the entire approach; soon other series of signals were being used to provide a sequence of patterns taken to represent characters, allowing names to be attached to the objects to which the universal constants applied. It was guessed on the *Persephone* that the signals being sent were part of some translation program which had been used many times before – while the humans were slow in response, having to recognize the pattern given and think up a return signal, the alien ship responded almost instantly to each signal received, apparently with full understanding. By the end of the day, the *Persephone* was transmitting a dictionary across to the other ship, which appeared to be ingesting and understanding the entire transmission.

The *Persephone* came to a full stop at the center of the closing sphere of alien ships. The ships were so close that one could be identified as slightly larger than the others. It was approaching a little closer than the others, and was the ship initiating all the translation communications. The *Persephone* waited while the ships closed to within 25 km, and the larger ship moved to within 1 km. Captain Adams had sent out instructions for about 30 of the crew to be present, in the closest they could manage to formal uniforms, in the rear landing bay if the aliens decided to meet in person. This group included all the senior officers except the Chief Engineer. A section of the landing bay had been converted to a communications and control center, and a constant record of all activities was being sent out through the communication line back to Loren Station. The tension rose on the *Persephone* as the alien ship stopped closing, and the expected imminent contact turned into a long period of waiting.

The translation work continued, as the alien ship stopped 1 km away and continued broadcasting. The alien communications were now in the humans' own language, and included requests for pronunciation guides.

After another 15 hours of transmissions, all communications stopped. Captain Adams sent out several messages with greetings, and requests for simple information such as a name to call the "guests" by, but there was no response. After a six hour pause, the alien ship made a last transmission: "Prepare to be boarded."

Captain Adams and the welcoming team filled the back of half of the landing bay. The alien ship slowly moved into position near the open landing bay, as all of its escorts moved to within about 5 km. As the ship moved close enough to see through the view ports used to assist in pod and shuttlecraft recovery, the crew got the first real look at their visitor. Instead of the tube shape and stubby "wings" of the *Persephone*, the alien ship had a more pancake-shaped body, with two extended wings. The front of the main body had what the humans guessed were missile launchers – they looked like they were designed to eject something, and were too small to be used for any pod or shuttle the *Persephone* had ever seen. The wings ended in what looked like turrets with gun barrels, each pointed at the *Persephone*. There was not the scattering of communications and detection antennas that sprouted around the *Persephone* – there were knobs and bumps on the alien ship, but the surface looked smooth, and even thicker than the *Persephone's* hide.

Watching it approach, the humans were sure they were seeing, for the first time ever, a spacecraft built specifically for war. As the description of the ship filtered through the waiting humans, many eyes turned to the Captain. Captain Adams waited calmly, but her face had become fixed, almost like a death-mask. Her thoughts seemed far away – there were no more orders to be given until contact was made, and she waited in silence. Chaplain Eisen was in the front row, off to Adam's right. While the others wore brown worksuits with a few symbols of rank attached, Eisen also had on his black robe worn for formal service – the only official dress uniform on board.

Stephen and Darron had been invited to the first contact in recognition of their roles as the first to recognize the aliens' presence. They waited in the back row, near where the auxiliary controls had been set up. Darron fidgeted, watching the people in front of him as they waited, and watching the operators at the control station beside him, even though he didn't really know what any of the controls did. Stephen looked bored, and just stood waiting.

Darron knew him well enough to know that his lack of motion or conversation was itself a sign of nervousness. Darron wasn't sure if Stephen was worried more about meeting aliens or about having to participate in a social encounter whose rules he didn't understand.

The reception crew waited as the alien ship moved up and extended a seal over the docking bay. When the sounds of the alien chamber filling with air had stopped, Captain Adams ordered the lock to be opened. The landing bay door lowered down, and revealed a chamber too dark for anything to be seen. As far as Darron could tell, all the humans had stopped breathing.

Eisen gave a wry smile as he heard in the awkward quiet the man just behind him, one of the decided atheists, muttering "please, God, please - don't let them have tentacles. Just no tentacles ..." Laser light swept out from the darkness, and washed back and forth over the humans. After a moment, all could hear the sounds of a number of people walking forward. Darron guessed that there were about a dozen, and then realized that the sounds sounded just like humans, walking forwards. Out of the dark came eight human figures, in suits and helmets. The suits were covered in small silvery scales, and looked more bulky than those on the *Persephone*. At first glance, there was a wave of disappointment and relief among the *Persephone*'s crewmen as the strangers were seen to be humans, not an encounter with an unknown race. Then the relief was gone as the realization sunk in that the strangers were not humans at all. The helmets were larger than reasonable, and the wrong shape; the torso was too large for the body; the lower legs were thicker than the top. Each suit had two inch spines sticking out from behind each elbow. From the realization that the strangers were in fact aliens the humans moved to the realization that of the eight, six were holding some type of weapon similar to a rifle. The other two had no weapon drawn, but wore bulky hand weapons on their belt. One of the aliens with two hands free stood slightly ahead of the others, about 15 feet in front of the assembled humans.

The humans could hear low guttural sounds from the alien's mouth, and "State your species name" broadcast in their own language from a mouthpiece on the helmet.

"We are called 'humans'", responded Captain Adams.

"Not the generic term. The specific name for the species of your planet. State your planetary name."

There was some whispering among the humans, as people started looking to their neighbors for support and advice. Captain Adams started to answer "Earth", but stopped, as "Earth" might be considered a generic term as well. Before she could answer, the un-whispered sound of Stephen Hunter answering Darron's whisper came from the back of the room. "No, 'Sol' is the sun. The planet should be called 'Terra', and we are "Terrans".

"'Terra'. You are 'Terrans'". The alien turned slightly to one of the gun-holders behind him. There was a momentary pause. The gun holder flexed his arms briefly, still holding his gun on the assembled Terrans. The lead alien turned back to Captain Adams and the others and stated, "There is no record of Terrans. What species have you contacted before today?"

"You are the first. It is an honor to …"

"You and your planet are claimed by the right of first contact for the Tavir Holding in the name of the Suvain Empire."

For the *Persephone*'s crew, nervousness was turning to fear, and to the cold certainty that the encounter with another race was going to be bad, not good. There was a low buzz among the crew, and few were still standing at the formal attention they had held so soon before. Then all attention turned to Captain Adams as she responded, "I and my ship, and my crew, belong to me, and to themselves. Earth, Terra, has no recognition any right of yours to rule. No declaration of yours will change this."

"Any resistance on the part of a primitive race is forbidden. You are the property of the Suvain Empire, and you must accept that fact, or suffer the consequences. You will immediately turn over all records and computer access to our crew. A prize crew will be placed on board to instruct you as we proceed to Terra."

All eyes turned back to Captain Adams as she absorbed this statement. She turned away from the alien, looking back towards her own people. She slowly lowered her head, and then turned back and looked back up to the alien. "You should expect resistance at every step. We are the property of no one, and we will accept no claim to the contrary. Any consequences of defending our freedom will be accepted. No records or access will be given. None of you are allowed on this vessel. We have no intention of taking you anywhere near our home world."

There was a shuffling among the Terrans, and the Suvain started to aim their weapons a bit more deliberately. The leading Suvain looked over the Terrans, paused for minute on the Captain, and then appeared to look carefully at the one Terran dressed differently than the rest – Frederick Eisen. The Chaplain was standing where he had started, steady as the rest of the Terrans sort of swayed back and forth around him. "Why are you dressed differently than the others?"

"This is my formal uniform for holding religious services," responded Eisen.

The Suvain turned back to the Terran who had been speaking before. "You realize that your refusals will not prevent our actions, and will lead to your deaths."

"Even if I agreed with your statement, it would not change my decision." Captain Adams seemed relaxed now, as if all decisions had been made, and nothing was left but to wait.

All the Suvain started moving at once. The gun-holders looked around and then to the one in the lead. The leader looked up and back for a second, then focused back on Captain Adams. He lifted a hand, and the other Suvain stood still. "Turn it off." Captain Adams did not respond. "Time to explosion?" This question was directed not at the Terrans but to a Suvain near the back. All the other comments between Suvain had not been translated and broadcast to the Terrans.

"18 minutes. " This statement came from the Suvain in back. The Terrans started talking, looking at the ship, and at the Captain. The Captain said nothing. The rumor started from the back near the control panels, and moved through the rest of the assembled Terrans. The ship's fusion reactor had been set to build up pressure, and blast the *Persephone* to pieces.

"You realize that we will leave, and you will be vaporized." Captain Adams did not respond. The lead Suvain turned briefly to the second Suvain without a drawn weapon. The second Suvain looked towards him, and then both turned towards Eisen. "You are a religious leader?"

"Yes." The Chaplain still stood calmly, watching the Suvain.

The Suvain turned back to the Captain. "Do you think your religion will defeat us? Does your religious leader tell you you will be safe?"

Eisen answered. "I have never told this crew that they would be safe." "You have no way to survive the destruction of your ship. Do you think your gods will save you?"

"Yes." Eisen paused and continued, "I do not think that God will prevent the explosion from killing me, or anyone else on board."

"But your god will save you? If not from the explosion, from what?" "From myself. From being someone who uses other people for my own gain."

"So your god will save me from you?" Most of the Suvain were flexing their arms, even as they held the guns steady.

Eisen shot Adams a glance. The aliens hadn't surprised him, and the explosion was something he had expected since his meeting with the Captain. But a theological discussion was not the usual expectation of where first contact with an alien race would go. The Captain wasn't intervening, so Eisen continued. "He can save you from yourself."

"I am the one with the gun. Why do I need saving?"

Eisen paused for a moment, then answered, "From all we have seen so far, all you have is a gun. You don't have love, or justice, or compassion.

You don't have anything really worth having, just some technology that is only good to encourage you to the very behavior that destroys you and others."

"Being the one with the gun is what matters at the moment."

"I have never told this crew they would be safe. I have told them that who they are is more important that what they have. One thing my religion does say is that he who is reconciled to his brother is greater than he who conquers a city."

All the Suvain moved at this statement. The guns wavered for a moment, and all looked over at the one in the lead. The leader glanced back at the others, who looked away immediately. He then turned back to Eisen and drew his gun. The gun was a bulky, misshapen thing that had a barrel nearly as thick as the grip. "Who have you been talking to?" he demanded.

Seeing the gun, everyone on that side of the ship moved away except for Eisen, who stood still, watching the Suvain. "You. As far as we are aware, no Terran has ever spoken to a Suvain before."

The Suvain reached up and pushed a button on his helmet. The faceplate rotated back revealing a face not far from human. No hair was visible, and the beginnings of ridges on the skull could be seen. The Suvain shot a glance at the Captain, and turned back to lock his gaze on Eisen. "I think you are what this crew trusts in as they are about to die. Why don't we see if your god really does save people." The Suvain pointed his gun at Eisen's chest, and fired.

The entire room flashed with heat and sound as a bolt of light blazed from the gun across to the Chaplain. Frederick Eisen's torso vaporized as the rest of his body exploded. There were scattered screams and shouts, and the Terrans moved away from the scattered body parts and blood. The lead Suvain turned back to the Captain. "Your religious leader cannot save you. Stop this foolishness, and turn off your reactor."

The Captain's face had jerked when the gun fired, and then returned to its former stoic immobility. Captain Adams met the gaze of the Suvain, looked down and carefully flicked a piece of Chaplain off her uniform, then looked back to the Suvain. "If you think I would take a murderer like you anywhere near the rest of my people, you are not just a thug, but an idiot."

The Suvain watched the Captain in silence for a moment. "A murderer? He wasn't someone sentient- just a primitive." The Suvain holstered his gun, and appeared to be talking to his comrades, without a translation to the Terrans. The Suvain turned his attention back to the Captain.

"There are two ways this could go. Your people and mine could turn to conflict, or your people could learn to work for us instead of dying. You are surely sending a record of everything to wherever it is you come from, as are we. If you continue in your efforts at sabotage, you will die, and we will step aside. Now that we know you are here, there will be a focused search for where you come from. Given a little time, we will find your trail back to the rest of you. You will start some desperate effort to arm yourselves, and when we next meet, the shooting will start at once. The path of conflict will be chosen, and it will end with the extermination of your species. Or you could decide to take us back yourself, and maybe the authorities of your people will have the wisdom to choose to survive."

"If your desire is to rule over our population, do not expect any of our authorities to give you any other answer." Captain Adams paused, and considered the Suvain gathered in front of her. "But you have a point. A longer association between our people might change our minds, or yours. But if you want to meet the rest of us, it won't be on your terms. I suggest a compromise. I turn off the explosion, and every alien ship but yours returns to your side of the field. You agree to follow this ship, at our pace and at the path of my choosing, back to a system inhabited by our people, and our "authorities". If you want to visit our vessel, you can ask. If you want information, you can ask. You, alone, can meet with our leadership, and take any answer back as you choose. And one more thing. For the entire time you are our "guest", you treat us as –Sentient? Not as a Primitive. And in exchange, we will refrain from losing our temper and killing you while you are isolated and alone."

The Suvain turned his head to the side, keeping his eyes on the Captain. The Terrans could see its lips moving as it had a quick conversation with the others. It turned back to the Captain. "Three ships, not one. With all respect for your hospitality, I do not intend to be isolated and alone."

The Captain thought for a moment, nodded her head toward the alien, and ordered over her shoulder, "Hold steady at the current pressure. No farther, but don't back it off." Behind her, a shaking crewman rapidly reset the fusion controls, and despite the specific order, set the control systems to back off the pressure a bit. "You are free to leave now. When only three of your ships remain in this region, we will proceed. Should any of your ships return to this space, all agreements are off."

"We are agreed." The lead Suvain barked out orders the Terrans couldn't understand, and the others shouldered their weapons and started to leave. Then the Suvain turned back to the Captain. "This is my Cultural Officer", he said, pointing to the other Suvain without a rifle. "Perhaps he could come and visit you during our trip together. He is skilled in the examination of primitive species, and would greatly appreciate the opportunity to come to know your people more fully."

"He should understand that any attempt to extract information from our computers or threaten any crewmember will be considered a hostile act. If he behaves and is unarmed, he is welcome as our guest. We would be glad to inform him of the ways of civilized society, and I will personally be responsible for his safety."

"Very well. Until our next meeting." The Suvain turned, and followed the others back to their own ship.

When the sound of the airlock being released could be heard, the Captain ordered in a voice suddenly hoarse, "Close the doors." The doors closed, and the first interview between Terrans and another race was over.

After the Captain had released the welcoming committee, Darron went straight back to his cabin. He laid down on his cot, and stared up at the ceiling. He was exhausted, but wasn't sure why. He felt guilty, but wasn't sure why. He was confused, but wasn't sure why. He kept playing out in his head all the ways that things should have gone, and hadn't. The image of the blast and the Chaplain exploding kept replaying in his mind, even though he tried to think of anything else. Logically, he knew that whether he had noticed the aliens or not, they would have come through the Intersections.

The image of the Chaplain exploding came back to his mind. He tried to convince himself that an early knowledge of the aliens' presence had been a critical advantage that helped save the ship and humanity. The image of the Chaplain exploding came back to his mind. It still felt like it had all started with him – because of something he had done, the Chaplain had been killed. Logically, he knew that an alien had pulled the trigger. The image of the Chaplain exploding came back to his mind. Darron gave up trying to force his mind to logic, and tried tears instead.

Steven had gone back to his quarters, and then decided to head back to his lab. He brought up the ship's primary network, and started checking for any signs of unauthorized access. After he was convinced that there was no sign of tampering, Stephen recorded all the security logs, and moved on to other possible vulnerable points. He was searching through the secondary networks when Darron walked in. Stephen said hello, and turned back to the console. He stopped and looked around when he realized that Darron hadn't said anything back. Darron was sitting in the room's other chair, staring silently at the floor. Stephen watched for a moment, as puzzled as he had been when Darron had walked in wanting to know about light flashes. "Hello?" he tried again.

"It feels like it was our fault." "What was?"

"The Chaplain, the aliens, everything."

Steven had a sudden urge to start working again, but couldn't just turn around on someone who had walked in and started talking. "If we hadn't seen the flashes, they still would have seen ours. They would have come through anyway. It probably would have been worse."

"I just keep seeing the Chaplain exploding. I keep thinking if we had done a better job, he would still be here."

This time, Steven did turn around, and buried himself in checking the logs. After a minute he answered, "I don't think there was anything to do. Our job was to tell the Captain something was up. And we did that."

"It feels like everybody sees us differently now. Like we made the aliens or something. Every time I see someone or think of someone, it seems like they are judging me for what happened."

Steven stopped working again and turned back to his friend. "The only guy who really has a complaint is the Chaplain, and he didn't seem upset at us at all."

"Did you know the Chaplain didn't have to be here? He should have been retired, but got special permission to come."

"He didn't have to stand there and keep talking to the Suvain", Steven pointed out. "But he chose to be there too."

Darron lifted his head at this, and stared at the viewscreen without seeing it. Then he gave a sad laugh. "I guess we can't be too responsible for what happened to the Chaplain – nobody ever really made him do anything. He was doing what he said he was called to do, whether any of us liked it or not. And I think he knew it was coming, somehow."

"He didn't seem very surprised by anything."

Darron looked from the viewscreen to his friend. "I bet if I could ask him, he would think my guilt was pretty funny. As if I could be responsible for his choices. As if his security was based on me, not himself, or God. It is strange, I can't imagine him judging me for his death, even though I sort of want to judge myself."

"The one I blame is the Suvain who shot him", Stephen responded. "But even then, I was thinking of his last sermon – about how the thing we were going to need was to forgive. He didn't act like he was going to blame the one who shot him."

"No, he just stood there like a rock, and took it."

Stephen frowned. "Well, not just standing still. He was shaking the whole time." Stephen caught Darron's glance and added. "I was watching him, not him and everyone around him. I think he wasn't nearly as calm as you give him credit for. I just don't think being afraid made any difference."

Darron nodded and went back to looking at the floor. After a moment he asked what Stephen was working on. He joined in for the next hour, looking through for anything suspicious. When he headed back to his cabin, he stopped at the door.

"We don't really know anything about these aliens, but do you think they have families? If they were humans, I would have said they reacted when the Chaplain quoted that part about brothers."

Stephen thought for a moment. "They didn't just react – they all looked at the big one. And that's when the gun came out, too. It wasn't a regular gun – I wonder what it really was?"

Darron thought for a moment. "Angulin cannons are illegal on Earth, but it looks like they aren't on Suvain, or wherever they are from." He headed on out, as Stephen turned back to shut everything down.

Darron did not see Steven for the next few days. He was working with the rest of the Physics team looking at every recording of the close alien ship, and every recording of the paths taken by the others. They had decided that a number of the bumps on the surface of the alien ship were probably sensors, imbedded within some sort of coating or armor plating. They couldn't imagine the front tubes to be anything but missile launchers, and the two turrets on the wings still looked like guns. There was a lot of debate about what they fired, but the growing belief was that they didn't have a shell like a Terran gun would – that they actually were driven by Angulins. If an Angulin released all its energy into a small object, in theory it could send it flying out at tens of thousands of miles an hour – a simple rock could be turned into a stream of molten slag that would blow through the *Persephone* from one side to the other. The paths taken by the ships showed an ability to accelerate faster than any Terran ship could achieve. No exhaust was detected, so it was guessed that an Angulin drive was in use on the Suvain ship. The *Persephone*'s main drive system also used Angulins; in addition she had a nuclear system as a backup, and for internal power. Darron was trying to see if there was any sign of radiation around the Suvain ship when he received a notice to meet immediately with the Captain in her office.

Darron found the Captain and the Personnel Officer already present. Stephen showed up just afterwards – he and Jon Sykes had been playing a game or something and had had to take a few minutes to clean everything up.

The captain began the meeting by asking everyone to sit down. Both Darron and Steven started to worry that something bad was about to happen - the Captain sounded almost polite.

"I have received a formal request to allow a visit by the Suvain "Cultural Officer". He would like to see the ship, and meet regular humans to get to know human culture. I have decided that as you were the first to discover the aliens, it would be appropriate for you to have the honor of escorting the Suvain around *Persephone*, and show him a little about humans." "Terrans," she corrected, with a glare at Stephen.

Darron, with eyes wide open and a heart full of fear looked over at the Personnel Officer for some helpful comment – for instance that someone else should show the alien around. Stephen sat stock-still, his face completely blank, looking at the Captain.

"Any computer access, the sensor control room, and the Angulin drive are off-limits. Otherwise, he may go wherever he pleases. Kindly show him every courtesy, and you are to freely answer any question he has about Earth culture and customs. Do NOT provide any information about the location of Earth or any human space station, or the existence of the three colonies.

Thank you for your assistance with this important assignment. You meet him the starboard airlock at 1900." The Captain graced them with a friendly smile. "Dismissed."

Darron and Stephen sat for a moment staring at the Captain, then got up and left without a word. The Personnel Officer turned to the Captain and cocked an eyebrow. Captain Adams smiled. "Oh, certainly", she said. "I could pick someone like you would who be a lot better at dealing with an actual living, breathing person. But then they might actually learn something about humans. It can ask those two anything it wants and unless it happens to be talking about bad movies or computer games, the chance either of them will know how people really operate will be near zero. We will have answered the aliens' request in full, and everything of importance about our race will be safe behind a solid curtain of cluelessness."

"Are you concerned that this might be considered deliberate misdirection?"

"It probably will be. But if they don't like my choice, they can complain."

The Personnel Officer thought for a moment. "Are you concerned that after a few days in their constant company, the alien might shoot himself?"

The Captain laughed for a moment, and then her face grew hard. "As far as I am concerned, if he did, we would be even."

Darron and Steven stood at attention in the starboard airlock at 1900. Neither spoke or moved as the airlock opened, a crewman stepped back to let the alien in, and then turned back to close the airlock. The alien stepped in, and looked towards the two motionless humans. Both Darron and Stephen were silent, waiting for something to happen. When the airlock was shut, the other human walked out, leaving the three standing in the corridor. After several minutes of waiting, the alien gabbled something and its headset asked, "I am supposed to meet Stephen Hunter and Darron Mason?"

Both the humans flinched, and then Stephen held out his hand, and said "Stephen Hunter". The Suvain looked at the hand, asked what he was supposed to do, and upon having a "handshake" described in some detail, took the hand and shook it, then Darron's. Both the Terrans looked at each other, wondering what to do next. After a brief conversation, they decided to ask the alien if he wanted to see their lab. The Suvain agreed, and the three walked out into the corridor and headed for the computer lab. Darron watched as Terrans saw them coming, stared, and stood out of the way. He could feel the eyes following him as they walked past. Stephen watched the Suvain most of the time. The alien walked through the halls with nothing that Stephen could recognize as discomfort or fear. It looked at the walls, the people, and the rooms they passed and Stephen got the feeling it was memorizing everything it saw. When they reached the lab and all three had crammed in, the next dilemma was trying to think of something to talk about. Finally they started a description of how they had first seen the alien flashes and recognized that they were not alone. The alien was interested in the entire story and had a lot of questions about when Terrans had started using Intersections, and how they found new ones. As soon as the conversation had moved over to technical questions about Intersections, both Stephen and Darron relaxed, and started talking much more freely.

The next two days passed in much the same way. The alien would show up, Stephen and Darron would take him down to the lab, and they would talk about whatever came to mind; the resulting conversation would tend to follow a line of questions coming from the Suvain. After the Suvain left, Darron would head off to the lab or his room, and Stephen would head off to some game he had going with Jon. The fourth day, the Suvain had a request. "You have stated that you are having a death ceremony where the body of the religious leader will be removed. Would it be permissible to see a record of the ceremony? Death customs of other species can be most instructive." Darron and Stephen came to a full stop and neither knew what to say. Both had been trying not to associate the friendly alien they had been talking to for the last several days with the murder of the Chaplain, but the question forced the memory back to mind. Stephen looked at the alien for a moment, and then turned to Darron.

"Do you think it would be safe? People were scared and angry when the Chaplain was shot. People look at us funny when we all walk around, and I think as things have started to feel more normal, I think they are less scared and more angry. Having someone there that reminds everybody of how he died would feel really weird."

Darron started to answer, but then looked over and noticed how carefully the Suvain was listening to the conversation. He refocused on Stephen. "I think the Captain will keep order. She has too many things to worry about already." Both were silent for a while, and then Darron continued. "You know what Chaplain Eisen would have said."

"He would have invited them to attend his own funeral." Stephen turned to the Suvain. "Sure. If you want, come to the funeral. You can bring the others if you want."

The Personnel Officer sat in the corner of the Captain's cabin. Crewmen Darron Mason and Stephen Hunter stood in front of the Captain's desk, avoiding looking at the Captain, the Personnel Officer, each other, and anything higher than the floor. Captain Adams sat with her right hand massaging her temple and her left hand drumming on the desk. She folded her hands in front of her, opened her eyes, and looked at Darron and Stephen. "You invited all the Suvain to the funeral?"

Both of the potential victims looked at each other, then back to the Captain. "We thought that Chaplain Eisen would have," Darron mumbled.

"Did you consider asking me first? Before inviting people onboard MY ship? Did you consider asking whoever was running the service? Did you consider that if 15 armed Suvain come to the service they might take over the ship on their way out? Did you consider that most of the crew will be present, and might dislike the thought of sharing a funeral with the one who murdered the dead man?"

Stephen decided that the best defense was a strong offense. "We thought Chaplain Eisen would have," he mumbled.

"May I point out to you that the Chaplain is not the Captain of this ship – I am. And, by the way, Fredrick is dead. It is my goal that the rest of this crew does not join him. Although if two have to be sacrificed, I have new candidates at the top of my very short list. You were given instructions, and nothing in those instructions gave you any sort of authority to invite ANYONE on board."

"I will tell him that it is our fault for the confusion, that they shouldn't come," Darron said.

"And have almost our first exchange with the aliens come across like we are incompetent? Nonsense. Since you have foolishly decided to speak for us all, and even told them of this before you told me, we are committed. I will be issuing a formal invitation myself. From now on, stick to your orders. ASK FIRST. And if you don't, I will be forced to demonstrate that humans, *Terrans*, have good discipline that is enforced by throwing offenders out the airlock."

After Stephen and Darron had fled, Captain Adams turned to her Personnel Officer. "Thanks for the heads-up. It is much easier to deal with those two when you tell me in advance what has been going on with the alien. Do you still feel the invitation is a good idea?"

Fergus MacDonald nodded. "From what I have seen of the tapes, I would guess that more contact between the races will lead to an increased chance of both sides gaining an interest in the other. The alien has proved quite adept at moving the conversation to areas which he desires to understand. Although he shows what I believe are signs of frustration at times, he moves back to information-gathering quickly. Our pair have interpreted your order that the alien should not have computer access to mean that he should not be given an account. Frequently, the two log in themselves to look up answers, and all three go through the requested information together."

"And you are tracking everything they view? What sort of information is the alien looking for?"

"His questions are usually leading to the social sciences. He had a few questions about our technology, but I don't think that is his primary interest. Early on, I think he got an estimate of the level of our abilities, and hasn't pressed for details or specifics. Darron and Stephen also showed some rare restraint, and were careful not to provide anything specific. They are much more free about questions concerning history, sociology, psychology, etc. I think they don't really see any of the social sciences as having any actual value, so they don't mind sharing the data."

"They are going through the data together? So Mason and Hunter may soon learn something about the human species? That will be a shock."

"Well, that could take a while, but the alien is learning quickly, and might be able to give them pointers." Both laughed.

"From what you have said, I would guess that the alien's study is not a risk, and may even be helpful." She looked questioningly at MacDonald.

"I would agree. And the tapes of the exchanges are providing some information on the alien, as well. For instance, I now believe that our initial inclination to view the aliens as emotionless is quite incorrect. I think that while we use facial expressions to show emotion, the "Suvain" emotions are often shown through arm movements. I think they are actually expressing either anger or fear when they draw their arms a little out and back – probably a sign they are ready to use those elbow spikes. When the Suvain is comfortable, the arms are more relaxed, and close to the body. I think a slight arm movement back and forth indicates laughter. Once you watch for a while, the movements seem natural, and you find yourself recognizing Suvain emotion about the same way as when watching a person's face when they are speaking."

"Is there anything specific the alien seems to be driving at?"

MacDonald paused. "He has come back several times to old Earth history – before space flight, even before industrial development. From his arm movements and his questions, there is something that he is finding confusing, or something that he thinks is missing or wrong. He isn't asking specifically for what he is looking for. Maybe he knows that Stephen and Darron won't know the answer, but I think it is more likely that he doesn't want us to know that something should be recorded, and isn't."

Captain Adams was silent for a moment, trying to remember what she had read about old Earth history, and trying to imagine what ought to be there. When she re-focused on the Personnel Officer, he said, "I am starting to wonder if there is something that we were expected to discover back then, and didn't. If there is some development or jump that everybody else made, and the alien is surprised that we missed something that basic."

Both were silent for a while, then the Personnel Officer continued. "The alien seems to have trouble with some answers, and has to go back several times to make sure he understands the responses he is getting. Other times, he understands completely, and moves right along to the next area.

From his responses, I think we are dealing with a political and social structure that is broken into two groups. He is very comfortable with the idea of a King, or Emperor, and he is very comfortable with the idea of family groups. I think that is why they talked about the "Tavir Holding" and the "Suvain Empire". I think that we are dealing with a society that is united under a single Emperor, but is divided into many different family-based clans. He is not comfortable with the idea of democracy. When the two described our elective government, it took several tries before the alien accepted that we actually have a government based on consent. He seemed to find the idea humorous, or silly."

MacDonald waited, as the Captain stopped listening, and stared down at her desk. Finally she looked up. "So we are dealing with a group of aliens with technology much greater than our own, who assume that power is held by those at the top, and those at the bottom have no say. And from what you say, anger and fear are similar responses – these "Suvain" probably respond to threats with aggression."

MacDonald nodded. "I would agree with both statements. Although their technological advantage may not be as drastic as it could be. They are clearly well beyond us, in just about every way, but their technology is still recognizable. It doesn't just seem like magic, because it is so far above us we could never imagine how a piece of technology could do such things. What we see of their abilities is close to what we think we will be able to do someday ourselves."

Captain Adams spent a few more minutes in thought and then ordered, "For now, we will let the interactions with the alien continue as it is. I am going to invite up to six unarmed Suvain aboard for the funeral. You will continue your review of all interactions with the alien, and continue sending the daily reports of your findings back to Loren Station. Provide me with the names of six reliable crewmen to serve as bodyguards and escorts for any visitors. Notify me if there is any change in the interactions with the alien, or future indiscretions on the part of our two representatives of the human race." MacDonald stood, saluted, and started to leave. The Captain stopped him with a final question. "By the way, what is the alien's name? Does it even have one?"

The Personnel Officer shook his head. "They have never thought to ask." He saluted again and left the cabin.

The six Suvain were welcomed aboard through one of the usual airlock transit tubes. The Captain, the Personnel Officer, the six identified orderlies, Darron, and Stephen were present as a reception committee. Two Suvain stepped out through the hatch, and then the Suvain commander stepped out behind them. He was followed by the Cultural Officer and two more Suvain. The Suvain were not wearing the full suits they had first come aboard in.

They now had on what looked like silvery tunics that stretched down almost to their knees, but left the lower legs and most of the arms bare. The sight of the limbs of the aliens went back and forth in the minds of the watching Terrans. At times the focus would be on the powerful upper arms, and at times the eye would be drawn to the forearms that looked puny by comparison. The alien heads were now uncovered, except for the headsets worn by each. The Suvain had no hair, and had three low ridges that ran from the forehead to the back of the skull. The first two to enter also had an extra overcoat which looked to be of thicker material.

The Captain stepped forward and welcomed the Commander aboard. She indicated the crewmen who would provide for any needs of the Suvain, and invited them to follow her down to the main mess hall when the funeral was going to take place. It was noticed that the Suvain had not followed the orders given – the two coated ones each appeared to have a pistol tucked away. This was motioned to the Captain, who stopped, pointedly looked at the two armed visitors, and then at the Commander. The Cultural Officer answered. "A Suvain commander always goes with an escort. A statement that no weapons were to be brought surely did not extend to the personal guard. We saw obedience to your instructions as fulfilled by our reduction of armament to the lowest possible number of arms consistent with a Commander's safety."

"The guarantee of his safety is my word, not those two guns," the Captain growled, and led the party to the dining area. The room was almost as filled as for Eisen's last service; those who had official duties in other parts of the ship were linked in by video. On the wall behind the makeshift podium was a viewscreen showing a section of tubing containing was left of Chaplain Eisen's body, sitting in the portside airlock. The aliens were led to a reserved location on the side where they had a view of the front. Their six escorts stayed between them and the crew. To most of the crew, the Suvain seemed emotionless, with no facial movement suggesting any response to standing in a large crowd of Terrans. To Darron and Stephen, positioned on the same side, the five newcomers looked normal, and the Cultural Officer looked nervous. He could pick up the current of anger that would flash through the crowd when something brought their attention to the Suvain guests. Darron touched Stephen's arm, and the two of them squeezed over to stand next to the Cultural Officer. Darron found himself looking at the Cultural Officer almost as one of the Terrans. Compared to the others, he was familiar, and sort of a friend. Darron realized he didn't really see the Cultural officer as an alien anymore, just a Suvain. But Darron realized he did see the others as aliens. He didn't really blame the Cultural Officer for the Chaplain's death, but found he did blame not just the Commander, but all the other aliens, for everything.

The Captain called everyone to attention. She began the service with several hymns, and then gave a brief description of Eisen's career in space. Darron noticed the aliens listening to the description, but also looking around at the Terrans. They had never seen tears before.

Captain Adams finished her description, and started to add personal remarks when she choked up and stopped for a moment. The Cultural Officer looked at Darron, and Darron started to say "She will be fine," and found his voice cracking as he did so. After a moment, the Captain continued.

"I served with Fredrick on three ships. I did not tell him that I had asked for him to be assigned to the *Persephone* when I was given temporary command. He was one of the finest men I ever knew. He showed us how to act in times of danger, and with his last words to us, he told us how to act to those around us, even those who mean us harm. He told us to forgive. He was right to say that forgiveness would be required. He was right a lot of the time. While we do not know what the future will bring, we know that Fredrick would have wanted our responses to the aliens to be based on a desire for the gain of both races, not vengeance for his death. The true honor of his memory will be the action to forgive and continue in the example he set." The Captain looked like she had prepared a lot more to say, but stopped. After a moment, she nodded to the other officers, who started a recording of an old hymn, played on bagpipes. All of the Suvain reacted with what Darron and Stephen could recognize as annoyance. He leaned over so the Cultural Officer could whisper.

"What is that? Some grief chant, or someone tormenting something in the name of the dead man?"

"It is an old earth hymn called 'Amazing Grace', played on some old musical instrument."

"Why?"

"I don't know. It is just what you play at every funeral in space." Darron was silent, as the airlock was opened. The pressure had previously been reduced so that the coffin slid slowly out of the ship into the void. The entire crew watched in silence as "Amazing Grace" finished, and the momentum from the expelled air moved the Chaplain's body away from the ship, and from sight. When the song had completed, the airlock was closed, and the crew was dismissed.

As people started to leave, Darron and Stephen turned to the Suvain, and waited while the Captain and Personnel Officer moved over to join the guests. Darron looked over, and saw that the Commander was standing in a posture he now recognized as relaxation. Seeing the murderer standing without fear as his victim's body floated away made something bitter in Darron come to the surface. The Cultural Officer saw his face change, and started to move his arms out in readiness for defense. The Commander had no such understanding of human facial expressions, and asked casually, "So when one of you gets killed, you want to forget the whole thing? You don't want vengeance, or retaliation?"

The nearby Terrans stopped moving and talking, and turned to Darron and the Suvain. Seeing the Cultural Officer starting to stand defensively in front of the Commander, the two bodyguards got ready to reach for their weapons. "What I want?" asked Darron in a low, precise voice. "What I want right now is to wait until you are transferring between ships, then release the containment on 423. The angulin would tear right out the side of the ship and right through you and all the rest of you. Then your crew could watch your body tear apart and fly off into nothing, which is where you belong." Darron stopped and took in a breath. He could feel Steve's hand on his shoulder.

"Crewman, stand down." Captain Adams calmly commanded. Darron leaned back and started breathing again. The Commander had listened to the entire statement, but saw his Cultural Officer relax after the Captain spoke. His eyes flicked over to the Captain, then back to Darron.

The Cultural Officer asked, "You said all that about forgiveness. But what you want is vengeance. Was the other just part of the funeral ritual?" Darron and Stephen knew the Suvain well enough to recognize that the statement was meant as an honest question, not an insult.

Darron just looked at the Commander for a moment, and everyone else was silent, waiting for his response. "You asked what I want. Forgiveness isn't what I want right now, it is what I am committed to. God help me, what I want is for you to die like he did. But what I should want is forgiveness.

So that is what I committed to choosing. Until someday when I finally want what I should want. Until I finally want what Chaplain Eisen wanted."

"You mention Chaplain Eisen. Is this part of your religion again? Do you think your god will punish you if you take vengeance?"

Darron had to think again, but then answered. "Maybe. But at the moment, it feels like it would be worth it. It isn't the punishment I am thinking of. It is that if I did blow you out into space, I would become someone just like you", Darron said, looking over at the Commander. "And what God offers is that I can become what I should be – that I can become someone like Eisen was."

Fergus Macdonald watched the exchange, and saw most of the Suvain flex slightly at Darron's statement. He was nearly certain that the motion indicated amusement – listening to a primitive describe how he didn't want to become like a mighty Suvain must not be something they usually heard. The exception was the Cultural Officer. He was standing with arms a little wide, and narrowed eyes fixed on Darron. MacDonald was sure that this was a posture indicating danger, and attention. It wasn't a response to a threat like direct aggression from Darron. MacDonald gave a short, tight-lipped smile. That combination of danger and attention reminded him of the response he saw sometimes from humans. When a human was playing Chess, and his opponent started making moves the player knew he didn't understand, there was that same combination – concern because something unknown was building up, and it was sure to be dangerous, and attention, as the player tried to put his finger on what the opponent had in mind.

The Captain ended the exchange. She notified Darron that he was to go to and remain in his cabin until otherwise informed, told the Terran escorts to see if the Suvain desired anything else before returning to their ship, caught the eye of the chief engineer, who left the room with two crewmen, and politely asked the Suvain if they had found the service enjoyable or perhaps informative.

"Most interesting and informative," responded the Commander as they walked back towards the airlock. "You Terrans are a much more emotional people than my Cultural Officer has led me to believe. And when emotional, you do not seem to consider the consequences to yourself – destroying your own ship, releasing the energy in the angulins mounted within your own hull, threatening a Suvain noble as he stands with his bodyguard …"

"We can be an emotional race. A funeral is often a time of great emotions for hum.., Terrans."

"I was impressed by your ability to restrain him so quickly with a word. Often Suvain are much harder to calm down once angered. And you will find that Suvain may take offense more easily than you imagine. Many of my rank would have killed him on the spot for the disrespect."

"Then we are fortunate to be dealing with a more restrained noble, who keeps his eyes on the more important issues before us."

They had reached the airlock, and the Commander stopped at the entrance. His arms moved back and forth for a moment in a gesture that Captain Adams thought was laughter. "There is a saying among the Suvain that a deal struck through flattery never lasts. Still, it is better than an insult."

"My crewmen have not informed me of your name, or proper title," said Captain Adams.

The Cultural Officer answered. "He is TavirAyan – the second son of the Tavir. His title, while he is the ranking member of the Tavir family present, is 'Tavir'." Seeing the captain was about to ask, he continued, "I am TavirGoDaiA – Fourth son of the third younger brother of the Tavir. While on a Tavir ship such as this, it is common for me to be addressed as GoDai."

"Thank you. " Captain Adams turned back to TavirAyan. "The repairs to our fusion drive are complete, so I intend to begin movement towards a Terran system in 20 hours. However, with the previous strain to the engines, I fear I must maintain a slower pace than normal, and as we were originally assigned the task of mapping this region of space, there may be a few small course corrections during the journey."

"I certainly would not want to put your ship under any undue risk. However, if the damage to your engines turns out to be so severe that the pace it can maintain is unbearably slow, I will decide to offer the services of an engineering crew capable of fixing all damage and allowing your ship to move with all the acceleration it can generate. While I appreciate your desire to fulfill your mission, should the mapping efforts be too extreme, I will be forced to conclude that I am dealing with a Captain who does not keep her eyes on the more important issues before us."

The Captain nodded her head in agreement. "Until our next meeting," she said, and waited for the two remaining Suvain to leave. As they turned to go, Godai said something to TavirAyan, and both turned back. Still speaking, Godai extended his hand to Captain Adams. Captain Adams took his offered hand, and shook it. When they had released hands, TavirAyan looked at Godai and then Captain Adams, and stuck his hand forward. The Captain hesitated for a brief moment, then shook hands with her counterpart. She watched the two turn and go, and ordered the airlock shut. She then turned and started walking back to her quarters. *I just shook hands with the thing that murdered Fredrick*, she thought. *Am I keeping my eyes on the more important issues, or just being weak?* She walked into her cabin and closed the door. *If he had lived through his own murder somehow, he wouldn't just be shaking hands with his murderer, he would be serving him coffee. He might even point out how much more it hurt to get shot in the old days.* She smiled, and then, safe from the eyes of the crew, began to silently cry.

Darron paced back and forth in his cabin. The size of the room meant that he took two short steps, then turned around and took two steps back. He laid down, but couldn't sleep. His mind kept running over all the things he should have said, or not said. He again paced back and forth and imagined all sorts of conversations that should have happened between him and the alien. He was a lot smarter, more prepared, taller, and in better shape in these imaginary conversations than he had been in real life. In some of the imaginary conversations, the alien was practically deferential. In none of the replacements of the actual event was Darron out of control emotionally. Now his replacement statements were wise, spoken with authority, and even the aliens were impressed. Occasionally the real event would intrude on his desperate imagination, and he would get embarrassed all over again.

Blowing up in public was a new thing for Darron. Emotions in general were fine things for other people, but he had never really thought of experiencing them himself. A part of him was glad that he had to sit alone in his cabin – he didn't know how he could face any of the rest of the crew after his display.

He heard something outside his door about 4 hours after his time-out, and did not recognize the sound of the guard posted by the chief engineer being told he could go back to his normal duties.

He had been in his cabin for 19 hours when he received a message from the Captain that if he wasn't on duty in five minutes he would be late, and subject to all associated penalties. He was fully dressed; he rushed to his station, trying to decide the entire way if he had time to stop and get breakfast. Arriving before the 5 minute deadline was up, but without having had time to get anything to eat, Darron moved to his workstation. He carefully looked at the monitor instead of anything or anyone else in the room. The chief scientist and two of his co-workers stopped everything to watch him enter and sit down. Darron focused intently on his display, and tried not to think of all the eyes focused on his back. He realized that his hair was not combed. He realized that he had not shaved. He realized that he had not washed up. He realized that he had not gone to the restroom, and that if he had to leave now, maybe he could burn a good 10-20 minutes before coming back – maybe the crowd of people watching him (all three of them) would have lost interest. The chief scientist broke into Darron's panicked thoughts with a comment that if Darron had been here an hour ago, he would know his assignment. Gratefully, Darron turned to hear of a task, any task, that would take his mind off of himself. The science team was to examine the motion of the Suvain ship as the *Persephone* began her trip back to Loren Station. Any information about rate of acceleration was considered critical, and the Captain wanted to know if there was any sign at all of particles being emitted by the Suvain ship, or radiation. The on-going attempt to detect any communication between the three Suvain vessels was to be continued. The speed with which the Suvain ship adjusted to the *Persephone*'s movement was to be recorded. The Captain especially wanted to know if the alleged missile launchers and gun barrels stayed locked on the Persephone all the time, or if there was any lag between the Terran ship accelerating and the Suvain ship re-targeting.

After notifying the Suvain of their intended course and acceleration, the *Persephone* began leading the Suvain back towards humanity. As the science team had expected, there was no sign of emissions or radiation – the Suvain ship moved easily while using nothing but Angulin-driven motion. The Suvain ship moved along with the Terran ship almost as if they were connected – it responded rapidly to the jerky increases in speed of the *Persephone*, and the entire time all weapons tracked the ship with hardly microseconds of delay. Captain Adams brought the *Persephone* up to 0.8g, and headed off in the general direction of the Intersection field to Loren Station. After the acceleration was established and things settled into routine, Darron was released to head on in to breakfast. He dreaded walking in where other people might be watching, or worse yet having people ask him about his explosion. He gave a relived smile, the first smile for almost 24 hours, when he saw both Stephen and Jon Sykes in the mess hall. Darron tried to ignore the glances from the others in the room, got breakfast and his previous day's dinner, and headed back to the two of them.

"We thought you might be coming this way during the off-shift," Stephen mentioned. Darron nodded, and then started eating breakfast and dinner in alternating hurried bites. "We have been running a little … experiment, and we thought you might want to see our next try."

"It was your idea, really," Jon added. "So we figure if it works, you should get a share of the credit." Darron went from confused to suspicious. "But if you are interested, be in the aft loading bay in half an hour." Stephen and Jon got up and headed out, leaving their trays for Darron to clean up.

Half an hour later, Darron walked into the aft loading bay. There was assorted gear packed around, but the main central area was open. About half way down the open middle area was a stand with a thick metal plate resting on it. About 20 feet away, near the ship end of the loading bay, Stephen and Jon stood near a small table that had a display with some drawings, and a long tube-shaped thing. They waved him in and motioned for him to shut the door. Darron walked over and saw what was on the display. He recoiled back almost as fast as from a coffee maker.

"Angulin guns are illegal, and probably dangerous!"

Stephen shrugged. Jon admitted, "Well, yeah, but nobody is ever going to know unless we tell them. And it might be useful to have an angulin gun around if the Suvain start shooting people again. And it isn't that dangerous. We built a little one and tried it a few days ago with no problem. But it hardly shot the charge at all. So we have a bigger angulin now – it should be able to provide more power." Stephen picked up the tube and stood to face the target. Darron started to study the sketches on the display of the angulin and internal anchoring devices.

Darron asked, "You built a little one like this, and then scaled up to a bigger version with the same increase in the anchors?" Jon nodded as Stephen dropped a bolt down the tube to serve as a projectile, and raised the tube.

Like many physicists, Darron was convinced that people needed a solid background concerning a problem before making a valid decision. Giving a command was practically an insult – instead a proper background should be established so that the person who was being informed would understand the rationale behind the suggestion that was being made, and determine whether or not the suggestion was valid. Given this belief, Darron never considered shouting "Don't push the button!" Instead he began to remind the two of things they probably knew very well and had not remembered in the excitement of making an illegal item that shot something very fast. He started to say that because of the non-linear relationship between the stored momentum of an angulin and the angulin's radius, the increase in size of the angulin would generate an acceleration which was much greater than that which could be controlled by a similar increase in size of the restricting anchors. This added increase which would not be properly controlled would primarily be released in the desired direction, but a small, residual portion of the energy would be released uniformly, which would then be channeled by the constricting tube into both a forward and backward velocity – the forward momentum being absorbed by the now-free angulin and the bolt, and the backward velocity being transferred to the individual holding the gun. As even the residual momentum transfer would be drastic compared to the inertia of a human weighing roughly 100 kilograms, there was actually significant risk, and so Stephen should not fire the weapon until the anchors had been replaced and, incidentally, slightly repositioned in the tube.

Stephen and Jon had long since learned to ignore boring backgrounds given by physicists; Stephen pushed the button to release the angulin at "… generate an acceleration…". The resulting events did not actually all happen at the same time, but since they were often only milliseconds apart, it sort of seemed that way.

The first two events did occur at the same time. The angulin released, and instantly went from a large wheel spinning very fast to a large wheel turning very slowly, and flying across the room fast enough to sink into the metal plate as it knocked the plate and stand across the room. The bolt sitting in front of the angulin caught a lot of the momentum and out-flew the angulin but unfortunately missed the plate entirely, shot to the back of the room, ricocheted back right past Jon as he fell down backwards, hit the back wall, ricocheted off to the side, and burrowed through a row of containers of spare parts and packing material which promptly caught on fire. The crack as it broke the sound barrier on its first flight across the room left all three people temporarily deaf. Paired with the forward motion of the angulin, the bolt, and the front half of the tube, was the backward movement of the back end of the tube and Stephen. The tube dislocated Stephen's arm as it rocketed back, and hurled him against the back wall hard enough to crack ribs and give him a concussion; he passed out fast enough not to notice that his left hand had been too near the tube and was now badly burned.

The next event was the recognition by the ship maintenance systems of what was registered as a major explosion and fire in the Aft Loading Bay.

This was immediately followed by the normal preventative measures – alarms went off across the entire ship, and suction was started through the vents to control the fire through removing the oxygen from the room. This was followed by the immediate commands of the officer of the deck for response teams to report to the affected area, for evacuation of all rooms close to the fire, for the dispatch of medical teams, and for the preparation to open the loading bay hatch to vent the contents of the room to space if the fire appeared to spread.

About this time, Jon got up, and Darron recovered enough to look at the fire, the smoke filling the room, and at Stephen on the floor.

Non-recovery personnel began moving forward away from the fire as the first damage control crewman reached the door. Jon and Darron had made their way to Stephen, and were starting to drag him to the door, but he seemed so heavy, and it was so hard to breathe all of a sudden. In response to a question from the officer of the deck, a bridge crewman activated the internal cameras and announced that crewmen appeared to be in the room. The officer cancelled fire suppression, and ordered that the victims be removed.

An off-duty crewman wearing boxer shorts, a tee-shirt, a fire extinguisher, and an oxygen mask opened the door within 45 seconds of the alarm. He helped Jon and Darron get completely out with Stephen and then turned to the charred container. Although the containers were melted and the contents destroyed, the fire was already almost burned out. The crewman finished off what was left of the fire, and looked around at the smoke-filled bay. Others were pouring into the room, and people were already getting Stephen to the medical ward. Jon had been concussed by landing head first after the shock wave from the bolt had hit him - when Stephen was taken care of and they were safely out of the room, he simply shut down, and slid to the floor. That left a coughing and befuddled Darron to respond to the Captain, the Chief Engineer, the Damage Control Officer, and about 20 interested listeners.

"Told them not to fire it," he started, then stopped. His mind really did not want to admit the size of the catastrophe, and so was lingering back at "confusion". The smoke and subsequent lack of oxygen did not help his mental state.

"Fire what?" someone demanded.

"The angulin gun." Darron was starting to cough out smoke and gasp in oxygen, and his mind was starting to admit that it could not stay in "confusion" forever – it was going to have to move on to "face-the-music".

"What angulin gun?" demanded the Chief Engineer. He led Darron back into the room, followed by the entire crowd. The Chief Engineer came up on Darron's left and the Captain on his right as Darron walked back through to the table and the tube wreckage. He could see a lot better now – the smoke was getting pulled out through vents. "We were talking about the Suvain and Stephen asked what the gun was that the Suvain used. I told him it was probably an angulin gun, and he and Jon made one. Two." He turned to the Captain. "I tried to tell them not to fire it – they hadn't scaled up the anchors properly when they increased the angulin size." He picked up the computer display from the floor, and it was promptly taken by the Chief Engineer.

"Did you ever consider reporting the existence of an illegal weapon on board, and letting Me see to preventing it from being fired?" asked the Captain in a unnaturally controlled voice.

"I just found out about it, they asked me ..." Darron broke off, realizing that he was getting his soon-to-be-court-martialed friends in even more trouble.

The Chief Engineer was looking over the design and asked Darron again, "They made a smaller version, and then just scaled up both the angulin and the anchors?" At Darron's nod, the Chief Engineer held out the display to the Captain. "It is not bad really – a pretty simple approach, that would have almost worked if the anchors had been the proper size. As it is, he's lucky to be alive."

"No", the Captain said in a low, icy voice. "No, he's not." She glared at the two of them. "So you know what is wrong with this? Why it did all this?"

"The anchors were too small. And he put something in front to act like a bullet, but it just flew all over. The angulin itself would have been enough," Darron answered.

Captain Adams stood without speaking, looking in disgust at Darron. She finally turned and looked around the room, where people were picking up tiny scatterings of debris, looking for any remaining flames, and standing gawking at the bent metal plate. After a moment she turned back to the two with the display. "Fix the design. Build it, test it, make me 10 by this time tomorrow, and 100 by five days from now. Oh – when you get ready for a test fire, Jonathon Sykes is to pull the trigger. That way if it kills someone it will be someone I am going to kill anyway. And if he dies," she continued, pointing at Darron, "you are next on the expendable list." She turned back to the disarray behind her, checked that the Damage Control Officer had everything under control, and stalked off.

When Jon was released from sick bay four hours later, he found that he was the target of numerous jokes about he and Stephen blowing themselves up and setting the loading bay on fire, and simultaneously he was a hero for making the angulin gun. Clusters of crewman would give him a hard time as they gathered around to hear all the details of the manufacture and the design of the weapon. Upon returning to his cabin, he found 53 emails containing quotes from introductory engineering classes describing size/energy ratios for angulins. When he then headed for the mess hall and found that all of his deserts and all Day 7 meals had been removed from his allotment for the rest of the voyage, four crewmen who overheard his shocked complaint dialed up their own desert for the day and gave it to him for free. He was still in the mess hall when he received a message from the Captain that as he had been released from sickbay, he was ordered to the aft cargo bay for special assignment.

Jon knew something was seriously wrong when there were no jokes, and lots of people looked at him with worried expressions. People moved aside to let him walk up to the new, larger table that sat where their old workspace had been. Several engineers were making final adjustments to a new tube, as the Chief Engineer and Darron watched. The tube looked wider than before, and even longer – it was about 4 foot long, and a handle had been welded on about a foot and a half from the end. It was held up with one hand and rested on the shoulder – a button on top across from the handle fired the angulin. Images of Stephen rocketing back jumped to Jon's mind as the Chief Engineer told him how to hold the angulin gun, and Darron started a long, nervous litany of how the original model was close, but the anchors were larger, and there was even a second angulin in reverse which would hopefully charge itself with any residual compensatory acceleration, and he had inserted a smaller tube inside the first to try to keep Jon's hand from catching on fire, and the angulin used was anchored better than previously, so hopefully even without the angulin shock absorber, any residual momentum would not actually cause permanent injury. Darron was still saying lots of things that Jon wasn't hearing as he saw a new plate being set up as a target, the engineers stepping away, and everyone looking to him as they stood far back from the fully assembled gun. Jon started toward the gun, stood for a second, then stepped up and lifted the new angulin gun to his shoulder. The Chief Engineer stepped up beside him and checked how Jon was holding the weapon. He remained next to Jon as Jon turned his head and focused on the target. Jon suddenly thought again of Stephen flying backwards, then looked at the metal plate and pushed the button. He rocked back but stayed upright, and the front of the gun cracked from the pressure wave ahead of the flying angulin. The angulin shot forward, blew the plate off the stand, and wedged itself halfway through the metal. Jon was slightly aware of the instant cheering throughout the room. The motion and sound had caused a wave of nausea that Jon had to fight down, and there was a slow realization that he was alive, unharmed, and had just become the first Terran to successfully fire a true angulin gun.

The Chief Engineer saw that Jon was having a hard time keeping up with things, probably due to his previous concussion. He assigned two crewmen to assist Jon back to sick bay for a last check, and then to his quarters. As Jon was escorted out of the room, he was aware that he and the gun were being cheered. At that moment, even his inevitable court-martial didn't seem to be a problem – the gun was a success.

Darron watched his friend leave the room, and then turned back to the angulin gun. He looked up to see the Chief Engineer walking back over to him. Darron shook his head at the cracked tube. "It works, Sir, but it looks like it is a single-shot device. We could never reset an angulin in the tube. The anchors have almost ripped out as well."

"True", the Chief Engineer replied, "but unless that skin of theirs is harder than it looks, I think one shot will be enough." He started to pick up the tube and then thought better of touching the smoking metal. "You can see the difference in their technology and ours", he said glumly. "We have a big tube that shoots the angulin. They have a miniaturized hand weapon that can probably be recharged, with an angulin many times more powerful than ours – strong enough to melt the shot into a plasma." He stood looking at the big, bulky tube and then looked at the ruined metal plate. "Still", he said with a smile, "one shot will be enough." He cut off Darron before he could interrupt. "I know, you have a bunch of improvements to suggest. Later.

This can be the Mark I version, and we have 100 of them to make in the next 120 hours."

Stephen was let out of sick bay 14 hours after he was carried in. The painkillers helped to some extent, but they combined with the splitting headache to make everything around him seem to be going much faster than he was. He could walk slowly on his own, but the three cracked ribs made every step and breath agonizing. His right arm was immobilized, and his left was bandaged from his hand almost to his elbow. He had slight use of two fingers and his thumb – the other two were in a splint. When released he had been informed that he was to head immediately to the Captain's office. He arrived and found Darron and Jonathon standing at attention, saying nothing. The Captain was sitting behind her desk. Stephen entered, and stood trying to figure out how to salute. He gave up after a minute, and continued standing, wincing with every breath. The Captain looked up when he arrived, waited for him to give up on saluting, and then began.

"All of you will be facing court-martial upon our return. You have broken multiple laws, falsely acquired and used ship equipment, destroyed ship equipment, started a fire which could have endangered the vessel, and placed crewmen in danger. You either took these actions yourselves, or failed to immediately notify proper authorities when such activities were discovered. All events have been recorded, and upon reaching Loren Station, a review board will be assembled to ascertain your guilt or innocence, and to assign the proper punishment once you are found guilty. In the meantime, since you have chosen to act without coordination with ship authorities and the crew, you will not receive the benefits of crew membership. All of your desserts and Day 7 meals have been removed from your allocations for the remainder of the voyage. In addition, you will continue with all assigned tasks, regardless of your current physical condition. To keep you busy, so you don't set the front half of my ship on fire as well, Hunter and Sykes will be assigned to an 8-hour guard shift in addition to their normal duties. This extra assignment will continue for the remainder of the cruise. Dismissed." Seeing the crushed look on Stephen's face as he turned to leave made the Captain add one final comment. "Hunter, once your right arm is cleared for duty, you are to report for AGM1 training. Until then, you stand guard without a weapon." Stephen responded with a despondent and drugged look, and then stumbled out of the office. Once the door had closed behind him, and Darron and Jon had started taking him to his room, Stephen asked what Agem training was. He assumed it was some other type of punishment. In the slow journey of 50 feet, the other two filled in Stephen on the development of the Angulin Gun Mark 1, and the current cannibalization of every non-essential part of the ship for the mass-production of enough weapons for almost the entire crew. By the time they had helped him into bed, he had started to realize that his angulin gun had not just ended his career; it had become a practical defense against the Suvain.

When GoDai had sent across a message to test whether the Terrans were open to additional visitation, the Terran ship was about to start accelerating. The Captain requested he wait for 12 hours or so, but that he would then be welcome to continue his research. His second request was also answered with a delay- he was informed that one of the crewmen he had been interacting with had been seriously injured in an accident, and was currently in recovery. He was requested to wait an additional 12 hours, with the Captain's apologies. There was an ongoing discussion on the Suvain vessel whether the Terrans had decided to be deliberately obstructive when a message from the Terran Captain was received indicating that as Stephen was now fit for duty, the Terrans would be most welcome to renew their association with GoDai a little ahead of schedule.

As always, GoDai had a set of questions he wanted to focus on during his time with the Terran representatives. When he walked through the airlock, they all took a back seat. Four Terrans stood at attention with long tube-like things that were certainly weapons. Two were standing against each wall, and facing the center of the room – none of the weapons were aimed at GoDai at the moment, but he would have to walk directly between them to pass into the ship. He then saw that Darron and Stephen were waiting for him at the other end of the chamber. Stephen was not standing up straight, and was making small squeaking noises over and over. His arms and head were bandaged, and he was looking down, rather than directly at the Suvain. Darron appeared different as well. He would meet the gaze of GoDai for a second, then look away, or at the floor. He was also a bit hunched over, and was showing what GoDai had started to identify as signs of stress for a Terran. GoDai hesitated at the entrance. He looked at the clear discomfort of the two Terrans he had met, and the new weapons where there had never been weapons or guards before. The thought that the Terrans might be intending to seize him as a bargaining chip seemed possible. He looked to the Terrans at each side, and the nearest looked back. The Terran transferred his weapon from one side to the other, smiled, saluted Terran-style, and said "Welcome aboard, sir." The Terran then looked away from GoDai, transferred the tube back to his right shoulder, and kept standing there. After a minute of thought, GoDai walked on into the room, up to Darron and Steven. The Terrans still did not really meet his gaze – Steve looked up briefly, and then back down. Darron looked all over, greeting GoDai as he briefly looked in his direction.

GoDai was considering whether he should grab Darron to use as a shield and try to get off the ship when Darron said, "Would you like to go back to the lab, like usual?" GoDai looked at the unmoving guards and back to Darron, and nodded, Terran-style. The three made their way very slowly down the hall. Terrans with the new weapons passed them several times.

GoDai had counted twelve weapons by the time they had finally reached the lab. He had also started to realize that the reason for their slow pace was that Stephen appeared to be seriously injured. After about five slow steps, Stephen would stop and make some more of the squeaking sounds, then continue. GoDai could not recognize any physical reason why Darron was mostly silent, and looked away. It appeared that the outburst at the funeral had marked a turning point in Darron's approach to the Suvain. As such resistance made Darron a useless subject, GoDai would have to request a different Terran to meet with. He stepped into the lab and sat in the usual chair as both of the others entered and sat down. GoDai noticed how carefully Steven sat down, and the number of squeaking noises that he made as he had to bend. He also saw that Darron seemed to be looking only at the floor, and was taking deep breaths. GoDai started to speak but Darron looked up and spoke first.

"Sorry for the blow-up with your captain." Darron looked at GoDai, then dropped his gaze again. GoDai realized that this behavior was Terran embarrassment, or guilt.

"There is lots of shouting on Suvain ships. And it is normal for primitives to get upset." GoDai answered.

"Yeah, but I am not a primitive. And the Captain didn't want trouble.

And you were a guest."

GoDai did not answer for a second. He already knew enough of Terran speech patterns to know that Darron's statement that he was not a primitive was not a boast – just a simple statement of fact. This inability to see the primitive nature of the Terran race was sure to lead the Terrans to resistance, and because of resistance, to large-scale death. "You do recognize the difference in the level of our advancement, and yours?" asked GoDai.

"Sure." Darron seemed to get much more comfortable now that the conversation had moved to technology and away from apologies. "Your ship can accelerate much faster than ours. Your acceleration is smooth, and those weapons of yours are way better than everything we have. Just look at your guns and ours."

"But that doesn't make you think that there is a difference between us?"

Stephen was leaning his head back against the wall with his eyes closed as he jumped into the conversation. "Let's say that a Suvain was at the beach, and a Terran ship landed next him. The Terrans would have technology, and the Suvain would have a swimsuit. Would you say that the Suvain was primitive then, just because he left his gun at home?" Stephen paused for a moment, either to let the Suvain figure out what "at the beach" meant, or because every breath hurt his cracked ribs. "So technology doesn't count."

GoDai had spent enough time to grow fond of the two primitives he was working with, and so tried to warn them away from this line of thought. "But technology does matter. If there is a fight, the high-technology side will win. You do need to remember that."

"But a big bully might win a fight, but that doesn't mean he's not a primitive," Darron said. "The little kid who gets beat up might be a better guy."

"You have to understand, the big question that will be resolved very soon is not whether the Suvain will die, or profit. The big question is whether the Terrans will die. And you need to realize that, so you don't die."

All three were silent after this remark, until Darron said slowly, "I don't want to die, and I don't want Terrans to die. I shouldn't want Suvain to die, either. But there is more to it than that. We have already had a Terran die. Your Captain shot him. Chaplain Eisen didn't have to die. He could have begged for mercy. He could have just shut up. But he showed us all that there are more important things than fear of death. If I had to judge which was primitive, I would say the one with the gun, not the one who died with self-control."

"Things keep coming back to the religious leader. Was he the one who tells you all this about self-control and forgiveness? Is this your religion again? You do need to remember – that man is dead. Following in the footsteps of a dead man is a bad idea."

"He is dead now. But he was alive before. Really alive. Everything about him was alive. Being dead in the future is worth it if you get to be truly alive now. And our religion says, fully alive afterwards too. I wish you could have known him. I wish I could have known him better." All fell silent, except for Stephen squeaking with every other breath.

"You speak of a person being primitive. Do you judge people to be sentient or primitive, rather than populations?"

Darron and Stephen were having difficulty answering questions they had never really started thinking about until the last few days, if ever. "I think everybody is as sentient as anybody else," said Darron. "But don't you have to judge whether someone is primitive by themselves? There are good people and jerks everywhere."

GoDai was silent for a while, going back over everything he had heard from the Terrans. Finally he looked at Darron. "So you judge an individual person to be sentient or primitive, and you think that your religion will make you sentient, which involves self-control and forgiveness to others. This life of control and forgiveness will make you fully alive. So you don't want to be like the Suvain with the gun, who happens to be alive right now, you want to become like the religious leader, who you say was really alive, but who happens to be dead because he annoyed the man with the gun."

Darron was having a lot of trouble following this, but Stephen answered from the wall. "Yes, that is about it. Except that Chaplain Eisen always emphasized that it was God, not 'your religion' that did the work."

"Do you think people really change? That primitive people really grow into someone different?"

Without thinking, Stephen tried to shrug, which cost him dearly. When he succeeded in making himself take a breath he responded, "Of course. It must be possible, because it had happened to the Chaplain."

Darron finally stepped in with the admission, "I didn't really think much about things until just a few weeks ago, when I really got to know the Chaplain. I don't know the answers to your questions, because I never really thought about my own religion until then."

"Look it up," said the programmer from the wall. Darron logged into the computer and the three spent most of GoDai's visit in a web search of Terran religions, and Chaplain Eisen.

As GoDai was about to leave, he finally asked Stephen if his injuries were permanent, and how he was injured. There was some hesitation and evasiveness at first, but the full story came out about the development of the angulin gun, the initial slight miscalculation, and the new AGM1. It took a while for GoDai to really believe that someone had tried to build an angulin gun, and then had fired it – practically releasing an angulin they were holding in their hand. He had all sorts of questions about how the Captain had responded when she found out, and finally expressed his satisfaction that Stephen's injuries were expected to have no lasting effects. The two Terrans escorted GoDai back to the airlock. GoDai counted another 19 AGM1s on the way back, although a few looked like they might have been the same as he had counted before. After thanking his friends for their hospitality, he accepted the salute from the new gate guards, and returned to his own ship.

GoDai called the Tavir, and said he needed to speak to him immediately. He reached the Captain's Annex off of the Command Room, entered, and sat down across from the Tavir. The Tavir looked at him sideways for a second, sniffed, and said, "It must be important if you have neglected to remember that showers are authorized for any crewman who has had to spend time around a Terran." Both laughed, and as he waved his arms, Tavir indicated to close the door.

"If you decide to take over their vessel by boarding, you should probably move in the next 10 hours," declared GoDai. "They are copying your gun, although theirs is a tube over half the length of their body. It actually shoots an angulin, and destroys itself after a single shot. But that shot will go through anything in front of it, and I suspect in an enclosed space could well kill everyone in the room. I counted about 25 they already have in service, and they are building more by the hour. They are taking apart every non-essential piece of machinery in the ship for angulins. They don't really know what they are doing yet, but even now they might be able to slow us down long enough for Captain Berserk to blow her ship up, and this time we would be next to it. It wasn't even the Captain who started the whole thing. Two crewmen built one themselves, and tried to fire it – that's why my official contact was described as 'injured in an accident'. That was somewhere around

25 hours ago. After they put out the fires, the Captain had the design fixed and started arming the entire crew."

Tavir listened to the entire story in silence, then laughed again. "I was deciding against a capture before they were armed, so I don't think that I will change my mind and rush them just because they have weapons." After a minute he asked, "Is this race truly suicidal? They blow up the ship they are standing in, want to blow out the angulins mounted in their own hull, make homemade guns and then pull the trigger …"

"No," said GoDai, without laughing. "They have the same fear of death as everyone else. Each time they have done something, or threatened something truly dangerous, they have a reason to do so. Blowing up the ship was a way to adjust the conditions you were imposing. Blowing out their own angulins was a way of getting revenge. Making their own gun was a way of ensuring that we would not be able to walk over and shoot anyone. From everything I have seen of their history, this race is a capable as anyone we have ever met to do something stupid. But they also are willing to take great risks to get what they want. And often, they show considerable ingenuity to find solutions to problems."

"Making weapons probably makes them feel better, but it also makes it more likely that if force is needed, that force will be much more drastic," answered Tavir.

"True. And the more I see of them, the more I think that personal intimidation is not likely to be an efficient means of persuasion. The other example of self-destructive behavior of Terrans is the acceptance of death by their religious leader. He gave a direct example that personal risk should not be a deciding factor in decision-making. As far as I can tell, the Terrans truly believe that a person can change – that a coward can become brave. The lesson the Terrans got by watching their religious leader die was that courage is possible."

"Not the lesson that getting shot is a bad thing that one should avoid?" Tavir was having trouble accepting the description given by his cultural officer.

"No. Right now, the dead religious leader has more impact on the Terrans than we do. They also learn other things quickly. One view of the gun has already led to the Terrans producing angulin guns of their own. They are studying this ship carefully as well – I would guess that they will be trying to duplicate ship weapons soon enough."

Tavir listened carefully, and then looked from GoDai to the display of the local Tavir Holding ships. "Unless their leaders are a lot more realistic than the crew of this ship, it sounds like force will be required. Messages are out to my father to pull in available ships, and my local fleet is already waiting for orders."

Tavir watched GoDai stare at the display, and continued, "I get the feeling you have grown attached to some of the Terrans. That is understandable. It is easy to get attached to one's pets. It isn't certain that this will end with the Terrans destroyed. These Terrans may be unrealistic, but those in charge probably have a lot better idea of how things really work."

GoDai looked back at Tavir. "There is something unusual about these primitives. They don't respond like I expect, and they have a remarkable ability to believe crazy things. For instance, they really believe that people can change – can become better than they are. The most common religious belief on the ship - there isn't just one – is that there is one God who created all things, and that when Terrans went wrong, the God who created the whole universe intervened personally. And, no surprise for a Terran religion, got himself killed. But then He was back, and now fixes people."

Tavir listened, and then started laughing. GoDai joined in. "So of all the races in the universe, God is fixated on this one?" asked Tavir.

GoDai got up to go to his shower, but stopped and turned at the door. "I knew they seem comic, but the Terrans may be more dangerous than they look. After the short period of time we have known them, they will soon have developed near-parity in crew combat abilities. Given time, they will be a threat to ships as well. I have to keep reminding myself not to underestimate them."

"A point well taken," responded Tavir, and GoDai headed out.

Captain Adams slowly increased acceleration over the next few days, and settled on a course not far from the direct path to the Intersection field back to Loren Station. The Chief Engineer met with the Captain and informed her that the 100 AGM1s would be completed on schedule, and that all the guns would be fully finished, not just the empty tubes that had made up all but three of the weapons seen by GoDai. As the number of AGM1s increased, the mood on the *Persephone* improved. After the Captain talked with the Personnel Officer, the decision was reached to offer to increase contact between the Terran and Suvain crews. Arrangements were made for eight Suvain crewmen to come to the *Persephone* for a visit with the Terran crew. Captain Adams set the visit time to be just after the entire run of AGM1s were complete. Careful orders were given to the crew that the Suvain were not to be given any reason to claim they had been given offense. Once again, there were strict restrictions against any mention of any Terran colonies, or any information that might give an idea where to find Earth.

The sixth day after the funeral, the first large Suvain visit to the Terran ship took place. The visitors walked through the security detail/ honor guard on their way through the airlock corridor. Several stopped to look at the Terran weapons, and against all regulations, the Terrans broke off from standing at attention to tell the Suvain that the new AGM2 was coming out soon, and that they should talk to the Chief Engineer to learn more. When asked by a Suvain where the Chief Engineer would be, Jon decided that being polite to the Suvain was more important than continuing to stand guard in his punishment shift, and led three of the Suvain back to the aft loading bay. One Suvain wandered too close to the physicists to escape and was dragged down to see the new black hole images that were being printed out and displayed all over the physical science lab. One Suvain acquired a coating of engineers, and headed off to be shown the fusion reactor. GoDai and a companion were greeted by Darron, Stephen and MacDonald, and walked off to a computer lab large enough to squeeze in five people. The last Suvain rashly accepted an offer to try Terran food and moved with a cluster of four Terrans into the mess hall.

GoDai introduced his friend, and was introduced to the Personnel Officer. The conversation took a very different turn than Stephen and Darron's previous talks when MacDonald started off by asking how many races GoDai and his friend had encountered before. The Suvain had met many races in the past – upon being asked how many primitive races they had discovered, GoDai confessed to being involved in three other encounters with previously-undiscovered races. He hadn't been on the encounter ship, but had been involved with the early evaluation process. The Terrans naturally wanted to know what had happened to the others, and GoDai decided that a little background might be helpful. He described how two of the races had rather quickly been convinced that resistance was futile, and were now living under Suvain rule, but without drastic losses of population, and much local freedom. GoDai was rather insistent that the subjugated races were actually advancing faster now than they had before, and both enjoyed the full protection of the Suvain against the attention of the other sentient races. MacDonald followed up his questions about the Suvain's previous experience with questions about the third discovered race. GoDai thought for a moment and then decided that the third race might also be a useful lesson for Terrans.

"They never really listened. They were the least-developed of the three, and we could never find a motivation method other than force. The race was more warlike than most, and were led by local warlords who ruled by demonstrations of personal valor. In the end, there wasn't any large-scale government to work with, and no way to convince the warlords that submitting to a stronger power was preferable to dying in a hopeless assault. We had to use nuclear weapons on almost all of the population centers. Even then, there was local resistance. In the end, we could only save about 20% of them from continuing to attack us. The planet is mostly used for mining at this point, although there is some hope that the remaining primitives are beginning to recognize that survival is better than the alternative."

This was a bit of an awkward topic for GoDai's friend and for the Terrans, so MacDonald decided to jump to a topic that might be more awkward for both Suvain. "So is the Tavir fighting with just one brother, or all of them?" He asked this while maintaining an innocent expression that was completely lost on the Suvain.

Both Suvain drew back, and drew back both arms as well. GoDai looked carefully at MacDonald for a few moments, then asked "You are watching the response of the Tavir to the religious leader?"

"Even we could see it," Darron answered for himself and Stephen. "When Chaplain Eisen quoted about reconciling with your brother, everybody got scared and nervous. You even thought we had been talking to somebody."

The second Suvain looked at GoDai with the universal signal that if someone was going to deal with the present hot potato, it wasn't going to be him. GoDai caught the look, and found it appropriate – GoDai was a closer relative to the Tavir, and so had more right to speak about family affairs.

GoDai chose his words carefully. "It is common for there to be competition in family-based groups over seniority, and opportunities to demonstrate leadership. It is also not uncommon for successful contestants, such as my present commander, to face a certain amount of resentment from less successful relatives." GoDai looked more carefully at MacDonald. "Of course, you should recognize that any such differences are common, and are trivial compared to the importance of unified policies towards primitive races."

"I am certain you are right. And such differences are common among Terrans as well. Actually, I have to admit that Terrans usually fight back and forth like cats and … Like creatures that fight back and forth all the time. We know full well that forgiveness and reconciliation are better than griping and sniping at each other, but we usually find ourselves poking at each other anyway. " MacDonald decided he had pushed his luck far enough and moved the conversation to less touchy topics.

GoDai eventually got around to asking a question that had occurred to him as he watched the Suvain heading down to the black hole pictures. "Why are you studying black holes? There is no singularity in this region – is there some other area you are trying to explore, but a gravity well is a threat?"

Both Stephen and MacDonald looked to the physicist for an answer. "There isn't any singularity here, of course, but the pictures of the mass and radiation emitted from the accretion disks are beautiful. And the compression waves that ripple through the ejected mass are amazing." Darron answered.

"You are looking at black holes, because you find a bunch of ejected matter – beautiful? And you don't get anything practical out of this at all – just pictures?"

"Well, they are really beautiful," answered the physicist. Darron was caught up in the thought of compression waves moving across each other in a recent image and did not notice the subtle body language that indicated that his Terran allies were firmly in the Suvain camp on the subject. "And it isn't without value," the physicist continued defensively. Doing something that had no practical application or gain of knowledge about the real universe was to Darron, like almost all physicists, a sign of ugly, inferior subjects, like theoretical mathematics. "It gives a useful case of fluid flows in highly compressible media." None of his audience knew or cared much about "compressible media". GoDai could easily tell that the other two Terrans found Darron's excuse for looking at black holes to be an obvious cover for his real motivation – he liked looking at the pretty pictures.

"Mass concentrations are usually not a big concern", tossed in the other Suvain. "If they are dangerously close to the door, the gravity distortions are huge, and easily visible."

Darron looked a bit suspiciously at the Suvain, and asked slowly, "Door? Do you mean Intersection?" He continued cautiously, "They are not doors, they are Intersections." Both the other Terrans looked sideways at each other for a moment, wondering if the entire "Not holes they are Intersections…" speech was about to be triggered. Darron looked back and forth at the Suvain for a moment, and then decided that the Suvain, like the Terrans, must have many crewmen on board who didn't have a technical background at all, and were therefore in desperate need of basic information about the mechanics of space travel, and about space itself.

"A Door is an object that slides back and forth to give access to a room," Darron explained. "A Door is a physical object. An Intersection is not a physical object. It is a co-joined region of space, where the set of points describing one physical location are actually identical to the set of points existing elsewhere in the universe, obviously causing an effective discontinuity in an otherwise continuous flight path should one be moving through one set and exit the Intersection within the other set. While a door is part of the wall between rooms, and therefore not technically part of either room, an Intersection is an overlap of sort between regions, and so is, in one sense, the entire opposite of a door." The unusual case of lecturing supposedly advanced aliens was so distracting that Darron stopped to draw a breath.

GoDai turned to his friend and stated, "The Terrans have not had space flight for an extended time, and so the terminology used is still based on the physical description of the door, not the more useful mapping terms used by those who are familiar with space travel, and are commonly using the "Intersections" as a means of moving from one region of space to another."

Darron, interrupted, got completely off-script and stalled out into silence as he considered GoDai's statement. The two Terran observers almost cheered out loud in admiration. On his very first try, a Suvain had stopped the "Not holes they are Intersections …" speech long before the usual ten minute time limit.

After a conversation that wandered around early space flight, architecture, claustrophobia, Susan Underwood forgetting not to drink coffee, caves on Earth, when the Suvain once met a species of primitives that were afraid of sunlight, and getting sunburn in unusual locations, visitation hours were over, and the two Suvain started to leave. As they walked back towards the airlock, GoDai stopped, and turned to Darron. "You study the universe because it is beautiful, don't you."

Darron started to protest that he really wasn't in to beauty, and that Physics was the most practical and useful thing in the entire universe to study, but then a memory of Eisen's excuse for being aboard ship came suddenly to mind. He started to say, "Physics is my vocation", but he was sure that the Suvain would not really understand the word "vocation", and was pretty sure that he didn't really understand it either. He was completely quiet for a moment, and then confessed, "That's part of it." GoDai stared at him for a moment, then everyone said their goodbyes and the Suvain returned to their own ship. MacDonald headed back to edit the recording made of the entire conversation, Stephen went to sick bay for arm exercises, and Darron went to his room to look up the word "vocation".

While GoDai was deflecting boring physics lectures, his fellow crewman was discovering the joys of Terran food. Most of the Terrans saw ship food as bland and sadly healthy, but to an alien, it was all an adventure. The Terrans began calling up their allocations from different days to give the Suvain a taste of a variety of foods. Eating or drinking substances from primitive races was officially forbidden until all items had been thoroughly checked, but nobody ever really obeyed the "don't eat" rule. As the Terrans tried to find something that the Suvain would actually eat and like, rather than eat, gag, and laugh at, conversations about food, how the different food was grown or raised, and different misadventures in the dining hall continued constantly. The Suvain's usual negative response was forgiven by the Terrans who knew that everything was foreign to the Suvain, and who gagged at the ship food themselves half the time. Between samples, the Terrans took pictures of themselves with the alien, and the Suvain used the display he had brought along to do likewise.

Everyone was having a good time until someone handed the Suvain a sealed container with a Day 6 drink – dark cola. Everyone stood back as the Suvain took a sip, then a drink, then gagged and shook his head, waved his arms, and drank the rest down. He placed the container down, laughed Suvain-style again, and asked, "What is that stuff?"

"Dark cola", someone answered. He turned and called up his own Day 6 drink, as the Suvain seemed to have found something he liked.

After the second container, the Suvain laughed again and said, "I think I can feel my brain cells dying. This stuff is great. What are the bubbles?"

The Terrans had no idea, but someone looked it up and announced that the drink was filled with Carbon Dioxide.

"Carbon Dioxide? That's poison", said the Suvain, as he chugged down his fourth container. After his fourth drink the Suvain looked straight ahead, arms motionless, and then collapsed face-first on the table, dead.

The Terrans stood in shock. None of them had any idea what to do. There was no way they could hide a dead Suvain, or find any way to avoid telling the Captain what had happened. They all began speaking at once, telling each other they hadn't meant any harm, and that they had no way of knowing they were doing something dangerous. As their imaginations had reached the angry Suvain captain blasting apart the *Persephone* and following on to blast the Earth, the Suvain sat straight back up.

"This is going to be outlawed so fast. But it isn't yet. How much of this do you have?" The shocked crewmen couldn't respond at first, and then someone started digging through the ship's records.

After returning, GoDai asked the other Suvain to immediately write down any impressions from their encounters with the Terrans. He noticed one Suvain looking at a poster of black hole emission patterns which had apparently been a gift of the Terran physicists, and remembered the Suvain was a scientist himself. The Suvain was not studying the patterns like a scientist – he looked more like someone viewing artwork. GoDai realized that someone was missing just as the last away team member came back through the airlock, struggling to carry a large cylinder with both arms.

When asked what he had, the Suvain slurred, "Liquid money. Until it's illegal." These encouraging words distracted everyone from GoDai's ethnological studies, and the rest of the time was spent trying the new drink, and secreting most of it away before providing the Tavir with a sample. It was after his sleep cycle that the new Suvain hero remembered that he had traded his display for *Persephone*'s entire supply of carbonated dark cola.

Stephen was still in pain from recovering ribs, still had an arm that worked only when it felt like it, and was exhausted from working double shifts and enduring physical therapy afterwards. When his personal alarm was triggered after he had been asleep for a single hour, he seriously considered trying to ignore it. The Captain's growls that Stephen had started as lazy and useless, and then went through being a useful, active crewman all the way to not just being a loose cannon, but actually building one came back to his mind - he was in way too much trouble already to not get up. Stephen staggered to his feet and lurched down to the mess hall. Twenty people were already there, clustered around something lying on the table. Captain Adams was present, and waved him up to the cluster. Stephen approached, and saw four people poking around with the Suvain display, trying different things that looked like commands, and filming everything that appeared on the screen. Stephen shook his head and looked again, then walked up and sat down in the middle of everyone in front of the tablet, and stared at the screen and the controls around the sides. Suddenly he was awake, and for one glorious moment, he didn't even feel the pain from his ribs. Behind him he could hear the captain telling him that she wanted every piece of data off the device, and that he probably had an hour or two to get it.

Six hours later, Stephen and his fellow hackers informed the Captain that they had gotten about everything they could get without days, or months, to try to figure out what the Suvain script actually said. The words were untranslatable and meaningless, but lots of them had been captured for future study. By pressing random controls around the sides, they had managed to get the display to start showing pictures of things, and eventually Stephen had managed to wander over to something that flashed a stream of pictures and graphs across the screen, all of which were greedily recorded by the Terrans.

When all of the easily-accessible information had been wrung from the tablet, Captain Adams put together a small selection of items the Suvain had expressed curiosity about and sent a message asking to be allowed to send over a package to the Suvain vessel. She added the display to the gift basket with a note that they had found it onboard – it had apparently been forgotten.

The Terran request to provide the gift basket arrived as the entire away team stood facing a wall, with the Tavir walking back and forth behind them, describing how the stupidity of losing a source of information to the Terrans could be construed as treason, and traitors were to be shot. When he was informed that the Terrans had returned the tablet, apparently intact and turned off, he dismissed the guilty individuals and returned to his cabin to issue a ship-wide order that Krola was not to be consumed without the expressed permission of the Tavir himself.

The next week Captain Adams kept the crew busy with a review of all ship- board systems, to make sure that nothing important had accidentally been dismantled for AGM1s. At the same time, copies of the recorded images from the Suvain display were made and sent to every department for analysis.

Recordings were always made of all conversations with the Suvain, and everything was being sent back to Loren Station, and from there on back to Earth. All of the writing on the display or in the discovered images was now sent back as a starting point for deciphering the written Suvain language.

Darron and Steven were given strict instructions that there was to be no discussion with GoDai about the display, or anything the Terrans might be learning from it.

When GoDai resumed his visits two days later, Darron and Stephen ended up spending most of their time trying to look up answers to all the questions GoDai was asking about early Terran science. Although both were in technical professions, neither actually knew much about the development of physics or early computing. Most history before space flight was a blur. They asked GoDai a few times if he would like to look at things that were more interesting or relevant, but he kept going back farther and farther.

Over the next few days, both Darron and Stephen got the feeling that something was wrong. The way that GoDai moved and held his arms and the way he asked questions had changed somehow, and even they could tell. In their limited experience with Terrans, both had come to the assumption that when normal people started acting irritated around them, it was because they had done something wrong. Both had also come to the defense mechanism of holding themselves more reserved to try and avoid repeating whatever wrong thing it was they had done already. This nervous silence to avoid saying the wrong thing did not improve the Suvain's mood. Finally GoDai's patience snapped, and with an unconscious lifting of his elbows – the Suvain equivalent of an angry shout – GoDai demanded to talk to someone who knew more about the Terran past and development. Darron and Stephen looked at each other with no idea what to do. Both decided at the same time to kick the problem up to someone else. Stephen called Captain Adams, and explained GoDai's request. Captain Adams had expected that someday the Suvain would demand to talk to someone competent. She said to tell GoDai that they had no official historian on board, but she would search through the ship records for anyone on the crew with training in history. GoDai was free to talk to any of the identified personnel about whatever history question he wanted information on.

Captain Adams promptly dumped the problem in her Personnel Officer's lap. MacDonald called to tell GoDai that he was going through the records now, and he would soon have a list of crewmen who might be helpful. GoDai nodded Terran-style, and waited without speaking. He was looking at a timeline of human history brought up by Stephen. 15 minutes later, MacDonald walked into the room with a printout with six names of crewmen who had studied history in addition to their primary subject in college. He read the names off to GoDai, who listened to the entire list, and then repeated the only name that sounded different than the others, as he had heard it before.

"You will bring Susan Underwood here immediately. I wish to speak with her right now. I do not want her informed that she is to speak with me, just that she is to come to this location."

MacDonald looked at GoDai for a second and then called Susan Underwood. He informed her that by request of the Captain she was to come to the lab immediately. When she asked what was happening, he informed her that this was an order, and she was to be present in three minutes. He then ended the call. He turned back to GoDai, looked at GoDai's tense stance, and asked, "Did crewman Mason or Hunter offend you, or refuse to answer your questions?"

"You should realize that attempting to lie to a sentient race is a very bad decision for a primitive race whose survival is still being decided."

Both Darron and Stephen reacted with shock and started to insist they had never lied to GoDai, or any Suvain, but their statements were overridden by Fergus's response. "They lied to you about history? That is impossible – to lie to someone you have to know the real answer. I would guess that they have to look up the answer to every question you ask."

"Precisely. Turn off that machine now." GoDai pointed to the computer terminal. MacDonald motioned, and Stephen reached over and turned the computer off. All four waited until the door opened, and Susan Underwood, after a moment of shocked hesitation, wedged herself into the small and crowded lab.

"Crewman Underwood, you are to answer any question concerning Terran history requested by this Suvain. You will answer all questions to the best of your ability. You will inform him if you do not possess the answers he is looking for, and you will not, under any circumstances, attempt to mislead him in any fashion, upon pain of court-martial. Is that clear?" Without waiting for Susan's answer, MacDonald turned to GoDai. "Please request any information you wish."

GoDai turned to Susan. "What energy source was used to raise the cathedral buildings in the Christendom Period?"

Susan was at a complete loss, and was still completely off-guard because of the unexpected and bizarre situation. She stared for a second, and then answered, "Uhh." She stared for a second again and then answered, "Well, they had people, and I think they used horses and things to pull stuff, and they had some simple machines, like levers and cranes. I don't remember that much for sure – I studied mostly post-industrial history at school."

"What was the time period of the Roman Empire?"

"Uhh, I think it was about 100BC to about 500AD?"

"Which empire followed it?"

"Well, there was the Eastern Roman one in the East, and in the West, there were a few big regional Empires, like the German one, but it wasn't as big as the Roman. There was more like a bunch of smaller countries."

"Which nation won your nuclear conflict?"

"Our what? Do you mean a war between nuclear-armed states?" Susan stood looking confused for a moment. "Well, a North American nation, the United States, was fighting a big war and used nuclear weapons at the end and the war stopped, so maybe you could say they did. But only three nuclear weapons have ever been used, so I am not sure what you mean by a nuclear conflict."

GoDai was silent for a moment, looking at Susan. The other three Terrans stood watching, noting that GoDai's arms were still flexed out – he was still angry, or upset, or nervous, or something else – just not relaxed. "What led to the development of scientific advance in Western Eurasia?"

Susan was completely lost. She did not have enough experience around Suvain to know if this was normal for the aliens or not, and had no idea why she was being drilled on Terran history. She was also nervous because whatever type of test this was, she had just flunked. "I am not sure." She admitted. "I studied mostly industrial history and later – I just had some survey classes on the older stuff. There is a fair amount of data available online if you want." She saw the Suvain's eyes flash around to the others, and looked over at MacDonald, who just shook his head no. She looked back to the Suvain.

"Uhh, well, in the Industrial Period, there was an increasing amount of knowledge, which sort of fed on itself ..."

"Before that."

Susan was at a standstill again. She tried, "Well, there was Roman and Greek stuff, and there were some monks?", and then gave up entirely. "I really don't know. I never really thought about it much. I am sorry. To get specifics about earlier periods, I would really have to check through the books in the current ship library, and to get really detailed, we will have to look through what they have at Loren Station. If you have specific things you want to know, and give me a list, I can have it sent back to my old university and I am sure they can forward the information to you. If I tried to tell you myself, I would just be making stuff up."

GoDai stood without responding, looking at Susan Underwood. "You have never looked at the development of science in Western Eurasia? Why not?"

"Well, I was more interested in the later stuff. Is there something special about the earlier period you are looking for?"

GoDai looked around at the other Terrans for a moment. He turned back to the computer terminal for a moment, and then back to Susan. "I will have a list of questions for you. I expect you to be able to provide the answers without delay."

"Of course", answered MacDonald. "If there is something specific you are looking for, we might be able to get answers for you more quickly."

"You do not know what I am looking for?"

The Terrans all looked at each other, and eventually all the others ended up looking at Susan. She finally turned to the Suvain and answered, "I would guess you are looking for something about our technology and what we are capable of. But why you are looking so far back, I really don't know. Did we miss something that you are expecting that we would have discovered?"

GoDai had been studying all of the Terrans as they watched each other after his question. "Thank you for your attempts to answer my questions.

You are free to use your memory storage systems if you wish. I will provide you with a list of requests very soon."

Darron and Stephen escorted GoDai back to his ship, and then returned to the lab, where MacDonald and Susan were still waiting. Both Stephen and Darron assumed that all of the trouble had been caused by their mistakes, and were too embarrassed to talk. MacDonald looked at them for a second, and decided to show mercy. "I don't think it was your fault. I think you answered as best you could, and I don't think you lied. I think what he wants to know is something we can't tell him, because we don't know what he is looking for. I am going to ask the captain to have the three of you assigned to a database survey of all the time periods GoDai has been asking about."

MacDonald dismissed them all, and headed off to talk to the Captain.

He described the entire encounter, and requested the reassignment of the three to the background search. He ended with the first warning he had given to the Captain in several weeks. "I am more concerned about this latest set of questions than anything I have seen for quite a while. From everything we have seen before, the Suvain are motivated by profit, and I think we have a good chance of convincing them that not killing us will lead to more profit than reducing the planet to a radioactive wasteland. But today was different. I think he was scared. I think there is something we aren't seeing that actually frightened him, and I suspect that a frightened Suvain is a very lethal Suvain."

Tavir had also noticed that GoDai had been acting strangely, and noticed when GoDai returned from his latest "visit", showered for a longer time than he was authorized, and then locked himself in his cabin for hours. Tavir accessed GoDai's account – GoDai was going over everything he had recorded from his conversations about Terran history. Tavir left GoDai alone, and went back to evaluating how much Krola could be sold under the cover of being a product of a primitive race, rather than a product of the Tavir Holding. Of course, sales would only last until the product reached SuvAa and was outlawed, but as long as the claim could be maintained that Krola was from Terra, the Tavir Holding could avoid any legal risk of damages from overuse. It was after his next sleep cycle that he was interrupted by GoDai walking into the Captain's Annex without any advanced notice or permission. Tavir sat back in his seat and watched carefully as GoDai stayed at formal attention rather than sitting down. GoDai stood for a second, then turned and shut the door, again without asking permission. When Tavir motioned to the seat, GoDai hesitated, then sat down without speaking. Tavir watched GoDai sit down all in one jerky motion, and watched his arms start to spread out slowly after he had sat down. Tavir wondered for a moment if extended exposure to Terrans could make someone dangerously unstable. He sat forward a little in the chair, giving himself easy access to the gun taped under his desk.

GoDai looked down at the desk, then up at the walls, and then directly at the Tavir. Tavir realized that GoDai wasn't mutinous – he was self- conscious, or embarrassed. Tavir waited for another moment, then tired of waiting and said, "Well?"

GoDai still hesitated for second, and then stated in a formal voice, "I am officially recommending Preemptive Extermination of the Terran species."

Tavir sat back in shock. He just stared at GoDai for a moment, then nearly fell over with laughter. As Tavir sat laughing, GoDai relaxed as if the worst was over.

"There hasn't been a race ever discovered that has required Preemptive Extermination. You seriously think this is the one that has finally been found that is so dangerous, they have to be killed off before they take over."

"Yes."

Tavir stopped laughing for a second. Then his arms started to widen and he asked, "How much Krola have you been drinking?"

"None." GoDai was still completely serious, answering with the same steady, slow voice as before.

Tavir gave in and started laughing again. "Terrans? So are the Terrans really smart? They are just so intelligent that once they get going, we will be turned into a bunch of peasants?"

"No."

"Are they strong?" "No."

"Do they breed really fast, and there are going to be billions of them by the time we reach this station of theirs?"

"No. At least, I don't think they breed any faster than anyone else, even though breeding shows up a lot in their stories."

"Do they have some secret technology they have been cleverly hiding this whole time? I know – they can control the minds of their victims and turn them into zombie-slaves."

"So you did read my notes about Terran alien mythology. No."

Tavir stopped and looked quizzically at GoDai. "They are just another spineless race. Sure, they have space flight, and the beginnings of technology, but what can you possibly point to that makes this race special? I can't imagine any competition that a Terran could win. Except maybe competitive suicide."

GoDai didn't answer at first, and when he did, he seemed to be talking as much to himself as to Tavir. "I can't find anything special about them at all. They aren't strong, they aren't smart, they aren't advanced, they make incredibly stupid decisions sometimes." He refocused on the Tavir. "But somehow, they are different. This race went from primarily animal power to space flight in about 2,000 years. That took us 6,000. Most places on Terra show the typical pattern – Empires go up and down, technologies advance and stall out. Land gets improved, and then wears out, and population and power moves. But there are places on Terra that don't fit the pattern at all. Some had almost continuous advance for the last 2,000 years. And something has pushed them forward, not just in science, but in other things. They aren't completely social, but somehow they work together – even though usually they seem completely self-focused. I can't find anything special about them at all, but they don't seem to fit any pattern. Their government is strange, too. They have had working governments that have popular representation."

"Why?"

"I don't know. I don't know why they pick such an unstable government, and I don't know why it doesn't fall apart immediately. I don't know why anything they do works –but it does. It is like they have something that causes them to succeed in spite of themselves. They may be just a spineless race, but there is something different here. And I am telling you – if we don't destroy them now, the day will come when whatever it is destroys us."

Tavir had listened carefully, and looked down at his desk for a moment.

The Tavir looked back up to GoDai and stated, "I will forward your formal recommendation for Preemptive Extermination on to my father, with the recommendation that it be sent to the Imperial Government for review. All of your records are sent back as per standard procedure, but if you would like to assemble a summary in support of your position it will be sent back as well."

Tavir nodded, and GoDai stood up and started to leave. He turned back for a moment and looked at Tavir. "If these people do have something dangerous, you may be the only one who has this single chance to act before it is too late."

"True. But at this point, I don't fear the Terrans. And if they have some secret thing that drives people forward and brings success, I am glad to hear it. Because we are here to take what they have."

Darron, Steven, and Susan now spent most of their time locked in the little lab working through the historical records requested by GoDai, trying to figure out some pattern to his searches. This was an unpleasant situation at first for all concerned: Steven and Darron felt terribly awkward working in close proximity to an actual member of the opposite sex, and Susan had to work in close proximity to two men who felt awkward working in close proximity with someone of the opposite sex. Both men tried to avoid the social unpleasantness by concentrating on their work, and slowly the fact of Susan's vastly different genetic makeup became just part of Susan.

Over the next several days, GoDai resumed his meetings with Darron and Stephen; now Susan joined in, helping look through the records for the data GoDai was requesting. GoDai had stumbled across something that Susan was actually knowledgeable about – he was searching for the beginnings of the Industrial Revolution. Susan had not had an audience who actually was interested in the subject for years, and broke into full lecture mode. She started with the major transformations of British production, and then moved to impacts on the British population. Stephen found much of the discussion boring – everything being discussed occurred before the development of computers, and therefore was not important. Darron kept interrupting with questions about the advances in Physics during the period. GoDai's questions kept trending back to whatever happened just before the example Susan was giving. Although the lecture was getting interrupted every two minutes, Susan was having a great time. There was no clear beginning to the industrial process – each time there was a significant development, some significant development could be identified even earlier. Eventually she ran out of answers, as GoDai's questions lead back past the only class she had had on the topic.

There was a sudden shift the next time GoDai came aboard. Susan had spent all of her time since the last visit studying the early industrial period, but now GoDai asked about human stories about alien encounters. Susan had no clue when Terrans started talking about aliens. Darron had seen a lot of the old movies but had no idea when bad science fiction movies had actually started. Stephen surprised the other three by knowing everything ever written about aliens. He could describe just when aliens had started to show up in human literature. He could describe the first stories about aliens invading earth. He could describe, with great detail, the early movies about encounters between Terrans and aliens. He could describe the changes in the portrayal of aliens over time, and the changes in alien encounters after Terrans developed space flight. Although Susan soon decided she was either in hell or hopefully purgatory, GoDai seemed interested in everything Stephen had to say. He asked a few questions about the early stories, and asked a few questions about what the aliens in the stories looked like. He seemed satisfied with the answers, and accepted when Stephen offered to show him a classic alien encounter movie. Stephen called up *It Came to Mars* and all four watched the movie, three voluntarily, and Susan because she was under orders. GoDai asked a number of questions during the movie. The movie began with an alien ship flying out of an Intersection next to Mars. GoDai was informed that there was no Intersection next to Mars. GoDai asked why the alien ship had only one alien. GoDai asked why the alien was killing all the human colonists instead of just asking for the phosphorus it needed to repair its ship. GoDai asked why the handful of brave colonists were fighting the alien with makeshift weapons instead of just calling for help. He then asked why all of the colonists' communication devices had happened to suddenly stop working just after the alien landed. He asked why the alien's death ray vaporized everyone it hit except for the main character, and only managed to burn off a lot of the main character's shirt. He asked why an alien intelligent enough to fly a spaceship couldn't find the controls to the automated lift that was taking him to the surface. He asked why the alien died from exposure to the cold, thin Martian atmosphere when the alien had apparently walked from his crashed ship to the colony domes without any form of exo-suit.

Susan had to admit that she was having a good time. Stephen was continuing to try to answer GoDai's questions, and the answers got more and more ridiculous. After the first few questions, both Susan and Darron were laughing at the movie, and at Stephen. Stephen didn't seem to mind, and soon could not keep a straight face while answering. Susan waited until the end to ask the question she had been wondering about for most of the movie. "Have you shown GoDai, or any of the Suvain, any other movie?" When both shook their heads, she asked, "So of all the literature of the human race,

the first thing you show an advanced alien race is *It Came to Mars*?"

"I thought we should start at the top," Darron answered seriously. "Do the aliens always die in your movies about aliens?" asked GoDai when the laughter had stopped.

"Not always", answered Stephen. "Sometimes the aliens are the good guys, or working with the good guy. But usually the alien is the monster."

"Does the alien ever win?"

"Only if he is the good guy."

"But if there is a fight between aliens and Terrans, the Terrans always win?"

"Well", said Darron, "it is Terrans who are making the movies."

"Do the leaders of your race take these movies seriously?"

Susan answered. "No Terran takes these movies seriously. In fact, most Terrans not only don't take the movies seriously, they don't take anyone who watches the movies very seriously either." As Stephen and Darron faked outrage and shock, Susan watched GoDai carefully. She continued, "The movies aren't trying to be realistic. Most realistic guesses about human encounters with aliens assume the aliens have a lot of technology the humans, Terrans, don't have. The usual calculation is that the aliens will end up eliminating most of the human race, even if they aren't deliberately trying to be destructive."

"I am glad to hear that your leadership takes a more realistic appraisal of the situation."

None of the Terrans responded for a second. Stephen answered slowly, "The movies are realistic in one sense. The Terrans don't just surrender to the aliens. You may find that there are leaders who will prefer surrender. But a more likely response is that you will end up fighting most every government on Earth. I think in the end, that path doesn't end well for either side."

GoDai did not respond for a long time, just stood up and stared at Stephen. He then thanked the Terrans for their time and their movie, and returned to his own ship.

He asked for another interview with Tavir several days after his introduction to classic Terran movies. He had been sent a wider of selection of Terran literature by Susan, and had started reading through some of the more famous works. GoDai entered the Captain's Annex and sat down again across from Tavir.

"Any second thoughts about the PE?" asked Tavir.

"Not really. I still think there is something here that is a danger. I still think that we need to exterminate it now, or it will be too late to keep it under control."

"Any guesses as to what the secret Terran power might be?" GoDai could hear the satire in Tavir's voice, but could also tell from his arms that Tavir was listening closely.

"No. Nothing really makes sense. I just can't believe these people could have succeeded on their own. I started thinking that maybe we aren't really the first sentient race they have encountered – maybe someone met them a long time ago, and has been moving them forward for some purpose of their own. I went back and looked again at the beginnings of their technological development, and looked more closely at their literature about non-Terran encounters. But it doesn't add up. Their technological development never shows the sudden change one would expect from an outside agent. It shows a slow but steady growth from well before the mass transformation of society. It is almost like a true exponential curve – the long, slow increase leading to the inflection point where growth becomes drastic and obvious. I thought that if they had been influenced by non-Terran activity, there would probably be some sign in their literature – some echo of the influence of an actual sentient race. But their "aliens" literature, if you can call it literature, starts well after the technological take-off has become obvious. And the things they imagine are nothing like anything you would actually find. It is all very much what you would imagine, if you had never seen the real thing."

"Were you looking near the takeoff point, or near the beginning of their science?"

"I was starting near the time technology started to re-define their society. I should say societies – there are lots of different types of Terran societies, with different histories and different rates and times of development. There still are. I am convinced at this point that their description of their government is not an elaborate lie. They really do have five or six major governments that are all sovereign. They have a unified government as well, but I am not sure it really is sovereign – I think it is just delegated power from all the others."

"Why doesn't one take over and establish a central, organized authority?"

"I am not sure. I think there are people from multiple different governments in this same ship. But I don't think that they value conquest as a sign of success for a government. This is especially strange as there are lots of examples of conquest and glorification of conquest in their histories – even the histories of the same groups that are still present today."

"So they used to be aggressive and full of life, and now are sterile and decadent?"

"I don't think it is just decadence. I think they could still be aggressive, and often are. But what they value is restraint, not conquest."

Tavir was silent for a few moments, laughed for a second, then stopped. "I am starting to see what you mean. How could such a chaotic, inefficient race ever progress?"

"One thing I have seen that is unusual is not just that they act aggressive, and value restraint. A lot of the things they value are the character traits they don't have. They are self-interested, and talk about valuing others. They are vindictive, and state that forgiveness is superior. Their histories are filled with greed and treachery and laziness, and they constantly state that none of these things are good. When they describe what is good, they don't describe themselves."

"A lot of people value what they don't have," Tavir pointed out.

"True. But when it really comes down to it, most of us think of "good" as "Sort of like me". These people have a different picture of "good" than anything you will ever see in a history of the Terrans."

"A lot of people want to better than they are. And we Suvain would agree that excessive commitment to any of the things you mentioned are bad."

"But usually when someone wants to improve, what they really want is not to be someone else, but to be more successful at being themselves. They want to become more like what they value, and less of what they don't like about themselves. But for these Terrans, being good includes learning to want and value the right things. When I look at the statements that drive the Terrans, at least the ones we are dealing with now, one of their goals is to be fundamentally different than they are."

"If I was a Terran, I would want to be fundamentally different than I was, too."

GoDai laughed, and then continued, "I have been given copies of more of their literature. I have read, or skimmed through works from several different Terran societies. *The Bible* is a religious work – the core religious text of the dead religious leader. It is hard to place. A lot of the descriptions of "good" seem to come from there, at least for the Terrans we are talking to now. It is written more like a history than a traditional philosophy text. *The Art of War* is from a different Terran culture. It is a military text from far back in Terran history. *Hamlet* is much later. It is not bad, for a primitive. The last one I have been reading through is called *The Distant Soul*. The book describes the struggles of a man moving from the Terran home world to a Terran colony. It is not a history, but is clearly written by someone who has experienced a colony being established."

"So the Terrans have tried so hard to hide the fact they have colonies, then hand us a book describing their colonies."

"Now do you see why I don't think they could get here by themselves? One of the things that was mentioned in the book was a Terran custom that when ships met in space the captain of one ship would invite the captain and officers of the other over for a meal. It would be an interesting experiment to try inviting over the Terrans over. It might be useful for the Terrans to see what a real starship looks like."

Captain Adams turned to her Personnel Officer as they waited with the rest of the dinner party outside the airlock. "So you still don't think that this invitation is designed to get all the officers off the ship?" she asked.

"It could be," MacDonald responded. "But I think if they wanted to attack, they would go ahead whether the officers are on board or not. I would guess that they have heard about the human custom of invitations, or it could be that they want to impress us with their technology. Or both."

"You guess? One far distant day when you are actually running your own ship you will learn never to guess about anything. It disturbs the crew to know that their commander is actually clueless. And most important, when you have to make a decision never let them hear the coin land."

Amid the nervous laughter, she turned back to her Engineering Officer. "Repeat your orders."

"In case of Suvain attack, begin self-destruction, and release all squads to push out the Suvain, and follow them back onto their own vessel. No orders from any of the dinner party are to be accepted. Self-destruction is only to be stopped upon notification from the boarding party commander from within the Suvain ship that the Suvain threat is ended."

Captain Adams turned back to the airlock. "Very well. Send over our request to come aboard."

After the visiting party had entered the airlock, and the bulkhead had shut behind them, the Engineering Officer turned to the nervous crewmen behind him. "Door guard – stations. Team 1, position as ordered." He then turned to the only individual who was not yet moving. "Is 423 ready?" he asked in a low voice. After receiving a silent nod from his chief assistant, the Chief Engineer continued. "Take Team Two to your station." As the crewman left, the Chief Engineer looked a last time at the closed airlock, and then headed to the bridge.

The Tavir, GoDai, and four other Suvain greeted them as they entered the Suvain ship. Captain Adams introduced each of the eight Terrans. In addition to the Personnel Officer, the Science Officer, the Information Officer, the Communications Officer, Susan, Darron, and Stephen had been invited. Captain Adams kept focused on the Tavir, as the other officers snuck looks at the alien designs and technology they were passing. Darron and Stephen were following along after Susan – neither was paying any attention to where they were going as they stared frantically around, trying to memorize everything they saw. Nothing they were passing had anything to do with Chemistry, so Susan did not mind too much having to take her time to watch the other two and make sure they did not wander off down some corridor.

The Suvain had prepared something that was probably made of protein material, and tasted sort of like beef, catsup, and fish all stuck in a blender. This had started as a Suvain delicacy, which the Suvains had then modified to suit what they had learned of Terran tastes. Several of the Terrans actually liked it, and the rest managed to get it down without giving offense. Most of the dinner conversation was led by the Captains, and concerned trivialities.

Both sides seemed to instinctually avoid touchy subjects like whether one group had decided to exterminate the other.

After dinner, the Tavir suggested a tour of the ship. The joint party moved through the ship, visiting the bridge, crew quarters, a joint off-hours room, and finally the weapons consoles. The Science Officer and Darron were all too pleased to discover they had been correct – the ship did have both missile launchers, and short range cannons driven by the ship's angulins. Their attempts to tell each other using only completely unobtrusive hand gestures that they had been right all along, coupled with their excited, smug grins made it completely obvious to the other Terrans that the prospect of being vaporized by these very weapons was insignificant compared to the joy of having been Right. After the general tour, people started to break up into their own interest groups. The programmers were off having discussions with their Suvain counterparts about the one uniform feature of every civilization ever discovered – hopelessly clueless computer users. The Suvain were soon showing the Terrans the interface page which listed the phrase "Is your informational device activated?" in 758 languages. Susan was off with the chemists, trying to convince them to give her a hint whether her research project into identifying Intersection fields through sampling trace interstellar matter for unusual concentrations of heavy elements had promise, and both Darron and the Science Officer were off to the science lab to view the newly- posted images of black holes, and a bizarre solar system that showed massive trails of matter being pulled off of two dull dwarf stars into a giant, brilliant blue star. They were soon being bombarded with the different theories about how a young star like a blue giant could possibly be in the same system as two of what had to be the oldest stars around, as they had already decayed down to brown. The picture showed the great contrast between the bright young star and the dull color of the older stars, and the matter trails varied through every color of the rainbow, all set against a varicolored background of stray hydrogen, soon to find its way into the blue giant.

The Tavir invited Captain Adams to accompany him to the off-duty area, which promptly cleared of all other personnel.

"I would like to thank you for a most enjoyable evening." Captain Adams began. "It was most kind of you to invite us aboard for a meal."

"I have been informed it is customary for your species to share food. And I thought a look at our ship might be both interesting and useful."

"Your weapons are most impressive. And your ship obviously does not require the near-constant refits of the Terrans – the angulin anchors are hardly noticeable, and your interior compartments are much more focused on crew comfort than on maintenance access."

"Thank you – it is always pleasant for a Suvain to hear complements directed towards his ship. The *ProfitTaker* has to put more emphasis on crew comfort. Our crew spends far more of its time in space than yours. In fact, most of the crew are far more connected to the ship than to any planetary system."

Captain Adams looked around for a second, and noticed again how all of the items in the room were different than on the *Persephone*, but similar. There were stools, and tables, and cabinets. Water and several other things were provided for the off-duty personnel. There were a scattering of what she guessed were some sort of terminals for computers. Colors were bright and varied all around the room, while the *Persephone* was a uniform gray, but nothing seemed truly *alien*. She turned back to the Tavir. "When we first met you, we had no idea what to expect. We had no idea if what was going to come in the hatch would be a slithering blob or something that had fifty arms. But of all the possible shapes in the universe, you look a lot like us." Captain Adams saw the Tavir arms flick out in a brief smile, and return to their previous relaxed position. "No offense intended, comparing you to a poor primitive species. But you seemed to expect what you would find. I assume your translation activities gave you an idea what to expect?"

"There is a considerable amount of information about your species present in the materials you sent across." Tavir began. "But we were not surprised that you are generally humanoid. Every species ever discovered that ranks even up to primitive has been similar. There are variations, of course. We have spines, and you are spineless. Our arms and legs are developed differently. But in general, we are of the same basic form. So is everyone else. For instance, no one has ever discovered a sentient race that has a bunch of tentacles. Animal life, certainly, but nothing you can hold a conversation with." Tavir was pleased to see that he was recognizing Terran responses enough from the recordings he had viewed to know that the Terran captain wanted to ask why this was so. "There are several theories as to why the universal form for intelligent life appears to be humanoid. One is that there is a common form because there is some sort of design or pattern that was used to create each race. Of course, no race has ever been discovered which is capable of designing or directing evolution, but one supposition is that such a race exists. A second view is that we are a later development of an initial space-faring race, which visited the entire galaxy before our evolution, and that all of us are the separately-evolved descendants of the initial race. This has difficulty in that no trace of the initial race has ever been found, and it is unexplained why the race would be capable of travelling across the entire galaxy, and then lose the ability to move from any of the planets it has occupied. A third view is that the humanoid form is simply the optimal form, and that through convergent evolution, the same solution, if you will, is reached by the random processes on each planet. This would suggest that every single environment is so similar that the same form, or roughly the same form, is optimal everywhere. For the lesser species, there is drastic variation even within the same environment, so the convergent evolutionists have their detractors as well." Tavir paused, and gave the Terran a bit of time to think this through. The "Why do you look like us?" conversation happened every time a new race was introduced to the galaxy.

After it looked like Captain Adams was ready for additional conversation, he continued. "I hear the strangest things from GoDai. He claims that Terran governments are often determined by a vote of all the population. Surely that must be a misunderstanding?"

"No, there is no misunderstanding. Most of the Terran governments are democracies. Most Terran leaders are chosen by a vote of the population over which they will have authority."

The Suvain looked at the Terran with what the Terran could not recognize as disbelief. "Which is more difficult, running an Empire, or fixing a fusion drive?"

"Running an Empire, certainly."

"So if your fusion drive malfunctions, or maybe needs repairing after someone tries to set it to explode, do you ask an engineer to fix it? Or do you ask everyone on the ship to vote on how the drive should be fixed?"

"I tell an engineer to fix the drive or get out and push."

"But on the more important, more complicated task, everyone votes?"

"The system is not based on efficiency. In fact, I am usually convinced that it is the most inefficient, stupidest system ever devised. It is based on the belief that no one has the right to rule over other people against their will – that every person should have the same rights before the law."

"So you consider the trained diplomat with experience of a hundred worlds and the day laborer who cleans his suit to have opinions of equal weight and value? Two day laborers who couldn't name the planet next door could outweigh the professional's opinion?"

Captain Adams had to stop for a moment; she was becoming more sure that this conversation could have wider repercussions than the casual conversation she had intended. "The opinions of the suit-cleaner and the professional may not have the same value. But they have the same weight.

They have the same weight because we believe that every human - Terran – has as much right to be heard as any other. The trained professional might be right more often, but that does not mean that he is somehow better, and gets to order the suit-cleaner around. And, in my experience, the professionals can be as clueless as the suit-cleaner. More so sometimes – the suit-cleaner at least does real work for a living. We don't think that anyone, just because of who they are or what they do is worth more than someone of different birth or with a different job."

"You really think that everyone is the same – no one is better than another? Surely you must have noticed that some are strong, some are weak, some are smart and some are stupid, some are trained and some are ignorant, some can handle money and power and some can't?"

"We do not think that people are the same in external capabilities. We think that people are the same in value. That every person has a basic value just from being a person that isn't measured by any external characteristic. So even though one is smart and another stupid, they are both people. So they both have the right to have an opinion, and they both can't just be told who is in charge. Of course, once they choose, they have to live with their decision – or in government the decision of the majority, even if they think the majority are clueless or blind. For instance, if someone joins the service and gets on board my ship, the decision is voluntary. But once he or she is on board, they do what I say. Period. If they don't like it, they don't have to sign up again when their term of duty runs out."

Tavir stood looking at Captain Adams for a moment. "You have reached space," he finally said. "You must have some basic understanding of reason, of logic. You must know that you have to make decisions on what you can see and measure, like whether one is born to a family of geniuses, and another to a family of fools?"

"We do know how to measure things. But I guess it is more a matter of faith, or something we realized before we had data to prove it. If you saw a Suvain in trouble, would you stop your ship to help him? And you wouldn't have asked first whether if he was smart or stupid – just being a Suvain would be enough."

"Whether I stop might well depend on the reward offered. You speak of faith – is this your religion again?"

"I am not sure. But it does fit with our religion. I have been listening to some of Fredrick's old sermons. There isn't any feeling that one person is better than another. The focus is not on people being good or glorious, but on God being good and glorious. There isn't much difference between a king and a peasant when you are comparing both of them to a perfect, almighty God. And there is the belief that God cares about everybody – peasants just like kings, smart and dumb, rich or poor. So if God considers someone worthy of value, who are we to say otherwise? Captain Adams stopped, realizing that she had said "our religion"; before she would have always said "Fredrick's religion".

The Tavir looked at Captain Adams for a moment, wondering if he was being made fun of. He did not know enough of Terran expressions to be sure that it was not an elaborate joke – this claim that a race which could travel in space based their social structure on a belief in the equality of all people, when the most basic observation showed differences between everyone.

Tavir considered how many different times the subject had come up, and from multiple groups of Terrans. He concluded that this couldn't be an elaborate joke – Terrans would never have been able to organize such an activity. He decided to change the topic.

"Did you get a lot out of the display?"

Captain Adams gave the Suvain an innocent expression which the Suvain could not possibly recognize. Then her mouth twitched and she answered. "Of course we would never think of trying to access information from a device from a highly advanced race. We were sure to return it once it had been found." Captain Adams noted that Suvain narrowed their eyes much like Terrans did. "But since it was turned on already, we couldn't help noticing a few things. There were a number of samples of your script, and the pictures were quite interesting. There were several images which looked like they were of importance showing a planet in a double-star system. Was that SuvAa, or perhaps the home system of the crewman who – forgot – the display?"

Tavir was confused for a second, considered who it was who left the display, and then realized what the Terran must be referring to. "Double stars, a small planet closer in, and a ringed planet in the distance?" Tavir thought through the descriptions of Terran body language, and remembered that the up-and-down head movement indicated agreement. "It is neither. It is a planetary system used for competitive flights of small spacecraft.

Thousands of Holdings send teams to achieve the fastest flight of the competition around a path that leads past both suns and out to the far planet. Most teams use the inner planet for gravity adjustments to their orbit, to gain a more efficient elliptical transfer orbit. DaiGal is quite enthused about the games, and even sends design and course suggestions on to the Tavir racing squad."

Captain Adams shook her head – another expression the Tavir could not follow. "It is strange that you look like us, but even more strange that we can be so alike. It is quite common among Terrans for people to be very focused on sporting activities and competition."

Both were silent for a while, and then Tavir moved back to the bizarre nature of Terran government. "If I am understanding GoDai correctly, your ship is not a privately-owned vessel, but is part of your official government fleet?" He recognized Adams' nod, and continued. "But GoDai also claims that you have a large number of different governments? Does he mean that you have different levels of government?"

"We do have different levels of government within each government, but we also have a number of sovereign states that are independent of each other." Captain Adams successfully recognized Tavir's reaction – he was having trouble deciding if he had understood the answer, or if there had been a problem in translation. "There are five major regional governments on Earth, and a handful of unassigned states. The regional governments themselves are collections of governments. There is also the United Governments - a joint government which is made up of representatives of the regional and independent governments. The *Persephone* is part of the North American Defense Force – the military organization of the North American Cooperative Zone. She, and we, are on loan to Earth Space Command – the exploration arm of the United Governments.

"And you have never had a single government take over and establish an orderly, central control over the planet?"

"We have had a few governments try, but none have succeeded. The joint governments have provided enough organization to allow trade between states, and people usually don't have a desire to be part of a universal government." Captain Adams recognized Tavir's arm movements as the equivalent of a frown, or a grimace. "Don't worry – if you are planning on negotiating with the Terrans, you can negotiate with the United Governments. There will representatives of the UG, and the UG will have the final decision. Of course, you will also be flooded with representatives from every other government. You will probably have to be polite with all the hordes, but the UG representatives will be able to make a formal agreement on behalf of the Terran population." Captain Adams thought she was still seeing the Suvain signs of disbelief. "You are hearing correctly.

There are multiple governments, none of which can order the others to take action, but all of which will come together and vote on what to do."

Tavir still looked like he was confused. "You don't distinguish between the elite and the weak. You don't have any organized government – no one ever had the drive to make one. How did you ever get off your first rock?"

Captain Adams laughed. "I wonder that too. Sometimes I think it is miracle that we are even alive, much less exploring space." She paused. "So if we Terrans are so pathetic, why does my personnel officer think that GoDai is afraid of Terrans?"

Tavir went completely still, except for an involuntary tensing of the arms, and then relaxed. "You Terrans are quick at understanding the Suvain, it appears. If you ever find out why GoDai has become irrational, let me know. I do wonder if spending too much time around Terrans is bad for your mental health".

Captain Adams paused and then asked, "Did you get a lot out of the dark cola?"

"Dakr Crola? That shows real promise. There is always money to be made selling people things that are only mildly harmful and unwise. It is not very difficult to reverse-engineer, although we will probably have you continue to manufacture the drug until it is outlawed, to avoid legal liability. It should bring a good, if time-limited, profit."

"We Terrans can introduce you to many things that are harmful and unwise."

"You do so much that is harmful and unwise, I am surprised there are any of you left."

"So am I, sometimes. But we have survived, and even multiplied."

Captain Adams paused, not sure if she wanted to go on with what she was thinking about. "Not all of us are unwise. It is unfortunate you shot Fredrick. He was the wisest man I have ever met, Terran or Suvain."

"You do realize he is dead. Actions which lead to your death are not wise. You do need to be realistic, and seek a path which leads to not dying."

"Fredrick probably would not agree with you. He claimed that true wisdom was doing what was right, regardless of the consequences. And in his sermons, he claims that "right" involves loving God, and loving people. In his last sermon, before you came over and shot him, before we had even begun to communicate, he talked about the need for Terrans to forgive Suvain and treat them, you, as we would want to be treated. Even though you shot him, he would argue that you have value and should be treated fairly.

Even now, he would insist that Terrans should want Suvain to prosper. But you need to understand, even though he did not lift a finger to defend himself against your gun, he would never have stood by while you oppressed his neighbor. He claimed that one sign of wisdom was that a person becomes a blessing to the people around him, not a curse. I really wish you could have had the chance to talk to him, because you are going to need wisdom very soon. This could end up with war, which will end us and hurt you, or it will end up with your accepting us as a partner rather than as an enemy or slave. And that will end in a gain for us, and large profits for you. Of all the people involved, on both sides, you are the one who will have the most important choices. You may be the only one who has this single chance to cause our encounter to a blessing for both sides, not a curse."

The Tavir, GoDai, and three other Suvain escorted the Terrans back to the airlock. As the other Terrans made their way into the airlock, the Tavir turned to Captain Adams. "I hope you enjoyed your meal."

"Certainly. Thank you again for a most enjoyable visit."

"I was not certain that you would accept the invitation. I thought there might be concern at having so many officers in a potentially hostile environment."

"Well, there was always the possibility that you would take the opportunity to seize the command personnel as hostages and demand the *Persephone*'s surrender."

"And you still came? That seems like an odd risk to take – different from your usual aggressive resistance to possible threats."

"I considered the risk acceptable. After all, the rest of the crew is standing by on orders to come get us in case of trouble."

The Tavir laughed. "I hear that your weapons are primitive, and likely to kill both the target and the firer. Still, with enough Terrans, that could be a good exchange. But don't let having them lure you into trouble."

Captain Adams stopped as she was about to head into the airlock. "That is very good advice. I am especially glad to hear that you are considering how having weapons can lead you into rash decisions." She could now recognize the Suvain smile.

"Quite true. Until our next meeting, Captain." The Tavir shut the airlock behind the Terrans, and both sets of crewmen turned to post-meal activities – the Terrans immediately went to record all experiences aboard the Suvain ship, and the Suvain placed air fresheners in the air recycling system and headed for the showers.

Word of the conversations with the Suvain spread through ship, not always accurately. Susan showed all of her notes to the other chemists. The Suvain had been careful not to tell her anything, but she was already good enough at reading Suvain reactions to feel that the Suvain she had been talking to knew she was on the right track. Stephen and the Information Officer were busy adding the phrase "If only there were an on-line manual I could read that would have answered this very question" in Suvain script across the top of the web page used for crew computer questions. Darron was eagerly describing to Jon the pictures of the blue giant devouring the brown dwarfs, causing several crewmen hearing little bits of the conversation from the other side of the mess hall to ask each other "Giants and dwarves are real?" As Darron was clearly excited about seeing pictures of dwarves being dismembered and fed to a giant, the next question was whether spending too much time around the Suvain could make you crazy.

Captain Adams set course directly for the Intersection field, and set the *Persephone*'s acceleration to a steady 1 g.

After the Terran visit, GoDai had been spending most of his time in his quarters. Tavir had accessed his console – GoDai was going back over the Terran literature. After four days, GoDai again requested access to the Terran vessel. Upon hearing that the shipboard religious services were scheduled, GoDai asked to attend. He met his three Terran contacts just before the service.

"What does your religious service consist of?" he asked.

"Usually there is some singing, some reading of Bible passages, and then a brief sermon, a talk, by the Chaplain." Susan answered. Stephen looked over at Susan, and started to ask a question. Susan continued. "This is the first service we have had since Fredrick was, was killed. I don't know who is going to give the sermon."

When they entered the transformed mess hall, it was already crowded with people. Over half of the crew had shown up for the service. The podium had been taken out of storage and reassembled in its usual place, but the figure of the Chaplain in his formal robes was missing. There was a lot of talking as people waited around; the talking turned to mumbling as the Suvain was seen to enter the room. Fergus MacDonald saw the Suvain standing in a widening pool of silence and stepped over next to podium. He formally welcomed GoDai to the service and began to clap. As the other Terrans joined in, GoDai turned to Darron. As Darron paused, Susan answered, "It is a sign of respect and welcome." After a brief clap, the Terrans went back to their previous conversations. A few minutes after the service was supposed to have started, Captain Adams walked in with one of the 80 or so crewmen that Darron and Stephen didn't recognize. Both walked to the front, and Captain Adams moved behind the podium.

"As the Chaplain is dead, an acting Chaplain has been appointed. This is acting Chaplain Soong." Captain Adams stepped away from the podium, and stood at in the front row of crewmen, facing the podium. A clearly nervous Soong stepped up behind the podium, dropped his notes on the floor, picked them up, and then announced the first hymn. He pushed the button for music, and people around the room joined in, or didn't, based on their comfort level and familiarity with the song. GoDai was interested in the first example of Terrans singing, but clearly nervous, or suspicious. He leaned over to Darron and whispered, "Do you play the same instrument, or thing, that made the noise at the funeral?" With Darron's whispered reassurance that bagpipes were almost never included, GoDai relaxed and began focusing on making sure he was recording all the noises being made.

After couple of songs, Soong, cleared his throat, coughed, and then looked at the floor for a moment. He then clicked to the passages to be read, and began from the 86th psalm. GoDai thought it was a usual text asking for help from a deity, but then when he heard the section about how "arrogant men have risen up against me", he began to wonder if the sermon was directed more specifically against the Suvain. The next passage was a description of the temptation of the religious leader Jesus, who was offered the entire world, but turned it down. The last section described the importance of love. He leaned over to Darron again and asked, "Does the new religious leader pick these selections?" Darron paused, started to speak, paused again, and repeated the question to Susan. Susan leaned over to the Suvain and described how there was a yearly calendar of readings that was followed.

After the readings, Soong brought up his notes for the sermon. He started reading, starting and stopping at first, but then speaking more smoothly as he started to think less of the 70 pairs of eyes and more about what he intended to say. He talked for a while about how much he had learned from Fredrick Eisen, both through his sermons, and through his conversations afterwards. He apologized for his lack of preparation, managing to point out that he had only heard he was the new acting Chaplain a few hours before. He eventually started reading from Luke 4:18 stating that "The Spirit of the Lord is upon me, Because he anointed me to preach the gospel to the poor. He has sent me to proclaim release to the captives, and recovery of sight to the blind, to set free those who are oppressed, to proclaim the favorable year of the Lord." Soong paused, and then continued, "The last time Fredrick spoke from this podium, he said that he felt that his time was ending, and ours was beginning. If the rumors we are hearing are true, our time could become any of many different futures. Depending on how things with the Suvain go, our future could be death for most of the human race, or slavery, or a war against people much, much stronger than us, or possibly, a future where Suvain and Terrans build each other up, not tear each other down. In our text today, Jesus read this passage, and then said that he was the one the passage spoke of – that he was doing all those things. The people that he read it to didn't rule their own country. Later on, he mentions a girl who is a believer in God who is a slave of non-believers, and how she is part of healing her captors, and bringing them to faith. We can't know how the future will unfold. But we can know that God's promise, of freedom for the captives, sight for the blind, the favorable year of the Lord, will be true regardless of whether the future is death, or slavery, or freedom and joy. God's love is not dependent on our conditions, or whether we are conquered or free. God's freedom is from our own sin, and nothing can stop that. There have been times when God's people have been killed, or enslaved, and the result is not that God loses, and his work to save the world from sin and death ends in failure, but instead, even the slaves are used to save their captors. So let us face whatever is to come with the same confidence and courage that we have always been called to. Let us have confidence that no matter what, God's word of salvation will not return to him empty. Let us trust in God's truth, no matter how dark things appear at the time. Let us remember that no matter what, we are called to love God, and love our neighbor." Soong stopped, looked around for a moment, and then announced that communion would be held for any who desired. He stated that communion was a public act indicating belief in Christ, and that anyone who did not believe should feel no pressure to participate. He then produced a cup with a dark fluid and a collection of pieces of re-hydrated bread. GoDai watched as some of the crewmen stepped forward and took a drink and took a piece of bread, while others filed out of the room. He, and many others, stopped and watched as Captain Adams stepped forward and reached for the cup. "Is that normal?" Stephen whispered to Susan.

"No, she always left at this point if she came to a service." GoDai and Darron waited as Susan and then Stephen walked forward. They returned, and started to leave, but Darron was standing, looking at Soong holding the cup. As people left, a few volunteers started to break down the podium for storage. The three others waited as Darron kept standing, not moving forwards or back. Then he walked forward just as Soong was packing up the bread and "wine". Soong turned, and served Darron, then turned away as Darron went back to his friends.

The four walked back to the tiny computer lab without speaking. Susan was silent. Stephen had noticed that Susan was silent and so he was silent, in case he had done something wrong. Darron was looking at the floor. When they reached the lab, GoDai followed the others in and then said to Darron, "Your actions are similar to when you felt the need to apologize." Darron did not answer.

"I don't think he needs to apologize." Susan stated. "GoDai, do your people, or you, believe in God?"

"There are a number of different theories about the existence of a deity, or deities. In general, I do not see the need to believe in something for which there is no evidence."

"Is there no evidence? Do any Suvain describe any experience with God? Or anything in the world that you see that seems hard to justify?" Susan asked.

"There have been a number of religions on SuvAa, but I have never heard of any credible description of an interaction with a deity, or anything suggesting one's presence. Your belief about your deity is hard to understand. The beginning of the service seemed like a usual request for help like you would hear from lots of different religions. But the second half was strange. It sounded like your new religious leader was saying that in times of trouble, you should not expect your god to save you."

Susan answered, "We do not expect our God to save us from trouble, but instead to be with us through it. We hope he saves us from trouble, and sometimes He chooses to. But his actual promise is to be with us, not that we will be protected from anything bad."

"So if bad things happen to you whether your god is there or not, what evidence is there that a god is involved?"

"He didn't say that God wasn't doing anything – he said that God is working in us, not just in our circumstances." Darron responded.

"So instead of looking only at whether someone has good or bad luck, you may also want to look at whether the person is changing." Susan added.

"And you see these changes as the evidence of God's presence?"

"Yes." Darron answered, and then stopped. Everyone was looking at him, so he started studying the floor as he continued. "When I think of Chaplain Eisen, I can see that he was different. In his sermons, he always insisted that the primary force that shaped his life, usually against his own will and desires, was God."

"People who believe something strongly may be influenced by their own belief. A strong attachment to a moral code can encourage obedience to that moral code."

"Believing something can be powerful force. But the Chaplain wasn't just obeying a moral code. He said he was learning to love. We Terrans can change, to some extent, but in the end, either he was changed because he believed a lie so hard he became someone different, or he changed because what he believed, and who he believed in, was true. If I have to choose between those two explanations, I will pick the second, because I trust in truth, not in lies. I don't see how a lie can create in you something new, that is beyond who you were before, because no matter how hard you believe something false, it is still false."

"Has there been any measureable change in the number of religious people aboard ship?" GoDai saw Darron jerk for a second, Susan start to speak and then stop, and Steve look at the other two for a second.

Then Steve answered. "There are a lot more people attending service. I used to go sometimes, and there would be about 20-30 people there. Now the room is filled."

"There is often an increase in activities such as religion when a primitive race first meets a sentient species."

Susan laughed. "Probably because of fear. Having your fate decided by another is a scary situation. Fredrick said there was a saying when he was a boy —that there are no atheists in foxholes."

This statement caused a pause.

"What is a 'foxhole'?" Darron asked. Susan realized she didn't know for sure.

"I think it had something to do with war, and people afraid of getting killed."

"So if your god doesn't help you, why do you get more religious if you are scared?"

"She didn't say that God never saves us from bad situations. And besides, when you are in real trouble, you might as well ask." Stephen put in.

"But if your god helps you sometimes, and sometimes doesn't, how do you know any 'help' isn't just random chance?"

"Well, we don't base our belief just on whether God chooses to help or not. And it is not surprising that God sometimes does what we want, or expect, and sometimes He doesn't. He knows what is truly good, and we don't." Susan stopped, as she saw GoDai's arms flex in and out for a second.

"When we first met, you talked about people being 'sentient' or 'primitive'. Susan said. "Are sentient races the ones who are advanced, and civilized, and in charge, and 'primitive' races are those who are undeveloped and barbaric, and generally stupid and behind?" GoDai listened and agreed that the definitions were correct. "So if you are dealing with a really primitive race, do they always understand why you do something? Or are there times when the primitive race just isn't advanced or smart enough to understand why you do things?"

"It is common for primitive races to not understand."

"And the difference between us and God is much greater than the difference between a sentient race and a primitive race. It is not surprising that we don't always understand God's choices. I would be worried if God always acted the way I expected – it would be a sign that my 'God' was no different than something I could just imagine."

"So you think of yourself like the primitive race?" Susan thought GoDai was just asking a normal question. Stephen and Darron could see that GoDai was nervous, or angry.

"Yes," Susan answered. "Basically, God is the one who is sentient, and we are all primitives."

"You believe that the Terran race is primitive?" GoDai asked again. He looked suspiciously at Susan, and then back to Darron and Stephen. "Is this why you judge people to be sentient or primitive, instead of populations?

Because you see all populations as primitive, and being sentient is something an individual achieves through religion?"

"We see all people, and all populations as primitive, and God as sentient," Susan answered. "And not really religion, but God, works in us to change us from primitive to being more like him – learning to love God and others, instead of just ourselves."

"So that is why you don't think that some have the right to rule over others. Because some might be better than the rest, but all are primitive."

"And because even though we are all primitives, God can make anyone sentient. There is no on one so high they are sentient, with the right to rule over everyone else, and there is no one who is so primitive that God can't save them. So no matter what someone's skills are, or how primitive they are, they are still people, with rights, and with as much possibility of being touched by God as any of us." Susan had been talking for some time now, and paused, to try to remember what she had just said, and check if it made any sense.

"Do you see the Suvain as just as primitive as Terrans?" None of the Terrans answered, but GoDai could already recognize the signs of a Terran who didn't want to say something embarrassing or insulting.

After a moment, Susan answered, "We don't see entire populations as more or less primitive. And the point of the analogy is that we aren't comparing to each other, but to God."

GoDai was looking at Susan when Stephen shrugged and answered directly, "We see Suvain and Terrans as pretty much the same. In terms of who is civilized and who is primitive, so far a Suvain has shot a Terran, and the Suvain are threatening the Terrans, not the other way around."

"Do all Terrans agree with you on this?"

Daron laughed. "All Terrans don't agree on anything. Seriously, I can't think of a single thing every Terran agrees on." GoDai was silent, and both Darron and Stephen could see that something was wrong. Susan saw both start to go into turtle mode, guessed the source, and asked GoDai what he was thinking.

"Those thoughts will get you killed. If you do not recognize that the strong rule over the weak, you are going to choose resistance, which will lead to your death."

"We do realize that the strong often do rule over the weak. If your hope is that we will willingly accept you as sentient and rightful rulers,

I think you will be disappointed. I don't think you will find anyone who believes you have a right to rule. But you may find people who believe you have the ability to rule." Susan answered.

"If there are Terrans who believe we have the ability to rule, it will be the first time I have heard of a Terran who believes something true."

"Well there are some things that Terrans believe that are obviously true. For example, 2+2=4," Stephen said.

"It depends if you accept Mathematics as true," Darron responded. "After all, Mathematics is really only a set of logical inferences based on an unproven set of postulates. It has no official connection to actual reality."

"And yet that reality is specifically described by what you dismiss as mere inference," Stephen countered.

As the argument heated up, and both Darron and Stephen forgot the existence of Susan and GoDai (except possibly as an audience to be convinced), Susan looked over at GoDai. She found that GoDai was watching the programmer and the physicist, and watching her. When he saw her look his way, he leaned over and asked quietly, "Would you say these two Terrans are typical examples of the Terran species?"

Susan laughed, distracting and briefly annoying Darron; he had been making a very important point and assumed that Susan was indicating disagreement. Darron continued, and Susan whispered back to GoDai, "Until you showed up, I was not even sure that these two were members of the Terran species at all."

"It would seem unlikely that I would have happened by chance to have been assigned to meet with two individuals so far from the normal."

"I am surprised that Captain Adams decided to have you spend time with these two. It increases the chance you will blow up the *Persephone*, just for the peace and quiet."

"Are they posturing for status? Or trying to impress a female of their species?"

"They have almost never met a female of their species, and Thank Heavens, have forgotten for the moment that I am a female of their species. No, they are arguing because they actually care about the answer. I think they are friends because they both care about the same things. And for most things they care about, they are the only the ones who care. Last week, four of them were arguing about which imaginary monster would win in a fight. It is hard to prove your point when both sides are making up all of the data."

GoDai made his way back to the *ProfitTaker*; he had a display given to him by Stephen. After showering and recording his notes, GoDai requested a meeting with the Tavir.

GoDai entered the Captain Annex, and after approval, sat down across from the Tavir. He placed the tablet on the Tavir's table. "This is a gift from the Terran information personnel. Apparently, during their visit, their information personnel and ours decided that it would be a good thing if the Captains of both ships have a private communication link. So they set one up for you. At least there was an agreement that Terran technology would be used on each end. They assure me that there is no security risk."

"Do you believe them?'

"How should I know? I would guess that it is okay – I would assume that our information fanatics know more than their information fanatics."

Tavir reached over and took the tablet, looked at both sides, and then set it down. "Have you changed your mind about the need to exterminate the Terrans? Or found any specific threats?"

GoDai fidgeted. "Nothing that anyone would listen to."

"I sent your report to my father. It was reviewed and sent back to SuvAa, under your name, not as an official statement of the Tavir Holding. We received notification of receipt of your recommendation. It will probably be considered with the usual government efficiency and timeliness. So I ask again – have you found anything specific to add to your recommendation?"

"There is one good sign – the Terrans are getting more religious. That is usually a sign primitives are afraid for the future. But that is about the only good sign. Everything else I see suggests these primitives are going to resist. About the only hope is that the Terrans in charge are a lot more practical than the crew of the survey ship. I can't imagine how these Terrans even function in the real cosmos."

Tavir watched GoDai, and thought that maybe he should pull GoDai back off duties for a bit. GoDai was starting to show irritation and defensiveness more and more often. He was still watching GoDai when GoDai burst out, "The other bad things are the things that no one is going to listen to. Usually when a primitive race is contacted, they are scared and confused. These people aren't. They are afraid, certainly, but they aren't confused. I am. If I am the sentient one and they are the primitives, why do they understand us, and I am so confused by them? Another thing I don't understand is how they knew they were primitive before they ever met someone sentient. Most races are sure they are the best thing in the universe until they meet someone real. And last, I don't see anything the Terrans are doing that copies what they see, except for making weapons. Weapons that are getting better already, by the way. I am sure that they are already producing a better version of their angulin gun, and I think they are already making plans for another improvement after that. When we met the Ravvois, they were making fake spikes to stick on their arms to look more like us. The Terrans aren't making spikes, and they seem more excited than impressed. Have you been in the physical sciences lab lately? There are pictures all over the lab about some special solar system they are all talking about. They first mentioned it a while ago. But then the only pictures they had were several graphs – they showed mass transfer or something, and timelines. Now the graphs can hardly be seen. The room is full of pictures that are color-enhanced, with all sorts of reds, and browns, and blues. They look like the Terran pictures our scientists brought back from their visit. We are sentient. They are primitive.

Why are we learning from them, not the other way around?"

Tavir listened to the whole outburst. He watched GoDai slump down in his chair, with his arms still tensed. "I am listening to what you say. We may disagree about the extermination, but I do take the primitives seriously. You are to spend the next 2 days away from Terrans, away from any tasking. I do not need to point out that it is not to be mentioned with other crew members that you are getting 2 days leave – everybody will show up with Terran Disease and need a week or two to goof off."

Tavir watched GoDai leave, and then turned his attention to the monitor sitting on his desk. He picked it up, and looked over both sides and all four edges. He knew that if there was some security risk due to the Terran monitor that it wouldn't be something he could see by looking at the hardware, but somehow it felt good to look. He pushed the round discolored area GoDai had indicated, and the screen lit up with three large squares – one marked "On", one marked "Hear", and one marked "See". He wasn't sure whether to be irritated that the information fanatics thought he couldn't understand anything more than three buttons, or grateful that they built an interface with him in mind, instead of building an interface with the 50,000 functions they probably thought were absolutely necessary. He also wondered how the Terran IFs knew how to write the labels in Suvain script. He pressed the On square. The On square moved to the top left, shrank, and was relabeled Off. Both of the other squares lit up with blue boundaries. He pressed inside the See square. There were several flashing things that started up, which Tavir guessed was some indication that something was happening. After about a minute, the entire screen was filled with the Terran captain.

"Welcome to the new hotline our programmers decided we should have," said Captain Adams.

"Was this your idea, or was it really developed by your programmers on their own?" questioned the Tavir.

"It appears that your programmers and ours thought this up after dinner. I have not decided whether to reward them for showing initiative and improving Terran-Suvain relations, or shoot them for setting up unauthorized communications with your ship."

"They are too valuable to shoot". The Tavir answered. "They may be annoying, but if they were shot, we would have to start maintaining our own information systems, and that would be more annoying than the information fanatics already are."

"If they are ever together in the same room again, I think I am going to assign a chaperone," answered Captain Adams.

"There may be a brief decrease in the frequency of Suvain visits. I have decided that GoDai needs a brief break from Terran interaction, and he will be suspending his visits for a short time."

"Have my crewmembers been failing to fully support his visits?" "No – there have been no improper actions by his contacts."

"Good. There was a file of information I had intended to send back with him, probably in a few days. If he is unavailable, you may want to send someone else over to pick it up. I am assuming we have been told the full story when we were assured that no file transfer is possible over this new link."

"What sort of information?"

"I have requested that a list be sent of all Terran representatives who be coming to meet you at Loren Station. In addition, I have also asked a few friends to see that whatever background information on the delegates be included, so you will have a better idea of who you will be dealing with."

"That information could be valuable. I am surprised that you would provide such information, as knowing the background of my negotiating partners may increase the chance of the Terrans choosing the rational course of surrender – a course of action you have always stated that you oppose."

"A better knowledge of the Terrans you are dealing with might also help foster clear communication that avoids a war," Captain Adams answered. "And besides, Suvain or not, you are a ship captain who is going to have to deal with politicians. Any captain facing that assignment deserves all the support a fellow captain can give."

"You have my thanks. Of course, as a ranking member of the Tavir Holding, you could say that I am a politician as well as a captain."

"You are a politician? You had me completely fooled. All this time, I had thought you were sentient."

Tavir laughed. "Again, my thanks for your provision of information. I will send GoDai or another crewman over when the information is available."

"Very well. Until our next meeting." Tavir saw the Terran's hand raise towards the screen, and the conversation was over.

For the next several days, both ships began decelerating sharply to reach the Intersection field at low velocity. Without GoDai's visits, Susan went back to her heavy-element studies, Darron went back to reviewing the recordings of the *ProfitTaker's* movements, and Stephen went back to building simulations. The Captain wanted a description of how fast the remaining Suvain ships could reach the Intersection field if they really tried. The only thing they had to go on was the acceleration rates the ships had shown when they first enclosed the Persephone. The *Persephone* could not sustain her maximum acceleration for very long; the Terrans had no way of knowing if the Suvain had actually been moving at full speed, or if so, if this was an acceleration they could maintain for long periods of time, or just a short burst. Stephen and Darron made a series of test runs making different assumptions about the Suvain abilities, and provided the results to the Captain. She did not find the results encouraging. They had deliberately wasted time heading back, but even if they had tried to fly as fast as possible, it still would have been nearly a three week trip. The most worrisome estimate was that the Suvain could go from one intersection field to the other in under six days. Should the Tavir decide to use force, this would give Loren Station practically no time to prepare. Captain Adams was sure that some sort of preparation was already underway. The messages coming in through the trail of communication relays no longer were emphasizing the need to delay arrival. She doubted if there really was anything that could be done for Loren Station if the Suvain decided to sweep out the local primitive infestation, but some sort of response was apparently nearing completion. They should reach the holes in about two days, given their current rate of deceleration. Captain Adams sent out a message to all senior officers to prepare their sections for crossing.

Each segment of the crew began the routine breakdown of equipment all around the ship. There were a few delays, as the Captain and the senior officers debated whether the compression for crossing would make the Persephone too juicy a target for the Suvain to resist, but nobody really expected the Suvain would wait this long, and then turn on a single ship. As much to feel like they were doing something as for any rational reason, the breakdown and compression sequence was changed to breakdown everything internal first, and only start the actual compression just before the crossing. Captain Adams called across to the Tavir, and sent over the location off the largest discovered Intersection. She then activated the location beacons which surrounded the Intersection, giving a visual signal showing the Intersection's location and size.

Stephen was busy making and storing backups of everything on the ship, in case something which was taken apart didn't come back on correctly. Both Susan and Darron were systematically saving off all information about each ongoing project, and then taking apart every piece of equipment and furniture in their lab. Each crewman in their off-shift went through all of their personal gear, and started storing it away in the 2 cubic foot boxes they had just reassembled. Jon was one of the crewmen who were always ritually disliked by everyone else as a crossing was prepared for. He would actually be a member of the bridge crew, helping to ensure that the ship was lined up exactly on the center of the guidance lasers being received from the location beacons. If a crewman died on voyage, it was the duty of his or her immediate superior to pack their gear, and label it for transport to the deceased crewman's relatives. As the Chaplain had officially reported to the captain, Captain Adams cleaned Eisen's room herself. It was a slow task; she was constantly finding things over which she stopped and reminisced.

Although packing things tightly became a skill of all crewmen, she could not find out how to get everything back in the boxes it had all supposedly come from. As she had spent every crossing on the bridge, she did not know that Fredrick wore almost every set of clothes he had while he was packed in, with smaller items shoved in his pockets, or that the large cross actually broke down, and had been held in his arms during each crossing. She did have the opportunity to save some space by throwing out the illegal coffee maker. She piled the coffee maker, the coffee, the water container and all of the assorted coffee junk into one of his boxes and took it out to dump it in one of the recyclers. On the way she found herself stopped in the corridor, looking at all of the gear. She turned around and began walking toward the crew quarters, summoning Soong. When he arrived, she took everything into his cabin, and gave him the box as well. "You are the acting Chaplain, so you have one extra square meter of space. There is still a bunch of stuff in the former Chaplain's room to be cleared. And if you find anything not allowed by regulations, like for instance a coffee maker, you should remember that if such a thing is ever observed by a superior officer, it would mean instant dismissal from the Fleet." She handed the open container to Soong, who looked at it, remembered the talks he used to have with his predecessor, and took the box.

When the deceleration was complete, and all possible equipment had been moved to storage, Captain Adams gave the order to begin compression. The sensor equipment on the wings retracted first – folding up and folding themselves into the hull. Once sensor storage was confirmed, the captain gave the order to retract the sensor wings. Both wings folded back into the main body of the Persephone. The aft landing bay, now empty of everything but a few scorch marks on the walls, was then pulled back into the ship, with walls folding themselves up like accordions. The Terrans had left the front and top sensors extended, and could see the Suvain ships all clustered around the Intersection. The Suvain ships were smaller to begin with, and so did not require as much compression. The Terrans watched as each Suvain ship folded its wings back onto its central hull, the left folding over the top of the hull, and the right wing over the bottom. The central section slid slightly inwards. In each case, the wings and hull folded over so that the weapon systems were still exposed, all clustered at the front of the compressed vehicle. On the *Persephone*, Captain Adams gave the order for crew storage, and all but the bridge crew headed back for packing. Each carried the bed they normally slept on, and lined up in their appointed order. Row by row, the beds were stacked, clicking into each other, leaving 15 inch spaces for the crewmembers to squeeze into. As each row was stacked, the assigned crewmen would crawl into the small space and wait for the next row to be slid over next to theirs, closing them in until the crossing was complete. One difficulty with packing the ship and the crew had been the presence of 100 angulin guns for which there was no assigned place, and which could not be taken apart.

A few had been successfully jammed into spaces in the machinery which had been cannibalized for parts when the guns were made, but most were left without a place. The extra guns ended up being packed with the crew as crewmen placed the ungainly weapons in their bunk before crawling in beside them. The only person in the entire crew glad to be loaded into the tiny space was Susan – once she was packed in everyone stopped offering her cups of coffee before the crossing. After everyone else was loaded, the emergency personnel loaded themselves in last. Once loaded, the crew had nothing to do but wait. They could also spend their time not remembering the space-travel equivalent of campfire ghost stories, describing in great detail how lost ships had been found in which the crew had packed themselves in, and then the ship had suffered a power failure, and the bridge crew died, and the ship kept flying, and the crew couldn't get out, but their compartment had life support, so they just floated on in space, trapped forever in their banks, unable to get out, and slowly they died of thirst, while they couldn't get out, and it was dark the whole time, because they were packed in, and they couldn't get out, and when they were found, some of them had eaten their neighbors, because they were starving, and they couldn't get out. Occasionally for a crewman packed in in a tiny space, with people all around him, and the light sources almost entirely blocked, who was hearing sounds he never noticed before, Bob's cousin's friend's uncle, *who actually saw such a ship*, could suddenly seem like a credible witness.

When the crew was fully packed, Captain Adams gave the last order to finish compression. The forward sensors and the sensors across the top of the hull folded back inside, and the forward extension of the hull pulled back into the compressed body of the vessel. The *Persephone* had become almost a sphere, flying slowly through space toward the Intersection. Once fully inside, the ship would exist in both sets of space at once – when the ship moved past the joint globe of space, it was random which region of space it would be found in. For a ship that exited into a different region of space, it would appear to fly into the Intersection, and then simply disappear – appearing instantaneously in the new region of space. For a ship which exited back into the region from which it came, there would be no change at all – everything would be a smooth flight with no evidence that any unusual space had been encountered.

The bridge was now the majority of the front of the ship, and the sensors built into the hull gave only limited communication and detection ability. Even after compression, the external hull still had several angulins available for last minute thrusting. Thrusting was required as the two Suvain escort ships suddenly flew right in front of the *Persephone* and headed into the Intersection. The first flew in and suddenly was gone – it had exited the Intersection into the other region of space. The other flew into the Intersection, and continued through without anything happening at all. It had exited back into the same region it had entered from, and so had no change of location at all – it was still on the smooth path it had entered with, still in front of the *Persephone*. As the Terrans slowed to give the Suvain ships room, a message was received from the Tavir, instructing them to hold back, the Intersection was not clear. A moment later, two transmitting beacons appeared in the Intersection, flying back out towards the incoming ships. As the Suvain beacons passed to each side of the *Persephone*, Captain Adams growled that if the Suvain were finished playing games with the Intersection, she intended to cross. The Tavir stated that the Intersection should be clear, and the *Persephone* slowly slid forward into the middle of the location beacons. Once inside, the *Persephone* was entirely contained in a small globe of space that was simultaneously part of the region of space through which they had been flying, and a completely different region of space around 100 light-years away.

Even though it was completely random whether a ship exited into the desired space on the first try, or had to come back around and keep trying again, over half the crew were praying that the *Persephone* would happen to succeed on the first attempt. This was not just the usual desire of the crew to get unpacked as soon as possible – not crossing seemed like it would be a failure in front of the Suvain. As the vessel moved into and out of the Intersection, the star trackers kept a constant view of the distant star field visible from the ship. When the star trackers all reported that the star field had completely changed, cheering broke out in the bridge. Captain Adams felt herself start to breathe again, and tried to remind herself that feeling smug that they had crossed on the first try was completely irrational. The navigation officer reported that given the Suvain course and speed, they should be exiting the Intersection in about a minute. Captain Adams rotated the compressed ship around to watch the Intersection, while announcing that the crossing was over, and unpacking could begin. When a full minute had passed, and no Suvain command ship had appeared, it was apparent that the Suvain had not happened to cross on the first try. The bridge crew began exchanging knowing smiles and nods, pleased at the thought that the mighty Suvain had failed to cross the first time like the *Persephone* had. It was completely random, but it felt like a victory anyway.

For the first time, one of the escorting ships hailed the *Persephone*.

The escort ship requested that the *Persephone* move away from the Intersection to ensure there was room for the other two ships to cross and the retrieval of the Suvain communication beacons. Captain Adams acknowledged the message, sent a response welcoming the Suvain into the Loren system, and gave orders to start moving directly away from the Intersection. The bridge watched as the Suvain ship also moved away from the Intersections, and began swinging around to pick up two transmission beacons which had been sent to the Intersection, but had not crossed. Just before Captain Adams started to give the order to unpack the ship, the second Suvain escort appeared out of nowhere in the Intersection. The entire bridge crew watched as it came through, and immediately changed course and accelerated away from the congested space. With both escorts through, all eyes turned back to the Intersection, watching for the *ProfitTaker* to appear. It seemed like far too long had gone by. Captain Adams asked for the position of the two escorts, and found that one was accelerating forward, cutting them off from Loren station, and the other had circled around the Intersection, and was now moving in the direction that the Terrans currently defined as up. All sorts of scenarios started going through the Terrans' minds – now that Loren station had been revealed, maybe the attack was actually going to begin, and the *ProfitTaker* was deliberately delaying, waiting for the *Persephone* to be destroyed by close-range fire from the escorts. Meanwhile, the *ProfitTaker* could be sending messages back to a fleet on the survey side of the Intersection, now that the *Persephone* wasn't there to see them.

Suddenly the *ProfitTaker* appeared. Captain Adams glanced at the clock – it had only been 7 minutes since the *Persephone* had crossed. Given that the *ProfitTaker* had had to circle around for a second try, and wait for the second escort ship, seven minutes was a reasonable time. Captain Adams let out a breath, and could hear the rest of the bridge crew doing the same. She stood watching the screen that showed the Suvain ships for a moment, and asked if there were any unusual communications that could be detected. Nothing was being transmitted by the Suvain ships openly – there could still be ship-to- ship laser communication, but nothing seemed out of the ordinary. Captain Adams looked around at the now-relaxed bridge crew. There were suddenly smiles again, except for one young crewman who was sitting very attentively at his station, watching the captain very earnestly. She looked back at him for a second, wondered why he was so focused, then failed to suppress a laugh as she belatedly ordered for expansion to begin, and for the crew to be unpacked. The young crewman immediately started the expansion process and sent out the broadcast to the crew compartments that the crossing had been successful and that unpacking was in process. It was rapidly decided among the bridge crew that no one had any recollection of forgetting the crew and leaving them packed for an extra five minutes.

IV

The Loren system had four planets. Two were small and close in to the star; they had been surveyed from a distance, but no one had ever even tried to land an unmanned probe for more detail. The fourth planet was a small ball of frozen rock. There had been three mining firms which had bought the rights to the planet, but none had ever established any successful mining operation. It was uninhabited, and had only the wreckage of the buildings set up during two exploratory missions. Loren Three was a gas giant. Loren station was orbiting the gas giant. Loren station had not been established in a circular orbit. It orbited around the equator of the planet, but the orbit was eccentric enough that its distance from the planet varied between 40,000 and 120,000 miles. This allowed ships to dock when the station was distant from the planet, and allowed for the collection drones to drop down to collect hydrogen when the station was closer.

Loren station was the primary point for exploration of this branch of Intersections leading out from Earth. An Intersection path to one of the three permanent Terran colonies led out from Loren station, as well as paths leading to four planetary systems with small mining establishments. There were also two lines of Intersections which were still under exploration; the *Persephone* had been the first to head out on one of the two when the Suvain were discovered. As the number of ships moving between New Chicago and Earth and the number of mining transports were steadily increasing, Loren Station was continually being expanded. The central assembly had been a simple tube with a fusion generator at the bottom and docking station on top. As the need for refueling became apparent, the bottom was expanded to support the operations of a hydrogen collector, which would drop down towards the planet to scoop up stray hydrogen, and then return to keep the fusion reactor running. As more ships used the station, the number of fusion reactors and collectors increased, and the docking station on the top of the station became the central pad in a ring of landing sites. As equipment and materials were shipped across from Earth, extra water tanks were added all along one side of the station, and the opposite side was slowly developed into a maintenance station that could perform most of the anchor maintenance needed by every ship. As a ship's angulins charged, released, and recharged,

the anchors attaching them to the hull would be under continual stress. No Terran ship could go for much longer than about 6 months in space without having to pull into a repair facility and reset the anchors. With the repair facilities at Loren Station, ships like the *Persephone* could make their regular maintenance stops without having to pull all the way back to Earth every time. Over time, the constant anchor pressure would stress the metal of the hull itself; even with regular maintenance, after several years a ship would require a trip to have the hull repaired at the Earth dockyards. Loren Station's next big jump occurred when a private investor obtained permission to add a string of entertainment rooms along the middle of the station. The cost of developing the rooms required a large loan that the developer was never able to support; he went out of business and the rooms sat vacant until a second company bought them up for practically nothing. The new company was now turning a steady profit providing distractions to the crews who were stuck at the station for months during refits. The expansions had led to a permanent population of nearly 2,000. The transition from a relay point to a floating colony had occurred ten years ago, with the opening of Disney Virtual World - Loren Station.

After the ship had fully been extended back to its normal shape and functions Captain Adams gave the order to start for the station. Long range scans quickly showed that there were a large number of ships present – far more than usual. It also showed that nothing was moving toward or from any of the four sets of Intersections that connected to the Loren system. Captain Adams guessed that all ships that could not be close to the station by the time they arrived had been stopped before travelling, so that the Intersections would not be revealed by the sudden presence of a ship. The presence of so many ships was soon explained as Loren station began broadcasting a series of greetings to the Suvain "visitors", coming from the representatives of each of the Terran governments represented. There was a delegation from the United Governments, a delegation from each regional government, a delegation from every major national government, and delegations from at least half of the smaller nations. In addition to the swarms of political representatives there were representatives from every interest group and organization that was able to get someone to Loren Station before the Intersection cut-off. Several of the major news organizations were present.

There was already a vast amount of information available about the Terran contact with the Suvain; unfortunately, most was nothing more than rumor or imagination. In a time of near-constant communication, having a collection of news professionals that presumably reviewed and verified information before broadcasting was considered critical.

Captain Adams pulled the *Persephone* alongside the *ProfitTaker* as both escort ships took up positions in front of the Tavir. She pulled out the captain-to-captain hotline and called over to Tavir.

"You were not kidding", he stated. "You really have hundreds of different governments, each of which think they deserve my time."

"Yes. They all will want to think they are considered important, but the United Governments is the one that will give a final decision."

"I suppose if I don't talk to them, they will blow themselves up in protest."

Captain Adams laughed. "If so, talk to as few as possible. Nothing could help the Terran race more than the removal of politicians. Remove enough of them and we might actually get work done."

"You listed which politicians might be present, and where they were from, but I am still unclear on who reports to who. I am not going to spend the time required to sit and have all the same discussions over and over with what – hundreds? of these people."

"I will contact the Fleet commander. He is used to dealing with the mess of them. I suspect he can set up some group meetings to pacify egos, and save time for real work."

"Very well. In the future, kindly ask all of your representatives to go through your ship in communications to avoid duplication."

"You want me in between you and that horde? What have I ever done to you?" Captain Adams sighed. "It may be for the best. I will forward your suggestion on, and start acting as your adjutant, taking your messages and making your schedules. At least until someone better at the job steps in."

"My thanks." Captain Adams could now recognize the Suvain arm movements expressing irritation. "There really are hundreds of them. Unbelievable. Until our next meeting, Captain." Captain Adams sent out the Suvain "request" to her superiors. She received a response that a "Councilor Extraordinaire" had been appointed for the United Governments and for the Earth Exploration Fleet. This individual, a Mister Aguilera, would be the focus for communication with the Suvain. He would forward all proposed schedules and Terran communications to the *Persephone*. Captain Adams decided that the crew would be in an unfamiliar situation when they reached the station due to all the attention that would probably be given to the first crew to meet the aliens. To ensure the crew stayed calm under the stress, she put everyone on extra shifts preparing the ship audit for the coming refit.

As the ships headed towards the station, GoDai visited several times. Most of the conversations were now about how all the governments were connected, and how the United Governments worked. Darron and Stephen were so completely useless for such topics that they and Susan sat with GoDai in the mess, where the Personnel Officer worked through GoDai's questions. Most of the time, other crewmen would cluster around as diagrams were drawn, famous leaders were mentioned, and maps were displayed.

GoDai's arms were flexing slightly without him even knowing it. While GoDai was trying to get everything straight, a message came from the station – The Councilor Extraordinaire was suggesting a schedule of events for the Suvain. He had arranged for a series of six dinners. The first five dinners each included representatives from a regional government, and every national government from the same continent. The sixth had left over odds and ends – national governments that were not connected with a regional government, and representatives of two of the Terran colonies. The formal meetings with the United Governments would begin four days afterwards. A list was included of the ships present at the station, and which landing pads were being made available for the Suvain ships. Instructions had been given to all ships that no one was to approach the Suvain ships within 10,000 km without a specific invitation from the Suvain. GoDai reviewed the lists and agreed to take them back to the Tavir. After a couple of modifications, the Suvain schedule was set. A series of messages then started back and forth between the *Persephone* and Loren Station; the cooks wanted to know all about what the Suvain liked to eat.

Once the audit was complete, the crew was put to cleaning the ship from stem to stern. Since the 6-month survey had been cut short by almost 2 months there was far more water available than usual to try and clean up the marks left by 120 people living in a tiny, unwashed container for months.

Each section was cleaned and reviewed by a senior officer and then the captain. Most sections were almost up to the captain's standards, except that burn marks were still being removed from the cargo bay. Once the crew had made the best possible attempt at the ship, they were given water to make themselves and their clothes as presentable as possible. Each of the crew only had a couple of sets of clothes to wear for the entire survey, so as presentable as possible was still not very good. Normally, no one would care – crews were expected to look wretched when they returned; in this case, the crew would be shown on displays across Earth and every Terran settlement. The captain and senior officers were more distressed at the condition of the crew uniforms than any one of them would admit. Worn uniforms seemed like a disgrace to the ship, and the coming disgrace was behind a tendency to snipe at the crew and find fault with lots of things that would otherwise be ignored. Then, without any request, a message was received from CE Aguilera. He was arranging for a ship to meet the crew before station landing that would provide brand new dress uniforms and barbers and stylists for the crew. There were a number of comments from both officers and crew that this was a useless waste, even as tension dropped around the ship immediately.

Soon after CE Aguilera saved the ship from disgrace, Captain Adams received a message she had expected and disliked in advance. Interviews had been requested with Captain Adams and members of the now-famous crew of the *Persephone*. Although reporters were not as disruptive as politicians, they were still annoying and slimy. In addition to the normal annoyance, the request was for a meeting as soon as the ship had landed, when the captain would have all sorts of other tasks. Captain Adams growled at the screen for a moment, and then memories of the aft cargo bay in flames came back to mind. Dark thoughts of revenge slowly bubbled to the surface. The captain smiled with true pleasure and activated her display to record a response. "In order to ensure you have true first-hand reports, the two people who were the very first to discover the existence of alien life will be made available for any question you would like to ask." She smiled innocently and closed the transmission. She then considered that the victims would still be *Persephone* crewmen, and their images would be broadcast across inhabited space.

Stephen had been on double shifts along with Jon since the failed first angulin gun, and both were showing signs of continual lack of sleep. She sent orders to all three disciplined crewmen that they were off their extra guard assignments, and they were to get enough sleep to look normal by landing.

According to the schedule set up by Aguilera, the *Persephone* was pulling in first, and the *ProfitTaker* coming in one day later. This was intended to allow enough time for each event to be properly celebrated and broadcast. After some argument, it had been decided to bring the *Persephone* in first, because once the aliens landed, everyone would be distracted when the human ship came back in. There had been a long discussion at Loren Station about whether to meet the aliens with celebration or with strict formality. Some of the representatives thought that strict formality might demonstrate to the aliens that humans should be taken seriously. The Councilor Extraordinaire had cautioned that the Suvain weren't likely to be that impressed with the Terrans, as they had seen lots of different races in the past, many of whom were a lot more impressive than the Terrans could ever hope to be. Another group of representatives wanted the alien entrance to be a huge celebration, with the feeling that the Suvain might be more interested in negotiation with a race that was so obviously excited to meet them. The Councilor Extraordinaire had cautioned that while it was fun to be greeted by a bunch of happy puppies, the greeting didn't convince you that the puppies were humans. Eventually the decision was reached to not worry about what the aliens would think, and celebrate if they felt like it, and be serious if they felt like it. As this was the only time that aliens would be welcomed to a human space station for the very first time, things were tending towards celebration.

As they closed for the final approach, the *Persephone* pulled ahead of the Suvain ships, and made the last arrangements for the landing. Captain Adams responded to the growing pressure of representing the entire North American Defense Force and Earth Space Command on camera by snapping at officers and pointing out small errors each time she moved past a crewman. A small ship came out from Loren Station, notified the Suvain of its intentions, and pulled up to the *Persephone*. The cargo transfer was quickly accomplished, and the little transport pulled away. Within the *Persephone* there were frantic efforts to make the crew presentable.

Uniforms were handed out, and every effort was made to make the ship look like the public's expectation of an elite starship. A list of instructions for the crew had also been delivered. Upon arrival, the crewmen were to disembark in their new dress uniforms, and move past a reviewing stand of important government representatives. After passing through the reception, they were to stand at attention in a long, impressive line, while Captain Adams officially reported the return of the ship to her superior officers. After the formal review and videos the crew were to file off, still in perfect order, into a room safely away from the cameras, where a party was to be held in their honor. Looking at the schedule, Stephen and Darron discovered for the first time that they were expected to part from the crew and proceed to a separate room for a special assignment.

The crew had not stood in line since the ship launched months ago, and then no one was watching. The crew could not practice walking out and standing in line – there was nowhere on board that was big enough for the crew to stand together. The captain spent multiple sessions with the officers, making sure that each officer knew which order they were supposed to walk out in, and which crewmen were following each officer. Each section was called out to practice walking in order to the mess hall and standing at attention in line. After the section had practiced a few times, the next officer would lead out all of his crewmen in the walking drill. The crew hadn't tried to look professional for ages. The officers led each section in practicing just standing at attention. For a crew that was used to wearing old clothes and acting as they pleased, the entire experience was agonizing. The Information Technology section was truly hopeless. It was always next to impossible to convince a programmer to obey an order they did not personally understand or agree with. Instead of simply doing what they were told, programmers inevitably did what they thought was the right course of action. Since programmers generally felt that appearance was irrelevant, attempting to convince the programmers that standing at attention was important went nowhere. After all, it was obvious that if the crew was going to be standing there for a long time, standing in a relaxed pose made a lot more sense than trying to force yourself into some silly fixed posture. As the fixed posture was less efficient, it was obviously stupid. If an officer was trying to force the front half of the line into standing straight and still, the back half was standing comfortably. When the officer had moved back and got the back half straight, the front half had relaxed. Finally the IT section was divided in thirds and stuck between other groups.

As the ships grew closer to Loren Station, most of the ships at the station moved out and signaled a greeting to the Suvain, and then pulled away to leave the approach clear for the visitors. Four pads were clear – the *ProfitTaker* was directed to the closest landing pad to the entry to the core living area of the station. Several smaller pads were made available for the escort vessels; the *Persephone* was allocated a space well away from the others. Both escort ships moved forward of the Tavir, and took up positions to each side of the *ProfitTaker* as it moved towards the station. The Suvain then slowed, and the *Persephone* moved alone to the station. As they pulled up, most of the crew were watching the displays showing Loren Station and the ships moored there. The ships were a collection of all different shapes and sizes. Every fleet had different ship designs they preferred, and different colors they painted their ships. The human crew had always looked at these ships as shining examples of human technology. The now-Terran crew looked at all of the ships and wondered if the Suvain would look at the station as a giant junkyard. As they pulled up, they could see the landing pads set aside for the Suvain. The largest pad was next to the largest ship at the station. The ship was a misshapen, bulging cylinder that looked far too large to fit through the Intersection back to Earth. As they moved past, Stephen stiffened, and started frantically looking around the crowded mess hall for Darron or Jon. As the people around him leaned away, he saw Darron and hissed across the room, "*Look at the name! On the ship! It's the Thunderchild! Look at the name painted on the hull!*" As Darron, and everyone else, looked as Stephen blankly, he hissed again, "*The Thunderchild*". As no one responded, Stephen gave up, shook his head at humanity in general, and went back to staring at the ship on the screen. The order went out that all crewmen were to change into their dress uniforms and prepare for landing. Everyone headed for their quarters. The bridge crew settled the *Persephone* gently onto her station, and the docking clamps locked.

Usually the landing process extended for several hours past the docking time. Once the ship was docked, the angulins had to be locked down and connected to the station's power grid. Internal systems were disconnected, and reconnected to station services. The crew usually performed all these tasks, and made any final shutdowns before the hatches were opened. In this case, there were the necessary adjustments made to ensure ship safety, and then the crew was ordered to line up for disembarking. A long tunnel had been extended to the airlock; it led into a long, low building which had been inflated and stabilized in the last month. Reviewing stands had been hastily built inside along the right, and the left was a long series of cameras. The crew was to walk down the middle, shaking hands with the important people at the front of the review and then continuing on in perfect order. When they got to the far end, the crew was to continue on through the main doors at the end. A handful of crewmen were to turn left after the review and head into a small side room for special interviews. The sections formed up in successive rooms in the ship, and then the hatch opened, nerves tightened, and the order was given to walk out in full view of all the Terrans in the galaxy. Everyone came to attention, and with nowhere else to go, the first section lead the long column out to the waiting worlds. They passed the admirals and United Governments representatives, shaking hands, and then stepped out to march along the long reviewing stand. Each section followed, trying to ignore the fact that they were being filmed the entire way. Every officer saw nothing but the irregularities in the line – crewmen who weren't properly erect, crewmen who were a little too far behind the man in front, crewmen who were nervously smiling, not stone-faced. Among the billions of viewers, a handful were naval officers or crewmen who judged the appearance of the crew. Everybody else just watched the crew walk through the review, and didn't notice a thing.

When the section with Darron reached the end of the Valley of Death, he found the Personnel Officer waiting for him. MacDonald indicated the door to the left, and Darron turned aside from the rest of his section. He watched as they escaped, and wondered what the "special assignment" might be. He assumed that since he and Stephen had spent the most time with the Suvain, there was going to be some special de-brief where lots of skilled people asked detailed questions, possibly about the alien weapons technology. He waited while Stephen came through and was collected. He noticed that the Personnel Officer seemed to be avoiding looking at either of them in the eye. Darron and Stephen followed the Personnel Officer to the door, saw it open, walked through, and found themselves in a small room with several very close cameras, and an attractive young woman with a microphone. As the realization that they were not free of the cameras sunk in, they heard as if from a great distance the statement that here were the two crewmen provided to provide a more personal account of the discovery that Mankind was not alone in the universe. Darron could see Stephen's face go blank, and his usual fidgeting stop. His fingers flexed a few times; Darron knew that he desperately wanted to withdraw into a small room and program frantically. As Stephen had stopped, Darron was a couple of steps ahead, and suddenly all three cameras were looking at *him*. He suddenly became convinced that there was something in his hair. Then he was suddenly sure that his uniform was not correct. Then he couldn't remember if he was supposed to be smiling, to indicate the Fleet had friendly people, or if he was supposed to be stone-faced, to indicate that the Fleet has serious people. He stood there, watching the attractive reporter step towards him, presenting the microphone. She had immediately realized that Stephen was not going to be of use, and had focused on Darron as her most likely source of a reasonable interview. She smiled, and Darron became very nervous. "So how did you feel when you first saw the light coming out of the holes?" she asked.

"They are not holes, they are Intersections", Darron said automatically, and the interview went downhill rapidly. Darron was truly lost being interviewed, and the "Intersections not holes" speech was very comfortable ground. He started off immediately into the discussion of the nature of Intersections, a subject about which everyone should be aware, and was so nervous that he was giving the speech at almost twice the usual rate.

MacDonald had followed the other two in, and had watched the inevitable disaster. He waited for a little while, and then, as the desperate reporter started to just cut Darron off, he spoke over the description, thanking Darron for his excellent information. The reporter gratefully turned to the new contact, and as Darron and Stephen fled, the Personnel Officer began describing the interactions with the Suvain. In the next week, the broadcasting company received 1047 messages from physicists from every system occupied by Terrans. Each message thanked the station for providing time for a description of the nature of Intersections – a subject about which everyone should be knowledgeable - and then pointed out that Darron's description, while excellent, was not quite correct or clear; a more complete description was provided. The reviewer at the station sent out 1047 responses each thanking a physicist for the very useful information, and deleted 1047 emails.

Darron and Stephen found themselves at the party being held inside. They were not exactly sure what had happened between the interview room and the party – someone must have directed them along to the right place. Once there, they discovered that alcohol was being served, and as the crew had been completely dry for months, about half were already pretty well gone. They looked around at the unfamiliar social situation, saw Susan Underwood, and moved to her as the only safe place in the room. She asked them how their interview had gone. When they asked her how she knew they had been interviewed, they were informed that the broadcast had been watched by the entire crew. In fact, people were watching the clip again, right now. There was a lot of laughter coming from that direction. Just then the Captain entered, and the entire room broke into cheers. She silenced the crew, thanked them for their service, and told them who to talk to to find their personal trunks and sleeping compartments on station. She then formally thanked Darron and Steven for taking the time to speak with the reporter. As the embarrassed two looked at her, she then smiled and mentioned that the next time they set her ship on fire, they wouldn't just be facing a reporter. This brought laughs from the entire crew, many of whom were laughing at anything. The crew was told to be ready for assignment at 8 the next morning, and the Captain released the crew back to the party. She then moved over to where Stephen, Darron, and now Jonathon had congregated around Susan.

"You are going to have a lot to do for the next several weeks", she told them all. "You have the usual clean-up on board, but also you are probably going to be asked to report on your experiences with the Suvain; people are going to want to know everything you picked up about them. Of course, internal cameras were filming everything, and lots of people will have been watching them over and over. But they will still want to hear your impressions. The Suvain will be coming in tomorrow, and we will all have to be there to greet them. After that, you can expect to be called out to sit with the Suvain during meetings, or even as they walk around the station. It has been decided that the

Suvain should have familiar faces in view as much as possible. And you are the most likely to be able to recognize if there is a problem. I know it is usual for a crew to have leave upon return, but these times are not usual. In fact, there may never be usual times again. I will see what I can do to get you some time off before we leave for Earth, but I can't promise anything."

Captain Adams paused. "If the human race does somehow make it through this, you four will have had a large part in our survival." A smile flashed across her face and was gone. "I never thought I would say this to some of you." She continued seriously, "Well done." She, and all four listeners, were silent for a moment. The Captain then continued, "You had better go get some sleep. It is going to be a busy day tomorrow, and most every day afterwards."

The four started to break up on obedience to the captain's suggestion. As he started to leave, Susan called Darron back. "Darron. What did you feel when you saw the light coming out of the Intersections?"

Darron paused, and thought for a moment. "I wasn't scared at first. It was more like knowing that people claim to have seen sea serpents, and walking in and finding one in your bathtub. At first it was more shock, and a sort of question about whether this was all really happening. The fear came later – as I started to realize that there really wasn't another explanation." Darron stopped, looked away, and then looked at Susan. "How about you?"

Susan looked at Darron for a second, then smiled briefly. "Mostly relief. It was hard to believe for a while. But the main feeling at first was relief." She saw Darron's look of confusion. "Remember, I wasn't one of the first group to know what was going on. For the rest of us, we just saw people sneaking around trying not to say things in public. And these people looked really worried. Most of the guesses about what was going on were pretty dark. My suspicion was there was something wrong with the fusion reactor that couldn't be fixed or controlled. When I heard "aliens", it was a lot better than the alternatives." Darron laughed, each bade the other good night, and headed off.

Darron found that his room had an actual bed, and found he had been sleeping on a cot long enough that sleeping on a comfortable bed was impossible. After a while he got up, logged on to the room terminal, and wrote his letter to his family. Each crew member was allowed a free 30- second transmission upon return of the ship. There were some communications allowed when a ship was in the middle of a survey, but they were mostly for emergencies. In the civilized world of Loren Station, a transmission could be purchased every several weeks. Darron looked at the blank screen and tried to think of something to say. At least this time there was news beyond "We finished a survey". Darron finally typed "Mom and Dad – I hope you are well. I am fine." He was stuck here for a while, not sure what to say. "We met aliens." Darron tried to think of what to say about the Suvain, and then added, "They are a lot like us." With the past summarized, Darron plowed ahead into the future. "We may all get killed." The letter now indicated concern for his parent's welfare, a description of the past, and a description of the future. Darron added, "Darron", and was done. Before sending the message, Darron re-read it half a dozen times. He became a little concerned that his mother might worry. He added, "We probably won't be.", and sent the message. He then looked at his transmission allocation, logged onto the ship crew site and put his other 29.994 seconds of transmission time up for bid.

Stephen could have slept, but was busy sending messages to each of the 8 gaming guilds he was a member of to say that he was back from the survey. His chance of actually joining in in any guild activity was basically zero, but now that he was back, he could log onto the local net and generate resources that could be forwarded to the inter-system gaming servers for guild use.

Stephen sent out a request from each for any guild news from the last 4 months, and added suggestions about a possible new online game where players played Suvain or Terrans expanding across the universe.

Susan sent a long message to her family, and then reported to her colleagues that it looked like the heavy-element study showed promise. She had run through all of her time, so she shamelessly purchased 5 seconds of Darron's time in order to send a message describing the trip to her friends, including the pain of being stuck with two nerds in a little box for days.

When Captain Adams was finally through the first round of reports to the senior officers present, third shift was almost half over. She started a letter to her son, gave up, and went to bed.

As the *ProfitTaker* approached the landing pad, the receiving line extended all the way back from the airlock to the reception hall that had been set up in the center of the station. The entire crew of the *Persephone* was present.

Darron, Stephen, Jon, and Susan stood right behind the officers of the ship. Both Darron and Susan were busy trying to keep Stephen in line. He kept looking at the massive ship next to the pad. He was trying to say something to the others without visibly speaking or gesturing. This was ending up in suppressed mouth twitching and occasional body spasms. Then the alien ship landed, and everyone's attention moved to the airlock. After an endless five minutes, the doors opened, and the Suvain stepped forward. There were four in the glittering armor they had worn the first day they boarded the Persephone, holding rifles. They stepped out and stood at attention as a protective honor guard. Once the four had stopped in position, the Tavir and GoDai stepped out to the applause of the waiting Terrans. Both were wearing armor, and wearing the same guns as before. The four guards came to attention and walked forward down the line of Terrans. Behind them came the two ranking family members, followed by a dozen more Suvain. They moved down the line, Tavir and GoDai acknowledging the dignitaries they were passing; all the rest stayed looking forward, taking no notice of the Terrans. As the Suvain passed, the Terrans began following to the planned grand reception.

When the Persephones reached the party, they found that no alcohol was being served, and no cola. Instead there was water and coffee, and a Suvain drink. CE Aguilera had questioned the Suvain about the chemical composition of a typical Suvain beverage, and had manufactured a large supply. The Suvain tried it, and seemed to think it was not too far off. The Terrans who tried it only tried twice if they wanted to prove their manhood by drinking something that tasted something like bitter apples mixed with rotting cheese. Once the formal walk down the reception line was complete, the iron discipline of most of the Suvain vanished. Suvain crewmen were scattered around in pairs, surrounded by crowds of curious and excited Terrans. The Tavir with a single bodyguard stood facing a huge crowd of dignitaries and senior officers. He was carefully talking around any question that might give specific information about the Suvain, and describing the size of the galactic empires which the Terrans had just begun to encounter. GoDai was the only Suvain moving alone through the room; he was awash in information about Terran customs and peoples, and was learning more in a few moments than Darron and Stephen had picked up in a lifetime.

Darron was afraid at first that he would be a celebrity, since he had spent more time with the Suvain than almost anyone else, and had even been on display, broadcast to Earth and every colony. He found that lots of people acknowledged him, but not many people seemed to want to talk to him at any length. He soon was wandering alone between groups of people at the party; he found himself a little disappointed that he wasn't the center of more attention, and at the same time, very grateful that he wasn't the center of more attention. He looked around for Stephen or Susan or Jon, but they were all busy.

Jon was in the middle of a cluster of Terrans and two Suvain guards. They were carefully standing where the Tavir couldn't see them, and having an animated discussion about the guards' rifles. There was a lot of low talk, then gales of laughter. Moving a little closer, Darron could hear enough to guess that they were speculating on how well the Terran guns would perform in combat. There also seemed to be discussions of various things that the Suvain had shot in the past. From past experience and the way the Suvain stood within a protective shell of Terrans, Darron guessed that the Tavir had been very specific that no information about Suvain weapons were to be shared with Terrans. From past experience and the way the Terrans and Suvain were talking, Darron guessed that very soon, some out-of-the way corner of Loren Station was about to become an unofficial and very illegal gun range.

Susan really was the center of a lot of attention. Lots of people must had heard that she had spent time answering GoDai's questions, and everyone realized that talking to Susan was a lot more enjoyable than talking with Darron. He moved past, and found that Susan was talking about how the Suvain had been interested in the Terran history, even old, pre-flight history. Several of the people talking seemed to know something about the subject, and were finding a way to keep the others interested. Susan looked up and caught his eye for a second. He gave a brief wave, but they were deep in some discussion, and he moved on by.

Darron finally saw Stephen. Stephen had been cornered by several senior officers from the Fleet. They were having some very serious discussion, in very low voices. He started over, and the officer facing his direction looked over at him with a glare that clearly indicated an order to stay away. Darron carefully headed back to the refreshment tables. The talk went on for a little while, and then Stephen turned back to the room. He very deliberately rearranged his face into what he believed was a normal, I-don't- know-anything-special-so-don't-ask-me expression. He looked sort of like a little boy who had just shoved an entire candy bar in his mouth and thought that if he held his mouth really still, no one would know. Darron considered catching him and making him tell, but Stephen was far too excited to stay at the reception, and was heading out. It occurred to Darron that this would probably get both of them in trouble. This reminded him that they were both already in trouble. They, and Jon, were scheduled to face a disciplinary hearing about setting a Fleet ship on fire. He looked back over to the Jon cluster and wondered if he should remind Jon that this was not a good time to be having illegal gun competitions. He thought for a second, and then decided that at this moment, not having actually been part of the conversation, he could still claim to not know anything about whatever was going on. A claim of complete ignorance seemed a safer way to go, and Darron carefully moved away from the gun enthusiasts. Looking around the room, Darron decided that he had been at the party long enough to have officially attended, and he headed back to his quarters.

Four hours later, GoDai walked into the Captain's Annex. The Tavir was just sending the last of the recordings of the meeting back to the communication beacon they had stationed on this side of the Intersection. GoDai waited for him to finish, and then sat down across from him.

The Tavir looked up at GoDai, and said, "I still keep thinking that this must be some sort of elaborate hoax. Sometimes animals try to prevent being eaten by carnivores by all standing in a massive group, so that the carnivore gets distracted by all of the targets. I just keep thinking that they must have a central government, and that the hundreds of other people are actually decoys."

GoDai waggled his arms for a second, and then answered. "To really believe that, we would have to believe that Terrans are capable of such a complicated hoax – that they are so good at deception that even after all this time, we aren't smart enough to see through it."

"You're right – that theory assumes a high level of competence. That rules that theory out."

"I no longer doubt that what we have been told all along is the truth.

There really are lots of governments, and lots of different levels of governments. There is no guiding authority over the Terrans. They really do vote on the decisions that matter most. The closest thing they have to a real government is the joint government, but even that doesn't have the ability to force other governments to do what it wants. There may be some hope of drawing out a few to use against the others, but it will be tricky - there is not much opportunity on the schedule to talk to any without a bunch of others present."

Tavir nodded in agreement. "We can try to get them to accept the inevitable by offering them a share in power under the Suvain. But this will be hard, as there are so many that would have to be bought off."

GoDai looked over at the display showing the Tavir's personal fleet moving to the Loren Station Intersection, and the Tavir fleet in transit to Transfer Point 7832, where they had first seen the Terran light flashes. He looked back to the Tavir and continued. "The government is different than in a lot of primitive races. Power is not held by an individual, but by a position. A person only has power because they occupy a position, and can legally exercise the power the position holds. If there is a problem with the person occupying the position, or even if they have just been there too long, the person is switched out, and the position still has all the power for the next person to use."

"So if this were a Terran ship, the crew could decide that someone else is going to be the Captain? Even though this is my ship, from my family, under our ownership? Perhaps I should limit the contact the crew has with these Terrans. Don't get any ideas."

"I think it may be different for people like ship captains. Although even Captain Berserk isn't a captain in the sense that you are – she doesn't own the ship, and will be moved to some other ship at some point. But since the governments aren't based on people, it will probably do little good to seize any collection of leaders and use force to get them to agree to anything. You can't hold a position hostage. As soon as you took people hostage they would cease to be occupying their positions, and the next group of people would step forward."

This time it was the Tavir who looked over at the display. "So the only approach left will probably be to start destroying population centers until they see reason. It is sad, really. These people had so much potential." He saw GoDai's eyes slightly unfocus, and asked, "What are you thinking?"

"They don't really have that much potential. They just have accomplishments. They aren't a race you would look at and see anything special. But they advanced three times as fast as we did. I still can't tell you why."

"You are still recommending extermination?"

"Yes. It would be sad, sort of like hearing that your young cousin has the plague, and has to be put down. But I still feel that there is something here that is different, and dangerous. Like we had better burn it out now, or we are going to look up one day, and everything will be Terran."

"So you still believe that something has driven the Terrans forward? That they have some magical thing that makes them succeed in spite of themselves?"

"It is hard to imagine anything else – how could they have gotten here so fast on their own?"

The Tavir looked at the display, out the porthole to the Terran Station, and then back to GoDai. "Okay, then find it. Find out what special thing it is they have, and you will either have made your case for destruction, or you will have found something very valuable to take and use ourselves. But the time you have is limited. If these people say no, talking will end very soon."

GoDai nodded, and then looked at the Tavir very intently. "If you are going to shoot, you had better start the shooting fast. We didn't come across a bunch of rock-throwers – these people didn't quite meet us half-way, but they met us in space, a long way from their home world. They are going to be preparing even as we speak. I would bet you they already have weapons on this station in case the shooting starts right here. And they have been watching us all the way to the station. I suspect they are already working on armed ships. We might be able to kill them like insects, but 1,000 insects are hard to get rid of." GoDai rose and started out, and then stopped at the door. "You might be able to prevent Terran ideas from infecting the crew by taking early steps against thoughts of mutiny. If you publicly execute someone now, it would demonstrate that you are the Tavir, and can do as you wish.

Someone unreliable, like AyanA. His arms were completely steady – the sign of a truly serious Suvain.

The Tavir narrowed his eyes and considered the suggestion. "So I should shoot someone now, to make the point. And the one I should shoot is our best engineer, who also happens to be the one to whom you owe money after you bet against, *against*, the Tavir team. Perhaps I should shoot someone else, someone who turns on his own family, and bets on the other side."

GoDai considered this. His arms flicked. "Maybe preemptive execution is a bad idea," he said, and headed back to his cabin.

Most of the *Persephone*'s crew had about a third of the next three days off. Captain Adams decided that all of the attention they were getting might be going to the crews' heads, so she put everyone on a full shift cleaning the ship a second time. The crew worked for three four-hour sessions, and in between attended briefings on the station. They were given their assignments as Suvain escorts, and every person was interviewed to record anything they had noticed about the Suvain. Well into second shift, crewmen were released from duty and had some of the time off they had been expecting. Darron had lots of things he had been planning to do when he had time off; instead, he spent all of every off shift sound asleep.

Over the next three days, each of the Suvain ships docked at the station. On day four the Suvain station visits began, and Captain Adams released the crew from all duties except acting as Suvain escorts. The Suvain showed up in groups from two to four, and were met by the same number of Terrans.

They were given full access to the station, and rapidly found the entertainment and drinking establishments. Wherever they were, crowds of Terrans immediately collected. The Tavir issued specific orders to all Suvain about avoiding Cola drinking. He was soon broadcasting the same orders every morning, each time with no effect.

The first formal dinner occurred the same day as the Suvain visits began. It was a tedious trial for Tavir, and one of the highlights of the lives of the Terran delegates. Captain Adams, Personnel Officer MacDonald, and CE Aguilera escorted the Tavir, GoDai, and the captain of one of the escorting ships to a table set above and in front of the room. There they sat while the head of the Committee of European States delegation expressed the welcome felt by all Europeans towards the honored Suvain guests, and expressed the deep desire for a jointly prosperous future. There they sat while the delegates from almost every one of the dozens of European states rose and expressed, usually at some length, the same thing. There they sat while a series of toasts were proposed to the Suvain people, the Suvain government, to peaceful cooperation, to the Tavir, and to most of the rest of the Suvain the Terrans had met. There the Terrans still sat, as a final reception line passed along the table and shook hands with each of the Suvain in turn. As the meeting finally broke up, Captain Adams leaned over to Tavir and whispered, "And to think, this is supposed to encourage you not to shoot us. By the 40th speech, I was ready to shoot us."

Tavir laughed and answered, "There were only 27 speeches. At least I did not get asked for a long comment in response. But you have to let each of them think they are important." The Tavir paused for a second. "Perhaps a response would have been useful. I get the impression that they think I am here to give them things. They need to understand that

I am here to occupy the natural place of the sentient over the primitive, and that they can submit to that reality, or get in its way and be crushed by it."

"Boy, you really know how to spoil a party." Captain Adams looked past Tavir to where GoDai on Tavir's left was leaning in and listening to the conversation. At Tavir's last statement, he had frowned, then gone blank, as if he was trying to remember something. She continued, "You may want to hold that thought until you are actually having negotiations."

"You are correct. And I do appreciate the greetings."

"Sitting next to you is quite an honor for a Terran. I am going to have to think of 5 crewmembers who deserve to be honored at the next 5 dinners. I wouldn't want to claim all the glory for myself."

"I would not think of having anyone else," Tavir declared. "In fact, I think I will suggest that you not only accompany me to each meal, but that you should make a speech in response."

"If I have to give a speech it will be on the importance of physical fitness now that the threat of war is hanging over us, complete with practical exercises for all of the guests to perform. If my crew starts eating as much as these diplomats, I will never get the ship through an Intersection."

"Terrans do come in a variety of shapes and colors. Are the large, round Terrans and the thin, tall Terrans different sub-species, or is the difference actually one of food consumption?"

"A little of both, but mostly food consumption. Over-eating is a habit of nearly every Terran society which has been able to afford it. I am sure that GoDai has already heard a lot about the Terran ability to make choices that are bad in the long term, but pleasant at the time." Captain Adams stopped, realizing that GoDai was not there. Seeing her stare at the blank spot behind him, Tavir turned as well.

The Tavir looked for a second at the empty chair to his left, then looked at MacDonald's empty chair on the far left. He turned back to the remaining Suvain on his right, who saw his questioning look and answered, "He just got up and left. He looked at you for a second, and then headed out. The Terran went with him."

"If he starts acting any more erratic, I am going to have to put him in restraints," Tavir announced. "As we have been abandoned in a room full of dangerous primitives, we should probably be off as well." The Tavir and all the others rose and after extended goodbyes, managed to work their way free of the room. As they neared the landing bay, the Tavir mentioned, "Actually some of you primitives are not as dangerous as you once were. I don't think you have threatened to blow yourself up in several weeks now," he said to Captain Adams.

"I don't have to. You are his problem now", she answered, motioning towards CE Aguilera. "But if I have to sit through two or three more dinners, I am not making any promises. At least a melting fusion drive doesn't talk at you for three hours before exploding."

Tavir waggled his arms for a second and said, "I think I will have to insist on your attendance just to watch. Until our next meeting, Captain." With final goodbyes, each of the four headed away for the night. Three of the four dutifully recorded their recollections of the evenings while the memories were still fresh. Captain Adams instead started to write to her son, wasn't sure what to say, gave up, and went to bed.

As the formal dinners continued their course, the United Governments assembly continued to meet. The Terrans with the most personal experience of Suvain were called in as a panel of experts to speak to the assembled diplomats. Darron, Stephen, Susan, and Jonathon were to report at 10:00 to describe the Suvain to the Terran assembly. They were to meet at 9:00 with CE Aguilera before going into the assembly. They were to meet with the ship's officers at 8:30 to make sure they were actually presentable. At 8:30, they all showed up and received a lecture on not disgracing the ship. By the time they headed off to the next meeting, Susan could see that she was the only one who was likely to say a word. Then she watched as CE Aguilera slowly drew the other three back out of their shells. Jon asked why they were being called as witnesses, since other people had surely been watching the tapes which had been made of everything. Aguilera said that even though others had watched the tapes, people often wanted to talk to the people who had had the actual experience. He admitted that he had spent hundreds of hours reviewing the tapes himself, and promised he would be there to assist if things started to go off-track. By the end of the second meeting, Darron, Steve and Jon were talking and confident, and Susan was looking at CE Aguilera sort of like how people watch a stage magician – she could see something amazing had just happened, and wasn't sure how it had been done. Then the four of them walked into a room with almost 400 people staring at them, and she felt like crawling into a shell herself. The four experts were led to a small table that had been set up facing the assembly.

Susan glanced over at the other panel members. All three looked like they were about to dissolve. She could hear Aguilera giving some sort of introduction, and then heard him say that since less was known about Susan's work than the others, maybe she could start by giving a short description of her work on the ship – he had heard exciting things about the heavy-element density program, and he was sure everyone would be interested to hear a brief summary of her promising research. Susan stumbled a bit a first, but it was a familiar and harmless subject; after a few minutes she had gotten over the paralyzing feeling of talking in front of the crowd. After she finished, each of the others was asked to give a very brief description of what they did onboard ship. As the others talked, Susan spent her time watching the other three. Stephen had determined from the looks in the crowd during his summary that the diplomats were not programmers and had relaxed – as people who didn't really count, the audience members were no longer scary. Jon was speaking almost normally by the end of his description – he was really there to discuss angulin guns, and had convinced himself that in the worst case, if all the audience suddenly grew furious and charged the stage, he could fight his way through the entire crowd and escape if needed. Since the worst case was dealt with, he convinced himself not to worry about lesser things. Darron was the only one still nervous; he was looking at the audience like they might be carnivores.

After he had given the panel a chance to calm down Aguilera offered the audience a chance to ask questions. The first audience member recognized was one of the senior delegates to the United Governments.

He stood and asked, "Given what you have seen, if we choose to resist, do you think that we have any chance of defeating the Suvain?"

Even before the delegate had finished sitting down Stephen answered, "No." Everyone in the room was suddenly very quiet. Stephen did not continue, but just sat, looking straight at the questioner. The delegate was unused to people answering with a definitive statement and no follow-up statements; he sat down as Stephen continued to make eye contact. Stephen still said nothing else as the audience moved from silence to lots of whispered conversations between neighbors. Susan looked at Stephen, and then at Darron. Darron was staring at the audience with a look between confusion and curiosity. Susan almost started laughing out loud. She recognized the look. It was a different physical motion, but the same action – he looked just like GoDai trying to understand a completely different species. She thought back to how she had joked about Darron and Stephen actually not being Terrans. Watching Darron now, she realized that while Darron and Stephen were Terrans, most other Terrans were completely bizarre to them. She could see that Darron was confused by something, so she covered the microphone, leaned over and asked, "What's the matter?"

"Why would they ask that?" Darron answered. He had not thought to cover his microphone, and the question went through the hall. All attention turned to him, but fortunately, he was only concentrating on Susan. "Why would they be wondering if we could defeat the Suvain Empire?"

"I would guess that they want to know if we have any choice other than surrender," Susan answered.

"How does the question 'Could the Terrans defeat the Suvain Empire?' have any connection to the question 'Should we surrender?'"

Susan and Darron looked at each other while Susan was silent, distracted by the question of whether dealing with Darron and Stephen was more like dealing with an obnoxious 2-year-old or solving a puzzle. Getting her mind back under control she responded, "What question would be more useful to ask?"

"Can we defeat, no, not defeat, resist, the Tavir Holding," Darron answered immediately. A muttering went through the assembled delegates.

Susan could see Stephen looking at Darron and nodding. It suddenly occurred to her how much of his off-shifts Stephen spent playing on the computer. Susan addressed Stephen, saying "When you say that the Terrans cannot defeat the Suvain, you mean that we do not have the strength to destroy all the Suvain fleets, conquer the Suvain planets, and force the Suvain Emperor to sign a treaty on our terms – if we let him exist at all." She thought of grabbing Stephen, shaking him, and shouting, 'Can't you see what he is asking? Instead of answering like this is all a video game?' Then she realized that Stephen probably couldn't see what the delegate was aiming at. Stephen wasn't sure why people did what they did most of the time, and so answered the exact question he was asked. Since people often weren't asking the precise question they intended, this led to greater and greater confusion.

Susan had heard a lot of bad things about elected officials over the years. But she suddenly respected one of them a lot more when the original questioner stood back up, and without anger or frustration asked Darron, "Why is that a more relevant question?"

"Because the immediate threat is not the Suvain Empire, it is the Tavir Holding", answered Darron. "Whenever GoDai and the Tavir would talk about how they are going to come destroy us if we say no, the Suvain Empire is mentioned, but the Tavir are the ones who actually are doing the attacking. We would only be fighting the entire Empire if we found some way to attack them, or if the Tavir Holding was unable to defeat us, and they had to call for help."

Susan saw that this was causing either confusion or concern among the delegates, so she jumped in. "While it is true that the Suvain Empire could destroy the Terrans, we have never even met an actual representative of the Suvain Empire. We have only met the Tavir Holding, and the Tavir Holding appears to be acting on their own. If they get in trouble, they can call on the Empire for help. But that would probably mean that the Empire would get any rewards. The decision, at least the first decision, will be made by the Tavir Holding. And that decision will be based on how the Tavir match up against the Terrans."

"They match up pretty well at this point," Jon said. "They have about 30 ships, and we are just getting started. Given a little time, we can probably put something together that can at least shoot back."

Everyone looked over at Jon. "How do you know they have 30 ships?" Darron asked.

Stephen answered. It sounded like this was something that Stephen and Jonathon had talked about for some time. "Well, the Tavir has 7 ships, and he has a couple of brothers. If each brother has about the same, and the head of the family has a few more, that is 30. And they are probably all armed, but the other six ships we met weren't quite as big as the Tavir's. And it may take some time for even the Tavir Holding fleet to get here."

The patient politician appeared to have become the de facto spokesman for the audience. "So 30 is really your estimate of the number of ships the Tavir Holding can call upon, not a number we know for sure. And we don't have any actual knowledge of how long it takes the Suvain to get here?"

Darron answered this time. "We don't really know how many ships they have – at least I don't. They never talked about such things at all. But if they had a whole bunch, they would have pointed that out at once. And there are limits to how fast they can get here. We have an estimated range for the acceleration rate of their ships; it is almost certain that they can travel faster than we can from Intersection to Intersection. But they still have to travel through the same Intersections we do. And even with their more advanced technology, I don't see anything suggesting they have any form of transport that we have never heard of – they are still limited by the distance between Intersections, and they are still well under the speed of light. And the Tavir were looking for Intersections when we first found them. They are probably an exploration team just like we are. So even if they call for reinforcements from the Empire, it will take quite a while for those reinforcements to get here."

When Darron stopped, there was a pause, and then Jon stepped in. "Even assuming the Tavir decided that they were not going to ask for help, I would expect that they could eventually wear down the Terrans. A small difference in technology could cause a significant difference in combat ability, and everything we have will be thrown together - they are using ships that have been designed for combat. But it would be a long fight." He stopped, looked over at Stephen, and continued. "How many ships do you expect to build? And we don't know for sure they wouldn't be able to distinguish real ships from shells." Everyone looked towards Stephen.

Stephen was now talking to Jon – the presence of the entire assembly had been forgotten for the moment. "Their ships are a limited size," Stephen pointed out. "They can't have an unlimited amount of ammunition. Even given that our ships are low tech, we can build ships faster than they can destroy them. If we keep building, they will eventually fire everything they have, and we can swarm them."

The Jon and Stephen show was clearly going to continue, so CE Aguilera stepped in. "Thank you for your comments. There will be a series of briefings about possible strategies for defense given by senior Fleet officers. Most of this discussion here today has been based on the sort of thinking which would be found in decision-making by Terrans. In your experience, is Suvain decision-making based on similar principles?"

After a pause, Susan answered. "Their decision-making processes are similar enough that I had never asked myself the question before. They look different, and they have different habits – like they use arm motions instead of face motions to express a lot of their emotions. But once you are around them for a while, you pick all that up, and everything seems normal. You see the arms move, and think of a smile. And there isn't much that you look at and think that it is really impossible to understand." She could not help adding, "There were a few times when GoDai didn't even seem like the most alien person in the room."

Darron realized that it was true – a lot of the time Susan was more foreign than GoDai. He answered, "I never really thought about it – after the first shock of seeing aliens that looked pretty much like humans, it was easy to see GoDai as a person, not as something strange. Of course, they are all different – a lot like real people. The Tavir is a captain, and deals with governments and stuff, GoDai deals with people, and the scientists deal with science. Although they sometimes seemed more interested in practical application than in pure research."

Stephen tossed in that the programmers seemed competent, and left it at that. Coming from a programmer, this was far higher praise than most of the audience understood.

Jon had not answered, and most of the audience turned to him. "They usually don't seem hard to understand at all. They do like weapons. They have lots of different types, both plasma and chemical-based." He saw Darron's confusion, and added, "They don't call them angulin guns. The angulin's momentum is transferred to the shell, which blasts the shell into a targeted stream of plasma. They are very effective at very short range. They can shoot through practically anything, but if you want to hit something more than about 30 foot away, you are better off with a traditional chemical- propulsion gun." He turned back to the unofficial spokesman. "From what I have seen, they think a lot like us. In a lot of the conversations we have had at the station, you wouldn't be able to say which were the Suvain and which were the Terrans. Except that they have shot a lot more exotic things than we have."

Aguilera gave the audience a few minutes to digest the comments, and then switched to a new topic. "Crewman Underwood, I understand you were not called to meet with the Suvain because of your heavy-element research, but instead were there to answer questions from the Suvain representative?"

Susan answered, "GoDai had asked a number of questions about Terran history. We do not have any specialists in History on the ship, so I was called in. I had studied History, but to be honest, I could not answer most of his questions. I had studied mostly the Industrialization period, and just before space flight. A lot of his questions were about Terran history even before Industrialization."

The audience spokesman asked the obvious. "So why are the Suvain so interested in the ancient past?"

Susan paused, and responded, "I don't know. We asked him a bunch of times if there was something specific he was looking for, but he never really answered. He was always looking for the beginning of things. Whenever we talked about something, his next questions were almost always about what had happened just before."

"A bunch of his questions were about the development of technology," Stephen added. "He asked a lot about the really old stuff, too. We tried to find out if there was something specific he was looking for, but I don't think he wanted us to know what is was. Most people thought that there was something we missed – some advance we should have made."

Susan started to respond, then stopped. She closed her mouth, and then looked a little sideways at Darron. She covered the microphone for a second and whispered, "If they had a whole bunch they would have pointed that out…"

Darron went blank, and then nodded.

"Is there something you would like to share with the class?" CE Aguilera asked.

Darron was embarrassed for a second, then said, "Well, not really something we know, just a thought. If the Tavir Holding had a lot of ships, they would tell us. If the Suvain had discovered something we didn't – if there was something we should have learned and didn't – they would have said so. It was pretty clear that GoDai wanted to convince us that we should just accept their control, because fighting back would be suicide. If he could show us that the Suvain are really that much smarter than we are, he would."

For the rest of the meeting, Susan and Darron answered questions when asked, but both their minds were elsewhere. When the briefing was finally over, all four were allowed to leave, and somehow found themselves together in one of the off-duty rooms.

Darron turned to Susan. "Do you think we have this all wrong? He isn't thinking how we missed something, he's thinking that we found something they didn't find?"

Stephen answered before Susan. "It would explain why he kept thinking we were lying, and why he almost seemed scared sometimes."

Susan asked, "Do you think that is why he kept asking about whatever was before whatever it was we were talking about? He was looking to see why we had succeeded, and kept thinking it must be something farther back?"

Darron had had trouble following Susan's first sentence and had lost the thread of the conversation. He squinted at Susan, trying to get back on track. For some reason, all four found this hilarious. After some of the pent- up tension had been released, Darron added, "This is exactly the sort of thinking that GoDai would be warning us about."

Jon answered slowly, "Maybe because this is exactly the type of thinking that we should be having. Maybe we really do have a chance to wear down the Tavir Holding if it comes to a fight. I am sure that work is underway, even as we speak."

"Sure", answered Stephen, "after all, they have already …" Stephen choked on his sentence and came to a garbled stop.

"Ah", said Darron. "This secret conversation that you are not supposed to tell anyone about." All three of the others looked at Stephen, who desperately tried to look normal. All laughed again, and the group finally made their way back to the ship.

As the dinners came a close, the Tavir was regretting telling GoDai to find whatever it was the Terrans had. He was apparently off looking for the Terran secret, since he was almost never around. He had started spending more time in his cabin, reading through Terran literature. When he came out he was usually off somewhere on the station, interviewing one or another of the Terrans. He showed up when he was supposed to at a dinner, but he seemed distracted. A lot of the time, he seemed to be watching the Suvain as much as the Terrans. When Tavir asked him if had found anything, GoDai started to speak, then stopped, closed his mouth, looked at Tavir for a second, then walked back to his cabin without a word. The Tavir wondered if this was sort form of breakdown, and thought of placing GoDai under an enforced rest period again. He decided that since MacDonald was there as a Terran escort, GoDai probably wouldn't do anything too crazy.

MacDonald was not there when GoDai left his room, walked off the ship without notification to the Tavir or the Terrans, and slipped over to an off-duty room where Cola was served.

Most of the time, Terrans tended to answer the questions that Suvain asked, so when GoDai wanted to know how to find where Chaplain Girelli was, people told him where to go. Six Colas later, GoDai showed up at the room where Girelli was sitting at his desk, working on a sermon. He walked in without knocking, and stood across from Girelli, slightly swaying, and shaking his head occasionally as the headaches washed through.

Chaplain Girelli had never been close to one of the aliens, and had no idea how to respond. He knew little enough about aliens to not recognize the slow widening of GoDai's arms. He only saw a sort of misshapen person wearing something like pants, a silvery tunic, and some sort of cloak. He started to stand and offer his hand, and then stopped, not sure what the correct greeting to a Suvain would be. Before he had decided, GoDai said "So you are the same clan as the other one. The one on the ship."

Girelli looked blankly for a moment, as GoDai's arms flicked and then widened. Then Girelli asked, "Do you mean Fredrick Eisen? The Chaplain?" He thought the lack of response was agreement, so he continued. "Do you mean what church I am affiliated with?" This lead to a jerk by the alien, but no response. "I am a Chaplain, and I am ordained by the Episcopalian church, just like Eisen was."

"So he's dead," GoDai stated. "Shot by a Suvain. We just shot your brother. So how do you feel about that? What are you going to do about it?"

Girelli was silent. He had not expected this conversation, and could not remember what instructions he had been given about talking with aliens.

Then he looked more carefully at GoDai, and decided that whatever the instructions were, this looked like someone who wanted or needed to talk. He motioned to the extra chair in the room. "Please have a seat, if you like," he began. GoDai remained standing. Although he had not expected an alien to walk into his room, Girelli had thought about Fredrick quite a bit. "What is going to be done about the murder of Fredrick Eisen will be decided by the proper authorities," he stated. "How do I feel about the death of my friend?

Sad. Sad for him, although I don't think he would be. Sad for those of us who won't get to spend time with him anymore in this life. Sad for you, too. You missed out on getting to know him. I had known him for about 40 years – he was one of my instructors when I first joined the service. He was one of the people it was really worth getting to know."

"Sad? That's it? You don't want to find a Suvain, and shoot him to even the score?"

"Sometimes, I am sorry to say. Although if I do give in to thoughts of revenge, I usually don't stop at wanting to shoot a single Suvain."

"Are you afraid of Suvain? Shouldn't you be? You seem to know that you are a spineless, weak, backward, foolish species."

"Humans are often weak, and foolish," Girelli answered slowly. He had never seen a Suvain up close, but he was getting the impression that this one was working himself into a frenzy.

"How did you know that? Before you met us? Who told you you were foolish? Who have you been talking to?"

"God."

GoDai stopped talking, and his arms flashed up and down and then went still. He stared at the priest for several long moments. "So that's the special thing you have. The special thing that makes a worthless race of primitives like you able to get all the way to space. You have God. So all the stories are true, and God is focused on this pathetic race of primitives. Out of the whole universe."

"God is focused on everyone. He made everyone, and his salvation is for everyone. And it isn't surprising that God works through a pathetic race. He often works through the ones that everyone knows can't do things on their own."

"So it is clear to everyone that God is the one making things happen, because everyone can see that you can't." GoDai was still for a moment again, and then reached out his arm towards the small vase of flowers that Girelli kept on his desk. Without looking, GoDai hooked the neck of the vase with his elbow-spike, and casually snapped his arm back, flinging the vase across the room; it shattered against the far wall. The random act of violence and the sound of breaking glass seemed to calm GoDai down.

Girelli was completely at a loss how to deal with the Suvain, so he migrated back to the thing he knew about – theological discussions. "If I tell you that God is working in my life, and then I accomplish something, like flying in space, or forgiving a Suvain for killing a friend, then either it is me accomplishing it, and lying to you or to me, or it is really is God, and I am telling the truth. In the end, you either have to believe that I am capable of the accomplishment, or you have to believe that God is. You will either end up believing in me, or believing in God. And if it is something like forgiveness, I can assure you you shouldn't trust in me."

"So I can either believe that God really did visit you, or I can believe, despite all the evidence, that Terrans really are specially competent. I don't like either choice."

"You probably don't. But what we like is irrelevant – what is true is what matters."

GoDai looked at the Terran, looked at the room, looked at the broken vase, looked at his belt, and looked back to the Terran. He drew out his plasma gun. "Would what I feel be relevant if I felt like killing you?" he asked.

Tavir had noticed that GoDai was missing a little before GoDai walked back into the ship. GoDai was informed by the ship guards that he was to report to the Tavir. He lurched into the Captain's Annex without permission, and collapsed into a chair across from the Tavir. Tavir sniffed, and decided that the ship-board tasks he was about to assign to GoDai would have to wait until after GoDai had spent several hours in the showers. He was about to ask GoDai where he had been, but another question occurred to him. He sat back and asked, "How much Krola have you been drinking?"

"Way too much," GoDai answered.

The Tavir leaned forward, hit a button on his desk to activate the ship intercom and announced, "This is the Tavir. From now on, the orders against Krola drinking are going to be strictly enforced. Krola will not be consumed unless with the permission of a senior officer. This is no longer the usual 'don't drink the stuff' order. This is now for real. Knock it off." He turned his attention back to GoDai. "So other than drugging yourself into brain damage, what have you been up to?"

"I thought I would get a little head start on the Preemptive Extermination", GoDai answered. "I decided that since you had gotten to shoot a Terran chaplain, it was my turn."

Tavir assumed that comment about shooting a Terran was not serious.

He asked "So have you changed your mind about the PE?"

GoDai sat up, then leaned back in the chair. Tavir flicked his arms at the insultingly relaxed posture; GoDai did not notice. GoDai looked back at his captain, and said, "You're too late. The effect is already spreading. You had to get rid of them before we really got to know them. We are already walking around, having shooting matches, putting up Terran pictures of singularities, joining their religions. We already spend as much time listening to them as they do to us. And we like what we hear. The way they see things is different. The physicists didn't learn anything about singularities from the Terrans, but the pictures are there. And now our own physicists look at the singularity like the Terrans do. Terran thoughts are spreading everywhere. To really clean out the Terran infestation, you would have to kill half the crew."

Tavir was silent for a second, then asked, "Joining their religions? Are crewmembers getting involved in Terran religious rituals?"

"It is not exactly a ritual. I joined one of the Christian clans tonight." "You what!"

"I joined one of the Christian clans. I think I am now an Epsekelapian, or something like that."

Tavir sat back in shock. He looked at GoDai for a few seconds, then said, "I realized you were under stress, but I had no idea things had gotten so bad. It is time for you to get off the Krola, and to have some time on board the *ProfitTaker*."

"It wasn't the Krola."

"Then what? What could make you go native?"

"You did." GoDai saw the Tavir's arms start to slide out, and continued, "You mentioned that the Terrans needed to recognize the reality of our coming, and that they would either bend to the new reality, or be crushed by it. When you said it, I realized I had heard something similar before – in one of the Terran religious books. It made me look at an answer I had avoided. But in the end, the answer I avoided was the answer that fit all the data. The Terrans aren't impressive, but they advanced faster than we did.

For some reason, they knew their place in the galaxy before they had ever talked to us. For some reason, they saw things in a new way – they saw beauty where we saw only practicality. They also knew from the beginning what a threat we were, and yet, they weren't awed by our presence. The very first encounter with the Terrans involved a Terran who was less afraid of us than he was committed to what he believed. I couldn't understand why the Terrans acted like we were like them. They could see our technological superiority, but they didn't see that as a reason to see us as superior. It was like they had already met someone else. But however hard I looked for some evidence they had met another species, there was nothing. There was one answer that was straightforward, but ridiculous – that the claims that they had met God were true. Then I heard what you said, and I realized that someone had told the Terrans that before. Their religious figure, Jersus, says almost the same thing. He also says that there is some big new thing they must accept, or be broken by the changes that will be coming. The more I read about him, the more he sounded like you. He shows up, tells everyone that he had come to change their entire world, and acts like he is not a typical Terran, but someone more."

"But he also said that he wasn't going to just change their world – he said he was going to change *them*. And that was at the base of a lot of the Terran thought – the thought that God would change them. It explained why they didn't care about our technology. They judge people by how they act, not just by what they can do. It explained why they weren't shocked by our presence – they had met someone much bigger already. And Jersus also didn't just say he was different. He showed he was different, and then called people to make decisions based on the evidence, not their expectations."

The Tavir looked at his former Cultural Officer in disbelief. "So how does any of this have anything to do with the secret Terran super-thing you kept looking for?"

"The Terrans advanced in spite of themselves. There is nothing about Terrans that makes them succeed. It isn't their ability that makes the difference – it is what they believe." GoDai sat back and seemed to go into lecture mode, or to be talking to himself about what he was thinking.

"Faith can be a powerful motivator. People who really believe in something are often able to achieve things that other people don't. People who really believe that God is on their side often have great courage, and can win battles they ought to lose. Faith can keep people going long after they ought to have given up in despair."

"But Truth is even stronger. People who are convinced that God is protecting them from plasma guns are really brave, but they still die. You can believe and hope all you want, but the truth always wins in the end." "The difference here is that Faith and Truth are on the same side.

People are believing in something that is actually true. To believe, you don't have to try and ignore all the evidence. To commit yourself to the truth, you don't have to try to avoid faith – your faith actually calls you to commit yourself to the truth. And the truth isn't dry facts – learning about the world isn't just practical, it is also seeing the beauty of the work of God."

Tavir raised his head in disbelief. "So you really believe that special thing the Terrans have is God. Well, that's not very useful. It isn't like we can just take God and bring it back to the Empire. You can't seriously believe that the Terran God is real – that God is driving them forward."

"I do," GoDai answered. "It wasn't what I was looking for. I certainly didn't believe in the existence of God, and if I did, I wouldn't have believed that God would care about primitives like the Terrans. If God cared about anybody, it should have been us. That was why I decided to shoot a Terran priest tonight. I had just gotten fed up with the Terran claim that God cared about them."

"You didn't really shoot a Terran, did you? Without permission?" GoDai laughed. "Well, I really scared one. I found out something tonight – if some Terrans are surprised and scared, they lose all ability to move. They just sit there, and can't move at all for a while. I thought about shooting him, but it really wouldn't have done any good. I would still have been arguing against the only rational explanation I could find. So I put the gun away, and told the priest about what I was thinking. He invited me into the clan. So I joined the Terran religion."

The Tavir was trying to decide whether to tell GoDai to get off the ship and not come back, or to tell him to go to his cabin and stay there for the next 5 days until he sobered up. He finally said, "I can't believe you left the Tavir Holding and joined some other clan."

"Left the Tavir? What are you talking about?"

"You joined another clan!"

GoDai sat up, "It is a religious group. Of course I am still a Tavir." "So if we end up shooting the Terrans, whose side are you on?"

"Ours, of course." GoDai was silent for a second, and to Tavir, he looked confused, or like he was trying to figure out some difficult problem.

Finally GoDai continued, "I think I am more strongly committed to the Tavir Holding than ever before. I am not sure why. Maybe it is because what really binds a Holding together is the love for one's clan, and love is what God calls us to. I don't really know."

"Go recover from the Krola. I will decide what to do with you later."

GoDai stood up to leave. "Shower or straight to sleep", he wondered aloud.

"Shower," ordered the Tavir. "We have to be in the same ship as you."

Movies about aliens were suddenly popular again. Most of the Persephones were gathered for the station-wide showing of *Space Serves Death Cold.* The movie was being shown in one of the largest meeting rooms, and broadcast across the station. Most of the Terrans on the station had been told several times already that Fredrick Eisen had been in the movie. As most of them had never met the *Persephone*'s chaplain, they didn't attach much significance to the story.

Somehow it seemed to Susan that the appropriate place to watch the movie was next to Darron and Stephen. She found them, with Jon, at one of the front tables. All three had saved back food coupons for the event, and the table was covered with the unhealthiest food Susan had seen in a year. She sat down next to Darron, and refused the generous offer to share in the junk food. She then decided to try just one, and promptly ate all through the movie right along with the others. Soon after she arrived, the lighting dimmed and the movie began.

Susan could immediately feel the change. There were lots of scenes that were so ridiculous that the room was filled with laughter, but now there were long silences as well. Susan glanced at the audience, and saw Darron doing the same. The station personnel looked normal; it was the Persephones that were reacting strangely. When the alien's ship came up behind the "Stargazer" all the Persephones seemed tense. When the alien burst through the airlock and attacked the handful of Terrans – no, "humans" – it found inside, most of the audience seemed grim instead of entertained. When the Stargazer's captain panicked, babbling words of peace to the alien before being grabbed by tentacles, dragged forward and eaten, eyeballs first, the Persephones didn't react with horror, but with disbelief and disdain.

There were lots of parts that everyone still enjoyed. There was the usual stilted dialog, the scientist who knew everything about every branch of science, the beautiful communications officer, and the brave lieutenant who led the resistance to the alien attack. But all through the movie there was the undercurrent of muttered comments by the audience – descriptions of what the crew should have been doing instead. Every Persephone broke into cheers when the dining room scene began, and one of the crew was in the back, praying over his food. Steven's observations about the extra tentacles had spread around before the movie; the dramatic entrance of the alien, guns in tentacles, was interrupted by all of the people frantically counting.

The movie started to feel awkward for Susan when someone turned to the heroic lieutenant, who had just saved the communications officer, and said, "You two have been closer to the alien than anyone else. What do we do?" After that, it was hard not to identify Darron and herself as the two characters. As the two characters started to look at each other as often as at the monster, Susan looked at Darron and the others less and less.

When the characters finally painted the giant eyeball on a grenade and moved towards the alien, Susan risked a glance at Darron. He saw her look over and whispered, "I can't see GoDai falling for that." Susan shook her head in agreement, and looked back just as the lieutenant suddenly kissed the communications officer, and shut the door with her on the side away from the alien. After a final glance at the woman behind him, the hero advanced into tentacle range, and pulled the pin as he was enveloped by tentacles and dragged forward. Susan snuck a look back at the others. Even though it was a cheesy scene, everyone was dead silent. Susan could see Stephen leaning forward in his chair, Jon with eyes narrowed, and Darron with a grim face and distant eyes. The audience was still silent as the alien greedily grabbed and swallowed the giant "eyeball", and then exploded. All of the Persephones stopped paying attention after the alien died. The final happy ending scene where the communications officer led the rest of the survivors into the room to find that the hero who had been next to the blast, thrown across the room into a bulkhead, and then left without an exosuit in the room as all the oxygen was sucked out, was somehow still alive seemed harder to accept than the alien itself.

The four at the table stayed behind as the room emptied. After a few minutes of concentrated snacking, Darron asked, "So has the movie changed, or is it us?"

There was general laughter as everyone answered "Us". "I didn't really see the creature as an alien anymore, just a monster," Stephen said.

"Aliens are commonplace now. It is the tentacles that are unbelievable," added Jon. "It is sort of funny to think that that alien was supposed to be scary. Sure, it eats eyeballs, but the casual discussion of exterminating your entire species is a lot harder to get used to."

"I think if that thing had come on the *Persephone*, the Captain would have had it sitting on command and performing stupid party tricks," Darron stated.

"One AGM1 would have done the job. They always have some crazy scene at the end", Jon stated, "when the real goal is not to have to walk around with an explosive in your hand in the first place."

"The stakes were so much lower, too," Susan said. "Granted, if you are on the ship, whether you live or die is rather important, but there wasn't any feeling that if you mess something up, everyone on Earth is going to die."

"I don't think that whether everyone lives or dies will end up being determined by us," Darron replied. "I think that no matter what, they are going to decide to resist the Suvain. Then whether Earth lives or dies will depend on the ships they must be building right now to fight back."

"And by the Tavir," Susan added. They were all silent for a few minutes, then Susan continued. "And no matter what, everything, especially us, will never be the same."

"Of course we will fight back", Stephen declared. "Why wouldn't we?" The others looked at Stephen, and Susan realized something that the other two had known all along. Stephen was having the time of his life.

Encountering aliens and having the entire fate of mankind hanging in the balance was like living out his greatest dream.

"You do realize", she asked him, "that we may all die horribly?" "I don't think we all will", Stephen declared. "They have to move through the Intersections – they can't just appear here. It is going to take quite a while for them to assemble the attack fleet, and we can use that time to prepare."

"Even if there is something we can do to prepare", Darron countered, "a lot of us involved are not going to come back." Susan looked at him, and knew that her previous claim that no one took the old alien movies seriously had been wrong. Darron had the same look now as he had had when watching the last scene of the movie. For Darron, watching the movies was sort like burning into his mind how someone should respond when the crisis came. Looking at him now, Susan thought that if he was in the same situation as the movie, Darron would act the very same way. He would do what he had watched over and over. He would make sure that the communications officer was safe, and then move to destroy the threat, even though he would know that the happy ending scene was not going to occur.

Of course, being Darron, he would never stop to kiss the communications officer first. Instead he would probably point out that only one person was actually needed to trigger the explosive, and that the basic purpose of excess males in a biological population was to ensure genetic diversity in the next generation, so that individual genetic weaknesses shared by a small sample of male progenitors did not lead to a widespread genetic weakness in a species, and with a total population of roughly 12 billion Terrans, which suggested nearly 6 billion males, sufficient genetic diversity was assured to the Terran race, and so the loss of a single male was insignificant, while the females of a species were directly responsible for the birth of the next generation, so in any case where there was the choice of the probable loss of a male or female Terran, it was only rational for the male to be lost so the female could survive, so Susan should stand on the other side of the bulkhead. And once he made sure Susan was safe, he would turn to face the alien, and find out whether the alien was still there, or if it had wandered off while he was talking about genetics.

"I think focusing on not having to grab bombs and hurl ourselves at aliens is probably a good idea," Susan declared.

The glob of Terran representatives had finally settled themselves into a series of meetings with the Suvain. The Tavir decided that he needed GoDai, even if he was mentally unstable. The Tavir brought a collection of the ranking Suvain to each presentation, along with four fully armed and armored guards. They had the usual Persephone escorts, who entered with the Suvain and sat next to them in the front row. Captain Adams had been sure to promise Tavir that she would stay awake the entire time. The Tavir assured her that staying awake would not be a problem. After the usual round of introductions, the Tavir was invited to speak. After a few kind words about the Terrans' hospitality, the Tavir came to the point.

"We have been very interested to learn more about the Terran species through our interactions with the crew of the *Persephone*," the Tavir began. "While this has been entertaining, many of the views expressed by your crew of researchers are different that the views I would expect to find from experienced political leaders like yourselves. While a group of scientists with little knowledge of the world might think that friendship and mutual respect guide the interactions between peoples, a group like yourselves will know that decisions are really based on force."

"The Terrans are a pleasant species. But the central fact, the fact that determines your place in the universe, is that we are technologically advanced, with the strength of 300 planets, and you are technologically primitive, and have hardly left your own world. Any contest of strength between the Suvain and the Terrans will end with the Terrans destroyed. I am sure you are trying to come up with something to stop the Suvain ships. This is not realistic. Our ships have been developed over centuries. Our crews are experienced. Our weapon systems are tested and effective. If you choose to resist, your ships will be destroyed. Your population centers will then be destroyed by nuclear weapons you have no way to defend against. The remaining Terrans will be a broken subject population, with no hope of recovery."

"This is not your only option. You can choose to accept that the Suvain are a sentient race, and you are primitive. You can choose to accept that the Suvain will rule the Terrans regardless of what choice or decision you make. Given the reality that the Suvain will rule, you can choose to accept what you cannot prevent. If you accept Suvain rule, your population will survive. You will be a race that can grow under our protection. Instead of destruction, you will have a secure place in the galaxy."

"You should understand that there are threats in the galaxy which you have not yet met. If you refused the Suvain and we did not take action, others would. We are not the only ones exploring this Intersection cluster. You could have met the Volsin, or the Zatheur. Even if you accepted their rule, your race would be destroyed. The Volsin have thousands of rules they impose on every subject population. Any failure to conform leads to the Volsin exterminating all offenders. I have met your species. You would never be able to obey sufficiently to survive. The Zatheur terraform every planet they control. Your entire race would be put to work changing your own planet into a world which would support the Zatheur, instead of you. Or you will encounter the VolatarA. The VolatarA see every other race as slaves. They torture and kill those primitives they capture, and automatically break any possible resistance by destroying every population enter and center of production and technology of the planets they encounter. Given that you are going to be controlled by one of the sentient races, you are fortunate that we are here – we could be the only chance you have of existing as anything other than slaves. And you don't have that much time. Rumor is the only thing that travels faster than light. By now, half a dozen sentient races know you are here, and will be checking around for scraps."

As the Tavir continued, Captain Adams started to sneak looks at the assembly. All were listening, but she didn't see much response to the Tavir's argument. She wasn't sure if the Tavir understood Terran body language enough to recognize how his audience was responding. As the meeting continued, she started to wonder if she understood politicians well enough to understand their body language herself. A few of the audience were clearly worried, and several were defiant, but most looked emotionless. She shifted attention back to the Tavir as he finished his first statement, and open the floor to questions. She could see he was a little angry or frustrated, but he wasn't showing any real emotion for a Suvain. She started to wonder if he would try to demonstrate that he was serious by shooting some of the delegates. Daydreaming about the Suvain shooting people, she did not recognize that the last question, repeated twice, had been directed at her. She asked for the question to be repeated once again. She stood and turned to the assembled crown of politicians.

"You have asked whether the Tavir has been true to the agreements he made when we first met. He has. He has resisted any impulse to shoot Terrans. He did not order his entire fleet to accompany us, but restricted himself to the ships agreed upon. His crewmen have behaved themselves. He made no attempt to seize the *Persephone*. From everything I have seen, he acts just the way he says. If we choose to surrender, we can expect that he will occupy the planet, and run the planet for the benefit of the Suvain. If we choose to resist, he will make every attempt to destroy our fleets, governments, and population centers. If you do decide that the Terran race should surrender, from everything I have seen, there is little fear that the Suvain will have us disarm, and then destroy us anyway. This will be true as long as the Suvain are making a profit from exploiting the Earth."

The Tavir acknowledged her statement, and Captain Adams sat back down. The Tavir turned back to the delegates for other questions and responses. He was distracted for a second when he saw that the Suvain he had brought with him were whispering among themselves. He looked long enough to see the left elbows drop for a second – some bet had just been made. He looked back to the Terrans, and refocused on the politicians. When the first meeting was finally over, and the Suvain were returning to their ships, he found time to ask what the bet had been about. He was not surprised to hear that the bet was about the final decision of the Terrans. He was surprised to hear that there were three sides to the bet. One captain was betting that the Terrans would submit and accept occupation, one captain was betting that the Terrans would resist and be destroyed, and GoDai was betting that the

Terrans would resist and both sides would be destroyed. He was trying to convince the others that he should get really good odds, because if he was right, he would probably be dead, and they wouldn't have to pay anyway.

The Tavir looked at GoDai, and wondered again which side he was really on. "So are you just saying that, or do you really have some reason to believe that the Terrans have any chance of resisting? When you say you will probably be dead, is that because they will kill us, or you will be on the other side, and we will be killing you?" Both the other captains turned in confusion to the Tavir, and then GoDai.

GoDai started to answer and then turned to the other two Suvain. "He is upset because I joined a Terran religion. He is convinced I am on their side now."

Both the other two stopped. One captain asked in disbelief, "You are with the Terrans now? But you were calling for the Extermination!" Seeing GoDai look accusingly at the Tavir, the captain explained, "My ship forwarded on the message. Everybody has heard about the PE call."

"It was good advice at the time", GoDai growled. "It is a bit late now. I don't know anything in particular. But I am sure they are working on something to fight back with. Probably lots of somethings. And when I talk to them, sometimes I get the feeling that there are things they are trying not to say."

"So find it", the Tavir answered. "If you actually can tell me that there is something to be concerned about, maybe we won't all think that you are a lunatic."

GoDai used the excuse that he needed to search out the Terran secrets to leave the ship and go to the first church service he had ever attended. Girelli was waiting for him outside the conference room reserved for the service. A number of the crew from the *Persephone* were present – Girelli had contacted all of the Terrans GoDai knew and asked them to be present. The two walked into the crowded room, and GoDai was walked up to the front row of chairs. A bunch of station personnel fell silent as the Suvain came into the room. The Persephones welcomed GoDai without concern, assuming that he was present on another observation assignment. He stood when the others stood, and listened to the songs being sung without attempting to join in.

Now that there were a roomful of Terrans, GoDai was starting to feel very nervous, and the smell was almost overpowering. The others could see him getting nervous, and started to shy away from the moving spikes.

Girelli spoke about God's revelation to Peter that Gentiles could be saved. "The Jews were God's chosen people. Peter had come to know of God's love for him, and for the people like him, but this day, God showed him that people very unlike him were loved too. Through his vision, Peter learned that it isn't how people are described that are important. What matters to God is us, not what we are like. If you say you have blue eyes, you are the noun, and blue-eyed is an adjective that describes you. For all of us, there are clouds of adjectives that describe what we are like. We could be fat, or thin, or rich, or poor, or smart, or Italian, or blue-eyed, or a music lover, or any of thousands of other things. We have seen God's love for us, and it is easy when we see someone with the same adjectives as us to think that God loves them too. But while God cares about us, not just about what we are like, we tend to look at others, and judge them by the adjectives that describe them. If someone is described by a completely different set of adjectives than you, it is easy to think that God won't love someone like them. What Peter was shown that day is that it does not matter how someone is described – that God loves everyone, regardless of what words describe them." Girelli walked over to where the communion table was set up. He looked to GoDai, and extended a hand. GoDai realized with a shock that he was suddenly afraid of a room full of primitives. Almost in a daze, he felt himself get up and walk forward to the waiting minister. Girelli stood beside him and announced, "That day God showed Peter that His love extends to everyone. This is the day that God is bringing the same lesson to us." He turned to the table, and served GoDai as the entire room sat in complete silence. He motioned to the congregation, and everyone began standing and moving forward. Some shook GoDai's hand, some nodded, and some were just really uncomfortable. After a final song, the service ended.

GoDai sat down with Darron, Stephen, and Susan. They were silent for a second, and then all the Terrans started talking. All laughed, either Suvain- style or Terran-style, and GoDai felt himself start to relax. It was strange for GoDai to find himself truly comfortable and relaxed among a group of primitives. It was also strange to realize that he didn't see Terrans as primitive anymore. When he admitted this to the Terrans, everyone laughed again. "You don't see Terrans as primitive anymore?" asked Darron. "But, I thought you had read Terran history?"

"All this time," said Stephen, "and we still have him thinking we aren't primitive."

"Okay", said GoDai, "maybe I should say no more primitive than anyone else." He thought for a second about Terrans and Suvain, and then about his conversation with the Tavir. "You do still remember I am Suvain? There is a feeling onboard ship that I am not trustworthy, because I am part of a Terran religion. But you do realize that I am still Suvain, and when the shooting starts, I am going to be on the *ProfitTaker*, not the *Persephone*?

This statement was followed by an awkward pause.

"Of course you are still Suvain", answered Susan. "God has never called you to be anything else. If the shooting starts, we will all be hoping that you survive. Of course, both sides will still be shooting. And if we die, and you do survive, it will be important that you are still Suvain, because you will have the task of continuing to tell your people about Christ."

"You won't all die", said GoDai nervously. "I am sure that your governments will have to face reality after the major population centers are gone. There will still be a number of people outside the radioactive regions that will be alive."

"Has it actually been decided then?" asked Stephen.

"I don't think it has officially", answered GoDai. But I don't see either side looking like it is going to back down."

"That will be really bad for both sides", declared Stephen. All looked at him. There was a certainty in his voice that everyone, even GoDai, could recognize.

Darron started to say something, then looked at GoDai and stopped.

GoDai saw everything go quiet, and looked around at his Terran friends. "I am a Suvain", he said, "and if there was anything I heard here that was of relevance, I would have to report it."

"I am a Terran", answered Darron with a smile, "and if there was something to hear of relevance, I wouldn't be told." GoDai looked around as all of the other Terrans glanced at Stephen, who stared nervously straight forward. He then looked around in confusion as all the Terrans except Stephen erupted into laughter, and Stephen shook his head at all of them.

"It must have been hard to accept the beliefs of a primitive race", said Susan. "What made you change your mind?"

GoDai learned back a bit, and everyone saw his arms raise a bit and widen. "When we have met primitives before, we were always impressive. We had greater technology, but we also had a longer and greater history.

Dealing with them, we always knew which side was which. But here, I could see a primitive race that wasn't impressed. You were impressed by our technology, but not by us. It was clear that you had met someone more impressive in the past. It wasn't another alien race, but it was someone who was great enough to transform your entire society."

"It was the only explanation that made sense. I didn't see any middle ground. Either what your religious leader was true, or it was an elaborate lie. I didn't see any way a lie could have done anything but held you back. But if everything was true, things made sense."

After the group finished talking, the Terrans walked GoDai back to his ship, and had started heading back to their quarters when someone suggested they stop by the same off-duty room they had now met in multiple times.

Captain Adams had watched the Suvain entrance into the Christian Church from the safety of a cluster of officers near the rear. She had moved forward for communion surrounded by similar uniforms, and had made it back to safe anonymity without awkward greetings or salutes from her crew. She looked forward to where GoDai was talking with Stephen and the others, and suddenly had the distinct feeling that she should set her affairs in order. She battled with the strange and defeatist thought for a moment, then headed back to her quarters on the *Persephone.*

She sat staring at the screen for a second, trying to think of what to say. Finally she gave up and started with the basic facts, just like any other order.

James Adams: my will is on file. Everything is to go to you in the event of my death, assuming my death is not simultaneous with the death of all society and banking systems anyway. I am afraid it will not be much after a life in the Fleet. This is more of a traditional allotment; I realize that you are no need of financial assistance. From the Christmas messages you send, it appears that your legal work is a distinct success, and has brought you all of the financial security you and your family will need. I do not know if I have much time left in this life, and there is more than finances for which I am responsible. I worked for years to achieve promotion and command, and by random chance have been thrust into a situation in which I have had more chance for decision making and career accomplishment than I could ever have imagined. Now that in many ways I have achieved my goal, I have realized that my goal was not what I should have been shooting for from the beginning. I do not regret going into the Fleet; I think it was what I was born for. What I regret is that I let the intoxication of promotion overshadow what I now realize was what really important – you and your father. It is too late to apologize in Martin's case. I did not come to the funeral because I thought it would be awkward. I should have been there anyway, if only for you, and for the man who treated me far better than I ever treated him. As you are still living, I have the opportunity to say that I regret that I put other things before you – I was wrong. My thoughts turn to you often, and to your two children. I cannot send a physical gift, so 7 credits are attached in order for a gift to be purchased for each. I think models of the *Persephone* are being sold, perhaps that would be appropriate. If you do not feel so, you are to use your own initiative in the selection.

May God keep you and yours safe. Regards, Rose Adams.

GoDai spent the next three days avoiding every assignment with the claim that he was tracking down the Terran secret. By the second day, Tavir had decided GoDai was now useless and stopped even calling him to the meetings with the Terran delegates. After Tavir returned after the latest meeting the third day, GoDai gave him a hour to calm down, and then sent him a request for a meeting. After another hour, GoDai was told to come to the Captain's Annex. He walked in to find his captain already irritated and looking for something to snap at, or maybe just shoot. GoDai walked in, saw his Captain's mood, and thought for a second about waiting a day. Then he flexed his arms, walked in, and sat down.

"So do you have something important to say, or have you decided that wasting your own time wasn't enough?"

GoDai laughed. "I thought about waiting until you were in a better mood, but you aren't going to like what you hear anyway, so maybe it is better this way. At least you won't be wasting a good mood. I found the Terran secret, but you have decided you don't want it. Now, I think I have found something more about the Terran activities. This one you might care about."

"So if I will care about it, why don't you just tell me?"

GoDai flicked his arms and leaned back in the chair. "Why don't I start at the beginning?" Ignoring Tavir's comment "Why don't you start at the end?", GoDai said, "I wondered where the Terrans would get ideas for defenses against the Suvain. The most likely place was from the Suvain.

The Suvain they have met is us. So after seeing the *ProfitTaker*, what would they try to duplicate? I was rather sure they had already identified the missile launchers and the point defense cannons. Of the two, the missile launchers are a lot more complicated, so I thought that the point defense cannons were more likely. The cannons are not that different from the "angulin guns" the Terrans were already building after seeing your hand gun."

"They will have developed missile launchers by the time you finish," interjected Tavir.

GoDai smiled and leaned further back in the chair. "So I thought that cannons were more likely, but even cannons need to be aimed. And even if you can track a target to aim the weapon, the light-time delay between the cannon firing and the warhead reaching the target is enough that every shot in the warhead has to be self-directing at the end of the flight. I can't believe the Terrans have multi-shot warheads, effective target tracking, or miniaturized self-guiding munitions. So if the Terrans are making weapons, they will have to be fired from very close to the target."

"So they have a bomb or something hidden nearby?"

"Not really hidden. As the captain of this fine ship, you have the privilege of a window. What do you see?" GoDai sat up and looked pointedly to the window.

"That big misshapen cylinder that the Terrans call a ship," Tavir answered. He looked out the window; GoDai could see him moving from irritated to serious.

"After I started looking at things sitting next to us to see if they were dangerous, I noticed that ship has a name painted on the hull. It is named the "Thunderchild". I am not really sure why the Terrans name things like they do, but I decided to find out where the name came from. It comes from a book. One of the first times the Terrans ever imagined what an encounter with aliens would be like was a story written by a Terran named "H. G. Wells". In the story, the aliens attack the Terrans, and one of the only acts of resistance that is successful is by a military water ship – the "Thunderchild". The ship fires from very close range, and kills two aliens, saving lots of innocent Terrans, even as it is destroyed."

"Another Terran that dies. Typical. Why are the Terrans so focused on death?" Tavir muttered, still looking at the *Thunderchild*.

"Maybe because death is the prerequisite for resurrection," GoDai mused. He brought himself back to the present with an effort. "Once I was looking carefully at the ship, I could see something unusual. Unless the Intersection between here and Terra is enormous, that ship would have to compress for transit out of this solar system. When you look at the regular cylinder, you can see panels that look like they will separate, probably to slide beneath each other – the cylinder telescopes down into a ring. Along the middle, it looks like the plates could slide both ways – so once it slides down into a ring, the ring tightens into almost a solid block of metal that is probably pushed through the Intersection. The cylinder isn't really a ship – it is a cargo hulk that was brought into the system and then had some angulins stuck in to move bulky objects back and forth. If they want to move it out, they could just take the engines out, and compress it again to move it back to Terra."

"But the bulges along the side are different. I had GoAyanA make a detailed image of the entire side of the ship, and we went over the hull very carefully. The bulges have been added later – probably not long ago. They are fixed in place – we didn't see any way they could compress. And they are not attached evenly. The top is just sort of tacked on, and the bottom is attached differently – it looks almost like there are joints. So if you had, say, a dozen giant angulin guns stacked underneath, you could have explosives that would blow the cover off to unmask the guns, and then fire straight across at whatever was sitting next to you. And, as the Terrans were so polite as to give us what they assured us was the most prestigious spot on the station, what is directly in the line of fire of all those cannons that might be there is… us. I don't know if the Terrans know how thick the hull of the *ProfitTaker* really is, but they took the precaution of not having anything on the other side of the ship just in case the shots passed entirely through."

GoDai stopped as the Tavir went completely still. After several minutes, the Tavir asked, "Who else in the crew have you talked to about this?"

"No one except GoAyanA."

Tavir turned to his terminal and said, "Ship-wide broadcast. Left side shift are to assemble in the off-duty room tonight at 6, Right side shift at 10. No exceptions." GoDai could hear the announcement from the adjacent bridge, and knew that a corresponding message had been displayed on every monitor in the ship. "Do you think that this is some attempt to hold us hostage?"

"No. I think the goal of the Terrans is to not surrender, and not to have a war. They have been informed many times that their two goals are mutually exclusive, but I think that is still what they want. Destroying, or trying to threaten, a Suvain ship would make a war almost inevitable. I would guess that the ship is there in case we start shooting."

"Maybe I should shoot a handful of Terrans to show them that they need to take what we say seriously. It might be useful, and it would certainly be enjoyable. Or maybe I should make sure that anytime crewmembers are out socializing with Terrans, they are armed. There is probably more socializing than there should be anyway." Tavir stopped talking as he saw GoDai go still for a moment. "So what is it about crewmembers and Terrans you ought to be telling me?" Seeing GoDai hesitate, the Tavir continued, "I have had a lot of frustrating meetings lately, I have been told that a bunch of primitives are pointing guns at my ship, and my cultural officer has lost his mind. Shooting someone, or just beating them senseless, might be very relaxing. At the moment, you seem like the only available target. So I ask again, what should you be telling me?"

"Well, if it is any consolation, our crewmen are probably armed." GoDai made an elaborate display of sliding his chair back a little, so he would be beyond Tavir's reach. "There is a rumor onboard – a rumor, which I have nothing to do with, and just heard – that there has been a bit more contact with Terrans than we might have thought. Granted, all movements off ship are supposed to be registered, but there is more than one way off the ship. The Terrans have interfaced computers, like ours. On their network, they have all sorts of useful things, and they also have a set of fantasy games – people take on roles of people in some imaginary setting, and usually fight things or blow them up. It seems that a few of the crew of the *Persephone* are involved in such things in their spare time, and now, their friends on the *ProfitTaker* are too." GoDai made an elaborate display of moving his chair even farther back. The Tavir had gone still again, but GoDai was out of range, so he continued. "It seems that their Terran friends made up Terran names for them, and they joined into the same games the others play, without anyone knowing they are actually Suvain." Godai tucked his arms in in a sign of submission. "Note – I am not talking about myself. And the Terrans might see the Suvain shooting each other as a sign of weakness."

The Tavir sat back and shook his head. "You claimed that if we decided to exterminate the Terrans I would have to shoot half my crew. At the moment, that doesn't sound like such a bad idea. I would ask you who these people are, but you would claim to have forgotten, and after I shot you, I would not be any farther ahead. So I think I will just shoot the entire IT group instead. First I think I will ask for all the excuses for why they thought that the rules about leaving the ship and contact with Terrans didn't apply.

Then I will shoot them."

"I did not actually say it was the IT group. The rumor says that they say they were not actually leaving the ship, and that they were actually not interacting with Terrans – just imaginary characters. It is possible that this is not really a bad thing. If the individuals whose names I never did hear haven't been telling the Terrans things, it might be a way to find out what the Terrans think when they don't know we are listening. We would need to make sure that the Terrans in the games really don't know that some of the players are Suvain, and we would have to remember that Terrans who play in the games might not be representative of the Terrans in general."

"So you think that if I question the crewmen I might get useful information?"

"Well, maybe if I question them, they may be a little more ready to speak up. I could try to track down who the game-players really are and see what their impressions are of the Terrans."

GoDai looked out the window at the Terran ship for a while. Then he mused, "So my rebellious IT crew will be interrogated by a rebellious Cultural Officer. So the information I will be receiving will be coming from a group of people who run around in a fantasy world, and gathered by someone who runs around joining primitive cults. That will be a great basis for decision-making."

"I wouldn't see joining the primitive cult as a sign of bad decision- making."

"This is the same primitive cult that their first religious leader was part of. Aren't your holy men supposed to work miracles? Or foretell the future? I don't remember many miracles – plasma went through him just like anyone else. And he wasn't very good at foretelling the future – he sure didn't predict he was about to explode." Tavir paused, waiting for GoDai to react, but there wasn't an outburst – instead GoDai was just sitting looking at Tavir. He started to say something, then stopped, then answered in a very controlled voice.

"I mentioned before that after joining the Christians, I was more committed to the Tavir Holding than ever. I think I also mentioned that one of the key beliefs in Christianity is a commitment to the truth. So being committed to the Tavir Holding means that I may have to tell you the truth, even if it is going to be something you really don't like." GoDai stopped, and looked carefully at the very still Tavir. "I think the religious leader did predict things. Before we first communicated with the Terrans, he stated that the Terrans were going to have to forgive."

"Contacts between races are always troublesome. It is not a great flash of insight to realize that the inferior race is going to have to forgive."

"Perhaps", GoDai said carefully. "But that was only what he said to the Terrans. He also talked to us when we came aboard. And of everything he could say to you, what he chose to say was that someone who was reconciled to their brother was greater than someone who conquers a city." GoDai paused as Tavir's arms flashed out and back. "One of the biggest threats or opportunities to the Tavir Holding is this discovery of Terra. One of the other threats is the rift between you and your brother."

"Competition is essential to the survival of a Holding. It is how you ensure that the most fit is chosen to be the next Tavir. If my idiot brother understood that, he would accept his defeat gracefully."

"I understand that competition is healthy. But your brother is not an idiot, as you well know. You would never accept anyone else calling him an idiot, or treating him as you did. You know he will never accept defeat gracefully when that defeat was encouraged by slanderous statements slipped to your father – statements which you knew at the time were not true."

"This 'commitment to the truth' could get you killed."

"Perhaps. That is why I didn't want to bring up the subject. Just like everyone else has not wanted to bring up the subject for a very long time. But someone needs to say something because this is the worst time for the Tavir Holding to be divided amongst ourselves. If we come to some agreement, it is going to take all of us to control the Terrans. If we don't, it will take all of us, or more, to fight them."

"So whether it was chance, or good guessing, or telling the future, he did tell the Terrans what they needed to hear, and he told you what you needed to hear." Tavir was still not moving. GoDai decided he had pushed the issue as much as he dared and stood up to leave.

"If we all need to stand together, who are you going to be standing with if the shooting starts?" Tavir asked.

GoDai stopped and looked back at his captain. "If the shooting starts, I think we will probably among the first shot. But when we are shot, I will be standing right beside you."

Tavir was silent for a moment, then his arms moved in a tight, short smile. "You will be standing right beside me? You do remember that if the ship is under attack, your station is in Auxiliary Controls – you are supposed to be far enough away from me that a single shot cannot kill us both at the same time."

"It gets really boring down there, and there is no one to talk to. Besides, if the ship has been hit so many times that the primary control systems are out, there probably won't be much to command anyway. It is a lot more fun to come up here and watch." GoDai walked out, ignoring Tavir's parting comment that GoDai was assigned to Auxiliary Controls so that he wouldn't get in the way.

It was the next day when the Tavir called for CE Aguilera. After he was escorted onboard by four jerky Suvain who took every opportunity to show that they were armed, CE Aguilera had guessed what was behind the "invitation". He saw the Tavir standing behind his desk, looking out at the *Thunderchild*. Aguilera looked out as well, then took the seat across from the Tavir.

"If we really wanted to hide it, I would have named it the 'Helpless Puppy'."

Tavir arms flashed, spikes clearly visible for a moment, and then he sat down. He snapped, "My unstable cultural officer tells me that the "Thunderchild" in your book saved the life of Terrans. That one is going to get you killed."

Aguilera could not resist looking back out the window. "Yes. It will." He looked back as his "escort" left the room, shutting the door behind them. Turning back to the Tavir, he continued, "In a way, that is the entire point of the ship. No one really believes that if both ships took off and had a duel, the *ProfitTaker* would be in any danger. But if you sent out your crewmen with orders to capture the station, you won't be able to stay here as a base of operations, or to provide fire support for your attack force. You will have to pull the *ProfitTaker* back to a safe distance. Even though that isn't very far, it means that your attack force will be isolated, and even given your weapons and armor, we can deal with the number of crewmen you can send."

Tavir answered, "And as soon as you do, I blast the entire station full of holes from well outside any defensive capability you have."

Aguilera nodded. "So the end result of your attack would be the death of your attack force, and destruction of the Terran station and everyone on it. The ship is there to ensure that if there is a fight at Loren Station, it ends with the destruction of the Terran presence, not leaving any person or computer for you to use to find the Intersection field that leads back to Earth."

"We will find it anyway," Tavir pointed out.

"But it will take you time. If the shooting starts, we will want every second we can get to build ships for defense."

Tavir looked out the window, then flashed his arms again. "You just don't seem to understand that time is not your problem. Your problem is that you are a primitive race with primitive technology, and you have just met someone real. In a long time, or a short time, you will be dead if you don't listen. And the time you have to listen is getting short. Everything you are doing here is obviously a delay, to get more time to build more ships that will just be vaporized in space anyway. If your real emperor, whoever that is, wants to come and talk to me, he can. But an endless series of meetings with that crowd will go nowhere. If I don't get your answer soon, I will assume you have rejected our terms."

Aguilera nodded in agreement. "I try to point that out to the crowd every meeting – that we will have to come to some conclusion. I really wish this was all an elaborate display, where we all pretend to argue about useless things to gain time. But endless meetings in a crowd of politicians is pretty much how things are done by the Terrans. Believe it or not – you probably won't – things are moving much faster than normal."

Tavir was moving from spike showing to stillness. "In that case, perhaps bothering to negotiate with you is a waste of time. From what I have seen, cleaning a useful planet of your species should not be that hard – everything you do to defend yourself involves you blowing yourself up."

"I have no particular desire to explode. But if that is what it takes to ensure that the Terran race does not end, that is what I will choose. That is a risk I have already taken. After it was confirmed that you existed, and were heading to Loren Station, all regular station personnel were given the chance to evacuate. Their places were taken by volunteers who were told from the beginning that this station is never to be captured intact. Every single person on the station is a volunteer. You have known us long enough to know that the last thing any Terran wants is to explode. The only reason that the Terrans keep talking about blowing ourselves up is because we are the only things we can blow up at the moment. We actually like blowing things up, and if the war begins, by the time you are moving on Earth, we will be able to blow up more than just ourselves."

Tavir flexed his arms again. "GoDai tells me that you have some understanding of dealing with those greater than yourself, who knows from where. But he is clearly wrong. You do not comprehend that you are faced with destruction, from a race you apparently cannot understand. It is a pity. You would have been worth more as a subject species than as radioactive ash, but that appears to be your choice."

Aguilera leaned back. "I actually think we do understand you. The only thing surprising about you is that there is nothing surprising about you. You are more like me than most Terrans are. You say that we don't understand you. I think you don't understand us. When you talk about technology, half the time that translator device of yours just sounds like gibberish. But when you are talking about politics, or culture, or clans, there is a word in our language for everything you say. In the social sciences, we are familiar with everything you say, and with everything we see. In fact, we see your society as almost, if you will pardon the word, primitive. I think we understand very well what your intentions are, and have a reasonable idea of your capabilities. I think we also have a pretty good guess of what life as a subject species would become. We have plenty of examples from our own history of what life as a subject population is like. Unless the Suvain are a much more generous and loving people than the Terrans, there is not much actual future as a subject race."

The Tavir pushed the button to summon the guards and said flatly, "There is no future at all for an opponent race. So are these statements of yours the official response of the Terrans? All of the horde have agreed on this? Or are there some I shouldn't be shooting?"

Aguilera responded, "Nothing I have said is an official statement from the United Governments. You said that our Emperor could come make his statement. We don't have one. I am not speaking as an official representative, I am speaking as a friend. You wanted more information on where things stand. I am giving it to you. The official statement will come from the United Governments, when the delegates finally agree. What they will end up agreeing to, I can't promise. And if you do decide to start shooting, you will have to shoot at everyone, and everyone will be shooting at you. We know very well what happens to a target population that does not stand together against an outside force."

Tavir had seen the guards arrive on his monitor, but did not yet open the door. "From what you say, and your time in building that piece of debris", he said, motioning to the *Thunderchild*, "your answer seems to be already determined. And therefore, so is the future of your race."

Aguilera did not move. "Even if the United Governments do choose surrender, trying to get everyone to live peaceably while you are the occupiers and we are the occupied will be next to impossible. If I thought like you did, I would have no hope at all. But if I had to bet on whether we Terrans will survive, I would put my money on our survival and success."

Tavir narrowed his eyes. "After everything you have seen and heard, you still put your trust in a homemade can with a few guns in it?"

"No", Aguilera answered, "I do not trust in the ability of the Terrans to defeat the Suvain Empire in massive fleet combats. In the end, I am trusting you."

Tavir widened his arms in surprise. "You are trusting me? I thought I had made my position clear. Maybe I should shoot a few more of you – you do not seem to think I am serious."

Aguilera laughed. "Oh, I know you are serious. And I do not trust you because I think you are a really nice person who would never think of nuking people. You made that very clear the very first time you talked to a Terran. I trust that you are a person who will be focused on making the decision that is best for you. I think you can be relied upon to care more about your own success than you are about your own pride, or habit. And I think you are smart enough to realize that we are in the same boat." Aguilera paused, he could see that Tavir was confused by something – the translator had taken the idiom literally and created the Suvain phrase 'We are sitting on the same starship.' This was so obvious that Tavir could not see why it had been stated. Aguilera clarified, "We are both going to go up or down together. I do not think that the Terrans could ever fight against the entire Suvain Empire, but if you want to get all the rewards of claiming the Earth, Terra, you are going to have to take it yourself. And against the Tavir Holding, we will probably still lose, but we won't go down alone. There are about 12 billion Terrans. Even if you kill a million Terrans for every Tavir you lose, the Tavir Holding will be crippled by the time you are done. And what the crippled Tavir Holding will have won will be a crippled world, with no significant population to exploit, and whose most valuable resources and production facilities are radioactive waste."

"But attacking the Terrans is not your only choice. If you decide that demonstrating your superiority is not as important as profit, you will not insist that the Terrans surrender to you, or to anyone. Instead, you will jump at the chance to be the middleman between the Terrans and the galaxy. In that case, you will have trouble just handling the load of all the trade that you will now control. Even if you are only taking a small percent of the value of the trade for yourself, I would bet that that will be a bigger gain for the Tavir Holding than you have ever had. And if Terran history is any guide, you will be taking a lot more than a small percentage. Or course, you won't be the only one to benefit. We will gain access to goods and knowledge that will build us up as well. I think you once told Captain Adams that a deal based on flattery never lasts. The real foundation of a deal that will last is that it really is the best option for both sides. I think that you have an opportunity that has to be rare for any race, or Holding. And I think you are a person who can see that."

The Tavir answered, "Is this a formal statement from the Terrans, or just another friendly comment?"

"A friendly prediction," Aguilera answered. "As of now, there is no formal statement about what Suvain-Terran cooperation would look like, but if such discussion took place, it is a natural solution – I can't imagine the Terrans arguing against it."

Tavir flashed his arms for a second. "It all sounds so good, but how long do you think it would really last? How long would it be before you decided to try to cut out the middleman?"

"Not forever", Aguilera answered. "Over time, the Terran trade would increase to a point that one Holding could not support it, and Terran knowledge of the galaxy would increase to the point that we could sell the excess trade on our own. The Tavir profit margins would go down, and the Tavir would not be the only source for Terran goods. But that time would be a long time coming. We have so much to learn, and even if the Tavir Holding eventually won't have the ships to move all the trade yourselves, you will still have a massive trade with Terra. And if the problem with an agreement is that it will grow so big you can't handle it all yourself, that is not necessarily a bad problem to have."

Tavir just looked at Aguilera for several moments, then pushed the button to open the door. The guards entered; Aguilera rose, said goodbye to the Tavir, and was escorted from the ship.

The now-customary meeting in the off-duty room was unusually sparse. Stephen had been called by several of his fellow game-players and had spent all of his off day sitting in front of a terminal typing. Jon had been roped into helping fix one of the sensors that was a little loose in its mooring – every time the ship banked, it slid back and forth a few centimeters and produced data that was almost right, but just far enough off to cause problems. Jon had been tagged for the exo-suit operation to tighten the antenna in place. This left just Susan and Darron. Darron had been working with Susan long enough that instead of being nervous at eating a meal next to one of the stranger sex, he had completely forgotten that she was, in fact, one of the stranger sex. Instead she had been promoted to "one of us". Although interacting with Darron and the others was much more comfortable for Susan now, she would have been horrified at the thought that she was now one of the group. Darron filled Susan in on why Stephen was missing, and Susan filled Darron in on why Jon was not there. Susan was about to suggest they all get together later when Darron said, "The summary of your heavy-element study sounded pretty promising."

"You read it?" Susan was surprised –outside of her immediate team, not many people expressed much interest in the Chemistry research that was performed on board.

"Sure", answered Darron. "Of course, it is sort of slumming, for a Physisict to read about Chemistry…" Darron said with deliberately exaggerated superiority.

"You're right", Susan said. "For a high and mighty Physicist to read about actual data in the real galaxy, that could be very disturbing. What would happen to all of the hours spent on printing out pretty pictures and wild, irresponsible theorizing, if Physicists actually read about people who were doing real work?"

"That is very good point", Darron answered. "After all, nothing interrupts grand theories about the nature of reality like paying attention to actual data." Both laughed, and Darron continued. "If

I am understanding you, you are finding the concentrations of heavy elements do show a measureable increase near Intersections, just like you predicted."

"Yes and no", said Susan. It does look like there is a statistically significant variation, but it is smaller than I had hoped, and less focused than I thought. The technique is probably more suited to finding the general region to search for Intersections, rather than identifying a specific location."

"But that is still a significant advance", countered Darron. "If we have a better idea where to start looking, we can start the detailed searches sooner."

The conversation continued for some time, with Darron asking for clarifications, and asking about ways in which the original study might be expanded. After a while, Susan changed the conversation by accident when she mentioned that she had the feeling that the Suvain used a similar approach. The reference to the Suvain brought the subject of aliens back to the front. It was a subject that was never very far away.

"It is strange," started Susan. "I could tell by the way they acted that they knew about density searches, and were not supposed to tell me it worked. But I can't watch them and tell if they are about to shoot me."

"I don't think they know themselves", answered Daron. "And most of them aren't going to decide, just be informed of a decision. Some of them would want us as friends, not enemies, but they aren't the ones, or one, who says what to do."

"Whatever they decide, we will be the first to know", said Susan. "I was supposed to be transferred to continue the study, but I was reassigned to the *Persephone* in case the Suvain want to hear more about early Terran history."

"I didn't know you were about to be moved off the ship – was staying onboard your choice, or yet another great idea from our oh-so-wise commanders?"

"I received a notice from the Naval Office thanking me for volunteering to continue to act as a Suvain contact. I have a feeling Captain Adams wanted me to continue, and sent in my request to stay here. She was going to order me to anyway, and this way it goes on my record as a good mark for volunteering for a dangerous post."

"If you had the choice, which would you have chosen?"

Susan was silent for a moment, then answered, "I would stay here. Maybe it is because this is the most important thing going on right now, probably one of the most important things ever, and I might be able to be of service, and maybe it is because this is an important, historic event, and I just want to see it up close." She saw Darron start to smile, then get a blank, distant look. It seemed almost like an actual human emotion had stirred somewhere inside the physicist. She asked "What are you thinking about?"

"I had a very similar conversation once. I was talking to the Chaplain, and he pointed out that we were likely to all die, and asked if there was anywhere else in the universe I would like to be. Of course, there wasn't.

Every once in a while, I still dream of seeing him die. I really wish he could have seen what has happened." Darron paused, then looked down to the table in front of Susan. "And every once in a while, I still feel like it was my fault – like I should have done something different."

"You couldn't uninvent the aliens, or jump forward and push him out of the way. Do you really think that when he died, he was thinking 'if only Darron Mason had done something differently'?"

"I don't think he would even be upset with the Tavir", answered Darron. "I guess I am not as good at forgiveness as he was."

"I suspect that forgiveness is something that takes time and practice. He had both. If we aren't vaporized as well, God willing, we will have both someday." Susan pushed her chair back. "I have to get going. I want to tie up the loose ends on the report before we are sent out again. I wonder if the leave we aren't going to get accumulates over time, or if we just lose it?"

"Probably just lose it", Darron predicted as he stood up. They said goodnight and both headed off. Susan was sort of surprised to find that she had been glad to see Darron take her work seriously. She thought of how Darron and Steve were friends because they cared about the same things; she had not really expected to find common ground herself.

Darron walked back to his rooms, and the strange thought occurred that if Susan had been transferred, the ship would have seemed empty. This irrational thought was clearly ridiculous; the volume of a single individual compared to the volume of the entire ship, especially when unpacked for normal flight, was tiny. This led to questions about what the total volume of the entire crew was if compared to the volume of the ship, and then to estimates of what percentage of the ship's volume was occupied by crew and equipment during flight. He was still working on different ways of estimating volumes when he reached his temporary quarters and found that there had been a change of plans – the *Persephone* was leaving very soon. This announcement had not come from Captain Adams. Stephen had been talking with his Suvain friends from his on-line game, who had been talking with their Suvain friends who were running the tracking systems that were checking on the heat emissions from the Terran power systems; the extra heat emissions in the power cables that were recharging the *Persephone*'s angulins had been identified, indicating that the ship was being readied for flight much faster than before. This information went to the other Suvain as fast as it went to the Tavir. This led to the Suvain asking Stephen why he was leaving soon, probably in the next few days. These questions went to everyone playing the game; people all the way back to Terra were soon taking bets on the *Persephone*'s course. Darron received a message from another member of the Physics team asking if he could use half a square foot of Darron's space allocation when they lifted off; this message came an hour before Captain Adams received the final confirmation that they were leaving as planned. When the official notification that the *Persephone* was leaving arrived it included an attachment to be filled out by the recipient - from now on, every crewman could choose to stay behind, or to volunteer for the hazardous duty of space travel. Each crewman opened the form and found that Captain Adams had helpfully checked "I wish to volunteer" for them in advance.

The next evening, Darron, Stephen, Jon, and Susan gathered one last time in the same off-duty room as usual. This time, the room had a number of other crewmen - several were trying to inhale six months of alcohol in advance. The four at the corner table talked about the normal blend of aliens, shipboard life, and aliens again; then Darron headed off to use the restroom. When he re-entered the room, he could be seen standing around, looking for their table. He eventually noticed the correct location and came back to the table, where the other three were laughing.

"So how many times have we come here?" asked Jon. "Uh, quite a few times", stuttered Darron.

"And how often did we sit at this table?" continued Jon.

Darron was considering this, trying to remember, when Susan stage- whispered, "Every time?"

Stephen jumped to his friend's defense. "Why remember the table? When you come in, you can just look around until you see your friends. And you can't stand there lost for too long when the room only has eight tables." "I found the right table eventually", Darron pointed out as he sat down.

"The confused look was priceless", said Susan to the other two. "He's going to play the Physics card soon", predicted Jon. "Why remember the table when you are busy contemplating the birth of the universe?"

"I don't think he was contemplating the birth of the universe", said Stephen suspiciously. "He seemed very focused, before he returned to the world completely lost."

All three looked at Darron. He looked around for a second, then realized the implied question.

"I was wondering if it would make a difference if the *Space Serves Death Cold*' monster had 6 tentacles or 8 if it was in a fight with the *'It Came to Mars'* monster", Darron answered.

All three answered at once. "Not really", said Stephen. "Unbelievable", said Jon, laughing.

"I think I am moving to that table", said Susan, pointing to a table where two relatively attractive men from the ship were laughing themselves into drunken oblivion.

Darron had no real answer to this, so he just sat without speaking. "So you observe how many tentacles a movie monster has, but not the table you were sitting at?" asked Jon.

"Well I am not completely unobservant", muttered Darron defensively.

He knew he was in trouble when even Stephen started smiling.

"We visited the Captain's quarters that night we found about the Suvain." Stephen mentioned in a friendly voice. Darron saw the other two look at Stephen, then look back at him. "So what color were the walls in her room?"

Darron saw both the others look confused, then start smiling as Darron didn't answer. "Well, I was just there once", Darron said.

Jon nodded. "That is very true. And that was a long time ago. You go into the mess hall every day. What color are the walls in the mess hall?" and all three looked with suppressed glee at Darron.

Darron stumbled for a moment, then hazarded a guess, "Something light colored - white?" He could tell by the laughter that white had not been the right answer.

Susan gave a sidelong glance to the other two, and then risked the question, "So what colors are the walls in your room?"

Jon saw Darron was obviously lost, and suggested, "Or could it be that every wall in the ship is painted gray?" When all the other three laughed, Darron joined in.

Darron gave up. "What difference does it make? There is no question of importance that requires knowing the color of the walls in the room."

"As opposed to knowing the number of tentacles of a movie alien," agreed Susan. "Now, that is truly important."

"It can be a valuable thing to deeply consider literature." Darron solemnly pronounced. "Lots of people selling literature have said so." With this profound thought in mind, all four returned to the ship.

Captain Adams was re-reading the answering letter from her son; the ship was ready for launch and she had sent out recovery parties for the handful of missing crewmen. She noted again that her grandchildren were well, and had enjoyed the receipt of gifts from their grandmother. After four times through the brief email, Captain Adams carefully detached the attached picture of the two smiling children, each holding the *Persephone*, and pasted it across her terminal. The Captain was trying to work up the courage to respond when there was a buzzing from the display with the Suvain direct line. She found it, turned it on, and pressed the "See" button. She nodded to the image of the Tavir covering the screen.

"You are leaving tomorrow," the Tavir stated.

"Who told you that?" Captain Adams asked.

"It is not hard to determine," he answered.

"Don't worry, we aren't headed back to Earth."

"Other places may be just as dangerous for you at the moment. The rumors of a planet to loot have already spread. Most of the races exploring this cluster will be headed this way."

"We will have to keep an eye out then. " Captain Adams answered. "I am going to send a ship with you- the *DoorFinder*," the Tavir informed her.

"Are you afraid that we will start talking with people we shouldn't?" asked the Captain.

"I am afraid that someone is going to steal my property," the Tavir answered.

The Captain laughed. "We will try not to get stolen. Of course, if you truly worried about your property, you could always go back to SuvAa and guard it."

"It is statements like that which make me fear for the future of your species. Besides, the Tavir only own one building on SuvAa – just the clan political interface center."

"Your family is not from SuvAa?"

The Tavir straightened a little and answered, "The founders of the Tavir clan were among the first inhabitants of the seventh Suvain colony – AyanAdyer. Tavir personnel have often been at the forefront of Suvain exploration."

"Are the Tavir famous among the Suvain?" asked Captain Adams. Tavir's arms flicked in a brief smile. "We have had our part in history.

But there are many such clans among the Suvain. Some are travelers, such as ourselves. Others are devoted to trade and industry. Of course, above all this is the family of the Emperor."

Adams shook her head. "It seems strange to hear of an Emperor, from such an advanced race."

"It seems strange to us that you leave the most important decisions to the most untrained." Tavir countered.

"If the Tavir are just one of many clans, it must be a great honor to be representing your species."

There was a gesture by the Tavir that Adams didn't recognize. "There have been many discoveries of new species. The Tavir are not a large clan, but we have been rising for several generations."

"Are you spread throughout the galaxy, or do different clans focus on different areas?"

The Tavir laughed. "We put all our cash into buying the concession for this cluster. Everyone is here."

Adams was silent for a moment. "So this really is the big bet for the Tavir. Either the cluster doesn't pay off, and you go bankrupt, or it does, and you go way up. That is a lot of responsibility – your family's future is probably in your hands."

The Tavir's arms flicked. "Well, we don't choose command to avoid responsibility." The Tavir's arms flicked again. "GoDai tried to claim I was responsible for even more than my family, before he lost his head and went native." The Tavir's arms flashed for a moment, and he changed the subject. "So is your clan also focused on exploration?"

"No, we really don't have the strong clan connections you do. At least, not where I am from. I am starting to think that is something we can learn from you. I am the only one of my family in space."

"So what drove you to leave your home, and choose this career?"

"I have often wondered why I went to the academy to become a ship captain. I think the real answer is that I like ordering people around." Both captains laughed. "And space travel is one of the great transitions of the human, Terran race. There was also a feeling that if people were moving forward I wanted to be part of it."

Adams saw Tavir start to speak, then flash his spikes and stop. She wondered for a second why her statement had made the Suvain angry. She noticed that the Tavir didn't appear to be focused on her. After a few moments, she saw him reach down to activate the intercom, and heard him order GoDai to the annex. Since the Tavir was already irritated, she went ahead and asked, "So has GoDai been giving you bad advice since he went native?"

Tavir's arms flashed again. Then there was the movement again that Adams couldn't recognize. "No," Tavir answered. "No, he has given me good advice. I am pretty tired of hearing it."

"That is one disadvantage of a clan-based ship. If someone keeps giving me good advice, I can just have him transferred to some other ship."

Tavir started to laugh, and then his arms flashed again. After a second he answered. "Maybe I should just send GoDai with you. Then you would have to listen to him, not me." He stopped, then continued. "No, that won't work as punishment. He would probably enjoy it." Adams could hear the door open, and saw Tavir look away, and motion for GoDai to enter. Captain Adams wondered if GoDai had already been in the next room, or if people really responded that fast when the Tavir gave an order.

The Tavir looked back at the display. "Very well. Try not to wander off, and don't blow up next to DyanIanTavir's ship. Ship explosions are rare, I wouldn't want to miss it."

"Don't worry," Captain Adams answered. "When I blow up this ship, you will have the very best view."

The Tavir laughed and answered. "Until our next meeting." Captain Adams turned off the display.

GoDai sat across from the Tavir and waited. Tavir was looking away, trying to decide what to say. Listening to Adams talk about joining the Fleet, he had been about to say that he thought the Adams clan would have a great future in Terran history. Then he had remembered that the Terrans would have no history. Then he realized that that he knew that would be a loss. The Tavir gave up trying to describe his conversation, and instead smacked the display across the room. GoDai sat carefully; such outbursts were not that unusual for Suvain.

"So you claim that Terrans are sentient," the Tavir accused. "Yes," GoDai answered. When there was no outburst from Tavir, GoDai watched him suspiciously. "So do you," GoDai stated. "Maybe they do have mind-control," Tavir said bitterly.

"No," GoDai answered.

"They aren't that competent."

"No one in the family will ever understand."

"Then you will have to be the one who makes the decision." GoDai stated.

"My father will be the one who makes the decision." Tavir answered. "And sentient or not, this concession has to pay off for the Tavir clan."

"Then you have to be the one who convinces your father that our real opportunity is through controlling trade, rather than an expensive war."

"Or we could go back to Plan A and call for a Preventive Extermination, and be done with it."

"It is too late. No one would understand the real threat." Seeing the Tavir's eyes narrow at the reference to a threat, GoDai continued, "We always thought the threat was some race that was advancing so fast, or already had, that their technology would be too great an advantage.

Whenever we look at a new race, we always ask ourselves whether they are going to have better ships or better weapons than we do. We never really thought about looking to see if their culture was a threat."

Tavir flexed. "I would admit I am still of that opinion. If a ship is about to shoot at me, I usually count the incoming missiles, rather than worry if the ship I am about to vaporize has 'culture'."

"So would I," answered GoDai. "But the real threat to our way of life is not that we are going to be destroyed. It is that we are going to be changed. The Terrans have truth. They have truth because it was given to them, not because they somehow figured it out. And truth and error never live side by side forever. Sooner or later, the two must come in conflict. You can see the effect in the Terran society. And as that truth spreads to our society, it will have the same effect. The truth will change us or destroy us."

"So I should not just exterminate the Terrans, I should exterminate everyone who has been contaminated by Terran beliefs." Tavir pointed out.

GoDai flicked his arms. Then he answered seriously, "Yes. If you want to go ahead with the PE, that would be the required course of action."

"I can't believe that you think this religion is going to destroy the Suvain, and you still choose to join it."

"I didn't say it will destroy the Suvain. I said the truth will destroy the Suvain, or change us. It is the thought that we might be changed that excites me about the possible future."

"You really think we need to change? To be like *Terrans*?"

"I think we need to change into Suvain. Into what the Suvain were created to be." GoDai saw Tavir was suspicious, or confused. "We are sort of like a ship bundled up for going through a door. What the truth will do is not turn us into Terrans, it will be like unpacking our ship - becoming the same ship, but configured as it has always been intended to be."

The Tavir looked at GoDai without speaking for a while, and then answered, "It is amazing. Ever since you went native, you have been giving advice. Sometimes you say things that are completely reliable, and sometimes you spout nonsense. And I think I have heard enough about culture and change and ships unfolding. I can imagine what response I would get talking to my father about the Suvain "unfolding like a ship into a Terran whatever". The decisions reached are going to be based on strength and profit, not gibberish about unpacking ships."

Tavir continued, "I want a summary by tomorrow of what you have seen of the negotiations here, and your estimate of the possible and most likely Terran responses to Tavir occupation. I think things are going to be done here very soon. From what I have seen so far, I am not optimistic. We have said all we are going to say, and I suspect that they aren't going to be coming up with an acceptable surrender anytime soon. Given their chaotic political system, I am not even sure they could if they wanted to. It is time to go back and get ready for the next stage of the occupation."

GoDai stood to leave, but the Tavir stopped him with a final question. "So if we are leaving, and will probably only be coming back to destroy any resistance, do you want to come with us? Or stay here with your new religious clan?"

GoDai stared at the Tavir. He had thought the question was another way to harass him about his attachment to the Terran religion, but from Tavir's posture, it looked like he was really serious. "I am a Tavir. I belong with the Tavir. Like I said before – when you die, I am going to be standing next to you."

"You are that confident that we cannot defeat a bunch of primitives – Terrans, whatever …" GoDai could see Tavir's arms raising.

GoDai kept his arms level and answered. "Obviously the Suvain can defeat the Terrans. I think it is likely that the Tavir can defeat the Terrans. But I also think it is likely the Terrans will manage to kill a lot of Tavir during the fight."

GoDai looked at his commander and added, "A little while back I bet against the Tavir ship in the races. I bet we would not be in the top 100 finishers. I did not do so because I am not a Tavir, I did so because a realistic appraisal of the Tavir design and the other designs suggested we would be farther back. And if there hadn't been an unusually large solar flare that disabled the flight controls of the ships that had saved weight by throwing out shielding and backup systems, I would have won the bet. I am just bringing this up as an example, of course. I am not still irritated that I lost money because of a once in a thousand chance of a stupid solar flare as the ships made the turn. My point is that I am trying to evaluate the situation as it really is, not as I, or you, would like it to be. And that evaluation suggests that the Terrans will resist, and that they will have a lot of armed ships by the time our fleet is here. Their ships will be pathetic, but there will be a lot of them. And the Suvain ships in front will probably be the ones they can actually target. And you, and I, will be on the ship in front. You will insist on leading your group in. You found this race, so your father will grant your request."

GoDai looked at his scowling captain, and stopped. There wasn't much else to say, anyway. The Tavir eventually narrowed his eyes, looked at GoDai and stated in a calm voice, "There are a number of successful leaders who claim that the most valuable asset you can have is a subordinate who doesn't just confirm your opinions, but tells you what he really thinks is true. After a brief pause, Tavir flashed his arms and announced, "Those people are morons. I am so sick of hearing all your estimates and advice. This whole "truth" fad is going to stop. From now on, when I ask your advice, I want to you to tell me exactly what I want to hear."

GoDai arms flicked for a second, and then he stood, knees together, arms tucked in, head bowed. "Of course, my lord. I will be sure to only tell you things that I have confirmed in advance you agree with." Tavir snorted, GoDai laughed for a second, and fled as the Tavir made a show of grabbing for any other throwable object on his desk.

When Darron awoke, he could feel that they had left Loren Station during the night shift. He guessed that the Captain had wanted to leave without dealing with a crowd of reporters. The floors and walls of the room had a tiny vibration - the strain from the angulin anchors always transferred out a little through the entire hull. Whenever the ship was accelerating, there was the slight feel of the metal responding to the strain, and the occasional low background noise of sections of the hull grating as they exchanged pressure. After the quiet of the ship as it sat locked onto the station, the motions and sounds seemed almost like the ship was stretching and groaning as it came back awake. He shook his head, and got dressed. Everything was completely normal. This was no different than any other launch. He had spent almost two years in space, and that is where he was going now.

Darron started to take a shower, and then remembered that he was onboard the *Persephone* again — there would be no more showers until the mission was over. He realized he was wondering if he would ever take a shower again, or if that was a memory from his life that was past. He started walking down the hall to breakfast, and suddenly remembered how everything had felt the morning after he had discovered the aliens. Now everything seemed shiny, and the light seemed glaring. He walked in and moved over to collect his food. He was moving back to a table, and then stopped and looked around the room. He had been moving to the center table, even though it had several people already sitting there. He looked around, and tried to figure out why he didn't want to sit at one of the tables on the edge, like usual. He looked at the tables, then looked at the walls next to them. The walls were gray, he carefully noted. The tables were white, and the walls next to them were gray, and the space behind the walls was black. For a second, the walls melted away, and Darron could see through to the endless space beyond them. Space was black, and empty, and endless.

Anything could be out there, and Darron would never know until the ship ran across it. He moved to a table away from the wall, and tried to eat. Breakfast included something called "eggs". Darron couldn't remember having real eggs since he left Earth. He remembered the food he used to eat before joining the Fleet, and thought how much he would have liked to have eaten truly good food once last time before they had left. The rational part of his brain started to point out that there had been lots of real food on Loren Station; then he realized that he did not expect to come back from this mission. Space had always been interesting before; now he really believed that there was something alien, waiting out there in the dark. And when he met that hidden alien, it was going to be the end of the *Persephone*, and him. Stephen would be dead too, but he would probably enjoy something as exciting as being blown up. The thought that his life would end was scary, but he also found a feeling of sadness - Susan would be gone. Darron shook his head to clear out such thoughts, and started on his food. Throughout his eggs, Darron kept his head down - every time he looked up, he could see through the walls to the dark void that surrounded them. He put up his tray, head down, and walked, head down, the 30 feet to his work station.

The other physicists were already there. Darron mumbled a greeting, deliberately loud enough to have satisfied social convention, and low enough not to be clearly heard - that might spark conversation. He watched the face of his superior as the morning's assignments were given out. After the first sentence, his mind had wandered back to the invisible aliens waiting in the dark. After not hearing the current assignments, he nodded, and went back to what he had been assigned to before - the assignments never really changed anyway. He stared at the monitor, and thought about how close another ship had to be for the normal radar to detect the incoming ship. While daydreaming, he went through all the normal motions of work - staring at the screen, moving his head to different angles, looking down at printouts, frowning at the screen. After about 20 minutes, he returned to reality enough to notice that things were quieter than normal, except for what might be suppressed snickering. Darron focused on the printout, and discovered it wasn't his list of readings from the accelerometers, it was the Chief Scientist's list of tasks and manpower estimates. He actually looked at the monitor, and saw that it had long ago switched over to a picture of some mountains on Earth. He thought it looked like a picture of the "Yosemite" park that the Chief Scientist talked about all the time. Then he looked around, and everyone started laughing. He sheepishly got up, moved over to his own terminal and sat back down. He started to bury himself in his work, but in a tiny room with four people, there wasn't going to be any way to escape. He turned around and asked, "Do you think there is a way to see ships further out than on radar? You know, in case there are other ships out there? It would be good to know about them at least as soon as they know about us."

The laughter stopped, and everyone started thinking about the new problem. After a couple of minutes, the Chief Scientist cancelled everything else, and the entire group began brainstorming about finding aliens.

The second day out, Darron and Stephen picked up their dinners, and then went to sit next to Susan. She had returned to her usual duties, and so had not been working with them. She saw them coming, and was surprised to find that she was not annoyed. She slid over, and the two sat down. "Your study was on heavy-element densities," Stephen announced. "How well can you track densities in open space?"

"Not very well", Susan answered. "Why?" She asked suspiciously. "We have been trying to come up with ways to see alien ships earlier than just seeing them on radar", Darron explained.

"A passing ship must have some impact on the stray molecules in space," Stephen added. "So do you think that a ship would leave a measureable trail?"

Susan looked at them both, then looked up to see Jon sitting down at the same table. "Space is pretty empty. We have to spend a lot of time in the same area to get enough data. If we looked right around an Intersection, maybe? But even then, I doubt it."

Jon looked around, and was brought up to speed by the others. "We find Intersections", he stated. "Granted, we have to be really close to them, but we can still see them. We send out sensors to the far side of the Intersection field. The sensors can fly independently, and can receive and transmit. Send them out first." Everyone stopped and thought for a few minutes.

"Finding things is basically a form of communication", Darron mused. "I really should have thought about asking the communications personnel first."

"Yep", answered Jon, and started eating.

Darron brought the idea back to the Physics lab. After things were fleshed out, the recommendation was forwarded to the Captain.

The third day out, things went back to their post-alien normal. The *DoorFinder* had suggested future contacts, and Darron, Steve, and Susan were called back to Suvain baby-sitting. They had moved back into the crowded lab and started going over the records of the Suvain actions at Loren Station when the Captain informed them they were back on normal duty. The Suvain request had been clarified - they didn't want to sit and have history lectures, they wanted to get together over dinner. If the dinner happened to be accompanied by Dark Cola, that would be even better. A few days later, the visits started, with clusters of Suvain coming to the *Persephone* to drink Dark Cola and watch Terran movies, or to show Terrans their own entertainment. As the ships headed out to the Intersection, the pattern of the every-third-day party was quickly established.

Four days after the departure of the *Persephone*, the Tavir notified CE Aguilera that he would be leaving in the next few days. He recommended that no ceremony should be held when they launched - they were not leaving as friends, as they had heard no statement of submission from the assembled delegates. The last few days saw most of the Suvain heading out for a last few hours of shore leave before returning to the discipline and routine of ship life. The Tavir noted that although he had specifically stated that they were not leaving as friends, nearly every Suvain who returned had gifts or souvenirs of some sort - usually dark or light cola. He then caught a group of 17 Suvain led by GoDai leaving together the night before the launch. He called to GoDai, "What's going on here?"

About half the group jerked away from the glare of the Tavir. Most of the other half looked at GoDai. "We are attending a last religious service before we leave", answered GoDai.

"All of you have joined that stupid religion?" Tavir asked, arms sliding outwards.

"Some of us", answered GoDai. "Others are just curious."

"Why would you possibly want to waste time watching some primitive religion?" asked Tavir.

"Come and see", answered GoDai.

The Tavir looked carefully at the number of Suvain leaving the ship at once. He looked over again at the *Thunderchild*, and then thought about how all the Christians were leaving the ship. He thought about ordering them all back on board, but decided that if something was up, he wanted to find out what it was. "Wait here", he ordered. He went back to collect his gun, and to collect 3 armed and armored bodyguards. He ordered the communications officer to notify the other ship to go on alert until otherwise notified, and to call out the remaining crew. The guns were to be manned, and the doors closed until he personally ordered them to open. Then he walked down the ramp to the waiting crewmen, said to "GoDai, "Fine - show me."

The sight of 21 Suvain walking together towards the station caused everyone in their path to stop and stare, then get out of the way. The presence of weapons and armor was immediately noticed. There were several hurried conversations about possible Suvain attacks, and guards across the station were cautiously picking up weapons almost as fast as questions and rumors could travel. GoDai led the huge glob of Suvain to one of the main meeting rooms, where a temporary chapel had been set up. There were nearly 200 Terrans already present, and more were still trickling in. There were shocked looks when all the Suvain marched in, and the Terrans rapidly cleared out a section for them to sit. The Tavir watched while about half a dozen of his crew went up and exchanged greetings with the Terran religious leaders, and lots of the other Terrans present. Most of the other Suvain were looking around curiously at the Terrans, and answering greetings that came from people all around.

Tavir guessed that the noise that happened next was Terran music. A number of the Terrans were singing along, but not the Suvain. He wondered if that was because the Suvain still had enough sense to know how stupid they would look, or if the primitive music was too far from Suvain musical structure to be followed. After a long period of noise, one of the Terrans in the front started speaking. He greeted everyone, and then mentioned the presence of the Suvain. The Suvain looked around suspiciously when the assembled Terrans began clapping; GoDai and several of the others spread the word that this was a sign of respect among the Terrans. Tavir listened as the Terran in front launched into a long discussion which made frequent references to one of the books that GoDai had been reading. Near the end of the speech, Tavir started to pay attention, as the leader quoted "As far as it up to you, live at peace with all men".

"It will not be up to most of us whether we can live in peace, or whether we will be at war. It will be up to us whether we face the future, either peace or war, with faith or with fear. For myself, I usually look at the future with fear. I have to deliberately remind myself that God has given us his word that nothing can separate us from his love. Either what will happen will be something which God desires, or something that God allows. And if it is something that God allows, it is something that cannot prevent God's plan for us, and for all of humanity." Girelli paused, and restated, "His plans for us, both Terran and Suvain. God does not promise us victory in war. God promises us that whether there is war or peace, He will be with us. He promises that through His love, we will be redeemed, regardless of our circumstances. Whether there is war or peace, God's love and His plan of salvation will continue. It may continue because our two races learn to live in peace. It may be that there is war, and God's plan of salvation will pass into the hands of the Suvain." There was a pause, and Tavir could see lots of people turn and look at GoDai. "While there may be war between races, and there may not, remember that the real war is between our rebellion against

God and His love. And in that war, there are already both Humans and Suvain on each side. And in that war, there is no question of the ending - God's love will sweep all before it. This may not be in the way we would prefer it to happen, and we may not live to see the end. But we can face whatever future there might be with faith that God is in control, and that God will be close to us, regardless of the choices of Humans … Terrans… or Suvain. And whether there is war or peace, the time will come when the shooting ends. And if we are alive, we will still have the same duty, whether we are free or slaves. We will still have the duty to choose forgiveness, and repentance, and love. And that duty is our blessing, for the path we are called to is the path that leads to life. May God give each of us wisdom, and faith, and courage, and love - a love that extends beyond the boundaries of our race, and beyond the boundaries of our circumstances."

Tavir watched as the assembled Terrans, and some of the Suvain, joined in a prayer for peace, and then was surprised to see the service end after a short blessing. He looked around, and saw several of the other Suvain doing the same. "That's it?" one asked. Tavir saw that Girelli had walked down to where they were, but the question was directed at GoDai. "They don't have sacrifices or something, to convince the god to give them victory?" the Suvain asked.

"No", answered GoDai. The Suvain looked at him for a moment, then they turned to Girelli.

"We don't offer a sacrifice to God", Girelli stated, "unless you consider a life of obedience our sacrifice. But that is really for our gain, not His."

"I was waiting for some time where your god promised you victory, but I must have missed that part." Tavir stated.

"God does not promise us victory in war. He promises us victory over the sin that is the thing that really kills us." Girelli answered.

"What is 'sin'", asked another Suvain.

"Sin is when we choose ourselves and hatred and death instead of God, and others, and love, and life. Sin is choosing not to obey God, which is really the same thing, because His command is to a life of love for Himself and others."

"Maybe if you did offer sacrifices, you god would offer you victory", a Suvain suggested, and there was a lot of arm-waggling.

Girelli laughed. "The only sacrifice is the one God made, to draw us back to Himself. And if there is going to be a sacrifice, that is the only direction that really makes sense - what would we have to give to God anyway?"

"So your God makes a sacrifice, and so you are free, not from us, but from 'sin'?" asked a Suvain.

"God gave Himself as a sacrifice for us, and so we can be free from sin.

And none of us are yet fully free from sin, just, by the grace of God, hopefully moving away from choosing sin to choosing life and obedience."

"So your god demands nothing, and gives nothing in return?" asked Tavir.

"God demands our entire life, and gives us His entire life in return. You could say that He demands everything, and gives everything."

"So your god doesn't give you anything, and tells you to think about other people, instead of yourself. Why do you believe something like that? It doesn't seem worth the effort." asked a Suvain.

"I believe it because I think it is actually true", answered Girelli. "When I say to have faith, I don't mean to try to believe things that you know are false, I mean to stay with what you think is actually true, even if it doesn't feel like it at the moment."

"You are getting back to the whole business about 'truth' that GoDai has been talking about all the time", Tavir declared.

"Yes," answered Girelli, "being committed to what it actually true, not what we want, or what we feel like at the moment, is a core part of our faith."

"And I do get something out of my faith," continued Girelli. "The few times I have really cared about other people, or really cared about what was true, and not just my opinion, or really was humble enough to listen to others instead of just lecture them, the few times I have really been obedient to God's will, those times have been worth anything."

"So if you are committed to the truth, not your opinion, how come all of you politicians can't agree on anything - probably not even what to eat for the next meal?" inquired Tavir.

Girelli shook his head. "Another part of the Christian faith is that only God is truly good. The rest of us are really messed up - and often Christians most of all. The change from the selfish, bitter, fearful people that we are now to the free people we were created to be is a long process, and most of us are very, very far from the freedom that we will, God willing, be brought to. We are so far away, most of the time, from what we were created to be, that the biggest struggle is often just the fight to want to be changed."

"So you are not how you are supposed to be, and your god is turning you into what you were supposed to be. But it will still be you - just in a different form, like a ship packed for crossing unfolding back into its proper configuration for flight?" Tavir asked.

Girelli thought for a second then agreed, "Yes - like a ship that is all tied together, being slowly opened up to its real form - the one it was built for."

The Suvain started to leave, and Tavir announced, "I think this is the weirdest religion I have come across."

Girelli nodded in agreement. "True things are always weird, when you really start to look at them." Terrans and Suvain exchanged parting statements and handshakes, and the Suvain moved back to the *ProfitTaker*. After they were safely back aboard, the Suvain ships stood down; the rumors that the Suvain had just gone to a church service and then went home slowly filtered across Loren Station to the Terrans awaiting attack.

Once they had returned to the ship, the Suvain began to disperse. Tavir and GoDai shamelessly took over the break room. When they had settled in, Tavir looked out at the station and narrowed his eyes. "Are all of your religious services like that?" After GoDai nodded, Tavir looked back at the Terrans. "All that did not sound like a speech about surrendering."

"No, it was more likely to encourage endurance."

"And you really believe all that. About a dying God who comes back, and changing to be a different person - one who thinks about others, instead of just themselves?"

"Yes. But I am finding that change takes a long time. So far, the more I try, the more I can tell that I fall short."

"So when we come back and reduce the Terrans to radioactive ash, are you still going to believe all this?"

"I hope so. Whether there really is a God does not depend on whether there is a war or not."

"So even if the Terrans are crushed, the religion will continue?"

"If the religion is true, it will continue, regardless of our decisions. If it is not, it will waste away like all the others."

"And it is the religion that you say it real danger?"

"If it is true, it is the religion that is the real danger if we are against it, and the real opportunity if we accept it. If it is false, Christianity is just a trap for everyone who falls for it."

Tavir thought about this for a few minutes, then answered, "So there isn't any threat then. Well, that was a fun trip over to the crazy side. Make sure everything is ready, we leave tomorrow." Tavir got up and headed back to his cabin for sleep. GoDai sat alone in the room, staring out at the Terran station. Finally he got up, and returned to his room.

Despite the Tavir's statement that he did not want any ceremony when the Suvain left, there were Terrans all over when the ship made final preparations to lift off. As the lines were disconnected Terrans kept coming up to and talking to the Suvain, and handing them things. The Tavir ordered the Suvain to keep the Terrans away, and found himself giving the same order over and over as his crew ignored the order as soon as Tavir walked away. The exasperated captain finally ordered every Suvain but himself inside, and ordered the Terrans to finish disconnecting the power cables themselves. When everything was done, CE Aguilera walked up, informed the Tavir that everything was clear, and held out his hand. Tavir hesitated for a moment, and then shook hands. As the Terrans moved away, Tavir walked back inside the ship, and closed the door. All crewmen were ordered to general quarters, and the Tavir growled as people wandered off to their rooms to put away their loot and then walked back to their stations. The *ProfitTaker* trained all weapons on the *Thunderchild* and lifted off. After both Suvain ships had cleared the station, the Tavir allowed the crew to stand down. He walked through the ship, looking at all of the Terran junk that crewmen had bought or been given, and were now taking back to Suvain space. After giving an order that every Terran item was to be checked for explosives or transmitting devices, Tavir gave up and just watched Loren Station fade into the star background.

Tavir saw that everything was in control on the bridge, and stepped into the Captain's Annex. He sat down and stared out of the window towards the Terrans. He considered ordering all of the crew to toss all of the Terran gifts out the airlock, but he did not think it would make much of a difference. A message to the crew about the dangers of becoming emotionally attached to the animal you were going to eat for dinner would probably do little good. Thinking of GoDai's discussions about being changed from inside, he realized that GoDai had been right all along - to truly get rid of the Terran influence, Tavir would have to throw all of the infected crewmembers out of the airlock as well. Dealing with the Terrans was far more complicated than dealing with primitives. The Terrans were probably building a fleet, which would have to be suppressed. That alone would take all of the Tavir clan resources, if not more. Assuming all went well, the Terran wreckage would have to be organized; assuming that the Terrans recognized their hopeless position before it was too late, it would take as many Suvain as the Tavir could muster to stay on top of the new subject race. All of this had to happen in spite of the distractions caused by the Suvain tendency to actually like the Terrans. GoDai had been correct again - it was going to take a united clan to face the Terrans.

Once the Tavir had set course for the Tavir clan gathering that was forming up two Intersections away, he collected all of the reports and summaries prepared by various crewmembers and forwarded them on to the Tavir station being assembled as a base of operations. He added his own comments to the reports to the family, and sent along several messages in his personal code to his subordinates at the clan command center. Once the reports were in and the course was laid, there was time to relax, and to be annoyed at the rumors that the Suvain Christians were meeting every couple of days to practice the Terran religion.

VI

The *Persephone* had crossed over the first of the two Intersections leading to New Chicago when Jon, Steve, and Darron came and sat next to Susan. They had watched some of the movies together, but she could tell by the effort everyone was making to look normal that something was up.

"You're a Chemist, right?" asked Steven in a low voice. Since everyone knew she was part of the Chemistry team, Susan did not bother to answer, but just waited for whatever unwise statement was going to come next. In her experience, usually when a non-Chemist expressed an interest in Chemistry, stupidity was not far behind.

"We have the AGM2 now," continued Steven. "But if there was fighting in close quarters, such as on-board ship, explosives can be as dangerous as a gun."

Susan sighed. "Explosives can be as dangerous as a gun even if you aren't in combat on a ship."

"That's why Darron said we should come to an expert," countered Jon.

Susan shook her head and looked over at Darron. "You were the one who suggested I should be involved in this?"

"Of course", Darron answered. "You are the best Chemist we know. And after all, Chemistry is about blowing things up."

"I am the only Chemist you know", Susan pointed out. "And there is a lot more to Chemistry than blowing things up."

"Okay, the fun part of Chemistry is blowing stuff up," answered Jon. All three looked at Susan with complete confidence that this statement was impossible to contradict.

She shook her head again, and looked back to Darron. "So what is it that you want?" Darron took a deep breath, and Susan jumped back in before he could get started. "I am only asking out of curiosity. I do not have any explosives, and if I did, the last thing I would do is trust you with them."

"What we have been discussing", Darron began, "is how close-quarter combat is often fought with explosive devices rather than just guns. What we need as something small enough to be held in the hand and thrown, or fired out of an AGM2, that will blow up and take out everything, or everyone, in a room. You see them used in a lot of the games that mimic old combat - they are called 'grenades'."

"They used one at the end of *Space Serves Death Cold*," Stephen pointed out helpfully.

"I see," answered Susan. "And what did Captain Adams say about your building this new weapon? Or was blowing up the Aft Loading Bay not enough for you?"

Jon and Darron answered at the same time.

"That was actually just a small fire. We mean something that will destroy everything in the compartment." answered Jon.

"If you say the device is feasible", Darron declared firmly, looking at his two friends, "we will be writing up a proposal to the Captain to study the subject."

"Can you make a grenade?" asked Steven, "using the materials we have aboard ship?"

Asking if manufacturing the explosive was possible automatically put the honor of all Chemists at stake. "Of course, we could make an explosive," Susan answered. "Keeping you from killing yourself is an entirely different matter."

"If you say this is possible, then I will write the description for the Captain", Darron announced.

The request to develop homemade grenades was reviewed at the daily officer check-in. While the officers considered the proposal, the Personnel Officer looked at the Captain in disbelief.

"You actually taught them to ask for permission", he said in awe. "I didn't think it was possible to teach that group anything."

"You would be surprised what sufficient punishment will do," Captain Adams answered in a thoughtful voice.

"Are you going to approve the request?" asked the Chief Engineer.

"Do we need explosives right now?" asked the Captain.

"I think there are only about 20 Suvain on our constant companion", answered the Chief Engineer. "If it came to a fight between the crews, I don't think we would need more than the AGM2s."

People looked at the Personnel Officer, who answered, "From everything I have seen, I don't think there is much risk of the Suvain starting a fight. For one thing, there is at least a couple of Suvain on board a lot of the time - they know if they try to attack us, the movies and cola will stop."

"So we don't really need to develop more weapons, but we could let the most irresponsible bunch in the crew build lots of small explosive containers, and probably store them all over the ship. At least if they blew up the forward loading bay, the ship would look balanced again." Captain Adams frowned at the request, and then continued. "But this would be something for the Chemistry team to do during transit. And it wouldn't hurt to have thought through how to build the explosives, even if we aren't building them now." She turned to the Chief Scientist. "Tell the Chemists they can make up the blueprints, but no actual weapons. If the lunatic brigade wants to help, they can, but they are never to be left alone with anything dangerous."

Once the authorization to proceed had been received, the Chemistry team dropped everything else. While Chemistry was about more than blowing things up, it was important for everyone to know that Chemists were better at blowing things up than anyone else.

After a couple of days, the Chemists had found a number of different ways to make incredibly dangerous explosives out of the materials available on the *Persephone*. The main difficulty was finding a way to contain the explosives safely, and still be able to trigger it upon command.

Susan met with Darron each dinner and went over the status of the Explosives project. On the third night, Susan described how they had found the perfect material - they could manufacture small quantities of an explosive that would combust as soon as air was introduced.

"The only difficulty left is how to contain the fuel and then trigger it when desired," Susan explained.

"What container is it in now?" Darron asked.

"It is held under pressure in a small tube. We thought of having a seal that would open, but the material is too strong - if we try to put in something that opens, the entire thing could go off- the seal just isn't tight enough."

"So you need a way to break the container from the outside. Preferably from a distance?" asked Darron. When Susan nodded, Darron said, "It is too bad you can't shoot it. But then you would have to be in the same room with it. And from what you say, that would be a bad place to be."

"Very," confirmed Susan.

"In the games, the old explosives were thrown. You triggered it, and then threw it before it went off." Darron thought for a few moments. "If you can't shoot it, maybe it could shoot itself. What if you stuck a small angulin gun on top, and then triggered it, and it shot down into the container?"

"You would probably want some delay, so the gun would have to have an external trigger that started a timer that fired the gun," Susan suggested." The two sketched out a design over dinner, and Susan left to show the Chemistry department the new approach.

Two days later, Susan asked Darron to join her in the aft loading bay. When he arrived, she was waiting with something behind her on the table. When he approached, she reached back, picked up a small cylinder about a foot long, with a button on top, and placed it in Darron's hand.

"Here is the prototype," she declared. She reached over and pointed out the button on top. "You just press this, and the gun fires and breaks the cylinder."

"You just press this button?" Darron asked, and as Susan nodded, he pressed the button.

He saw the sudden horror and shock on Susan's face, and realized that he was not holding an empty container, but an actual prototype. He could hear her shouting, "You pressed it, you pressed it..." and then starting to shriek "Throw it, throw it!" Darron had no idea how long the timer was. In a panic he threw the container towards the other side of the room, and then, with nowhere to hide, just stood, wincing away from the bomb. He was in front of Susan, and looked back to tell her to run. "At that point, Susan lost control and began laughing.

"Did you really think I would give you a real explosive?" She started to say more, but broke out laughing again.

"That is not funny", Darron declared. "You shouldn't mess around with explosives. I thought we were going to die."

Susan snorted, turned so she could point to the shadows of the scorch marks on the wall, and answered, "Of course, you would never think of playing around with really dangerous things, which might set the ship on fire. And if someone tells you, 'if you push this button, it will explode', you might want to try - not pushing the button."

"You practically told me to", Darron complained. Susan started laughing again as they walked over to retrieve the cylinder. For some reason, Darron was having a hard time maintaining the proper sense of outrage when Susan was laughing.

Susan picked up the container, and looked it over. "Let me make it up to you. Engineering is making a copy with the angulin gun attached, and we will need to try it out. With the real one, you have five seconds between the time you press the button and the time the gun fires, hopefully cracking the container. The explosive won't be inside, but the container might shatter, so you will want to be a ways away when it does."

Darron had to admit that getting to throw the fake bomb was pretty good compensation, until he found his face showing up on screens around the ship. The monitors in the loading bay had captured the entire exchange, and an enterprising crewman had zoomed in on Darron as he stared in panic at the bomb in his hand. The image was quickly transferred to all of the enterprising crewman's friends and then throughout the ship.

A day later, Darron took the new prototype, watched as everyone scurried to the far side of the room, pressed the button, counted to one, and then threw the cylinder behind a barricade that had been set up. He ducked away just before there was a loud explosion from the far side of the bay. A crowd of people swarmed around the smoking fragments of the bomb. There was loud cheering, and another weapon had been added to the *Persephone*'s armory.

The *Persephone* was traveling through an empty region of space known after its discoverer as the Kansu Transfer; at normal accelerations, after four weeks they would reach an Intersection that led to New Chicago. The Kansu Transfer had three identified Intersection paths, each leading to a solar system. The first discovered connected to a cold system with a small mining outpost. The mining outpost was one of the Terran's first establishments outside the Sol system - from there an Intersection led directly back to Earth. The discovery of the Intersection to New Chicago had allowed the Terrans to discover a planet suitable for the site of their second colony. A third Intersection had later been found which led to Loren station. As Loren Station also connected back to Earth, this formed an inner loop of Terran Intersections. The Kansu Transfer was not exhaustively explored; mapping to check for any other possible Intersections that led to regions of empty space had not been completed.

Captain Adams started sending out sensors the second day after they crossed over the Intersection. The *Persephone* would push up to maximum acceleration, and then release the sensor. The *Persephone* would then back off to a lower acceleration, and the sensor would burn its onboard angulin all the way down, accelerating ahead of the ship. After the angulin was run down, the sensor would stop accelerating, and the ship would slowly catch up. As the ship retrieved the first sensor, another would be sent out in its place. After things had settled into a routine, the crew was starting to have a rather pleasant trip. There were frequent movie nights, with the attraction of watching the strange actions of generally friendly aliens. Sensor juggling was an interesting variation on just flying through space. Going back to familiar tasks was a form of relaxation after the slew of meetings at Loren Station. There was even the chance that someone would blow something up by accident while making charged cylinders for bombs. An alert crewman took the opportunity to trigger the "Intersections not Holes" speech when the entire Physics team happened to be eating at the same time - bets had already been laid on how soon another Physicist would jump in to correct the first responder. Jonathon Sykes won with a prediction of 37 seconds. As the Physicists forgot about the speech entirely while arguing about the details, Jon happily collected his extra Day 2 dessert. It was this relaxed atmosphere which led Captain Adams to make the tactical error upon which she blamed all of their subsequent troubles.

After a movie night in which Suvain and Terrans had not shot each other, far from the political meetings of Loren Station, and far from the tasks ahead at New Chicago, Captain Adams went off shift. She looked at the cot, took the blanket she had snagged from Chaplain Eisen's possessions, removed her uniform, and went to bed, completely relaxed and comfortable. After she had gone pleasantly and thoroughly to sleep, the pounding on the door began. She woke up slowly, unable to place the sound at first. She started to tell whoever it was to come in, then stopped. She looked around for a second, found the uniform, and began cursing herself for inviting trouble by going to bed as if she wasn't going to have to get up. Putting on the uniform took her enough time that she was almost awake by the time she opened the door. The Chief Engineer and two other crewmen were waiting outside. She stepped back and motioned them in. All three squeezed inside, and the Chief Engineer managed to shut the door.

The Chief Engineer announced "The forward sensors have detected several light flashes, occurring at regular intervals. There are no objects known in the area the flashes are coming from. The flashes are concentrated in very narrow frequency bands, and are the same each time." He paused, as the Captain cut in.

"So these look like radar searches coming out from one or more ships?" As all three crewmen nodded, she continued, "Where are they relative to us?"

"Az 330, El 0.5", answered one of the crewmen. Directions in space were always set by whatever ship was in flight. For a ship near a planet, choosing how to identify a location was usually based on the objects around the ship. "Up" was defined to be away from the center of the planet; you were always getting pulled "Down" by gravity. The other two directions could be chosen based on other nearby objects; a ship near a planet might pick the planet as being "Down", the direction to the star of the solar system to be "Forward", and make the third direction "The way you point if you stand facing the star and put out your right arm". Then when the ship started moving away from the planet out to an Intersection, a new set of directions would be decided on. Any set of directions could be chosen to represent up, forward and right or left. The Terrans, as almost every other race, always set the galactic plane as the base for their reference frame, and judged "Forward" as pointed towards the destination they were flying to. "Azimuth 330, Elevation 0.5" indicated that the probable alien ship was a bit to the left of their current path, and not very far above them.

"Are the flashes the same frequency as the Suvain use?" asked the Captain.

"No," answered the Chief Engineer, meeting the Captain's eyes.

She looked away for a second, then answered, "So the Suvain told us there were others headed this way, and we probably just met them." She looked at all three, and no one challenged the statement. "Meet me in the bridge ready room in five minutes. Also call Personnel, the lunatic brigade, and Communications." As they all started to leave, she added "And someone get coffee for everyone," and shut the door. Once everyone was gone, Captain Adams sighed, and allowed herself to sag a little. The entire scenario of meeting new aliens was going to have be started over. She remembered that at least she and her crew had a little experience now, and then thought that this time, Eisen wouldn't be there. She gave a tight little smile, thinking that maybe Eisen wasn't here, but his Commander was. She gave a quick prayer for guidance and strength, adjusted her uniform, and headed for the conference.

Susan looked around at the crowded room. She would have been horrified to learn that she was now included in the "lunatic brigade". Half the senior officers were present, along with several of the bridge crew, and the four crewmen who had spent the most time with the Suvain. Most of the group was still trying to come fully awake. The Captain opened the discussion by asking the Chief Engineer to summarize the new situation. By the time the introduction was over all of the participants were alert, and turning to the Captain for instructions.

"How close are they expected to come, and how long will it be until our closest approach?" the Captain asked.

"Do we have any idea what the velocity of the other ship is?" asked Darron.

"Not really - the flashes are coming from pretty much the same direction," answered the Chief Engineer.

"Do we have the frequencies of the light flashes?" asked Darron. Darron picked up a spare display, and the Chief Engineer sent over the requested data. Darron immediately lost all interest in the conversation, and started looking through the provided numbers and typing on the display.

The Captain looked at Stephen. "So do you think that they have detected us yet?"

"Have there been any change in the pattern of their transmissions?" Stephen asked. After people shook their head in denial, Stephen continued, "So they probably haven't seen us yet. But if they are anything like the Suvain, it can't be long."

"Do we know they aren't more Suvain?" the Captain asked. "We don't know much of anything for sure," answered the Chief Engineer. "But the frequency is different than what we have seen the Suvain use."

"All of the Tavir clan ships have standardized equipment - if they are Suvain, they probably aren't someone we have met." Stephen added.

"If they are new, what are the chances they are hostile?" "According to the Suvain, they will be very hostile," answered MacDonald. "Of course, the Suvain could be lying. It is in their best interest to claim they are a better choice than the alternative. But I would guess that they are not. They see us as so unusual, I think it is likely that the other races they have been dealing with are not that different from themselves. I think that it is more likely that they will have a similar response to us that the Suvain have had."

"If they are hostile, what are our options?"

"An exact answer cannot be determined from the frequency data alone," Darron answered. "An estimate is only possible if we make a large number of assumptions ..." Everyone looked at him in confusion for a second, then the Chief Engineer realized how far back they had lost Darron.

"Just tell us how close and how long," commanded the Chief Engineer.

Darron was caught in mid-explanation, and couldn't continue for a moment. He started back on his assumptions, but was cut off again by the Chief Engineer saying, "Given all of your assumptions, how close will they be, and when will they be that close?"

"Close. 10 or 15 million kilometers. About 60 hours from now. They will pass in front of us, from left to right." Darron answered, and then sat in horrified silence as everyone took his statement as accurate, without asking for all of the assumptions, limitations, and approximations that were required to come up with any answer at all.

"Now that we are all back in the meeting," the Captain stated, "If they are hostile, what are our options?" The repeated question was met by silence. Everyone looked at the Captain, at each other, or the table, and waited for someone else to answer.

"Other than blowing ourselves up?" asked Susan eventually. There was nervous laughter from several points around the table, but no one bothered to answer. "And we are assuming that we have talked with them, and they won't listen?" she continued in a quiet voice. Again, there was no answer. As nobody was taking charge of the discussion, she continued speaking. "One of the books I sent over to the Suvain as an example of Terran literature was 'The Art of War'. I glanced through it just in case GoDai had questions. One thing it emphasizes is that your opponent will always get his information about you from how he sees you. So you should always look different than you really are."

"So we are supposed to look strong and powerful, since we are completely unarmed," asked MacDonald.

"That is what it sounds like, but looking dangerous is going to be awfully difficult." responded the Captain.

"I don't know if would do any good, but we would be a lot better at looking helpless and pathetic." MacDonald mused, to general laughter.

"The *Persephone* is unarmed, be we aren't," answered Stephen. "We cannot affect their ship, but if they are trying to board, almost everybody has an AGM2." added Jonathon.

"And what they will see is the ship, not the crew," continued Stephen. There was a pause as people absorbed the fact that using an AGM2 against an alien might have gone from an interesting idea to a probable, actual future.

The Captain changed the subject. "I don't want to lead them anywhere significant. We have been speeding up in the direction of the Intersection for New Chicago for 6 days. How far off from that course can we get in 60 hours?" asked the Captain, knowing it wasn't very far. Everyone looked over at Darron; his face had gone blank, and his fingers started tracing out triangles.

After a minute he answered, "Assuming we are using maximum acceleration as much as possible, maybe by 15 degrees. With all of the built- up velocity from the last six days, we just can't change course that fast; there is just too much inertia."

"What if we don't use all available acceleration, but hold it down to about 1 g?" asked Captain Adams. "I would rather they don't know what our maximum acceleration really is."

"Restricting ourselves to 1g?" asked Darron. "With that restriction we are looking at maybe a 10 degree course change. No matter what, we are going to be headed almost straight for the New Chicago Intersection field."

"Are they moving as fast as we are?" asked MacDonald. "Are they going to have trouble closing with us, because they are going so fast they are going to fly right by?"

"If they are like what we saw of the Suvain," Darron answered, "they probably can change course enough to close. They might not be able to stay near us – it might be a close approach, and then we fly apart again. But they can close the 10 million kilometers if they really try." Daron looked at the assembled group and added desperately, "you know this is practically made up. All we really know is effective velocity in our direction shown in Doppler shifts in the received frequencies. I am having to make huge assumptions in their ship capabilities. And we don't really know anything for sure."

"What if we kept speeding up? To make the close approach as short as possible? That way we might be close to them, but they wouldn't be able to pull up and board," asked the Communications Officer.

"We could," said the Captain. "But where would we go then? I don't want to show them any Intersection, so we have no way out of the Kansu Transfer. And if they want to close, they will be able to eventually. We might take them on a long chase, but unless they decided not to, they would eventually run us down."

Everyone fell silent as the Captain sat back in her chair. After a few minutes she stated "If they threaten to blow us up unless we surrender, we refuse. If they do shoot us from a distance, we die. If they try to board, we fight. The most important priority is that the *Persephone* is not captured. This is the same situation as with the Suvain. The important thing is not that we get back to our home. The important thing is that they do not get to our home. All of us, and the *Persephone*, are expendable. The *Persephone* will look like we have no defense. No reference will be made to the fact that we are going to defend ourselves if attacked. If they behave themselves, great. If not, they are going to have to come onto this ship if they want to get anything out of the *Persephone*. We have 60 hours to be ready if that happens.

MacDonald, I want you to divide the crew into groups who will operate together in case of a fight."

"Squads", interjected Jon.

The Captain looked over. "Crewman Sykes will work with Officer MacDonald in forming the 'squads'. She turned to the Chief Engineer. "I want the fusion drive re-set to overload if commanded. Make a review of every ship-board system we have – I want to know about anything that could be used as a weapon. Mason – you are assigned to assist. She turned to the Communications Officer. "They are going to know we are here soon anyway. Re-route the sensors towards the alien craft. It can't hurt to know as much as possible. Underwood – you are to report to the lead Chemist. I want the bombs completed before we might need them." Turning to the bridge crew, she said, "I want everything possible recorded about the transmissions, and when they get close enough, the ship that is sending them. A full report is to be sent back to Loren Station every two hours, no matter what. Change acceleration, set a total acceleration of 1 g. For the next six hours, accelerate towards azimuth 90. From that time on, begin acceleration against our current velocity – 1 g acceleration, azimuth 180. If we are going to meet them eventually, let's act like we are doing so voluntarily."

Everyone sat forward, ready to be dismissed, but after a pause, Captain Adams continued, "One final question. Assuming this ship is not Suvain, how do you think the Suvain will respond?"

"They won't want anyone to get more information than they have," answered Susan.

"They might order the other ship away. If they can't, they will ensure that there is nothing left for the other aliens," MacDonald said quietly. People looked at him, then at the lunatic brigade, and then back to the Captain.

"Probably so," she agreed. "Dealing with the Suvain will be my problem. I want a follow-up meeting of all the officers in four hours. Dismissed." She waited until the room had emptied, then returned to her quarters. She threw the comfortable blanket in the corner and laid back down, fully dressed, to get sleep while she could.

Captain Adams had not bothered to tell everyone to keep silent about the probable new contact. The entire Chemistry team knew something was up as soon as Susan announced the Captain's order to build the grenades. The change in acceleration was felt across the ship, as the angulins were activated and the anchors caught hold. As the disks spun down, and pulled at the anchors, the ship hull grated as the momentum transferred through the ship. Captain Adams half-woke at the sound of the strain, and placed her hand on the side wall of her cabin. Feeling the vibrations going through the hull, she relaxed, knowing the course change had been performed. She fell back asleep without having truly woken up. The handful of people finishing up third shift could hear and feel the change, and knew that they were no longer headed straight for New Chicago; they all mentioned this to the new shift coming on duty. Darron reported to his usual shift to tell the lead Physicist that he had been reassigned. Once the others heard what was going on, everyone stopped all their other tasks and went to meet with the Chief Engineer. Most of the engineers had dropped everything and were there as well - the entire meeting was moved to the Aft Cargo Bay. By the time the officer meeting was held, nearly every person on board knew that contact may have been made with a new set of aliens.

Captain Adams listened to the reports stating that each group had started its tasks, and then sent everyone back to work. She then returned to cabin, and took out the communication display. The Tavir had left his display with DyanIanTavir; Adams pushed the button to start a call. After a long delay, the face of the Suvain captain appeared. Captain Adams described the light bursts that had been recorded. She asked, "So are they yours? More Suvain?"

The Suvain was alternating between having his arms tucked in a little and his arms flexed out a little. He answered, "That does sound like a ship radar. It is not one of ours. Given the strength of the signal you describe, we should pick it up in the next 8 hours or so. That is about the time they will see us coming, unless they have already picked up the sensors you have sent out in front. I assume that this is the reason for your sudden course change a few hours ago?"

"Yes. I don't think we can avoid them, so we are going to go ahead and move next to them. Do you have any idea who this is, if they aren't you?"

"Most fleets use a standard set of equipment. Send over the information on the transmissions, and we can probably tell who we are dealing with."

"We will send the data over now." She gave a tight little smile at the uncomfortable Suvain. "Then why don't we talk again in, say, three hours."

The Suvain nodded his agreement without speaking, and ended the connection.

Captain Adams had the information sent across, and then checked to see that all tasks on board were continuing. She sent out a request to the lunatic brigade to send her all information they had collected about all of the non-Suvain races that the Suvain had mentioned. After the three hours, she retired to her cabin, and called the Suvain. The call was answered immediately. She looked at the picture for a second then asked, "So are the little arm jerks a sign of stress for the Suvain?"

She saw the Suvain's arms flash for a second, and then the Suvain answered, "We agree with your assessment. They are the long-range sensors of a ship, or maybe two." He started to speak, then paused. "The frequencies are some of the ones used by the VolatarA."

Captain Adams took a second to call up the information sent to her about the VolatarA. "According to what we have heard from you, the VolatarA policy towards other races involves killing half of the prisoners they take in front of the others, in order to encourage the others to talk."

"That is common. The VolatarA are known for their tendency to see themselves as the only truly sentient race in the galaxy. All of their ships are armed – usually more heavily than ours are, and their technology is quite advanced."

"Not good news," answered Captain Adams.

"No", said the Suvain. "Maybe if you had surrendered to us when you had the chance, we could have claimed that you were legally ours and they should stand off. They might have listened, or they might not, since we are certainly outgunned, and probably outnumbered. But by now, they will surely have heard they you exist, and that you are insisting you are not Suvain property. I can't imagine that they are not going to close to take your ship."

"Probably so. If they destroy us from a distance, there is not much we can do. If they board, we will fight."

"The VolatarA are not very good at making peace after the shooting starts. If you shoot at them now, then when they trace you back to your home planet, you may have difficulty surrendering. And if you shoot at them now, they may claim that since the firing started before you surrendered to us, you may not even be able to get our protection."

"We will have to take that chance." Captain Adams could see the Suvain captain sort of shrink down, and knew he was embarrassed.

He straightened up and looked at Captain Adams directly. "If there is a threat, my orders are to ensure your ship is not captured intact."

"We have expected as much. You have nothing to worry about. The *Persephone* is never going to be taken intact. It is unfortunate. I had promised the Tavir that I would not blow up the ship until he was sitting beside me, but I may not be able to wait. If there is any chance that she might be captured, the *Persephone* will be nothing but radioactive slag. You will have to film the whole thing to send to Tavir, with my regrets."

"My orders are very specific."

"So are the orders I have given my crew. If they fire from a distance, we will destroy the ship. If they board, we will fight back. If there is any chance of losing, we will destroy the ship. We have more incentive to see that the *Persephone* is not captured than you do."

"If I let that ship be captured, it could be more than my life is worth."

"I would assume you are going to want to stay around to see what happens no matter what. You have a missile launcher. Why don't you wait to see what happens? Then if things are going badly, finish us off."

"That is stretching my orders, but I don't think it will get me killed. Just make sure to kill yourself. In the meantime, we will send over everything we have on the VolatarA ships. They use pretty standard designs, so we should know what we, you, are up against. The VolatarA often operate scout ships in pairs, so it is likely there are two out there to deal with." The Captain paused, then continued. "We can move some of you on board this ship if you choose. If you want to get a few people out of this alive, we could take maybe 15 back to Loren Station."

"Thank you for the offer. But we are going to stay together – live or die. But before the end, I will make sure to send over any movies which you desire."

"I am sorry that this has happened so soon, and to you. Good luck," answered DyanIanTavir. Captain Adams nodded, and they ended the connection.

Captain Adams ordered a ship-wide meeting an hour after she had spoken with the Suvain. At the appointed time, every crewman stopped, turned to a display, and watched as the Captain's face appeared all around the ship.

The Captain began, "As you all know by now, we have another alien contact. It appears to be another race, not Suvain. We will meet them somewhere around 50 hours from now."

"It is possible that this race will be friendly, and give us party gifts, and promise to aid us in maintaining our freedom. It is more likely that this race will be like the first we have met. In that case, they will be demanding our surrender just like the Suvain did. We are going to be stuck between two different groups that both want to eat us."

"There are probably going to be demands for surrender, and threats, and promises. The answer we give will be the same, no matter what. This ship is never surrendering to anyone, ever. We are going to fight anyone who steps aboard. If we are given a choice of giving up or dying, we are going to die. This ship is never going to be captured intact by anyone. The fusion drive is again being set to overload on command. The destruct sequence will be broadcast across the ship. Every person has the duty to see that this ship, and the information it contains, is not captured. If every other person on this ship is dead, it is your job to see that the command is given to vaporize whatever is left. We are not out here alone. There is a Suvain ship watching everything we do. How we act will be remembered. The example we are going to set is that no matter what, Terrans will fight to the death for their freedom."

"If the aliens will accept peace, there will be peace. If not, we will either be killed from a distance, or will fight them aboard ship. If aliens attempt to board this ship, our duty will be prevent the capture of our vessel, and our objective will be to take theirs. You are being divided into teams that will fight together if combat is required. Team assignments and team leaders will be announced in 8 hours. Training will start in 16." Captain Adams started to end the transmission, and then added, "The weekly church service is scheduled in five days. It is now moved up to tomorrow. Dismissed."

The *Persephone* was buzzing with activities, rumors, and predictions when Captain Adams met with MacDonald to go over the 'squads' which had been formed. She looked down the list at the names, and asked "So what am I looking at?"

"Most of the crew has been divided into six squads", answered MacDonald. "Each squad is broken into three teams of five. There is also a squad leader and a chemist to carry the grenades to use in support."

"That is seventeen people in each group? With 122 total on board, which will leave … 20 others left over?"

"Yes. The other 20 will be available to run the bridge, stay on station at the reactor, and the sick bay."

"The leaders don't look like they are the officers of the ship", the Captain pointed out.

"They are not. We have two people who have some military experience. One actually served for a tour of duty, and the other worked his way through college by weekend military service. We have three people who have at least some experience with police service. So those five are five of the squad leaders. The last is the Chief Engineer. We thought that if we did break into the VolatarA ship, we might need to figure out the alien technology we were seeing."

Captain Adams looked down for a moment and then shook her head.

"So how much experience do these people really have?"

MacDonald gave a rueful grin, and answered "We do not have a soul on board who has ever shot at someone, or been shot at." He paused for a moment, as the Captain's shoulders slumped. After she took a deep breath and straightened back up, he continued. "We have 13 people who have some experience with hunting, so they have shot something, if not people. So they have been appointed the leaders for 13 of the teams."

The Captain looked down at the table again. "None of us have any idea what we are doing, and none of us have faced anything like this before. I wonder if I should just blow up the ship now."

"We do have weapons, and we have numbers on our side. The biggest fear is that most of us will either run away, or get behind something that looks solid, and stay there."

The Captain snorted, and started looking over the list again. "If that is the biggest threat that we have, then we will be fine. Whether we fight or hide is something entirely under our own control. All right, send out the lists, and tell all of squad leaders to meet with me in two hours." She set the list down, and switched the chemists between Squad 3 and Squad 6. She saw the questioning look from MacDonald and said, "So our biggest danger is that we will run away when the time comes? So tell me," she said, pointing to the last two names now side by side on the list, "Do you really think Darron Mason will run away if Susan Underwood is watching?"

While the Terrans were trying to figure out what to do, the first reaction was observed from the coming ships. The light flashes suddenly doubled, and then focused right around the *Persephone*. Within a few hours, the messages began. They were not sent to the *Persephone* – the VolatarA were telling the Suvain to back away. The Suvain sent the message traffic on to the *Persephone*; the Terrans could listen as the two groups argued over whose possession they were. The conversation moved from demands to threats to insults from both sides. It was an odd flame war – with the light-time delay between the Suvain and VolatarA, each side had to wait for about two hours to hear the response to its latest barrage of abuse. The message traffic had the side benefit of giving a much better calculation of the time the ships would come together. Since the time the Suvain ships sent their messages was known, measuring the time between the Suvain message and the VolatarA response gave a much better guess of the distance to alien ships. Soon after discovering the Terran and Suvain ships, the VolatarA had changed course to close with the revealed ships. Since the VolatarA appeared to be able to accelerate at 3g continuously, the ships would come together in about 36 hours. This was very close to what Darron had predicted for the time of the close approach. Everyone else seemed to think this was normal; Darron thought it was a miracle.

As the ships closed, the VolatarA finally sent a message directly to the Terran ship. The message was in VolatarA; it was automatically translated by a translator provided by the Suvain. The VolatarA message informed the Terrans that they were now VolatarA property, and that any resistance would mean the death of the crew. The *Persephone* was ordered to maintain her current acceleration. Captain Adams sent back a response declining to surrender, and expressed the Terrans' wish for a peaceful encounter. The light-time delay to the VolatarA ships meant that the Persephone had to wait 45 minutes for the message to reach the VolatarA, and for the VolatarA message to return. After 45 minutes that seemed like 45 hours, nothing happened. There was no return message from the VolatarA, and after a while, the Captain ordered everyone back to their previous duties.

The Suvain had sent over a map of the usual design of a VolatarA scout ship; Stephen had made a copy and then disappeared. The squad leaders had been briefed, and had met with their squads; Stephen had been AWOL. Two hours before training was supposed to start, Stephen reappeared by publishing the location of the new Steel Champion scenario he had just created. There were questions from the Captain and from many of the crewmembers about what "Steel Champion" was. When she was informed that this was a video game where groups of people ran through corridors and shot at each other, Captain Adams decided not to ask how the game had appeared on her ship's computer. She became a bit suspicious when she found that the game involved people dividing into groups of five and that Jonathon Sykes played the game frequently. The map created by Stephen was a copy of the VolatarA ship as described by the Suvain. Stephen had also changed the graphics to make the view of the corridors and rooms as similar as possible to the provided description of what the inside of a VolatarA ship looked like.

Although basing real life actions on a computer game was an appalling thought, the Captain had to admit that practicing moving down the corridors as a group could be helpful.

The official training sessions started when the expected encounter was about 35 hours away. Each squad met together in the forward loading bay. The squad leader described how the teams would be numbered, and how to talk over the intercom. Each group was trained in basic first aid, with specific descriptions of how to seal off severed limbs. Each group had one member who would be given samples of the limited supply of painkillers.

Actually firing an AGM2 was likely to destroy the weapon, so there could not be lots of target practice. In order to get some idea of shooting the gun, a couple of copies were taken apart, and the angulins taken out. Much smaller angulins were put back in, so the gun would fire without stressing the barrel. Each crewman at least received a couple of chances to shoot the gun at a nearby target. Each squad practiced dividing into teams, and having each team move down separate paths to the same objective. After one squad had trained for a few hours, they were replaced by the next. The replaced squad was then taught how to play the Steel Commander game, and all logged in together and practiced moving as a group through the alien ship. By the end of each squad's training session, the trainees usually felt like they had learned something, and the trainers felt like things were generally hopeless.

While the squads were trying to learn what to do, the officers were meeting trying to figure out what to do with the squads. The decision was made early on that everyone would be wearing exo-suits at all times. The exo-suits each had transmitters to allow anyone outside the ship to be tracked to assist recovery if needed. The goal was to track the location of all personnel at all times through the transmitters, and plot the location of each team from the bridge at all times. Then the officers could coordinate the activities of each squad, even though the squads couldn't see each other.

Even if the squads could work together, there was still the question of what to try to do. A monitor with a diagram of the VolatarA ship had been setup as a display, and the different rooms were numbered for reference. According to the Suvain, VolatarA scout ships had about 25 crewmen. The Terrans had no idea where the VolatarA crewmen might be, so the squads ended up getting aimed at different parts of the ship – at least that way there could be some planning as to where they should go.

Captain Adams had moved the weekly chapel service again so that it would come at the end of the last squad's first training session. Acting Chaplain Soong was again giving the sermon; he had felt prepared until he walked in and found over 100 people mashed into the Aft Cargo Bay. Almost every Terran on board that was not on duty was present, and the Suvain had heard about the service. There had been considerable curiosity on the Suvain escort ship about the religion that they had heard was spreading onboard the Tavir's personal vessel. Six of them had come to watch the service. After reading and several hymns, Soong stood up to speak. He had modeled his sermon on the last sermon by Chaplain Eisen, talking about God's love shown in Jesus, and God's forgiveness. Near the end of the sermon, Soong referenced Eisen's call to forgive. "Chaplain Eisen told us that we would need to forgive. And we did need to forgive. When we met the Suvain, their first action was to commit …" Soong paused. He hadn't expected Suvain to be in the audience. He then continued, "to commit an atrocity – an act we needed, and need, to forgive. And it has been forgiveness that has given us the small chance we have to have a beneficial life with the Suvain, instead of a short life against them."

"We are about to meet another alien race. From everything we have heard, they are far more aggressive than the Suvain. While the Suvain were willing to talk, everything suggests the VolatarA are only going to be willing to shoot. We will still need to forgive, and those of us who survive will probably have far more to forgive. But willingness to forgive the wrong actions of another is not the same as accepting the action while it is being performed. If the VolatarA are shooting people, it will be our duty to fight their actions just like it will be our duty to fight the desire to hate the VolatarA afterwards. I will not promise you that if the shooting starts, you will be fine. I will promise you that whether we live or die, there is nothing that the VolatarA can do that can prevent God from continuing His work in the world. God has been working out His plan of salvation for the last 2,500 years – I don't think He is going to stop now. Our meeting the Suvain did not surprise God, and neither does our meeting the VolatarA. Whatever the future holds, our duty will be to face whatever comes with faith, not fear.

Whatever the next few days hold, it will be something that we have never faced before. When that something comes, we will have to decide whether to press on, or to give in to fear. So I will end with the first half of Chaplain Eisen's last benediction: Be strong and courageous."

After Soong finished, there was an additional song, and the service broke up. "So, your god tells you to be brave, but does not tell you that you are going to win the fight, and live through the whole thing?" one of the Suvain asked their neighbors.

"No, He tells us that He will be with us no matter what, and that no matter what happens, that will be enough." Susan answered.

"And that is the statement you want before getting into a fight?" continued the Suvain.

Darron answered, "I can't speak for everyone, but the statement I would like to hear is 'You are going to win the fight, and live to the end, and everything is going to be fine.'"

After the meeting, each squad had one last training session. For another hour each set of three teams moved around in the loading bay. This time, the squad was briefed on a specific target that each team was supposed to move towards once they were on the VolatarA ship. There was another session of the computer game; afterwards, the teams were sent out to prepare the ship in case boarding combat was necessary.

The *Persephone* had sets of bulkheads crossing through the interior compartments. These provided sets of secure barriers that could be used in case of hull failure in different parts of the ship. A line of bulkheads had been identified that separated off the starboard side of the ship from the bridge and the fusion drive. Teams were soon busy moving equipment from the starboard side to the interior two-thirds of the ship. Others were set to work preparing the containment anchors on the angulins on the starboard side. Vibrations could be felt throughout the ship as all but three doors through the established line were sealed shut. The chemists had been relieved of other tasks in order to make grenades. As a break from playing with incredibly dangerous chemicals, they practiced throwing dummy cylinders around obstacles setup in the Aft Loading Bay.

After finishing their assigned work, each team was given the impossible order to relax and get some sleep. Most wandered to the mess hall and started eating Day 7 meals. Most were surprised to find that Day 7 meals for future weeks were still locked. The Captain had continued the lock on meal removal – people could not eat the meals scheduled for future weeks, on the assumption that future weeks would still occur. As the meals from the current week were available, lots of meals were called up, especially desserts. The mess hall became more and more crowded as a lot of people stayed after stuffing themselves to watch the movies that Stephen and Jon had starting playing on a large monitor. The old alien movies always showed humans blasting aliens, and living happily ever after. When Captain Adams eventually came in and saw the movies being played, she said nothing, but instead went and got out her Day 5 meal as usual. She watched the movie currently being played, and watched the crewmen watching the movie. After she finished, she told Stephen that after the current movie finished to shut things down and go to bed. She returned to her cabin, and laid down fully dressed on the bed. When she woke up four hours later, she logged in to check for any changes. No messages had been received, but there was a fair amount of computer activity by about 20 crewmen. She looked in at their current activities, and then sent out a broadcast message that playing Steel Commander did NOT count as additional training; they were to knock it off and go to bed. The collection of crewmen storming the underground lair of the Lizard King of Zzithringg complained to each other, but finally logged off. Captain Adams watched the computer use drop back to normal, and then started back to bed. She glared at the blanket, and then decided that nothing more could go wrong anyway. She took off her uniform, pulled up the blanket, and had five hours of deep, untroubled sleep.

Darron would have woken up just before the start of first shift if he had ever been able to sleep. When he gave up and headed for breakfast, he found that almost everyone was up already as well. He played around with his food for a few minutes, but then gave up and threw the rest of the eggs away. The VolatarA were expected to reach the *Persephone* in six hours. The bridge crew were still sending occasional messages to the

VolatarA ships. Nothing had been received in response. While a few of the crew were making last preparations, Darron wandered around with most of the rest, trying to kill what might be the last few hours he had left. He realized how little he knew about the people he had served with for the last several years. Looking at them now, thinking that they might all be dead in a few hours, he thought he should at least have learned some of their names. He thought about logging on and joining the Steel Commander game that had started again well before the Captain had woken back up, but spending his last moments staring at a screen did not seem appropriate. Eventually he wandered back to his usual work area. The Lead Physicist was there already. He had printouts scattered around as if he was doing last checks on the approach of the VolatarA ships, but was just sitting staring at the mountains shown on his screen. Darron said hello, then sat down at his usual station. He looked over the latest readings of the VolatarA accelerations. They had maintained a full 3g acceleration for days. Darron was not sure the Terrans had ever made a ship that could sustain such high accelerations. The latest numbers looked different than usual. The two incoming ships were close now – they were making the final approach to the *Persephone*. The tracks of the two ships had separated – one ship was heading directly in, and the other was cutting back on its acceleration by a slight amount.

"These are different," Darron said. "One ship is holding back."

The Lead Physicist focused on Darron's display. He nodded, and called the bridge. "The two ships are separating," he reported. "One is coming in as expected, the other is holding back. If they continue as they are now, they are going to be standing off a little bit, maybe tens of kilometers, when the other matches velocity and pulls alongside." The two physicists could hear the Captain ordering all squad leaders to the bridge. After the Lead Physicist stopped talking, and did not start again for five seconds, the bridge shut off the call. The two talked for a few minutes about what groups they were in, and about how much the Suvain had liked the Black Hole pictures. As the conversation started to taper off, the ship-wide broadcast system started to squawk. All crewmen were ordered to report to their assembly areas. After wishing each other luck and awkwardly shaking hands, both headed off to get on their exo-suits.

Darron knew that there was still three hours until the VolatarA ship finished its approach, but when he put on his exo-suit he was already sweating. He did not put the helmet on, but did try to find a way to find some knob to turn to cool down the suit. The suit had built-in heating, since the suit was expected for use in space, but it had not been designed for use in hot climates. He finally gave up and started out for the mess hall. After he was a little more than half way there, he turned around and walked back to his room. He picked up his AGM2, and headed to the mess hall. He found a swarm of people already there. Squads 5 and 6 were both gathering in the room, and at first, Darron couldn't remember if he was supposed to be meeting on the hull side or the center side of the room. He would have just walked over to the people in his group, but he couldn't tell which ones they were – all the exo-suits looked the same. Darron looked helplessly at the ocean of silver and tried to refocus on peoples' faces, since no one had their helmets on. He finally recognized Susan standing on the far side of the room. He walked over, and found most of his team and his squad already there. The Chief Engineer was standing in front of what was becoming three rows of crewmen. Darron moved to the end of the third line. Susan was already there, standing behind the three groups. She was wearing a vest over her exo-suit; it held four cylinders. Although covered in explosives, she looked silent and calm. Darron could see her lips moving a little, and knew she was praying. He looked around for Steven and Jon, but they were not there. Jon was in Squad 1, and was in the forward loading bay. Steven was in Squad 3, and was in the aft loading bay. It took it Darron a few minutes to realize that the Chief Engineer had already started talking. He tried to pay attention, but found himself going back and forth between his own squad leader giving instructions and the sound of the squad leader for Squad 5 talking on the other side of the room. Darron turned with everyone else when both leaders stopped talking, and activated the display. The Captain's voice could be heard from the display, which showed the diagram of the VolatarA ship.

"All squads are going to be given the description of what each squad will be doing; if one squad is failing, another will be told to take over. There is one VolatarA ship drawing alongside. The other is watching from a distance. The Suvain have backed off, but are certainly recording the entire encounter. Should the VolatarA attempt to board this ship, we will board theirs. All starboard angulins have been prepared, and will be released when a solid lock with the VolatarA ship has been achieved. Squad 1 will board through the main airlock. Squad 2 will follow up Squad 1. Both squads will ensure that any VolatarA attempting to board the *Persephone* will be dealt with. Squad 3 will move forward to secure the bridge of the enemy ship.

Squad 4 will move behind Squad 3 and be ordered to assist Squad 3 if needed, or to move up behind Squad 5. Squad 5 will move through the ship to the airlock on the other side of the VolatarA ship. Squad 6 will move to the missile launcher shown at the aft of the ship. All personnel will be tracked and commanded from the bridge. When we take the first ship, the second ship will either fire from a distance, or when they see their partner in trouble, they will try to board to assist their friends. If so, they will be met by Squad 4 and Squad 5, and we will continue on to the second ship in turn."

"There is nowhere to go but forward. We have to capture the ships, or die. After we capture the ships, all crewmen will be assigned the task of looting every piece of technology we can fit in the *Persephone* to take back to Loren Station. Until we finish the last ones off, the VolatarA will be watching. The Suvain will be watching. Today is when we show every vulture race out there what they are up against. May God in Heaven go with you, and may He let us teach all these people a lesson they will never forget."

The monitor stopped talking, and both squad leaders called the squads to attention. Darron heard Squad leader 5 order his squad to the Starboard assembly room. He watched as the squad leader called out for Team 51, Team 52, and Team 53; each time, 5 crewmen walked out as a group. After the squad leader and the chemist walked out as well, he could hear the Chief Engineer saying something behind him. Darron turned back to his commander, and didn't hear a word of the commands being given. People were walking out as Darron stood looking around, and then everyone around him was moving. When he saw the other four members of Team 63 moving out of the room, he followed the rest. After a room or two, it registered that Susan and the Chief Engineer were walking behind him. They passed through the narrow doorway left in the bulkheads into the now-empty starboard side. They passed Squad 1 and Squad 2 waiting near the airlock. This took a while – there was very little space, and everyone had to try to squeeze past each other. The training had always been with a single squad in the roomiest part of the ship; it was a shock to find that two people in exo-suits could get stuck next to each to other in some of the smaller corridors. They eventually all collected in their assigned place in the aft. There was still over an hour to wait. They could feel the ship jerking as small adjustments were made. The angulins were mostly off-line in this area, so the ship movements were much greater than the crew was used to feeling. They could hear other sounds that were harder to identify. After a while, someone suggested that it might be the sound of the external antennas that stuck out all over the hull being folded back down into their slots in the hull. Then there was a grinding sound, coupled with vibrations that Darron could feel through the walls and floor.

He did not recognize the sound, and then realized that that was the sound of the last doors through the bulkheads being welded shut. He looked around at the room; it suddenly looked like a tomb. He had been blindly following the others until now, but the sound of the last exit being sealed suddenly brought him face-to-face with his present situation. He had a sudden desire to run back, now while there was still time, and get back where it was safe. He looked around at everyone else – several others looked as panicked as he felt. But no one else was running, and something in Darron wouldn't allow him to go first. It might have been a trace of courage, or possibly a desire for Terrans and the *Persephone* not be disgraced, most likely a desire not to look bad in front of his friends, or maybe leaving the safety of the group was scary, even if going backwards. He heard the welding finish, and the chance to go back was gone.

Susan stood in the room behind - there was not room for everyone in the room. She was not part of any team, and found herself wishing that she was – standing four feet from the nearest person somehow seemed like she was all alone. When she heard the welding start, she could see the others jerk in response. The sound only made her more aware that she was carrying enough explosives to bring down a small house. There was nowhere to go but forward, and there was no other choice anyway. She couldn't really run away when she was a critical member of the team; besides, Darron would be watching. She waited, wanting to talk to someone, but everyone was looking the other way. It appeared that no one wanted to face the sound of the escape route being sealed. She could have talked on the exo-suit intercom, but there had been strict orders to everyone to keep all channels clear of chatter. With nothing else to do, she checked and re-checked each of her cylinders.

Jon stood with his team near the airlock. He had checked his AGM2 several times, and those of each of his team. He had pointed out that they were the first team of the first squad – they were Team 11. Somehow having the first number of all the teams had convinced all five that they were a special group, chosen specifically because they were the elite of the ship. Of all the squads, Squad 1 was the most likely to run directly into the VolatarA. Unlike the others, Team 11 was laughing and talking. Jon was giving a long description of the firing of the first angulin gun. Everyone had heard the story before, or been there themselves, but at the moment the story seemed new and hilarious. Then the order came to put on helmets. Jon looked at the other four, smiled, and pulled his helmet down over his face.

Instead of being nervous and motionless, Stephen was excited and pacing around. As there was only about three steps he could take back and forth, and those three steps were between the other members of the team, Team 32 was about to shoot Stephen. Finally someone thought of asking Stephen what his favorite alien movie was. After a pause, Stephen started talking about a movie that may not have been his favorite, but was the one most on his mind at the moment. The movie ended with humans and aliens having a big firefight through the Terran ship, a firefight which the Terrans of course won. The droning was easier to ignore than the pacing, so tensions cooled. Then the others slowly started listening. Stories of how humans beat aliens were sort of calming to listen to, and by the time the order came to put helmets on, the team was a little sorry not to hear the end of the story. After helmets were put back on, Stephen could still hear the sounds of angulins starting to strain. After what seemed like forever, the order was given for all the teams to get back from the outside wall and lay down.

Captain Adams had been sending messages every couple of hours to the VolatarA ship. None were returned until the VolatarA ship was within an hour of the rendezvous with the *Persephone*. Then an order was received for the Terrans to halt all acceleration and rotate to present an airlock. The Captain sent a message back that as a free Terran ship, they were not under orders to obey. She then gave the order for a full stop to acceleration and rotated the ship.

The Captain's next message stated that the *Persephone* would not allow any boarding of the ship. Such an attempt would be seen as an act of war.

As the alien ship closed, it sent orders that the crew was to assemble in an open area of the ship. All computer equipment was to be turned on and left accessible. Any resistance would result in the death of the entire crew.

Captain Adams ordered that the message be logged, and no answer to be given. The entire exchange had been forwarded back to the communication beacon that was relaying everything to Loren Station. She then ordered that all transmissions to the beacon be stopped until further notice. The VolatarA were too close – a transmission might be noticed. As the final approach was made, all of the communication antennas and sensors on the close side of the ship were folded back down to allow the VolatarA to get a good lock on the hull. One ship was docking, and the other was standing a little ways off. The Suvain had backed away to a safe distance, and were on the far side of the *Persephone*. The message was sent to all squads to take up last positions. The bridge crew all watched the monitor that showed the location of each exo-suit. They could see the little dots sliding back from the hull, as everyone moved back and laid down.

The alien ship closed, and there was a jolt through the ship as the two came together. Watching the VolatarA lock on looked to the captain like seeing a parasite latching onto a host. Captain Adams sent a final message stating that any attempt to board would be an act of war, and telling the VolatarA that this was the last communication they would receive. If they backed off now, there would be the opportunity of peace. There was no answer at first, and then an order was received to open the airlock.

The Captain shook her head, paused for a moment, and then growled, "That's it then. You want an open airlock, you will get an open airlock." She turned to the bridge crew. "Let them go."

A waiting crewman pushed a single button. Immediately, every angulin on the starboard side was activated, and every angulin anchor on the starboard side of the ship was fully released. Five angulins immediately converted massive amounts of angular momentum into linear; the spinning disks stopped rotating, and started moving forward fast enough to rip out of the hull of the *Persephone* and tear through the alien ship. As the five angulins blasted through the hull, the entire frame of the ship writhed from the shock. Debris from the hull sprayed out after the angulins, and a sound like two trains colliding head on blasted back into the *Persephone*. Several of the crew did not have the exo-suit sound dampeners on full; the sound blew out eardrums and left the crewmen stunned. In two places, sections of the hull did not give way entirely at the same time, and parts of the hull were twisted back away from the blast onto the exterior of the hull. This shot hull fragments back into the ship; one shot through the main lines leading to the bridge and the entire bridge went dark. The squads had been distributed in rooms one back from the hull; even the slight blowback from the blast was enough to knock everyone around like bowling pins. One of the forward angulins stuck just long enough to transfer some of its momentum into the hull; the walls of the room held long enough to transfer momentum to the back wall. This tore the door off of the room in which Squad 4, Team 2 was lying. In seconds, all of Team 42 was sucked out after the angulin into space. The three who did not lose consciousness were screaming, but as everyone else was shouting as well, the screams went unnoticed. The two ships were knocked apart from the shock, but were pulled back together by the magnetic locks which had been applied by both ships.

The angulins had been directed by releasing the angulin anchors microseconds apart, so that the angulin would turn as it started moving. Targets had been chosen by referencing the ship charts provided by the Suvain. The forward two angulins had been aimed at the bridge of the VolatarA ship. One was off target, and ripped through the adjoining rooms, blasting through the entire ship and out the other side. The second tore directly into the bridge, destroying everything in its path, until it impacted against the wall on the other side. The walls of the bridge were strengthened bulkheads, and they managed to contain the blow – the angulin tore into the room, but did not pass through the bulkhead on the other side. Instead it crashed into the wall, dug part way through, and exploded into a shower of molten fragments that sprayed into the next room, and back into the bridge. Anything or anyone who might have survived the first passage of the angulin was eradicated by the shower of white-hot shrapnel. Four VolatarA had been stationed on the bridge – in an instant, the VolatarA crew had been reduced from 27 to 23. An additional VolatarA had been walking to the bridge, without the precaution of an exo-suit. The first angulin through had blasted past him, and carried him in its train of destruction out into space. Fortunately for him, he had been sufficiently injured by the instantaneous experience that he was not really conscious in the half a minute it took him to fully die. Had the Terrans any knowledge of his fatal catastrophe, they would have simply noted that the number of enemy crew now stood at 22.

Angulins 3 and 4 had been focused on the airlock, where the VolatarA were expected to be congregated. Both tore through the middle of the VolatarA ship, and passed through to exit on the other side. The airlock was vaporized, along with the eight VolatarA which had been waiting to board the *Persephone*. The angulins tore through the room behind as well. Four more VolatarA had been in the area, ready to move in in support of the first group; one of them suffered a direct hit from an angulin and disappeared, but the other three were alive. An additional alien had been on the other side of the ship when the walls were torn apart and he was sucked out into blackness. He had taken the precaution of putting on his suit just in case; there were standing orders that on any encounter with a foreign ship or possible combat, exo-suits would be worn at all times. The suit was not torn apart by the blast, and the crewman was left flying slowing away from the ship, with no weapons, and no way to take any action but wait until his four-hour air supply was exhausted. With the losses amidships, the number of VolatarA onboard was reduced to 12.

In the aft portion of the ship, the fifth angulin made its destructive way. It had pulled slightly during release, and struck not far from the very back of the ship. It blasted through the hull on both sides, and ripped the back three compartments off the ship entirely. The still-connected rooms began a slow spin away from the rest of the ship. One of the rooms had contained the auxiliary controls for the vessel – one crewmen had been stationed there. He had quite properly had his exo-suit on, but had been thrown across the room onto a metal row of consoles by the blast. The contact tore a hole in the suit, knocked him nearly senseless, and broke both his right arm and right leg. The integrity of the room was giving way as well as the fractures throughout one of the walls were getting expanded by the air rushing out. In a daze, he managed to pull a strip of the torn exosuit material around one of the legs of a console. He then held his new tie-down with his right hand, and with his left, reached down for the repair kit on the right leg of the suit. He fumbled around, leaving the floor entirely as the room continued to move, and he, without artificial gravity, drifted at a slightly different speed. He fumbled in the pouch, found the patching material, and shook a piece open. He placed it across the suit tear, holding the end of the strip of material to the suit as well. The patch automatically stuck itself to the suit, but with the extra strip present, there was still a leak. A second patch piece was found, and laid across the seam of the first. The hissing stopped, and the suit began to register a constant pressure. Tied to the room, in a now-sealed suit, the crewman gave up the fight against the pain. He was left with a draining air supply, passed out, dangling from a table leg in the now-empty shell of auxiliary controls.

Eleven VolatarA were still alive and onboard when the Terrans began their attempt to storm the ship.

The surviving VolatarA were in no condition to resist. Even if alive, they had been knocked across the rooms they had been in, blasted by the sounds of metal being rended, and completely out of touch with other crewmen.

Unfortunately, the Terrans were not in much better shape. They had known the shock was coming, and had some idea where everyone was supposed to be going. But they were also mostly stunned and tossed about as well. The angulins had blown open the VolatarA hull in multiple places so that the groups could cross into the other ship, but the rooms in each ship had been destroyed. The squads had to get back up, get back together, get the doors open to the outside rooms, and get over the gap between the ruins of the *Persephone* and the wrecked rooms of the alien ship. By the time that the Terrans had gotten themselves together and started across to the other ship, the VolatarA were picking themselves up and trying to find each other.

Squad 1 was the first to get back in order and head across. The room they entered was the ruins of the VolatarA airlock. Among twisted metal, and what they did not recognize as the remains of the VolatarA, they could see scattered debris, and on the far end, a hole leading into the alien ship. The lights in the new cavern had been destroyed, and everything was dark until people began switching on the lights on their helmets. Shafts of light extended down the hall as Team 11 entered the alien ship, led by Jonathon, first of all the Terrans. As the squad started to move in, Squad 2 was getting into order behind them.

Squad 3 was thrown around like everyone else, and took five critical minutes finding themselves, and getting over to the new gaping hole in the other ship's side. There was nothing to oppose them on the other side – no VolatarA had been in the area and survived. As the squad moved across, they found out that this section of the ship had lost lights and artificial gravity.

As the squads started to move across, they found themselves drifting away from ground with their steps. The ships had a small rotation, and the teams found themselves moving in nearly random directions through the ruined rooms of the VolatarA ship. Squad 4 was trying to form up behind them. There was lots of confusion as Squad 4 tried to find out whether the missing team members were ahead or behind them. After a while, they gave up and the squad members who had gotten back together headed on across after Squad 3.

Squad 5 got up and had a several minute delay as everyone got away from the Chemist. The Chemist carefully checked each grenade before telling everyone that he wasn't about to blow up. The squad then opened the door to the empty space where the outside room used to be. There was no ship to climb into. The angulin had torn the stern of the VolatarA ship off completely, so when the Terrans looked out, they saw the rest of the VolatarA ship off to their left, and nowhere in front to go. They milled around for a few minutes, until someone found a cable they could pull out. The leader of Team 51 took one end of the cable, took a running start, and hit the small angulin on the back of his suit. He was aiming off to the left, and ended up in one of the torn-apart rooms that were left sticking out into space. He grabbed on to something that gave way, then grabbed at something bolted to the wall. Once he had gotten across, he tied off the cable and waved for the others. One by one, the rest of the squad followed. Instead of moving directly into the ship, they were now right along the other hull, moving through rooms parallel to the hull instead of deeper inside.

The orders to stay off the communications channels unless directed to speak had been ignored after the first few seconds, and with everyone talking, shouting, or screaming at once, it was impossible to hear anything that was being said. Each Squad leader ordered for silence again and again, adding to the general babble. One by one, squad leaders used hand signals to get his or her personnel to turn off every outside signal but those from their own squad. Even then, it was hard to hear anything above the constant stream of things that people decided really were absolutely critical to tell the rest of the squad. Squad 6 soon heard nothing and saw nothing, except that there were still Squad 5 people in the way. As Squad 6 waited to move out after Squad 5, and found that Squad 5 was not moving forward, the rumor quickly took hold that Squad 5 couldn't move forward, probably because the aliens were pressing forward instead. The squad started finding places to defend from, expecting to see the VolatarA swarm towards them any minute.

The bridge was completely black. Emergency lighting took hold 2 seconds later, and critical equipment started to come back on line as the backup power systems took hold. As each system came back up it started screaming warnings about loss of hull integrity, angulin failure, loss of air pressure, hull stress, and many other things the ship designers had never really believed could actually happen to a starship, at least one that wasn't already too far gone to save. The bridge crew frantically turned off the audible alarms, and scanned through the list of errors flooding the screens to find any damage they hadn't deliberately inflicted themselves. The Information Officer was desperately trying to find why everything was down, and bring back the main power. The monitor with the display of the VolatarA ship and all of the little people-dots had not been considered a critical system - after backup power came back on, it remained stubbornly blank. In the first four minutes after the angulins fired, Captain Adams commanded "Get that display back! Show me where they are!" seven times. The captain was reduced to sending runners down to the sealed bulkheads to make sure that the VolatarA were not forcing their way into the ship. Even as the systems came back up and were brought back into some form of service, it was clear that the bridge had completely lost all control over the boarding parties.

Jon led Team 11 into the new tunnel stretching into the alien ship. The first rooms on the sides of where the airlock used to be had been torn open by the angulins. Jon passed them by and moved toward the next set of doors.

The right side door was completely blocked by debris; the left had been blown open. Jon led the group up, then turned off his light. He waited until the rest of the team was up; he could look past them to the rest of Squad 1 moving up along each side of the new tunnel. Once people were close to the opening, Jon pointed to the light on the helmet of the man behind him. His partner took the light off, as Jon hunched over. They flashed the light over, then back. There was a flurry of shots that poured out of the opening. The VolatarA were not using the angulin guns the Suvain carried. They were using a chemical-based weapon similar to an automatic rifle. Shots ricocheted all around the tunnel as shots scattered off the metal across from the doorway. The second the shots stopped, Jon moved into the room, across the doorway from where his team fired an AGM2 into the room, and flashed the light back in. As the VolatarA ducked from the angulin bouncing around the room and fired again towards the light, Jon lifted his gun and fired at one of the muzzle flashes. The VolatarA was torn apart and died immediately; Jon dropped behind a part of the wall of the room that was now piled on the floor. As the other two VolatarA broke for cover, Jon announced, "one down, two more."

Jon was flat on the floor as the surviving two VolatarA shifted fire to the debris in front of him. Squad 2 had kept the channels to Squad 1 open, and so all of both squads heard that the first VolatarA had been hit. For the first time, the truly barbaric nature of cross-racial combat came home to the Terrans. There was no sense of guilt or shame in the rejoicing felt by the Terrans over the death of a VolatarA. It was easy to de-humanize the enemy when the enemy was not, in fact, human. At the moment, the Terrans did not see the VolatarA as people - they were more like a variety of carnivorous ape. To the VolatarA, the Terrans were the moral equivalent of a swarm of rabid gerbils.

Everyone could hear the Squad leader calling in the rest of the squad. "Jon, stay down. Get the grenades in – put one in to the left. Team 1 and 2 – as soon as the flash goes by – both go in – Team 1 right, Team 2 left." Squad 2 could see Squad 1 pull near the opening, and could hear the Chemist saying he was going now. There was a shadow of people moving to the door, and then explosions. There was a massive blast, followed by more. The exosuits automatically detected the blinding flashes and darkened the viewscreens of the helmets of Squad 2 to prevent eye injury, and all of the Terrans dove for cover as the blasts rolled down the tunnel. The force of the blast and loose debris rolled across the prone squad, and back into the *Persephone*. When things had calmed down, Squad 2 looked up to find tunnel littered with debris, and the bodies of Squad 1. Things were still exploding, and chunks of metal coated with the equivalent of rocket fuel were still burning. The VolatarA ship had effectively been shattered- so much of the ship's atmosphere was venting out of the fragmented doors and walls of the interior of the ship that there was enough oxygen in the tunnel to maintain the white- hot blazes. The entire group stood in shock, looking at the destruction.

Someone noticed that one of the scattered Terran bodies was moving and two moved forward to get the possible survivor back to the *Persephone*. Slowly the squad began moving through the wreckage of their friends, the VolatarA ship, and the VolatarA.

Squad 3 was moving forward, thinking the path of destruction from the angulins would lead them to the bridge. They were following the path of the angulin that had missed its target, so most of the squad was actually moving across the alien ship, just aft of their intended target. They had lost a full team. Someone from Team 33 had gotten all turned around in the darkness and the lack of "down", and had drifted over to a missing door. Thinking this led towards the bridge, the crewman went through, and was followed by the rest of the team. The ruins of the corridor inside had an open hole leading to stairs up to a higher level. Thinking the bridge might be above them, they headed up the stairs, not knowing that they were entirely upside down relative to how they were when they boarded the ship. Instead of moving up,

and toward the bridge, they had just moved onto a lower level, and were heading into the middle of the ship.

Squad 4 was supposed to move into the ship, and wait amidships, between the bridge and the airlocks on the other side of the ship. Instead, they saw the lights ahead of them, and followed right after the main group of Squad 3. They had managed to keep the 12 remaining crewmen together as a relatively tight group. They were going the wrong way, but were at least going the wrong way together.

Squad 5 had gotten across to the alien ship, and had started moving through. After about two rooms, someone in Team 52 realized they were going the wrong way, and announced that they all needed to turn to the right. Team 52 turned at the next opportunity; Team 51 continued straight. Team 53 moved up, saw the two moving different directions, and wasn't sure which to follow. They asked the squad leader; this message was lost in the stream of questions about where they were and where they were going. Eventually, they got through to the squad leader who said that everyone was to go the same way he was. As Team 53 had no idea which way that was, they were still lost. Finally they guessed wrong and followed Team 52. Team 52 had already moved out of sight, and the teams were soon moving in three different directions. Squad 6 had gotten across and moved up behind Team 53. With no idea that they were following the blind, they trustingly trailed after the group in front of them.

Captain Adams was about to make a request to the single armed individual on the bridge that he hand her his AGM2. She was at the point of just wanting to shoot someone, anyone, or maybe the blank monitor. Then the sounds of about ten people all talking at once on the leader frequency filled the bridge. The Information Officer had gotten audio connections restored with the assault squads. The display was still blank, but at least the bridge crew could hear something. The Captain shouted into her communication set "Everyone shut up! Everyone shut up! Now!" After repeating this about five times, the channel was clear. "I need to know where you are," Captain Adams unwisely continued. This was followed by about a dozen voices, almost all of which were saying they didn't know. The Captain repeated the Everyone Shut Up order another several times, and then tried again. "Squad Leader 1," she demanded. "Where are you?" She then said to the bridge in general, "Someone get a printout of the ship. With the room markings." There was no answer from Squad Leader 1. "Squad 1, where are you" she demanded again. There was no answer.

"I think he's dead", said Squad Leader 2 in a shaky voice. Then with a more steady tone, he continued, "We have passed through the airlock and are moving further in. There are wounded here."

Captain Adams paused, along with the rest of the bridge. She took a breath, and in the same tone of voice as before, demanded "Squad Leader 3, where are you?"

"Almost at the bridge," he answered incorrectly.

"Squad 4?"

"We are right behind Squad 3." "Squad 5?"

"We are moving towards the other airlock. The back of the other ship is gone. One team is lost," answered the lost squad leader of Squad 5.

"Squad 6?"

"We are right behind Squad 5."

The captain turned to the bridge crew, as someone finished printing the ship layout. "You three," she said, "find something to mark where they are. Walker, I want you to ask every squad leader, then every team leader where they are. In order, by squad and team. I want their location marked, and where they are headed. And have them say how many VolatarA they have met." She turned back to the controls on the bridge as the questions began, and positons were marked. After the long delay when no one from Squad 1 answered, Squad 2 started the chain of responses. Seeing the marked locations, which were all over the alien ship, and sometimes on top of each other, it rapidly became apparent that the squads were wandering around, and dissolving as people got lost. But it was also apparent that the Terrans were pressing into the VolatarA ship, and not the other way around. Captain Adams shook her head in despair at the chaos. "If they had any organized resistance, we would all be dead," she stated to no one in particular. "But we aren't dead, so they must be as confused as we are. And if they are too confused to guard their ship, they aren't going to be coming here anytime soon." She spoke into the ship communications system. "Sick bay – you are authorized to go to the amidships door through the bulkheads and unseal it.

Treat wounded as necessary. And you," she said, turning to the one armed member of the bridge crew. "Go with them and stay there. Let everyone know you have orders to shoot the first person of any squad who tries to get back in this ship."

Squad 2 was trying to get back on track after seeing the carnage in front of them. Two people moved to the down crewman, and started trying to get him back to the ship. Others were walking back and forth, looking at the other Terrans and VolatarA scattered around. Several were staying back, trying not to look at anything. The squad leader finally got people's attention. He sent Team 21 back with the wounded crewman, and didn't protest as a handful of others started sliding back as well. The Team Leader was told to get people back, and guard the entrance to the *Persephone*. The squad leader gathered the other 8 people together, and got them moving further into the ship.

Most of Squad 3 was standing in a glob, trying to figure out where the bridge was, when the lights came back on. As people were blinking in the light, the artificial gravity came back on as well. With the lights on, they could see a corridor just to their left, and thought it looked like the way to the bridge. They moved out with Team 31 in the lead. The VolatarA engineer who had just restored the lights and gravity stepped out into the end of the corridor right in front of the Terrans. He had been heading for the bridge, and had no idea that he was anywhere near aliens. He stopped and stared at the mob that was only ten feet from him. The Team 31 lead had his AGM2 up, and when he saw the VolatarA, automatically fired. The angulin went straight through the VolatarA, who died instantly, before he even recognized the shot was coming. The angulin then hit the back wall square and ricocheted straight back. It went through the unfortunate VolatarA again, hit and killed the team lead, and went through to smack into the person behind him. The entire event occurred so fast that almost everyone was standing in shock, wondering what was going on. When people recovered enough to react, the rest of Team 31 forgot everything but their dead and wounded friends. The Squad leader sent them back with the wounded man, and pressed on with his other six, still trying to find the bridge.

Squad 4 heard the shots in front of them, and met the remains of Team 31 coming back. The Squad leader decided that the squad should be closer to the inside of ship. He led the group back to the right, and the two squads separated.

Squad 5 had divided up completely. Squad 6 had been following behind, but then had entered a room that looked like it might be the VolatarA mess hall. This gave them a point of reference, and they asked the bridge which direction they should be going. According to the chart, there was a straight path from the mess hall to the weapon station they were headed for. The squad gathered together, and moved on, thinking that they finally knew where they were going.

The bridge was a bit calmer now that they had some contact with the squads. There was a constant stream of messages coming from the squads, and occasional orders and location references from the bridge. As most of the orders referred to room names, and the squads had lost all idea of which room was which, most of the orders were useless. Captain Adams turned her attention on the second enemy ship. The other VolatarA knew something was wrong, but was standing off, probably trying to get some response from its partner ship.

The Squads had mostly come apart, and were wandering randomly through the alien ship. The remains of Squad 2 ran into a single VolatarA who had gotten his gun after the angulins hit, and found good cover with a view of the door into the room. The first Terran to start into the room was hit and fell back wounded. The Terrans tried to get the Chemist forward, but there were shots coming through the door and bouncing off the walls into the squad. One hit the Chemist, and the Chemist went down wounded. The bullet had passed right between two grenades, and the entire squad hustled the Chemist far to the rear. The entire squad was stalled, when Team 51, thinking it was going in the opposite direction, happened to come up directly behind the VolatarA. There was a flurry of shots, and another alien was down.

Team 52 had moved through the entire ship directly to their destination.

They had reached the airlock on the far side of the ship. Squad 5 was supposed to be first line of defense if the second ship did try to board and help their friends. When the second ship started to come aboard, Squad 5 was to call for help and everyone was to come to their aid. The five members of Team 52 felt very, very alone. They had not seen another Terran since they had parted from Team 51 and Team 53. They had no idea whether the other ship was about to connect to the airlock and come across. The five crewmen started piling up whatever they could find as cover, and waited.

Squad 6 was moving towards one of the alien ship's weapon systems.

They had no contact with VolatarA, until they stepped into the room directly in front of their objective. The room had several metal cabinets that had fallen down on the near side of the room, and a collection of equipment that had been piled up on the far side, in front of a door that led on towards the missile launcher. After three Terrans had entered the room, two VolatarA raised up and fired; in seconds, all three Terrans were down, as well as another who had been inattentive enough to step into the room as the firing started. The fourth was alive, and was drawn back into the next room by his friends.

All three teams blended together as Team 62 tried to help get the wounded man back, and Team 63 caught up and moved into the room. The Terrans were milling around behind the door. They could try rushing the room, but they would be completely exposed to the firing from inside. No one had any experience in attacking defended rooms. The squad sort off milled around, with the VolatarA occasionally shooting through the door. Finally, the Chief Engineer stated, "Grenades."

Everyone turned to Susan Underwood. She could feel everyone's eyes on her as she took a step towards the doorway and stopped. She could try just throwing a grenade through the door, but the VolatarA were behind good cover – they probably wouldn't be killed by the blast. To make sure that the grenade had an effect, she would need to get it to the back of the room, over the top of the VolatarAs' cover. That would mean stepping out into the room as she threw. With both of the aliens waiting, she knew that there was no chance they would miss. She started to take out one of the grenades; every action seemed like it was in slow motion. She tried to remember what Soong had said about not being afraid, but couldn't remember anything clearly. She finally got the grenade ready to throw, and stared at it, then at the door. The door looked sort of like an open grave.

Darron had seen Susan start to take out the grenade, and knew what was going to come. Suddenly, the thought came back that the ship would be empty without Susan, but this time, it was the whole world that was empty. He saw her turn towards the door, and said "Susan". She stopped and stared as he started to walk forward. He walked up, and they stood facing each other for a moment. "Wait a second", Darron said. He said quietly, "You are going to push the button and throw on two?' When she nodded, he continued, "Wait there", pointing to the wall next to the door. He looked at her for another second and then said, "Count to three and push the button." He started to say something more, but stopped. She nodded, and didn't speak.

Susan took a breath and said, "One". As soon as she spoke, Darron started for the door. As she got to three, Darron was running into the doorway. As he crossed, he hit the angulin on the back of his suit, and shot himself into the room. He was diving forward, aiming for the space behind the fallen cabinets. The VolatarA saw him coming through and both started to fire. He was moving faster than they expected, and one missed behind him; the other did not. Darron's body was flung to the side as he smashed into the wall behind the cabinets and then fell to the floor. As the VolatarAs' guns turned, following Darron's motion, Susan stepped around the door, and lobbed the grenade towards the VolatarA. She flipped back out of the room as the VolatarA spun back to her. One and a half seconds later, the grenade blew up right behind the aliens. They both died about the same time as they realized the grenade was coming. The confined blast blew the makeshift barricade out into the room, and then spread across the room. The blast hit the two cabinets, and sent them over against what was left of Darron. The flames flashed back out through the door, and as soon as they went by, half a dozen Terrans poured into the room. They spread out, looking for any signs of life from the VolatarA.

The second that people had gone by, Susan ran to Darron's body. She could see that the suit was torn along the leg and in the side, and an arm was bent under one of the cabinets. There was still motion: the free arm was moving, and the unshot leg was bending back and forth. She turned back and started shouting for the crewman with the painkillers. He came forward, and the two of them got the cabinet off Darron. Susan started grabbing patches, and slapping them on the torn suit – Darron's suit was already mostly decompressed. The assisting crewman had found the worst holes in Darron's ruined left leg, and slapped on two medical seals. Each one stabbed into Darron's leg and expanded across the wound applying pressure to stop the bleeding; at the same time, it shot local anesthetics around the wound. Susan had used every patch on Darron's suit and started using her own, holding the torn leg of the suit together and sealing it shut as the makeshift medic moved up to Darron's chest and applied a shot that would hopefully turn off most of the pain. Darron was conscious again, and starting to focus on things other than his leg as his nerves were being turned off. He saw Susan was there, and alive.

The Chief Engineer was trying to get people back together. Behind the VolatarA was a shut door; no one was going anywhere near it. The excitement, tension, and fear of getting past the VolatarA was over, and with the release, the squad just stopped. People were milling around, looking over at Darron, looking over at the wreckage of the VolatarA, or wandering back in to the room they had come from. The Chief Engineer finally got the Team leaders' attention, and got the two of them to round up their teams. As people came together, someone asked about Darron. Everyone looked at the cripple, then looked at the Squad Leader. The Chief Engineer looked at Darron like everyone else, then looked back at the next door. He shook his head. "We can't take them back to the ship," he stated. "Anyone going back would probably get lost. They are safer here. We will come back when things are over."

People started to move towards the door. Susan and the pseudo-medic were still next to Darron. He was watching everyone start to leave, and realized that he was going to be all alone in the alien ship. As Susan started to rise up to leave, Darron reached out and grabbed her arm. "Don't leave me alone," he whispered. Susan looked, and could see Darron's terrified face through his visor. She looked back to the medic, and then leaned down to pick Darron up. The medic took the other side, and together they lifted Darron to at least one foot. They started staggering forward, following the rest of the squad. As the others reached the door, the Chief Engineer looked back and saw the three of them. He decided to ignore the disobedience, and focus on getting through to the next room.

When someone finally opened the door, there were no defenders on the other side. The room the Terrans edged into was the gun turret for a missile launcher – the target the squad had supposed to secure. The nervousness turned into chatter, and then into shouts and cheers clouding up the entire voice channel. People started crowding into the room, looking at the controls marked in a language they didn't understand. Above the controls were a series of purple lights. Across the center of the room ran a large casing that held the missile. About it was a huge monitor that showed a dark background, with stars visible, and what looked like the location of the second VolatarA ship. In addition, there was a circle in the center of the monitor. As everyone came in, Susan and the medic sat Darron down on a small shelf, and started looking at the controls with everyone else. People were wandering around the room, arguing over what the different controls might mean. Finally a group of people gathered around a square panel that stood out slightly from the wall. A crewman reached out and gently pushed on the top. The panel moved, and so did the room. The room jerked a little, and the background on the monitor moved just slightly up. There were cheers from the Terrans. As the panel was tapped to move the circle, the conversation switched to how to actually shoot the missile. The Chief Engineer said, "We press that button," and pointed to a button on the other wall. As everyone turned, he continued, "That is the only one which is covered so you can't accidently press it." The cheering turned to suppressed excitement as a crewman moved over and lifted the cover, waiting for the order to fire. All eyes turned to the monitor, where the VolatarA ship was sliding into the center of the circle.

Darron was watching, along with everyone else. The room was moving a bit slowly, but the burst of adrenaline and excitement that had come from actually seeing an alien missile launcher had brought him mostly awake. He watched the screen with the circle and the alien dot. Then he frowned and looked around again at the rest of the controls. He looked back at the missile, and back to the screen. He watched as the crewman stood at the button, holding up the clear protective cover. The VolatarA ship was in the center of the circle, and all eyes were turning to the Chief Engineer for the order.

Memories of an earlier disaster stirred in Darron's brain. "Don't push the button!" He screamed.

Everyone stopped and looked at Darron. Darron looked at the Chief Engineer. "This weapon must be designed to fire at targets which are very far away. The initial pointing of the launcher can't be the way to target the weapon, since the light time delay between the time the weapon is fired and the time the weapon reaches the target will be significant – even small variations in target speed could not be accounted for and would cause the weapon to miss. The missile must be self-targeting – the target must be loaded before the missile is fired. Then as the missile closes, it will make corrections as needed." Darron stopped, and sagged back against the wall.

Everyone turned to the Chief Engineer. "You tell the weapon who to shoot, and after you fire it, it curves around as needed to hit the target," he translated.

"And it is probably loaded for the *Persephone*," Darron added.

"We are about to shoot ourselves," finished the Chief Engineer. There was a click as the cover was dropped back over the button.

Everyone was now milling around in the middle of the room, staying away from everything. The Chief Engineer took a deep breath and ordered, "We are going to move on. Team 63," he said, "stay here. Keep the ship in the circle. If they get close enough, we fire anyway. If they are close enough, the missile should hit before it has the chance to make any turn." He started to emphasize to Darron to stay as well, but Darron was now limp against the wall, so he did not bother. The wounded man from Team 62 was set next to Darron. People milled around, and then Squad 6, down to one team and two extra people, headed back out to look for other weapon stations.

On the bridge, there was growing confidence that the attack squads were going to clear out the attached VolatarA ship. Attention had shifted to watching the second ship. The *Persephone* had no weapons – no way to strike at the ship as long as it stood off from the fight. Captain Adams had started pacing back and forth across the bridge, reduced to a spectator, waiting for the VolatarA ship to make its decision. She listened as reports slowly came in of individual VolatarA being encountered and killed. Terran casualties were piling up, as each VolatarA was usually discovered by a Terran team seeing a team member fall down, or fly completely apart. If the Terran team did not run for cover immediately, the VolatarA was in trouble. If they did, once the report was in, other teams wandered towards the area, and the VolatarA would finally be overwhelmed by numbers. As the bridge crew tried to keep track of the wayward teams, the focus was starting to shift to trying to keep the Terrans from shooting other Terrans by mistake.

Captain Adams and the others watching the displays suddenly saw flashes register on radar behind the *Persephone*, around the *Persephone*, then towards the distant VolatarA. The radar returns disappeared, and heat flashes registered all other the VolatarA ship. After the flashes died down, the VolatarA ship was gone – replaced by scattered radar returns, slowly separating. All conversation on the bridge slowly came to a stop, as person after person realized that something had happened. Everyone ended up staring at the radar display, looking on as the pieces of the VolatarA ship slowly separated. Some one finally noticed that the Suvain were closing. The silence was broken by a broadcast from the Suvain that echoed in the silent bridge. *"Persephone.* Permission to board." All eyes turned to the captain, who didn't answer. She was starting at the screen, not moving. Finally, as the Suvain repeated the request, the Captain turned to the communications officer and nodded. She then ordered the engineering team shut down the reactor, and repair any damage.

"Are there any left?" came the message from the Suvain. After the Terran response that they didn't think so, there was a short blast of Suvain swearing. "We will check around the area," the Suvain answered.

There was a brief moment of disbelief and shock, and then the bridge exploded in cheers.

Captain Adams let them cheer, as the realization sunk in that she was going to live through the day. She enjoyed the relief for a moment, and then got herself back to work. She got the attention of the bridge crew, and had them start telling each Squad to hold in place. "Don't tell them anything else at this point. They need to stay focused until everything is taken care of." She turned back to the blank screen that was supposed to be showing the assault squads. "Go through each squad, and see if they have wounded. If so, each squad is free to break off and bring them back. They are to broadcast their position at all times – I don't want us to start shooting each other now that it looks like things are almost over. There was a last final message that a VolatarA had been encountered, and then all of the fighting was over.

The teams were straggling back aboard bringing the wounded to sick bay when the Suvain called again, asking again for permission to board. The Captain gave permission, and met them at the airlock that still existed on the port side of the ship. Six excited Suvain came aboard, fully armed and armored. For a second, Captain Adams wondered if they had come aboard to take the *Persephone* while the Terrans' guard was down – she had not given any orders to implement if the Suvain turned out to be hostile. As she was thinking this, the Suvain came forward, more excited than the Terrans had ever seen them before. With them was the team leader of Team 42. He was walking along behind the Suvain, alive, and apparently well. He saluted, and said he had wounded. People stepped forward as two other Terrans and a Suvain appeared, carrying another team member. As people started taking the wounded man to sick bay, Captain Adams looked at the Team leader, the wounded crewmen, and the two others; she counted to four, not five, and looked back to the Team Leader. He met her gaze, looked down, and shook his head in the negative. The Suvain captain walked up to Captain Adams, and said, "Next time, leave some of the fun to your friends." He waggled his arms for a second, and then said, "We found one of yours that didn't make it, and a couple of VolatarA. Where do you want them?"

"Just bring them here," she answered. "Thank you for picking up the crew." She took a deep breath. "And for dealing with the others."

The Suvain laughed again and answered. "Officially, we didn't.

Hopefully the missiles hit before they got off a message that we had fired. We picked a path that was shielded by your ship for as long as possible."

"It looked like there was more than one missile, but you only have one launcher?" asked Adams.

"We fired four, with a timed start to acceleration. The first ones waited until the last was launched, and then all fired towards the target.

We didn't think we could get more than four out without something being seen. We had to use the point-blank warheads –there wouldn't be enough velocity built up for the usual kinetic-energy shots to go through the hull."

"And these four were enough to destroy the entire ship?"

"The shots didn't really destroy that much themselves – but they break the hull, and the ship's own angulins finish tearing everything apart. Of course, a real warship would be designed to take a much greater beating; those VolatarA are really scout ships, just like us."

Captain Adams was distracted by two Suvain carrying a torn silver figure towards them. Crewmen all around turned to watch as the body was brought forward, and two Terrans moved forward to take it. Then everyone stopped as a VolatarA with hands bound was marched forward by a Suvain. Another was being half-dragged out behind him. Captain Adams realized that when the Suvain had said that they had picked up a few VolatarA, they meant living ones, not corpses. It was the first look she had ever had at a VolatarA. The alien was tall, a bit thin, and looked enough like a human that he might have passed for one on the street. Everyone looked to Captain Adams for orders; she stood staring at the prisoner, wondering what to say. "What is the usual method of dealing with captives among the Suvain?" she asked.

"It depends on the situation," he answered. "If there is some problem keeping them, they might be shot, or if they have valuable information, it is dragged out of them. Or locked up, or maybe parole." "What is parole?" asked the captain.

"Parole is when both sides agree to stop fighting until there is agreement to start again. If a prisoner gives parole, they do not try to kill anybody, or destroy the ship, or gather information. And the people giving parole agree not to kill or torture or imprison the prisoner. They are more like a guest aboard ship until there is an agreement that they are released, and can be a combatant again. Parole is more common than you might expect – it is easy to end up facing a ship much more powerful than you, so you can end up getting captured without having done anything wrong. Since that can happen to anyone, having a way to capture and be captured without instant death can be useful."

Captain Adams turned to the prisoners and said, "Bring them here." When they had been marched forward, she looked up at the uninjured one and said, "Do you agree to parole?" The alien stared back at her until the message was relayed through a Suvain headset.

There was some talking back and forth between the Suvain and the VolatarA, and then the VolatarA answered via the Suvain, "I will give parole to be in effect for as long as I am on this vessel." When the semi-conscious VolatarA was indicated, the standing one continued. "I will give parole for him as well, as he is incapable of doing so himself."

Captain Adams, and every other Terran, turned back to the Suvain, who nodded. She turned back to the VolatarA and announced, "Very well.

Welcome aboard." She saw the Personnel Officer, and ordered him to take the VolatarA back with a guard, and find some empty place for him to stay. She then ordered the wounded alien taken to sick bay.

The Suvain watched them go, and then said, "We will head back. I suspect you will be busy for a while. But we should get together soon, to celebrate the victory."

"We most certainly will", answered Captain Adams.

The Suvain started to return to their ship. One stopped and asked, "Will you be having a religious festival? To thank your god for winning?"

Several people heard the question, and looked to the captain. She realized that she had never thought about such a thing. "Yes," she answered firmly. "We will."

VII

The nerve blockers had worn off while Darron was still on the alien ship. He had promptly passed out. Darron woke in the sick bay, where he was lying on his own cot. The tiny room was crammed with six patients – Darron had a broken arm, bruised ribs, a ruined leg, and had lost a lot of blood. He was in the best shape of anyone actually in the room. The less-severely injured were scattered around in the adjacent rooms. The ship's supply of drugs and blood was running out fast; half a dozen crewmen who had been dragooned into service went from patient to patient handing out what was left. The lucky few who were uninjured found themselves at risk of attack again as the ship's medical officer turned vampire and sucked a pint of blood off anyone he could catch.

Darron had been told that the last supplies of nerve blockers were going to the two crewmen who were the most injured. His previous drugs had worn off sufficiently for each breath to hurt. When he wasn't whimpering or groaning, he was usually thinking that the others were probably too far gone to survive anyway, so he should get the pain blockers instead. Occasionally he would feel a bit guilty about these thoughts, but then another of wave of pain would come by. He found out that he had been asleep for nearly 16 hours. After he had been awake for a few hours, he had moved from just "in agony" to "in agony and desperate for some distraction". His leg was immobilized, and one arm was bound up. Unable to move around, he was starting to get frantic when one of the new medical assistants found a way to hang a display over Darron's bed. Knowing his audience, the kind assistant set an extensive display of old science fiction classics to run on a long loop.

Darron welcomed the distraction, and found that with the noise and moving pictures, he could drift in and out of consciousness. He was still able to sleep through the night.

When he woke up, he found that he had a different neighbor. He did not recognize him, but this patient did not have the nearly-complete covering of bandages that the other man had. After a while, he asked one of the attendants where the first guy was, and the attendants grew quiet for a second, and then turned away without answering. After a while, Darron asked someone how many people had been killed. 24, they answered. Most from Squad 1. Darron thought there was something special about Squad 1, but couldn't place it. After he watched a movie for a little while, he looked over at his neighbor a little more carefully. The man was unconscious, probably drugged. Then he got a good look at the other's face and realized that he was lying next to an alien. The alien wasn't tied down, and Darron was nervous to be next to him. It seemed a lot safer if the alien was kept farther from people, like maybe in an airlock.

During the second day, Darron received his first visitor. Susan Underwood came in, and stepped over a little ways from Darron's cot. She looked down at him, and there was a tiny moment when the pain wasn't noticed. She didn't come any closer, and Darron thought she looked different – head down, not meeting his gaze. He worried for a second that she had been hit after all.

"Are you okay?" he asked. "Did you get hurt?"

Susan gave an attempt at a smile, and then confessed, "I didn't get a scratch."

Darron relaxed slightly, upon which all his ribs hurt again. "Great," he exclaimed.

Susan tried to smile, and failed. "They say you are going to be all right.

Well, maybe, mostly – I mean, not going to die."

"I think the leg is gone, but they keep insisting I am doing well enough I don't need painkillers," Darron complained.

"They have no painkillers," Susan answered in a low voice. They asked us..." Susan paused, swallowed, and continued, "They asked us if we could make them more, but we don't have anything to make them out of."

Susan was one of the stranger sex, and Darron was mostly thinking about pain rather than the outside world, but he could tell that something was wrong. There was the momentary instinct to say nothing and do nothing to make sure whatever mistake he had made would not be repeated, but he didn't really have the option to withdraw – he was unable to move from the cot. Instead he just asked again, "Are you okay?"

Susan answered, "It should be me in the cot. You didn't have to step through first. You don't deserve to be the one who is shot up. If anyone was shot up, it should have been me."

Darron tried to shake his head in complete disagreement, and found that that was a big mistake. His body had started to shake as well, and everything hurt for a moment. After several painful breaths, he just said, "No, you shouldn't."

Susan looked at the floor next to Darron. "You don't understand. When you first stepped up to me in that room, I thought you were going to say you would throw it. That you would take the cylinder. That you would be the one who had to step out into all those gunshots." She met his gaze and then continued in a small voice, "I feel so ashamed, because if you had asked for the grenade, I would have given it to you."

Darron listened to Susan's confession and got a confused look. Then he asked, "Who wouldn't?"

Susan laughed in relief, and reached down and took Darron's moveable hand. "Thank you," she said.

Darron was confused about he was being thanked for, but being thanked was the best thing that had happened that day, and so he just accepted the happy moment. She gave his hand a brief squeeze, and straightened back up. "I am going to have to get back to work." She shuddered. "You managed to avoid the really bad tasks," she accused. "We are trying to clean things up, and bring everyone back. A few teams are looting every piece of technology they can find, but most of us have to try and find what is left of what used to be our friends, and gather them for burial. At least we have most of the remains back. The funeral is tonight. I can see if it can be displayed here, if you want."

Darron nodded, and then asked, "Stephen must be going wild trying to translate stuff. Did Jon get burial duty?" His suddenly felt like the cot was spinning when he saw Susan's face change.

Susan started to answer, then looked confused for a second. "I haven't seen Stephen," she answered. "You haven't either?" When Darron did not answer, she continued, "Maybe I should check up on him – I don't remember seeing him in the recovery teams." Then she continued in a low, steady voice, "You know Jon was in Team 11."

Darron remembered hearing something about Squad 1, but that was way, way back, and he had passed out about 15 times since then. He just answered, "I think he is."

Susan realized that her statement meant nothing to Darron. "He was the team leader of Team 11." She could see the use of the past tense start to sink into Darron's face. "Squad 1 was wiped out. They found a bunch of them near the entrance, and Jon led Team 11 in. He hit one, and then they started to use grenades on the others. But from the one surviving recording, it looks like the VolatarA had shot out their own grenade just as Matthias started to throw. It went off, then every one of his grenades went off. The entire squad, and all the VolatarA, were blasted away in an instant. There was only one survivor, and he was badly burned. He died from his wounds. With his death, the number of losses went up to 24. There are about a dozen of you in sick bay." She paused for a second. "There were four of us in the Chemistry group. I am the only one who wasn't hit. One took a bullet to the chest, but fortunately the exosuit took a lot of the shock. The other is pretty torn up from one of our own shots that bounced around the room and into him." Susan started to go, and then said, "Do you want me to collect Stephen and come back later on?" She smiled at Darron's thankful look, and left.

After Susan asked the Personnel Officer where Stephen was, and the Personnel Officer asked the Information Officer where Stephen was, and the Information Officer asked the recovery team leader if Stephen was at his assignment, and the recovery leader said no one had seen him, and the message went back up the chain that no one had seen him since Squad 3 was released, the Personnel Officer looked him up through the ship tracking system. Then he ordered the acting Ship's Chaplain to go to Stephen's cabin.

Soong knocked, and received no answer. He knocked again, waited about 20 seconds, and then opened the door. He stopped for a moment, as his eyes adjusted. The lights were off; the room was dark except for a glowing display on the side away from the door, partially blocked by a human silhouette. Just as his eyes adjusted to the darkness, Stephen turned the lights back on. As Soong blinked back to normal vision, he could smell stale blood, and a stale person. Stephen was unwashed, unshaven, and looked exhausted. Stephen had turned off the glowing thing, and now stood facing Soong, eyes a little down.

"We hadn't seen you in a while", Soong began. "Is everything alright?"

"Fine," answered Stephen, with a wave of his hand. "I have been working on this."

"Did you hear the Captain's statement that everyone is authorized to take a full shower?" Soong had located the blood stench – Stephen's exosuit was lying crumpled as far away from Stephen as it could get in the tiny cabin. One side was covered in a spray of blood.

"I have been busy," Stephen explained. "I found things I could access from the other ship."

"You were not listed as wounded. Is that your blood?" Soong asked, indicating the exosuit.

"No", answered Stephen, briefly glancing at the exosuit then turning back to his display.

"Why haven't you thrown the suit away?" asked Soong.

Stephen stayed focused on the display, and answered, "I was able to bring up the information on a VolatarA display, and recorded it. I have been making a new interface", he continued. Soong started to interrupt, but then Stephen clicked on the display, and the glow came back. A glowing set of lights hung in front of Stephen. He moved his hands apart, and his side of the room was filled with an ocean of star systems. The systems were connected by lines of different widths.

In spite of himself, Soong was distracted by the first real Intersection map of the galaxy that Terrans had ever seen. As Stephen started to describe the map and how he was pulling out the data, Soong shook his head and went back to his point. "If it isn't your blood, whose is it?" Stephen stopped, and Soong repeated the question.

"It is what is left of Xian She." Stephen confessed in a low voice. "She was in your team?" Soong asked.

Stephen could not resist turning back to stare at his map, but continued, "The lights were out in the room we went into. I had turned off my light and moved across from the door. But Xian She didn't turn her light off. She came in, and one of them fired. There was a flash, and there was nothing left of her except the … what hit my suit. Bob and I fired back, and killed it, but she was gone. I really thought she had her light off. I reminded her about the light. I should have made sure, but I didn't."

Soong was silent for a second. Then he asked, "Have you gotten any sleep since the fight?"

"I have been busy", Stephen repeated. "This map could be the first way we have to identify where they might be coming from."

"You need to get cleaned up …", Soong began.

"I need to get this ready for the captain", Stephen answered.

Soong thought for a second, then stated, "Crewman Hunter. As the acting Chaplain, I am actually an officer at the moment. This isn't a request. One. You are going to shave. Two. You are going to take a shower." He openly sniffed. "A Long shower. Three. You are going to throw that exosuit into the garbage pile started in the aft loading bay. That is not what is left of Xian She. Her body was found, and she will be part of the ceremony performed in one hour. Four. You are going to attend the funeral. Five. After the funeral you are going to return here, and sleep. If you aren't asleep for at least eight hours, I am having you sedated. Six. In fourteen hours, you are to show that map to the Captain." He looked at Stephen, who had turned to face him, and stood in a posture not drastically far from attention. "I will give you a hand", Soong continued. "I will get rid of the suit for you." He walked over, picked up the suit, and opened the door. He pointed to the tiny compartment for personal effects, and watched Stephen as he got out a razor. As both left the room, Soong said, "You are a friend of Darron Mason, aren't you? After you have completed all orders, you might want to visit him. He is in Sick Bay."

The Captain had decided that one funeral would be held for everyone, instead of one at a time. If held one at a time, the funerals would last for days, and she was not sure that the bodies could be kept on board for that long. Soong was officiating the service. He had hardly ever been to a funeral, much less spoken at one. He had tried to find examples of what Chaplain Eisen would say, but the Chaplain hadn't performed any funerals on board. He stood and watched as the airlock was loaded with the gathered remains of 24 crewmen. Then people began to file into the mess hall, looking at the display of the airlock. He looked around, and realized that the room was not nearly as crowded as it had been. He tried to convince himself that there really hadn't been that big a change, that the room felt empty because there were a dozen people unable to attend because they were wounded, and others had to watch the wounded. Then he looked back to the 24 remains, and illusions could not be maintained.

Soong blundered through the service, forgetting what he meant to say, and mumbling things about hope in Christ and celebrating the life of their friends. After what seemed like an eternity, but was actually about 7 minutes, he called for the tape of Amazing Grace, and the sound of bagpipes filled the room. The Captain nodded, and their fellow crewmen were slowly released into the void.

Some of the coffins were normal sized; others were small boxes with representative DNA. Each had been decorated with something from the crewman's possessions. Darron could see the caskets sliding out, and saw one showing a printout of the Lead Physicist's mountains. As the others slid out, one of the small boxes slid outward with one of the old AGM-1s attached on top. Darron started to cry as he watched what was left of Jon head into space. People stood and watched until their fellow crewmen were gone.

Soong stood silently with the others, and after a few moments announced that the service was over. Everyone began leaving, and many came to thank Soong for his words. He shook their hands, and wondered what he had actually said. Finally the room was empty except for the Captain. She came and stood before him. He realized he was directly facing his superior officer and came to attention.

"When I appointed you to this position, I had no idea how hard the job might turn out to be. However, I am glad of my choice. Fredrick would have been as well. You have been dealing with a lot since the fighting. You are released from duties for the next 6 hours. I would suggest sleep." They saluted, and Captain Adams left the room, leaving Soong feeling lonely and alone for the first time ever on a crowded starship.

The Captain had told all of the officers to take time off right after the service, and then report to her eight hours later. She gathered all of them together in the bridge ready room. Although 24 crewmen were dead, none of the officers had been lost. There was a small undercurrent of guilt that the officers had survived, when so many crewmen they were supposed to be responsible for had not. Captain Adams looked at the drawn faces, and growled, "In case you have forgotten, we won. And a bunch of us are even still alive." There was laughter around the room, and then the Captain continued. "The fight is over. The cleanup is finishing as well. We have to start focusing on getting the ship, and every piece of information we can learn, back to Loren Station. We also need to get the crew back to regular work. Personnel – you are responsible for any remaining cleanup activities. I also want to know if there are any crewmen that need something more than just returning to duties.

Soong is at your disposal. Information – there are a lot of ship systems still not restored. We need them back up – for real, not just jury-rigged. There is also a lot of debris over there that might have things we can take back. I want one team on repair, and another on the VolatarA ship. I want anything that might be part of their computer systems that still exist brought over here. Engineering - we need to take any technology we haven't invented ourselves and get it back for study. For one thing, it looked like they have angulins made of denser material than ours. I want to make sure we have samples. But we also need to be working on getting this ship ready for transit. We didn't really worry about structural damage when we released the angulins – we were going to be dead in a little while anyway. But now, this ship has to accelerate back to the Intersection. And once we get there, it is going to have to compress to go back through. I want a second team checking for any hull failures, especially around the reactor. Another team is to start cutting away what is still attached from the starboard side – we will have to get it off in order to compress. Communications – the transmissions back to Loren Station have been restarted, but we still haven't heard anything back yet. In addition to listening to our side, I want you to get the sensors out again. If there are others out there, we want to know as soon as possible. We have to know for sure we are not being followed when we go through the Intersection. Science – I want you to go over everything you can find from the VolatarA ship. Anything that looks like it might be something we can read, or see, or listen to, or figure out, is to be identified and brought back here. If you can learn anything from looking at something, I want full sets of images prepared and sent back to Loren Station. Medical – as soon as someone is ready for tasks, I want them put back in service. I don't want people to just sit around and stagnate. I know you are short on supplies. Give the science team a list of everything you need. Maybe you can separate out some of what you need from the medical supplies still existing on the VolatarA ship. Any questions?

Soong turned to the Science officer. "I talked to Stephen Hunter a while ago. Hopefully he is asleep right now. He found a map of the galaxy on the VolatarA ship, and has been working on a 3-D display." There was a ripple of excitement through the room, and Soong continued, "He has worked on it since the fight – if he has been able to sleep, he really needs the rest before presenting his work."

The Medical officer looked a bit hesitant when he asked, "Are there any specific orders concerning the VolatarA prisoners?"

The Captain turned to the Personnel Officer. "For the Suvain, we sent in the lunatic brigade. Do you think they would be a good choice for the VolatarA?"

The Personnel Officer shook his head. "The lunatic brigade is not in much shape to be doing much of anything. Stephen is busy, one is dead and one is crippled. Susan is the last one left, and she is the only Chemist available to try to identify what the VolatarA drugs are made of."

Captain Adams nodded. "I doubt simple ignorance would be of much use – I would bet that everything the Suvain have learned will get spread around to everyone else pretty fast. So instead, let's try competence.

MacDonald, once you have given out assignments, you will be the primary interface to the VolatarA. Learn what you can, give up as little as possible. Other questions? No? Dismissed."

Darron did not know that Susan had been ordered off to the Chemistry lab, or that Stephen had finally passed out. He only knew that they had not shown up as promised. Lying there, trying to find something other than pain to occupy his mind, he gave in to general thoughts of self-pity. He finally wasn't able to pretend interest in the latest movie anymore, and turned off the display.

He rolled partway over and noticed the alien lying in the next bed. It was lying on its back, staring straight up at the ceiling. Darron could a see a small grimace with every breath, but the alien was not making any sound. Darron felt a little embarrassed that he was making a much bigger fuss than the alien, but decided that he must have had a lot more injuries than the alien had suffered. He was trying to sleep when the door opened and the Medical Officer walked in with the Personnel Officer and several others. They had another alien with them, and the entire group walked across the tiny room to the farthest cot. Darron couldn't see which patient was there – a small table blocked his view. Something interesting was going on, but Darron would have to sit up completely to see, and that was more pain that the distraction was worth. He stayed down, seeing just the top half of the crowd. It sounded like there was a conversation going on about a patient at the other side of the room. He could see Suvain headsets being handed out to the standing alien, and to the alien lying next to Darron.

"Look, I have no idea what to do," stated the Chief Medical Officer. "I have tried stopping the bleeding, applying bandages to obvious wounds, that sort of thing. But I don't have any reserve blood supply. I don't even know where the organs are in the patient. I am pretty sure there is internal bleeding, but I have no idea how to stop it."

"Why are you treating him?" asked the prone alien. "He is too far gone already to be of use. When you start questioning him, he won't have the strength, and will just die on you."

There was a pause as the Terrans tried to catch up. "Why are we treating him?" asked the Medical Officer. "He is a patient."

"It does not matter if you keep any of us alive", stated the prone alien. "For every one of us on the ship, we are going to kill 25 million extra Terrans, to make sure that you learn that VolatarA are never to be harmed."

Most of the Terrans reacted to this statement; the Personnel Officer did not seem surprised. He asked, "Do you think we are trying to heal him so that we can torture information out of him later?"

"Why else?" asked the VolatarA.

"We aren't going to torture you", answered MacDonald. "Besides, you gave.."

"We have given parole", the VolatarA said, "But as soon as we leave this ship, such protection will be gone."

"I can't say what others will do", responded MacDonald, "But I would be surprised if there was any attempt to use physical violence to get information. I doubt if you would have any information about a specific attack, and I doubt if we could get you to give up information about your ship. If we tried to make you log onto …"

"You are correct. If you made us log onto our information system, we would log on with a command that would erase everything before you had the chance to access it. Give us a few more minutes, and we would have the ship destroyed as well."

"Torture or not," interrupted the Medical Officer, "This man will not be any condition for anything but lying in bed for a long time. And I don't think he is going to make it all unless I can get more information. Do either.."

"Neither of us have the required medical training to assist with someone so severely injured." answered the standing alien.

"Then his only hope is to get the information from your ship's comp…"

"No. We will not be logging on for any reason, except to destroy everything."

The Terrans started talking; the prone alien looked to the other and clicked his tongue. People just started to notice as the standing alien turned to the table and picked up a scalpel. Before any Terran could react he turned and rammed it through the temple of the unconscious VolatarA.

There were shouts of shock and revulsion from the Terrans; the VolatarA calmly wiped off the scalpel and placed it back on the table. As the shouts turned to questions, the prone alien stated, "He had no chance with only primitive medicine. Better to end it quick than have him just lying there in pain." There was no answer given to this – the Terrans just stood in shock.

MacDonald started to answer, but was overridden by the Medical Officer. "You are right, we didn't know how to treat him. And even if we did, there wasn't much to try to treat him with. And even we knew how, and had something to work with, he probably would have been crippled afterwards. But while there is still any chance, I am not going to give up hope. Do not mess with my treatment of patients again. When there is truly no hope, I will tell you, you will not tell me. If I think you are going to interfere, you will spent the rest of your time in Sick Bay in restraints. Is that clear?"

"I am in command. His life is subject to my decisions, not yours." "While you are in this room, you are under my command, as was he. If you don't like that, tough. You are going to stay here until you are capable of moving about freely with no chance of further injury. When you are well, you can leave, and then you can go kill any VolatarA you feel like."

"If the captain of our own ship were injured, she would be under the same restrictions," added MacDonald.

"So you primitives have no idea of the authority of a captain either," said the prone alien in disgust. This brought laughter from every crewman, and groans from Darron and several other wounded who had been unwise enough to laugh with the others.

The Medical Officer turned to the Personnel Officer. "Get someone to remove the body. And all of you, out, now. I think you have disturbed the other patients enough."

As the group turned to go, someone said, "I think I will go disobey Captain Adams. After all, we Terrans don't understand a Captain's authority."

As the laughter started again, MacDonald assured the Terrans that the Captain did not actually shoot crewmen who were disobedient, no matter how desperately they deserved it.

"Terran captains can't execute crewmen for refusing orders?" asked the standing alien.

"They can, given certain conditions. I didn't say she couldn't, but that she wouldn't."

"Why not?"

"You can't get work out of a dead crewman," quoted the Personnel Officer and the Medical Officer together. The group was shooed out by the Medical Officer, and life in Sick Bay returned to boredom.

Several people showed up a few minutes later to remove the body.

Acting Chaplain Soong was with them. While the others retrieved the body, Soong moved over to the prone alien.

"We have collected the remains of your fellow crewmen", he said. "I do not know what your customs are about burial of your dead."

"Why do you want to know about our burial customs?" asked the alien. "I had assumed you would want the bodies for burial", answered the chaplain.

"Why would you bother with burial for enemy dead? Why not throw them out, or dissect them?"

The chaplain shook his head. "Because they are people. They may be your people, not ours, but they are still people."

The alien looked at the chaplain in silence for a few minutes, then stated, "For humans killed combat, the bodies are burned in front of their comrades. The comrades then swear to inflict punishment on those who killed them. I doubt if you would enjoy the experience."

"I usually would perform the ceremony", answered the chaplain after a couple of seconds. "Somehow, I don't think that would go well. I can have the remains placed in a room for cremation if you would like, and have the two of you brought to an adjacent room if you wish. You would then be free to say whatever you want."

"This is pointless," answered the VolatarA. "Trying to act nice to us now will not get you anywhere. You have already ruined any hope of mercy from the VolatarA. And after firing on us after surrendering, do not expect that any ship will be allowed to surrender in the future."

"We did not surrender," Soong pointed out. "We told you from the very beginning that we did not accept your authority, and that attempting to board the ship would be taken as an act of war. We aren't trying to win over the VolatarA. I am trying to treat the VolatarA dead the way I would like to be treated."

"So you know this will do you no good, but you want to do it anyway? Is everything your race does this pointless?"

"I don't see this as pointless. But it is true that often we do things that don't make much sense. Would you like us ..."

"If you are willing to spend your time on such things, we will hold a service for our dead."

"I will tell you when preparations are complete," answered Soong. "I will speak with the Medical Officer about having people avail ..."

"No one will be necessary. My shipmate will take me to the service. Nothing from you is required, or desired."

The next day, the service was held. The remains had been placed in a room of the ruined VolatarA ship, and all of the left over grenades were placed in as well. The VolatarA were notified that everything was ready, and the intact alien came and helped the other out of the sick bay cot. Four armed guards and Chaplain Soong were waiting to accompany them. They slowly made their way to a viewing area set up to show the room with the remains. The unwounded VolatarA thanked the dead for the joy their companionship had given in life. The wounded VolatarA promised the dead that those who had killed them would be killed, that the offenders' families would be destroyed, and the offenders' race would be punished. Then he pushed the button provided by Soong, and everything in the room was vaporized. The small group silently made their way back to sick bay, and broke up.

The Suvain had left soon after the fighting was over. They had come aboard to watch the thanksgiving service and the funeral, and had come aboard a last time to celebrate. After the celebration was over, they headed back to their ship, loaded with movies and Terran souvenirs; once aboard, they made for the Loren Station Intersection field with all speed. Captain Adams had the surviving crewmen working double shifts to prepare the *Persephone* for movement and to loot everything they could take from the VolatarA hulk.

She waited until the Suvain were far enough away that they had disappeared from view, even with sensors being sent in their direction. Sensors were being sent out in the direction the VolatarA had come from, but no additional VolatarA ship had been seen. When no alien ship was in view, the Captain gave the order to start moving the ship. A low acceleration was begun, and repairs were made to each section of the hull that looked like it was under stress. After repairs were complete, the acceleration was edged up, and the repair process started again. It was immediately noticed that the ship was not heading back to Loren Station. The captain had decided that it was worth the risk to move to the Intersection field that led back to Earth. After the course changes they had made to meet up with the VolatarA ship, it was easier to continue accelerating forward and to starboard to reach Earth than it was to take the time to reverse course entirely. As long as they could get a few days head start on the new course before the VolatarA moved another ship into sensor range, they should have a good chance of getting away unseen. After a week of careful repair, they had gotten up to a steady acceleration of 1.2 g.

As both Susan and Stephen pointed out, Darron missed all the work by lying on the cot complaining about his leg. If the Medical Officer had thought he had the necessary equipment and facilities, the leg would have been removed. But without secure ways to dull the pain, and without the room to have Darron recover afterwards, the decision was made to try to prevent gangrene and leave the whole mess for when the ship reached the Earth System. Stephen had visited just after he had gotten up from his mandatory sleep. When Stephen came into the room, Darron had been staring blankly at a display, remembering that he had been shot, and that so many had died. He looked at Stephen's smiling face, and wished for a second that he could be completely relaxed like Stephen was. Nothing ever affected Stephen. "So, I heard you were shot drawing fire away from Susan so she could throw a grenade," Stephen stated. Darron had not thought of how to respond when Stephen continued. "Very brave," Stephen continued. Then he smiled and shook his head. "Very brave. Although," Stephen said thoughtfully, tilting his head, "I wonder if it might have been possible to throw something else through the door to draw fire?" Darron snorted, which hurt his ribs again, allowing Stephen to continue. "Or possibly, throw a grenade through the door first. You wouldn't get it over the barricade, but as soon as it explodes, she steps around and throws the next one. There is no way that they could get back up from the first blast in time to stop the second." Stephen stopped as Darron seemed to slide back and forth between embarrassment and irritation.

"It was the only thing I could think of at the time. Sorry." Darron muttered.

"But after all", Stephen conceded, "Your plan – throwing yourself into the room – that was a great idea too." Stephen laughed as Darron started to protest then cut off because of his ribs.

"So do you always harass cripples?" Darron asked.

"Of course", answered Stephen. "Cripples are the only people to taunt – they can't catch you."

Both laughed, each glad the other was alive.

"You look like you didn't get hit", stated Darron.

"Not standing in the line of fire worked pretty well", answered Stephen. "Did you see any VolatarA in your area?" asked Darron.

A blankness washed across Stephen's face, then he answered, "Yes."

Some instinct in Darron changed the subject. "Now I see how much broken ribs hurt", he stated.

"Don't remind me", answered Stephen. "What are you watching?" The conversation moved to old movies, and stayed there until Stephen started to leave. As he said goodbye, Stephen stopped and confided,

"I found…". He glanced over at the motionless alien in the room and then continued. "When you are moving around, I have something to show you." Stephen visibly stopped himself from continuing and left the room.

Darron tried to concentrate on the movie when Stephen had left, but it was hard to replace actual human conversation. He looked aside, and noticed that the alien next to him was watching the movie out of the corner of his eye. He thought how boring it must be for a VolatarA to be lying in a cot in an alien sick bay – being treated, but having no one to talk to and nothing to watch. The Suvain headset had been left with the alien, so at least he could understand what was going on around him. The movie finished, and the next automatically began. Darron finally asked, "Do you want me to turn off the movie?"

"At least it makes noise," the alien responded. "Is all your entertainment about fighting aliens? Or was this something special to encourage the primitives before the battle?"

"Very little is about aliens. Not many of us were interested in such things." Darron answered. He hesitated for a few moments, then added, "My name is Darron Mason."

The alien turned his head far enough over to look directly at Darron. He answered, "VolatarA Borasal Kallim Duleka, acting commander of the *Winged Vision*."

"The *Winged Vision* was …"

"The *Winged Vision* is the second scout vessel of the Right Searching Hand of the Imperial Delegation."

"But you were on the ship that we …"

"The *Winged Vision* is the physical ship and the crew. The ship is destroyed, but as long as crewmen are alive, the *Winged Vision* is still in service, and the highest ranking survivor has responsibility for the rest."

"Are you badly injured?"

"I will recover. Primarily due to your willingness to assist me after I was found. That was a strange decision, as you should have realized that I am of no use to you, either for information or as someone who would offer you mercy."

"You are a person, are sentient, and you needed medical help."

VolatarA Borasal Kallim Duleka considered this for a moment. "So you treat any person? This is not an action based on the rank of the injured?"

"No", answered Darron. He asked, "Are you of high …?"

"My family is not of high rank, but I am Borasal," answered VolatarA Borasal Kallim Duleka. He saw Darron pause, and continued, "Borasal is a rank indicating an individual's level of training. The first name given to every VolatarA is 'VolatarA'. It is a constant reminder to every member of our species that we are VolatarA first, before any other commitment or personal achievement. 'Borasal' indicates that I graduated from training at a Provincial-level graduation ceremony. 'Kallim' is the name of the family group of which I am a part. The Kallim family is not of exalted rank, but is locally known and has produced a significant number of successful individuals. 'Duleka' is my individual name. In non-formal circumstances, such as a conversation in a hospital, 'Duleka' is all that is required to identify me."

"Is Borasal a rare level of …" asked Darron.

"About one in ten thousand VolatarA choose to continue education to the provincial level," answered Duleka. So there are about 200 - 250 million of us." Duleka saw Darron's eyes widen as he did the math and guessed that eyes widening were a sign of surprise to a Terran. "The Emperor is Lord of roughly 400 inhabited planets. Of these, around 200 have predominantly VolatarA populations. Within the empire there are about 2.2 trillion VolatarA, as a rough estimate. These are numbers you perhaps should have considered before starting a war against an enemy who outnumbers you by at least 200 to 1 in population and 400 to one in resources."

Darron considered protesting that the VolatarA started the war by docking to the *Persephone*, even though they had been warned not to. He decided that a war guilt argument would get nowhere, and discussing education was more fun anyway. He asked, "Did you go to a special university to get your advanced degree?"

"VolatarA education above the local and planetary level is normally performed aboard ship, rather than at a fixed location," answered Duleka. "All VolatarA receive training at the local level. This training is provided in local education institutions. At the time of completion, all graduates are brought forward as a group, usually 144,000 at a time, to a local graduation center where the local imperial representative personally reviews them. He or she then calls them to their oath of loyalty first to the Emperor, then their oath to the region in which they have graduated, and lastly their oath to their fellow graduates. About 2% take the tests to enter Planetary-level training. This is not a reflection of low ability among the VolatarA who leave training at the local level. Many individuals are very qualified, but choose other careers. Planetary graduates attend a ceremony with their class of 1.44 million. The class stands in a block, 1,200 by 1,200. There are 6 races in the galaxy who can claim to have the strength to resist the attack a single class of VolatarA could deliver. 6% of the Planetary graduates continue to the Regional level of training. Regional graduations are held at the regional capital, so the students fly from their home planet to the graduation site.

Regional training is performed on the transport vessels. Students also perform as the crew of the ship during the flight. The process is repeated for the 6% who continue to Provincial training. There are eight provinces within the Empire, and each year, each graduates two or three classes of students who achieve Borasal rank. The most stringent competition is for the last level of training. Regardless of how many students apply, only one class of 1.44 million are taken for Imperial training. The Imperial graduation is held on Volatar, and is overseen by the Emperor himself. The graduates are given the highest rank of education – 'Volasal'."

"So if you were not the commander of the *Winged Vision*, does that mean an Imperial graduate was in command?"

Duleka laughed, the same way a Terran would. "No. Command is given to the most qualified, or the most responsible. Our commander was of Planetary level, although he probably could have gone higher had he not chosen to join his uncle in the exploration fleet. Educational rank is primarily used in determining who is appointed to government administration, and for military command. While any person can be appointed to any position in theory, in practice it is rare for anyone to be appointed to a level of administration higher than their educational rank. As our ship was part of the Regional exploration fleet, a junior commander who was of Planetary rank was not unusual. The hand commander is of Regional rank, and the fleet commander is Imperial." Darron started to ask a question and Duleka said, "A hand commander is a leader of five other ships."

"But you were an officer on board?" Darron asked.

"I was third in command. Now I am first. While promotion is exciting, this is not the method of promotion I would have intended."

"So who made the decision to attack the *Persephone*?" asked Darron. "The commander," answered Duleka. "My advice was to warn off the Suvain by destroying your ship, then claiming the wreckage by right of conquest. The commander decided to board the ship, as more information would be retrieved."

"I am glad you were not the one making the decis…," stated Darron. "In retrospect, my approach would have been preferable, but we are speaking with information provided after the fact. The commander's decision is not solely to be evaluated on the results."

"So if you are training for a high government position, why were you off in a scout ship?"

Duleka laughed again. "I have long wanted to work in a Provincial foreign service. The Imperial foreign service is the final authority on all matters, and deals with all communications with external developed species such as the Suvain. Exploration of new space is run by more local branches of the service – Regional and Provincial. I decided that in addition to formal training, I should get as much first-hand experience of exploration as I could before applying for an entry position. So instead of the usual military service, I volunteered for duties with an exploration fleet. While definitely I have gained experience in actual exploration, this was also not the experience I intended."

"You are speaking with information provided after the fact. The graduate's decision is not solely to be evaluated on the results," responded Darron. Both laughed, and, exhausted from even the short conversation, turned their attention to the next movie. Duleka watched as a crippled Terran ship crashed on a planet which appeared to have large, scaly, flying creatures that could breathe fire; he then realized that he could not get away from his cot, or the movie soundtrack. He began to suspect that the Terran torture had actually already begun.

To Duleka's relief, the Medical Officer decided to move him out of sick bay after two more days of old movies. He had turned off his translator the day before. MacDonald came with several crewmen and helped Duleka move out to a room that had been prepared for both the VolatarA. He asked if he could provide a wider range of entertainment; Duleka agreed, and it became common for MacDonald to bring in some Terran classic to watch together with the aliens.

The Captain had set Stephen to work deciphering the map. He was working with a capture of a specific display, so if the map had had any way to show different sets of data, the ability had been lost. There was only one level of detail; it showed individual systems, with what looked like summary information at several edges of the map. There was data associated with each system; without being able to read the numbers, Stephen was still unsure what was being reported. He had looked at the prefixes given to different planets and regions, and guessed that the prefixes indicated ownership of the system. Once he found out that the VolatarA were no longer in the sickbay, he brought a copy over to show to Darron. Darron was thankful for something to do, but found it hard to concentrate. It took him a full day to notice that the large section in the center of the map which shared the same prefix was divided into eight sections, and to remember that the VolatarA Empire had eight provinces.

As things came under control on the ship, the extra shifts began to ease up. Susan had done what she could to produce something that could work as a painkiller, but there wasn't enough material available to make much of a difference. When she had some time off, she headed over to see Darron. She found him and Stephen staring at the map display, which was currently hovering in the air over half of the sickbay. She stopped, and stared at the display. The rumors of the map had spread through the ship, but this was the first time she had seen the real thing. She asked, "What are the lines?"

"Intersections," answered Stephan and Darron together. "The lines are of different thicknesses," continued Stephen. "We are guessing that the size of the line indicates the size of the Intersection connecting the system. Some of the lines meet at spots that do not have star systems. We think those are empty zones – like the Kansu Transfer. There is a lot of information around each star system." Stephen pulled one of the images towards himself and pulled it out to a glowing sphere about a foot across. There were four lines moving into the system, one large and three much smaller. The central star had a series of VolatarA symbols underneath. There were six rings around the star; each had a small planet. The fourth had a long series of symbols, and the second and sixth had short lists of information.

"Do you know what the symbols mean?" She asked.

"No," admitted Stephen. She looked to Darron, who shook his head. "We have sent everything over the communication beacons. Maybe the linguists will have better luck," Darron said.

"There is a lot of writing by the star," Stephen stated. "Stars have a size, and a temperature; maybe the other information is about the planet in the system?"

"We do at least know which systems belong to the VolatarA," Darron continued. "The beginning of the name indicates ownership, and the VolatarA provinces are marked."

"It is odd that the information about the system is placed next to the star, but the name is placed at the top of the list by the planet," Stephen commented.

Susan had watched Stephen pull over a star system; she pulled another over. She pulled her hands apart like Stephen had, and saw an entire solar system grow in front of her. "I thought you found a picture?" asked Susan.

"The map has a massive amount of data, too small to read. I built the interface later." Stephen moved his hand and pulled another set of systems over.

"I am not sure this interface is a good thing. It feels a little too much like playing God," Susan said to Stephen, as she slowly rotated the new system in her hand. "This one is like the other – a bunch of data at the star, and on several of the planets. Are the symbols the same too?"

"The writing is different each time, but the same basic pattern," answered Darron. He sat up a little, looking at the chemist holding a star in her hand. Then he sat up suddenly, gasped at the motion, and managed to sling himself to a full sitting position. "Chemistry", he said.

Both of the others looked at him. "The key to a happy life," stated Susan. "What were you thinking about the truly useful science?"

The Physicist laughed and looked at the star. "Stellar emissions are not the same. Each star gives light with different intensities at different frequencies – never the same."

"Each star has a different chemical content – the light frequencies of the starlight are as unique as a fingerprint," Susan answered. The two stared at each other for a second, with faces full of excitement. Susan began grabbing stars and handing them to Stephen and Darron.

"Each one has data in two columns," announced Darron. "With one to three symbols in the first column and a bunch of symbols in the second.

"That could be the atomic number of each emission line, and the intensity," suggested Susan.

"The first symbol on the left is alone, and is the same on every star," stated Stephen.

"That will be hydrogen," answered Susan. "So this symbol must be the number one." They all looked at the single vertical line that made up the first symbol. She started through the stars, pulling out the likely numbers for elements with significant emission lines. After they realized that there were a dozen symbols for numbers, and started converting the atomic numbers to base 12, the lists of symbols began to match what starlight should look like. By the time Darron finally gave out, they were reading the numbers on the chart, and had started to try to match the stars they were seeing to similar recordings of known stars.

They met each day for the next week, Darron and Susan translating the numbers and Stephen making a Terran translation of the map. Just before the ship was ready to attempt its exit from the Kansu Transfer, they gave a report to the assembled officers. A Terran version of the map was shown, and Susan described what information had been determined by reading the numbers off of the planetary systems. Information that they guessed was either population or tax revenue were given for about a quarter of the planets in the province nearest to the edge of the map. Susan stated that they had guessed that population was shown, because a little over half of the planets had two entries – possibly for VolatarA population and for the surviving populations for subject races.

"This section of the map looks unfished," Susan continued. "This is on the fringe of the VolatarA Empire. There are far fewer populated planets, and the associated populations are smaller than those farther in. On the edge of what we believe is VolatarA-discovered space, there is this star." She pulled one system forward and expanded the region around it. "Note that the star has one thin line leading in, and the star has no planets. This star has the same distribution of frequencies as a star we already know – Chicago Cygnus Delta. We have found an Intersection to the same star, two Intersections out from New Chicago. A second star was found that matches a star out from Loren Station. And we think this end of the line shown at the very edge of the map is actually the Kansu Transfer. If so, all of Terran discovered space is in this dark area off the edge of the map." Susan pushed a button and a miniature version of Terran space appeared just off of the edge of the VolatarA Empire.

"We know the VolatarA are not the only threats out there – for instance, who can forget the Suvain." Susan indicated the portions of the Suvain Empire which were included. "We can see the Suvain stretching out to where we encountered them, but we can also see three other races which are within an Intersection or two of Terran planets or stations. If we look at the numbers listed for the Suvain planets, and what we guess are the 'Zatheur', the 'Nemi-Vemzl', and the 'Volsin', the planetary populations look small compared to the planets deeper in. We suspect that Terran space is on the edge of each Empire - all of the empires are expanding forward through this section of the Intersection connections. The easiest access to us is through Suvain space."

"So Tavir was correct in saying that others would be following up the Suvain's discovery," Captain Adams stated.

"They only have a few steps to take to be here. And considering that the news of our existence has spread, they will be here soon." Susan confirmed.

The surviving two-thirds of the *Persephone* was finally squeezed back through the Intersection. There had been a delay after the ship had started to compress for transit – the starboard side was a tangled mass of metal that couldn't be pulled in. The compression had been started, and then stopped. Everything that wouldn't compress was cut off the ship. The compression was restarted, and then stopped. Everything that wouldn't compress was cut off the ship. After the fifth set of amputations, enough was gone that the ship could slip through.

When the Persephone crossed, she entered the "Beta Quadrant" region.

The name traced back to the earliest days of Terran exploration. The Beta Quadrant had been the second region discovered via the Intersections. A solar system with six planets had been discovered. None of the planets were at a habitable range from the star, but one of the outer planets had some rare metals, and a surface hard enough to build a station on. Mankind's first extra- solar colony had been established, pulling out sets of rare metals, and pitching them out to the Intersection field. Alpha Station had not been very profitable; after the thrill of building the new station, the population dwindled. The station was eventually sold to a small, family-owned mining company. The new owners had squeezed out enough income to stay in business, and the entire family eventually moved to the station. They had lived there ever since.

The United Governments had ordered the evacuation of Alpha Station, and the destruction of any materials or devices that could lead the VolatarA back to Earth. As the *Persephone* headed to the Intersection field to Earth, they could see the first ship leaving the mining colony. Only a skeleton crew was being left behind to sanitize the station. As soon as they finished, they would be taking one last ship back to Earth. They had to hurry – if the VolatarA entered the region before they got away, they couldn't get home without leading the VolatarA straight to their destination.

The Beta Quadrant passage was not an enjoyable one for most of the surviving Persephone crewmen. The truncated ship was now flying without constant work; even Captain Adams could not keep the crew busy enough not to remember how many crewmen had been lost. Without distractions, the memory of the stress and fear of the fight was closer to the surface.

It had been suggested that a ship meet the *Persephone* with a full medical team and a treatment center. This idea had finally been given up. The ship would be leaving Earth and moving into the Beta Quadrant. From there it would have to accelerate towards the Kansu Transfer. The *Persephone* would be accelerating the opposite direction through Beta Quadrant; if the two did not slow themselves down, when they met, they would flash past each other in an instant. If they slowed down to meet at a stop, the *Persephone* would have lost so much time slowing down that she might as well just head for the Earth Intersection. A relief ship had been prepared; it was going to wait on the Earth side of the Intersection, since the *Persephone* would have to slow down for the transit anyway.

Darron's days alternated between soul-crushing boredom, and the excitement of having a visitor, nearly always either Stephen or Susan. Stephen's visits usually involved playing with the galaxy map, or discussing how the multiple-race on-line galaxy game should work. When Susan was visiting, the conversations were usually about history, or watching a movie. This was Darron's introduction to non-science fiction entertainment.

Strangely enough, he enjoyed watching almost anything if Susan was there watching too.

The *ProfitTaker* was most of the way to her second Intersection transfer when the news was received that the VolatarA had been encountered. Tavir sent back a reminder that the Terran ship was not to be taken by the VolatarA. His order was not mentioned in any of the stream of messages coming back from his scout ship. Other than telling GoDai to pray to his new god that the Suvain wouldn't do something truly stupid like shooting at VolatarA, there was nothing Tavir could do. –All updates were sent on ahead to the clan command center. Just as the *ProfitTaker* started to compress for transit, the news arrived that the VolatarA and Terrans were fighting. Tavir ordered that the transfer continue; they would catch up on the battle reports on the other side. After they were through and the ship had returned to its normal configuration, the messages were received announcing that the Terrans had defended against the VolatarA boarding parties and that both VolatarA ships had been destroyed.

Tavir read the last messages several times, then called together his officers. He laid printouts of the latest reports on the table. "So, what do you think really happened?" Everyone looked around at each other, no one wanting to say what everyone was thinking.

"But how would we have shot them both?" GoDai asked.

"I don't see how we could have," Tavir answered. "Unless the VolatarA asked to be shot, we couldn't have fired fast enough to take out both ships. The Terrans had to be involved somehow. But I can't imagine the Terrans taking out both either."

"If we couldn't have hit two, and the Terrans couldn't have taken out both, then each ship must have accounted for one VolatarA ship," suggested GoDai.

"Can anyone suggest a scenario where both VolatarA ships are destroyed, and we didn't just get into a shooting war with the VolatarA Empire?" asked the Tavir.

"Maybe the VolatarA tried to board from both ships, and the Terrans overwhelmed both VolatarA crews?" someone suggested. There was a pause, then suppressed laughter from around the table.

"Maybe they made two giant bombs, and snuck one onto each ship?" was the next suggestion.

"If they made a giant bomb, they would have blown themselves up," countered the Tavir. No one contradicted this statement. The Tavir sighed. "So does anyone have a suggestion for how I explain to my father that the biggest investment the Tavir clan has ever made is going to be challenged by an entire VolatarA exploration squadron?"

"Blame it all on DyanIanTavir," suggested GoDai.

"Blaming everything on the subordinate you are directly responsible for is rarely a good idea," the Tavir pointed out. "We could claim that they shot first."

"We have no idea if that is accurate," cautioned GoDai.

"We don't know it is inaccurate. Until we do, we insist on the possibility. Until there is proof otherwise, I believe and you believe that it is very possible that the VolatarA fired first, and that they owe us compensation and an apology." The Tavir looked around at the others, noting them flex their arms in acknowledgement of the order.

"A bigger question is what we are going to do next," GoDai stated quietly.

"That is not our problem. The future will be decided by my father." stated the Tavir. "But no matter what," he added, "Terra is going to pay off for the Tavir clan, even if this ship has to defend it alone."

Now that the *ProfitTaker* had exited the Intersection and expanded, the radars began picking up contacts only a few days away. The rest of the Tavir's fleet was present, along with seven other ships. All were clustered around a large shell that had been pulled through piece by piece. As the base was being assembled, supplies had been pushed through the Intersection, then grabbed by a ship. The ship would speed the package up towards the base, building it up to a significant speed, and then let it go. A second ship would catch it, slow it down, and bring it over to be placed in the growing hull. Pack by pack, food, missiles, and charged angulins were filling the station.

TavirAyan announced his presence in the region, and set course for the new clan outpost. As they grew close enough to make out details off the radar returns, they could see the command ship of the head of the Tavir clan tied up to the base. They could also make out the returns from a new group of four ships moving to the base. TavirAyan's younger brother TavirDai had arrived with the first ships of his fleet.

Before they landed, a message was received from The Tavir himself.

He had read the summary of the combat provided by his second son TavirAyan, and had one question: If the VolatarA had fired first, as TavirAyan had suggested was possible, how come the Suvain were still alive to fire back? As there was no real answer to this, no answer was given.

TavirAyan watched as his brother rushed to get to the base first. Trying to speed up seemed undignified, so TavirAyan stayed on a more sedate pace and let his brother win the race without showing that a race had ever occurred.

TavirAyan was still a little over a day out when TavirDai docked with the station. He led his officers and advisors aboard, and was greeted by his father. They embraced, and then The Tavir welcomed the new arrivals to the base, turned them over to one of his assistants, and led his third son to a private room. The room was near the top of the station, and had a clear wall section that gave a view of the stars.

"Welcome to our new home," stated The Tavir. "I have a feeling it will be our home for some time."

"The station is coming together quickly," TavirDai answered. "I will have all ships of my fleet and TavirI's advanced squadron here within the month."

"Good. And look there," The Tavir answered, pointing to several small circles that were displayed on the station wall. "Your older brother is going to be here within a few days." The Tavir watched his son tense, and give a slight arm flash. He turned to face him, and TavirDai turned as well. "I received a most interesting message from your older brother. He stated that his assistant had found definitive proof that the anonymous accusations raised against you were false. So apparently we can all rest secure, knowing that you were not treasonous to the clan."

"I was never treasonous to the clan!" TavirDai stated, arms flashing wildly. "And everyone knew it. Of course he has proof that the accusations are false – he made them himself."

"Everyone knows that. Everyone always has. You were competing for the chance to lead the survey efforts into the cluster. If there was the slightest question about your loyalty, you would not be chosen." The Tavir watched his third son go completely still.

"So if you knew the charges were false, why did you choose to doubt me anyway?" asked TavirDai; his arms continued to be exactly motionless, a sign he was very calm, or about to break into a truly violent rage.

"I didn't," answered his father calmly. He turned back to view the outside. "I had been leaning towards selecting TavirAyan before any of this came up. The anonymous warnings were irrelevant. It was your reaction that solidified my decision." TavirDai did not answer, so after a moment The Tavir continued. "When the statements were made, you reacted with an explosion of anger and denials. Such a response could only make you look weak, and did not have any chance of advancing your cause."

"What was I supposed to do, pretend it never happened?" demanded TavirDai. His arms were flashing again.

"Of course not," snapped his father, turning back, arms flashing in response. "You were supposed to look to see how the situation could be turned to your advantage, just like you are to look at every situation to see how it can be turned to your advantage. At least your brother had the initiative to throw something up to trigger a response."

"And how was being accused of treachery supposed to be an advantage?" quizzed the son.

The Tavir's arms flashed in amusement for a second. "Well, for a start, you could have openly laughed, not reacted with anger. Then you could have become serious and stated that this really did raise questions about TavirAyan — after all, if he had the slightest real claim to the position, he wouldn't have to be making up silly lies. That argument might have carried a lot more weight." The Tavir watched TavirDai. He was not motionless or arm-waving now; he was listening.

"Dealing with a bad situation by closing your eyes in anger is not useful. You have to open your eyes to opportunity. I am telling you this for two reasons. First, whatever is going on, we are all going to have to be working together, not fretting about old grudges. We all have to think of the clan first. You and your brother are going to have to cooperate. Second, when your brother comes on board and starts describing how we are stuck in some weird place in between war and peace with a bunch of primitives, and one of the strongest races in the galaxy is now shooting at us, I am going to have a great temptation to just shoot him; I will need you to repeat what I have just said back to me."

For the first time, TavirDai arms flicked for an instant in a slight smile. "Opportunity," he intoned.

His father laughed. "Opportunity," he proclaimed. "And dinner. I have accumulated a little better than ship food."

The *ProfitTaker* attached onto the base airlock. TavirAyan and GoDai waited in front of the rest of the crew as the seals locked. When the row of lights were out, TavirAyan pushed the button and opened the hatch. His father, brother, and a dozen others were waiting. His father welcomed the crew to the station, and turned over everyone but TavirAyan and GoDai to several of the base crewmen; he then led the other two straight to a briefing room. The Tavir moved to the head of the table, with TavirAyan on his right, TavirDai on his left, and DyanIDai, an advisor to his first-born TavirI, at the foot of the table. GoDai joined eight others in chairs around the walls.

"Let me summarize the current situation," The Tavir began. "Among a number of minor positive discoveries, we have also found a habitable planet occupied by a race of primitives that have already reached space. While we have been entertaining the primitives, the VolatarA have moved in to take the ownership position we would have expected to have already secured. So we have apparently responded by starting a shooting war with one of the strongest four races in the galaxy. Does that about sum things up?"

TavirAyan flicked his arms. "That is pretty close. I will argue about the details later."

"This does raise several questions," The Tavir continued. "For instance, why have we been entertaining primitives instead of occupying their planet? And possibly of more importance, how are we going to get out of this intact, much less showing a return for our investment?" Every eye turned to TavirAyan.

"Why don't we start with the first question," TavirAyan answered. "I am more confident that I have an answer for that one. We have been entertaining primitives rather than shooting them because we have a once-in- a-century opportunity to take control of an intact developed planet. I found out rather quickly that shooting a Terran did not impress the others. And they are a race that has already reached space. If they don't submit, they will not surrender easily. We will take significant losses subduing the planet, and we will get radioactive ruins – not a very profitable prospect. It was an opportunity that was worth talking instead of shooting, and worth taking risks for. Besides, talking was not much slower than shooting anyway. It is going to take everything we have to break the Terrans, and getting everything together takes time. With our full strength on display, we have a chance to demonstrate to the Terrans that resistance really will end in destruction." TavirAyan stopped for a second, then flashed his arms for a second and continued. "This is too big an opportunity to give up. I know we have been growing as a clan for the last seven generations. We have been careful, building money and strength, finally to put everything on this exploration concession. But the opportunity we have found is too big to reduce to slag or to just slink away from. This is what we have been building up for all these generations."

"Perhaps," answered The Tavir. "But the second question is still present. Granted that this is a huge opportunity, how do we possibly take hold of it? We can't stand up to a full VolatarA Exploration Squadron, much less fight the VolatarA and then overawe the Terrans."

The room was left in silence, only broken by a shifting sound from GoDai.

The Tavir looked over. His arms flicked for a second. "GoDai. You were calling for a Preventative Extermination, I believe. It looks like you will get your wish – the VolatarA are about to do the job you have been calling for." Lots of arms moved in brief flickers around the room. GoDai laughed back for a second. "But if we are going to stand aside and let the VolatarA clean out the Terrans, we still need to find a way to make such an action pay off for us."

"I gave up on the PE some time ago," GoDai said with another brief smile. He continued quietly, "I was going to suggest that we call on our allies."

"We have no allies," answered TavirDai. "We could ask other clans for help, but they would want a significant cut of any profits, and the profits might not cover our expenses even if we win. More importantly, at this point, this is a minor border skirmish between one Exploration Squadron, and one Tavir clan. If we start calling in a bunch more Suvain, the VolatarA will call in assistance as well – probably significant elements of one of their local Fleets. And those will be real warships, not just the exploration ships we are facing now. Given the risk, I am not sure we could convince anyone to come, no matter what the profit share we offered."

Quite true," agreed The Tavir. There were signs of agreement from around the room, including TavirAyan. Then TavirAyan turned to look at GoDai, and his eyes narrowed for a moment.

TavirAyan turned back to face the table. "I don't think he meant the Suvain clans," he stated.

"The Terrans are already at war with the VolatarA, and have every incentive to continue the fight no matter what." GoDai pointed out. "We have allies if we want them."

"And using the Terrans against the VolatarA should not bring in any greater VolatarA response," added TavirAyan. "It is not any addition to the current set of opponents the VolatarA face, and it is hard to see the local VolatarA commander deciding to call for the Imperial Fleet to help fight primitives."

"And if we do manage to defeat the VolatarA, which won't be easy with just us and some primitives, then we attack the Terrans?" asked TavirDai.

"We can argue about the ownership of the planet after we ensure that there is still a planet to be argued over," responded TavirAyan.

"That argument will probably be decided by what percentage of each force survived the combats with the VolatarA," pointed out The Tavir. "If anything does."

"What strength do the Terrans have, anyway?" asked TavirDai.

"They have quite a few ships," answered TavirAyan, directly speaking to his brother for the first time. "We visited one of their space stations, and there were 16 ships present. This station is probably on the main lines to one or more of their colonies, but that presence was just the ships that happened to be in the zone when we arrived. They support three colonies that are populous enough to require local governments. I would not be surprised if they had 100 ships, although mostly of small size. And the Terrans are very fast at converting ships into weapons. In the few weeks it took us to reach the station, they had converted a transport hulk into a gunship. Not a good one, but an armed ship anyway. It will probably be 10 or 15 months before the VolatarA can get a concentrated fleet against the Terrans. They will have converted a lot of hulls by then. They will be more like armed targets than real combat ships, but they will still be a significant force in a fight."

"Is there anything that suggests the VolatarA are not the usual Exploration Squadron?" asked TheTavir.

DyanIDai answered, "We have been checking on the statements coming out of the VolatarA embassy; nothing is suggesting they see this as anything more than a bit of firing between an Exploration Fleet and a clan. If we back off now, we don't think there will be any more conflicts with the VolatarA. If we press our claim to the planet, we do not think this will be seen as anything but a border skirmish. We have also been checking out the gossip among the foreign trade groups, especially the N-Vs. No one seems to think that there is more than one Exploration Fleet in the area."

"TavirI has also been entertaining his contacts within the financial sector. If we pull out of the fight, there are some questions about whether we will be able to uphold future claims in the sector, or whether the VolatarA will see our retreat as an excuse to push us around. If we decide to fight, then we think we can get the loans we will need to ensure we have full sets of ammunition. But the interest rates will be high, and the collateral will be high. If we get in a fight and lose, we should expect to lose most of our assets outside the sector as well." DyanIDai completed his update and sat back; everyone then turned to watch The Tavir's response.

"So we either pull in our spikes, and let the VolatarA get not just the planet, but the edge in the rest of the sector as well, or we bet everything on a fight against an opponent with larger ships, and more ships than we can put in the field," The Tavir summarized. He turned to TavirAyan.

"You were appointed to lead the exploration of the sector – what do you suggest?"

"Fight," TavirAyan answered immediately. "Maybe we will lose everything. But there will never be another chance for the Tavir like this one. A developed planet is worth everything we have, and more. And a developed planet is not just more than we are worth, it is more than we could defend on our own. But in this case, along with the opportunity, there is also an expendable fleet that is surely willing to give us the help we need to actually compete for the prize. If this isn't the opportunity that we have been building up to this entire time, what opportunity could we possibly think would be worth it?"

The Tavir looked around the room – every Suvain was sitting up a little straighter; no one was sitting with arms tucked in at all. He turned back to GoDai. "You said 'Allies', not 'Subjects'", The Tavir pointed out.

"If we tried to force them to surrender in order to gain our protection, they would have no incentive to build the fleet we need them to build," GoDai answered. "And if we offered them nothing more than the choice of serving us or serving the VolatarA, it won't be much motivation to surrender in the first place. If they will be slaves either way, they might as well just fight whoever comes first."

"Then how would we make a profit even if we did manage to win?" "If we do win," TavirAyan answered, "their fleet may be too weak to resist us afterwards. If not, even if we have taken serious losses, we can negotiate from a position of strength. Even if we had to agree not to take full ownership of the planet, just an agreement that we control the trade to and from their systems will give us more low cost, marketable goods than we can handle."

"If we have taken serious losses, and they haven't, what sort of position of strength will we have?" asked TavirDai. "What will keep them from trying to finish us off?"

"They know they need us," GoDai answered. "They don't know anything about galactic trade, and they know they don't know. They know there are more than just the VolatarA out there – if they destroy us, soon they will be alone against the Zatheur, or the N-Vs. They know they need us, and we can get more out of them willingly than with a fight. And there will never be a better chance to squeeze them for a trade deal that is ridiculously in our favor than there is right now."

The Tavir looked down at the table, thinking of how many generations had carefully built up the family wealth; this had usually been accomplished by not letting themselves get carried away by wild schemes. But TavirAyan was right – if they hadn't been building up to try for something like this, what had they been building all this time for? "Maybe there are times when it is worth getting carried away," he mused quietly to himself. The entire room, dead silent as they watched him, heard every word. The Tavir looked around the room again, and looked back to TavirAyan and GoDai. "Whatever agreements we make with the Terrans only last for as long as the VolatarA are a threat. There isn't to be any more of the trade agreement nonsense.

They are a bunch of primitives - they can't be trusted to honor their word. We fight the VolatarA, and in the unlikely event that we are still alive, we deal with the Terrans to whatever extent our fleet will still allow." The room was filled with flashing spikes and words of agreement from the other 11 Suvain. The Tavir looked at his excited relatives and commanded, "We will be fighting the VolatarA soon enough. I don't want anyone getting overly enthusiastic and trashing our own station." There was laughter around the room; the excitement was still there.

"We have to make sure that this stays localized – that there isn't escalation on either side. That is going to have to be my main focus, at least for the near future." The Tavir stated.

"The Terrans will need to be convinced to work with us, and formal agreements will need to be set in place," TavirAyan stated. "They already know me, and I already have some experience navigating around the ocean of Terran government officials. "I would probably be the most likely choice to interface with the Terrans." There were nods of agreement from around the room, but TavirDai just sat with eyes narrowed, wondering what this latest power play of his brother might be.

TavirAyan continued, "I was appointed the leader of the exploration effort in this sector, but I will not be able to run the sector and deal with the Terrans. As I will be fully occupied, perhaps TavirDai should replace me as the sector commander?"

The room went silent. Everyone was watching the two brothers.

GoDai's eyes had gone wide, then narrowed again. "An interesting suggestion," The Tavir stated. "He would be a natural choice. Of course, that would mean that he was, technically, your superior." There were quick flicks of elbows around the room.

"That is true," agreed TavirAyan. "But we will have to have someone here, to move forward supplies, and to gather the rest of the Tavir clan fleet. Besides, there is still exploration to be done in the sector, and the light ships might as well continue. TavirDai is the best choice for the position."

"True", agreed the Tavir. "With one exception. I don't want command changing in front of the Terrans. When the combined fleet is together with the Terrans, TavirAyan is in command." With that restriction, TavirAyan is moved to the position of Terran representative, and TavirDai is promoted to sector commander."

The Tavir looked back and forth between his sons. "I expect full cooperation between the two of you." Both tucked in their spikes for a moment in acknowledgement. "So, we have committed our clan to the most risky scheme in its entire history. That is probably enough for one day.

Dinner is served in the main dining hall."

As the room began to empty, TavirAyan and TavirDai continued to sit facing each other. Finally TavirDai asked, "What are you after, anyway?"

TavirAyan did not answer or a second. Finally he answered a different question. "In the past, I lost sight of an important fact. What is important is not whether you or I are standing in front. What is important is that the clan is moving forward. That is something I am not going to forget again."

"What I am after now is Terra. It is the biggest opportunity the clan will ever have. And if we are going to turn this opportunity to our gain, several things are going to have to happen. We are going to have to convince the Terrans to not fight us, and to fight the VolatarA. We are going to have to get everything the clan has to Terra in time. For the first task, I am the most appropriate – I already know them. For the second – you are the most appropriate. So I should be the one to do the first, and you should be the one to do the second. This has the disadvantage that this means you are now my superior. But it is not important which of us is in front, what matters is that when this is over, the Tavir clan is still here, and the Tavir clan has control of the wealth of Terra."

The next day, the first planning meeting was held. The Tavir let TavirDai take charge. TavirDai described what ships and resources were already present, and asked TavirAyan for a summary of what was known about the Terrans. After TavirAyan's description, the two brothers moved on to list out the supplies needed to bring the current fleet to full readiness. The meeting ended with a conversation about what sort of terms should be offered to the Terrans. When the meeting ended, the Tavir and both brothers led the way to the dining hall. With the prospect of a fight looming, the Suvain were all in a good mood. After a dinner in which more members of the clan were introduced to the joys of Krola, and lots of boasts at the VolatarAs' expense, every group returned to their ships. TavirAyan turned and saluted his brother, received a salute in return, and turned to go. Halfway back to the ship, he stopped, and looked back towards the dining hall. The four other with him stopped as well, all in a good mood, arms swinging loosely. TavirAyan looked back for a few moments, then turned back towards his ship. He focused on GoDai for a second, then punched him solidly in the face, knocking him to the ground. TavirAyan calmly turned and started back to the ship. The others stood in shock for second, looking at the two of them.

GoDai automatically started to jump up and strike back, but after getting up, he just stood and watched TavirAyan leave. As they continued to the ship, TavirAyan started up in conversation again with the other three, happy and relaxed and excited, just as if nothing odd had happened. If anything, he was more cheerful than before.

GoDai followed the others to the ship. When they got there, the others broke off to their separate rooms, and TavirAyan wandered over to the Captain's Annex. GoDai followed him in. TavirAyan did not appear surprised at the company – he just walked over and sat down in his usual chair. GoDai sat down across from him without asking.

GoDai felt his jaw for a second, flashed his spikes and stated, "There are other ways of admitting you have lost an argument with a subordinate."

Tavir flicked his spikes for a second and answered, "Yes, but none that feel so satisfying."

GoDai waited for him to continue, but nothing more came. He finally asked, "So what was my final winning argument?"

Tavir flashed his spikes again for a second, then relaxed, and looked out the window. "It wasn't your argument at all," he explained. "It was the argument of the man I shot." Tavir looked back to GoDai and stated, "After dinner tonight I had to admit, it is a greater thing to be reconciled to one's brother than to conquer a city."

"So what are you going to do now?" asked GoDai.

"Well, I don't want to join a primitive cult, but I also can't ignore that you, and the priest, have been right all along. I wonder if there is any way that everything someone says is correct, but everything they base all of their statements upon is false?"

"Why don't you find out more about what we actually believe, before deciding if it is true or false?" GoDai suggested. "You know we believe in God, and that we believe that God became a Terran – Jersurs. Why don't you see what he said, and see if it is reliable?" GoDai turned the monitor around and brought up his private collection. He selected a couple of books, and sent them over to Tavir. "Read what he said. See if it really is the basis for the statements you have already decided are true."

"This is an all-or-nothing sort of thing, isn't it", asked Tavir. "In the end, there is no halfway."

"No", agreed GoDai. "After all, we are talking about truth, and there is no halfway about truth. A statement like 'There is a God' is either true or false, and there is no logical way to pretend there is any other case." GoDai stood up and turned to go. Then he stopped. "One thing that he said was that if someone hits you on the cheek, to turn the other cheek, instead of hitting back. For instance, I am letting that previous blow pass, and sitting and talking with you instead of getting a gun."

Tavir flicked his arms out again. "Or you are letting it pass because I am your superior, and because if it came to physical combat I would win?" he suggested.

"Well, true, and true. But I would still like to point out that such self- control shows strong moral character." Both laughed, and GoDai returned to his compartment.

After four days of planning, TavirAyan was ordered back to the Terrans to start negotiations. The night before they left, TavirAyan walked into the small conference room the Christians were meeting in. Everyone went silent; TavirAyan walked up to GoDai.

"So what do you do here?" Tavir asked. "Is it like the meeting I went to before?"

"Mostly," GoDai answered. "So are you here to watch? Or for something else?" TavirAyan did not answer. "You are welcome to watch if you want." TavirAyan did not answer. "Or, if you are here to join us, you walk up to the table on the left and eat one of the food capsules, and drink one of the water containers." TavirAyan did not answer for a second.

"This is that ceremony near the end of the book?" he finally asked. "Yes," said GoDai. TavirAyan did not answer. Everyone else was just waiting and watching.

"I think I will just watch for now," TavirAyan answered. The service was held as usual, and then TavirAyan, GoDai and the other nine went back to their rooms.

The *ProfitTaker* headed out the next day, with TavirAyan's ships in company. All had recharged from the base, and headed out with the highest acceleration they could maintain. They sent word ahead to the TavirAyan's returning disobedient scout ship; it was to wait at the Intersection for the rest to arrive. Tavir told GoDai that he could use the off-duty area for meetings. GoDai and the other Christians starting meeting every other day. Tavir came and watched; since the captain was there, a lot of the other crewmen came as well. Soon over half the crew would assemble, and watch GoDai and the others hold their service.

Even at maximum acceleration, it took a full two weeks to get back to the Intersection. Tavir was busy working on the offers he would give to the Terrans, and the threats he would declare if they hesitated. GoDai had been assigned the task of collecting together everything known about the VolatarA, and preparing training sessions for the crew. Most of the crew were kept busy running practice drills – repairing equipment while using only half their tools, practicing loading missiles, and aiming the point defense cannons at simulated incoming missile swarms. The tradition took hold that at the end of each successful session, the participants would share a secret cup of Krola. Between practices there wasn't much to do, so crewmen sat around and made bets on what Tavir was going to do to DyanIanTavir when he reported in.

As they approached the Intersection, everyone was waiting to see what excuses would be broadcast from the waiting ship. Nothing came. Finally, the fleet decelerated almost to a stop to squeeze through to the Loren Station solar system, and Tavir finally sent across an order for DyanIanTavir and his officers to come aboard to explain themselves.

Everyone who could find an excuse was watching DyanIanTavir and his three highest ranking crewmen as they came on the *ProfitTaker* and stood at attention in the airlock. They were met by an ordinary crewmen, who told them to follow him to the off-duty room. When they came in, TavirAyan and eight others were waiting. Everyone waited for TavirAyan to speak, but he said nothing, just stood looking at DyanIanTavir. Once he waited long enough for everyone to be nervous, TavirAyan finally asked, "So, were my orders somehow not clear?"

"You said to ensure that the Terran ship was not captured. The Terran ship was not captured," answered DyanIanTavir.

"Did you miss the part about not starting a war with the VolatarA?"
"We were very careful not to take any action against the VolatarA," DyanIanTavir claimed.

"Other than shooting them!" Tavir shouted.

"We made our ownership of the Terrans very clear, but backed away from the combat," DyanIanTavir countered.

"Nothing in your orders allowed for attacking the VolatarA."

DyanIanTavir decided the best defense was a strong offense. "A single unarmed Terran ship was putting up a good fight against two armed attackers. You would have done just the same", he stated.

"I would have followed orders," Tavir said with finality. This was such an enormous lie that everyone in the room just stood looking at the Tavir.

After a few moments, Tavir continued. "It doesn't matter what I would have done. You were supposed to follow orders. Now that you have gotten us into a war, do you have any suggestions? Maybe toss you and your ship to the VolatarA as a peace offering?"

"Join the Terrans," replied DyanIanTavir. There was arm waggling from around the room, as everyone waited for Tavir's response.

Tavir stood looking at his subordinate. The room went still, but Tavir didn't respond. Finally he stated, "You aren't going to join the Terrans.

Someone needs to go back through to where you met the VolatarA before. They will start their search there, and we need to know how fast they make progress. Of course, it is likely that they will notice your presence and that will be the last time you cause trouble. We brought along four extra reloads to replace the missiles you spent. The cost is coming out of the pension funds of your crew. Half of the cost is from the officers, and half of that is from you."

There was a gasp from the onlookers, but Tavir didn't notice. "If they do see you, do not lead them back here. You have already started a war; we don't need you bringing them to us before we are ready." Tavir watched DyanIanTavir acknowledge the order, then continued. "While you reload, I want you to recharge your ship from the fleet. This is the last spin-up you are going to get for a long time, so be sure to conserve your angulins as much as possible. I want to know when the VolatarA get there, how many they are, and how fast they discover their next Intersection. If their search is towards Loren Station, tell us at once." Tavir finished, and narrowed his eyes at his junior captain. "And if by some miracle you survive this assignment, maybe you will live to retirement. And then you will have just enough money to rent some tiny room on a planet somewhere. Sitting there, you will have lots of time to dwell on the importance of obeying orders." He dismissed everyone, and stalked back to his Annex.

Four ships closed in and joined to the scout ship. Power transfers began, spinning up the angulins on the *DoorFinder* to their maximum speed, feeding in as much power and momentum as the ship could hold. While the recharging was in process, DyanIanTavir went to the storage bay of the *ProfitTaker* to move across the four missiles that had been brought for him. He had already decided that if it came to a fight, the missile he was paying for personally was going to be fired last. Maybe if everything went well, the missile wouldn't be fired, and he could return it for at least a part of his pension. Nearly everyone else went with him. Surprisingly, there had been four extra missiles delivered to the Tavir base that hadn't been tracked on any manifest. As they weren't really part of the family assets, spending them really didn't cost anything. The crew could ask the Tavir about them, and he would surely get them recorded properly. But he was so busy. Maybe they should just stick them on the *DoorFinder* for the moment, while someone looked up where they came from. Of course, moving the missiles would take a long time, so maybe DyanIanTavir could give them a first-hand account of the fight with the VolatarA? The four visitors started a long description of the combat. With the questions from the audience, no one was thinking about loading the missiles at all. Eventually, the Tavir clicked his display over to the loading bay cameras and noticed his entire crew standing around, talking and laughing. The crew heard his outraged orders, and the comment that he was coming down in ten minutes; if the missiles weren't gone, he was taking the first crewman he met and personally throwing them out an airlock. He did arrive ten minutes later, just as the last missile was leaving the storage bay.

Extraneous crewmen were heading out each door. The Tavir saw the task was being completed, and headed back to his Annex. Then he replayed the security tapes from the storage locker back to where the four started their description, turned up the volume on the recording, and listened to the entire story.

When the *ProfitTaker* crossed over to the Loren Station system, messages from the Terrans were waiting. In addition to greetings, there was an invitation to come to Loren Station for negotiations concerning a joint response to the VolatarA. Tavir signaled his acceptance, and the fleet started towards the station. In the days they had before contact, Tavir reviewed the notes from the clan meetings, and wrote out possible agreements with the Terrans. Drills continued, if only to keep the crew busy. When the ships were about four days out from the station, the Christians were meeting again, and Tavir was in attendance as usual. When the service ended and the Christians started to eat and drink, everyone suddenly stopped. TavirAyan had gotten up and was walking forward. The people in front of him stepped aside, and TavirAyan walked up to the table, ate a food capsule, drank down a water container, and went back to his seat. He looked at everyone watching him, and stood up. "When we talk with the Terrans, no one is to know I have joined this clan. It would weaken our negotiating position." He then got up and walked out, followed closely by GoDai. There was a pause, and then everyone in the room behind him started talking at once.

The Terrans had set aside six landing spots together, with camera crews on hand to film the joint landing of TavirAyan's ships. The Tavir landed, and after ten minutes of securing the ships, each crew marched out in silvery armor. Each officer had a holster with a Suvain hand-gun, but the rest were unarmed. A cloud of delegates were waiting in the inflated tunnel, and began clapping as the Suvain emerged. The cloud somehow smoothly divided in two, leaving a wide path leading to the interior of the station. Station personnel led the Suvain to the prepared reception, and after they had passed, the Terran blob recombined as it followed the Suvain into the permanent structure.

Negotiations started the day the *ProfitTaker* reached Loren Station.

Tavir and GoDai were met by CE Aguilera, who led them to a meeting room; six Terran delegates were waiting inside. All rose, and CE Aguilera performed introductions.

"We have been appointed as representatives for the United Governments. Each of the Regional governments are also represented.

We have been authorized to discuss what joint action could be arranged between the Terrans and the Suvain, to the benefit of both."

"So I need to speak with you, and not individually with every one of the hundreds I talked to before?" Tavir questioned.

CE Aguilera smiled for a second. "Any agreements have to be confirmed by the larger body. But you only have to talk to us, and we have to deal with the other Terrans."

"Deciding on you seven must have been a painful process – from what I saw last time, every Terran would have expected to be here." There was laughter from around the room.

"I must admit, I have been looking forward to dealing with you, instead of dealing with us," CE Aguilera answered. "But you really do have to deal with this group, not the entire mob. If we can reach an agreement," he continued, "we are confident that getting approval for the agreement from the community at large will be accomplished." There were nods from the other delegates.

"This is better news than I had expected," Tavir answered. "A group of manageable size is a big improvement. Now, if you have realistic expectations, I have great hope for the future."

CE Aguilera nodded, and the horse trading began.

The talks ran on for days, even though CE Aguilera and Tavir had started with reasonably close opinions of what "reasonable expectations" were. The rest of the Suvain crews were enjoying their time as celebrities, being entertained by different Terran groups in succession. After watching his crew get looser and more tired each night for three consecutive days, Tavir ordered every captain to find tasks for their crews for at least 12 hours a day. There was enormous grumbling, and occasional accidental spiking of breakable objects, but the crews were pulled back into discipline before they became too unmanageable.

The officers kept themselves to the restricted leave given the crew. On the seventh day of the stay, Tavir informed GoDai that they needed to go to the religious leader that GoDai had visited before. GoDai called to say they were coming, and led Tavir to Girelli's office.

Girelli greeted them as they came, and offered each a seat. GoDai sat down, and Tavir remained standing. He stood looking at Girelli;

the other two waited for what he had to say. Tavir flashed his spikes a few times, and then said, "There is something I am supposed do. It is supposed to occur now." Both of the others kept listening. While reading, I found a statement by KaarenI that is probably relevant." Both of the others looked confused for a moment, and then GoDai turned to Girelli to explain.

"There is an old word in Suvain, 'Kaaren', that is similar to your word 'God'. 'I' indicates the first-born son, or heir. So 'KaarenI' would translate as 'The first born son and heir of God.'"

"All those primitive names are confusing," stated Tavir. "The title is easier. Anyway, there was a statement that if someone has a just claim against you, you should give them justice. This is to occur at this time, rather than at some point in the future. From GoDai's statement, you are of the same clan as the religious leader onboard the *Persephone*." Girelli nodded, and Tavir continued. "At our first encounter, the religious leader said something irritating, and I shot him, as a way of encouraging the Terrans to surrender peacefully. I did so under the impression that he was just a primitive; I had not realized that he, or Terrans in general, were sentient.

Knowing what I do now, I would have acted differently. I would not have shot your clansman." Tavir paused, and GoDai could see the slight arm flick inwards that marked a bigger apology than one could ever expect to see from a noble Suvain. "Do your people have some form of compensation required to account for the death of one of your own?"

GoDai started to explain to Girelli that this was a sort of apology from the Tavir, but he stopped; from Girelli's movements and facial expressions, it looked like Girelli understood what was happening. "No compensation is needed," answered the Terran. "There are lots of laws about murder in our society, but I think they are not considered relevant to the current situation.

More important than the law is for the wrongdoer to realize he or she has done wrong, and commit to do differently in the future, and for the wronged to realize that the wrongdoer is as covered by God's grace as they are. You have any forgiveness from us you need. And Eisen was a friend. I knew him well enough to know that he would not consider getting shot to be the thing that should decide our relationship in the future. He would say that we should desire your greatest gain now, just like he did before. Nothing would have made him happier than hearing this conversation, no matter what you had done, or what had happened in the past."

There was a brief arm flicker that GoDai recognized as relief. "So your people do not require any penalty for killing someone?" asked Tavir.

"There may be legal penalties for murder, but nothing is required for forgiveness. It was given by God to each of us, without anything from us in return. If you did something wrong, and it caused a harm that you could undo, you should undo what you can, whether you are forgiven by others or not. For instance, if Eisen had children that were now not provided for, you should provide for them, whether we forgave you or not. But that is for you, not for us. In this case, all of Eisen's children are long since grown, and provide for themselves – you need have no concern."

Girelli indicated the seat again, and Tavir sat down. Girelli continued, "I think if he knew he was going to be shot Eisen would not have minded.

After all, he died in the place God told him to be, doing the thing God told him to do. I can't imagine a better end."

"So that is it – we are considered even again?" asked Tavir.

Girelli laughed for a moment. "We are not 'even'. We are friends."

Tavir looked at the other two and then stated, "You know that my father may still decide to abandon you to the VolatarA. Or to move in to conquer you himself. Nothing has changed that."

Girelli nodded. "And if it comes to a war, you were made a Suvain, not a Terran. It will be your father's decision, not yours. Your responsibility is to encourage your father to do what is right."

Tavir and GoDai were silent, then Tavir stated, "I would tell you not to speak of this conversation to anyone, but that would be asking you act against your species."

"It is not acting against my species. I am the chaplain for the station. All such conversations with me are to be private, not shared with anyone. Everyone here knows this. I will not be speaking of what the conversation was about, and they will not be asking me."

Any possible gossip about the actions of the Tavir would have been forgotten two days later, when CE Aguilera and TavirAyan announced a joint request to speak to the full assembly of delegates. The meeting hall was filled to capacity; the negotiating team sat on the platform facing the crowd. Beside them sat TavirAyan, GoDai, and three other Suvain.

There was a brief introduction, and then CE Aguilera rose to the podium. He gave a brief description of the meetings held with the Suvain, and then announced that an agreement for common action against the VolatarA had been proposed. There were flurries of applause; CE Aguilera restored order by continuing to speak.

The description continued for nearly half an hour. The first clauses described military cooperation, including joint planning and joint fleets. The next section listed out Suvain rights to use Terran resources and bases.

Section three declared that all intelligence gathered by both races would be fully shared with each other. Section four affirmed that neither side would make any separate alliance or agreement with the VolatarA without the full knowledge and agreement of the other. The document ended with the commitment by both sides to act as allies "for as long as needed to force the VolatarA to accept the rights and liberty of each race". At the conclusion, CE Aguilera gave the audience time to applaud. He then formally requested permission to sign for the Terran race.

Of course, there could be no signing without the chance for everyone to ask questions. CE Aguilera waited for someone to ask the obvious. He acknowledged the first hand.

"From what you have described, this agreement only lasts until the war with the VolatarA is over. What assurances are we given that the Suvain will not attack once the war is over?"

"None", answered CE Aguilera. The entire room was quiet, but he did not continue. After a long pause he stated, "There is no discussion of any relationship between the Suvain and the Terrans after the war is won."

"We have made no attempt to convince the Suvain to make any binding settlement with the Terrans in the future. I believe that joint action against the VolatarA is required. This agreement will establish that joint action.

There should be no illusions about what we are doing this day. We are forming an alliance against a common enemy. When two nations form an alliance against a common enemy, the alliance lasts as long as the common enemy lasts. When the common enemy is gone, the alliance is gone as well."

"An alliance lasts if it the best option for each side. When the common enemy is gone, both sides will make decisions about what is best for them – decisions that will be based on an entirely new set of conditions and criteria. Those decisions will drive different agreements or conflicts. We could ask or demand that the Suvain promise us that after this war, we will be best friends. But those promises would be worth less than the paper they are signed on.

Instead of bringing forward a treaty that sounds good, and is not realistic, we are bringing forward a treaty that addresses our current situation, and will be real."

"There are many challenges ahead for the Terrans. What we must focus on today is the challenge right in front of us. If we do not turn back the VolatarA, nothing else will matter. We are not here today to ensure the future of the Terran race. We are here to ensure we live one more day. Tomorrow's troubles will have to be dealt with tomorrow."

VIII

The *Persephone* had returned to the Earth system, and had been sliding easily down to a repair station above Earth. Darron was on his second rehab assignment. He had been transferred to the hospital ship that had been waiting on the other side of the Intersection field. The medical staff had offered Darron two choices – the leg could be removed, or a metal shaft could be installed, with a computer-controlled artificial knee. Darron immediately chose the second option. He had lots of reasons why; Stephen announced (correctly) that Darron just wanted a computer implanted in his knee, so he could claim he was a cyborg.

Soon after the surgery, the medical team had Darron up and walking on the rebuilt leg. He had grumbled before about not getting to do anything, and now grumbled about having to exercise regularly. Grumbling did not help him avoid having to recover. The medical team had him walking around well enough in two weeks that he could be transferred back to the *Persephone*.

Stephen had planned a celebratory try of their new game, but Captain Adams put Darron to work as soon as he came back onboard.

Darron was surprised to find that part of his new tasking was to join in the entertainment provided to the VolatarA. There were gatherings every couple of days to watch movies or to sit and talk about Terra, the Suvain, or the VolatarA. He had not expected that Duleka would remember him from their brief conversation in sick bay. Darron was excited to see that he had been so memorable until he realized that the VolatarA appeared to remember everything he had been told and everyone he had met.

Soong was usually the organizer of the evening's activities. Of the Terrans, he was the only one who was at every event. It wasn't long before Darron found the entertainment duty his least favorite task. Unlike the meetings with the Suvain, now there were plenty of Terrans present. Darron quickly settled into his usual social role of the silent, awkward guy sitting in the corner. Stephen and Susan were there most of the time; Stephen sat by Darron, and Susan tended to end up in the front near the aliens.

In between awkward social events, Darron was sent to a part of the ship he had never seen before. His first day in Auxiliary Controls, he started around at the banks of green and red lights, wondering why anyone would have sent him somewhere both practical and important. He was met by one of the engineering team, who led him to the two seats in front of a bunch of displays.

One of the displays showed the solar system and the *Persephone's* current orbit. Darron settled down in front of the display and forgot everything else. He looked over the current path of the *Persephone*; she was making a rather steep drop toward the Sun. Her current course would swing around past the star, come back out towards the Earth, and then fly past.

Darron could see a series of dots on the path, and recognized them as the points at which the *Persephone* would be firing up the angulins, pulling back against all the speed the ship was gaining as she fell towards the Sun. With each maneuver, the *Persephone* would lose energy. Along with the red curve indicating the ship's current path was a green curve, showing the predicted course that she was expected to follow if the maneuvers were performed as expected. The green curve showed the ship slowing itself down over and over as it spun down around the star, and again as the ship pulled back up near Earth. Finally, a last set of maneuvers brought the ship into an orbit around the planet.

Darron had already happily lost himself in the ship's orbit when his new superior tapped him on the shoulder. Darron was informed that he was now the navigator of the reserve command crew, and his heart soared. Then he was informed that as a member of the reserve command crew, he had to learn to monitor all the other ship systems, and all good feelings went away.

Susan had been assigned to the bridge crew – some new system was being put in to track the status of the entire ship and equipment, and Susan was going to be one of the operators. Susan had pointed out that the new assignment really wasn't that similar to her previous heavy-element study. Her comment had no effect; her superiors appeared to consider the task to be one that a Chemist could safely be assigned to in what was about to become a warship.

Stephen was the only one of the three who really enjoyed his new tasking. Most of his time was spent in re-loading control software for the ship systems that were being put back on line. The rest was going to making "repair packs". Stephen was loading hardware drives with packages of system software that could be plugged into damaged equipment. The pack would then go through the device and replace all damaged software, bring the equipment back up, and, if possible, reconnect it to the rest of the ship.

Darron ended a shift in Auxiliary Controls and headed for the mess hall. He found Stephen already there, and Susan was heating her dinner. Darron and Susan were on the same training schedule; Stephen was able to pick his own work times. Darron sat down with Stephen; Susan joined them only on the condition that Darron not complain about his assignments. With complaints not allowed, the conversation turned to the changes planned for the ship. Nothing had been announced about what was going to happen.

Susan and Darron knew what new systems were being added to the Bridge and Auxiliary Controls, and Stephen was already getting instructions for connecting new elements to the ship network. Between the three, they had a reasonable guess of what was coming.

The starboard side of the ship had been torn off, but the center and portside were mostly intact. New systems were being added to the Bridge to control weapons. New targeting and communication systems had already been delivered when the medical ship docked with the *Persephone*. The cables from the new controls were all being laid out towards the missing starboard side. The consensus at the table was that the missing starboard side was going to be filled by a row of weapons.

"I heard new power cables from the angulins are being laid as well", Susan mentioned quietly. "It looks like replacement angulins will be coming. But they aren't balanced. At lot of the cables are near the middle of the ship, not nearly as many around the fore or aft. There are cables headed all across the starboard side; some are near the new angulin connections, and others aren't."

"There were two different kinds of weapons on the *ProfitTaker*", Stephen pointed out in a low voice. "Some were like a giant angulin gun, and some were missile launchers, like we saw on the VolatarA ship."

"One big difference was how the weapon was charged", Darron responded. "The big guns looked like they fired a shell - the gun itself was powered by the ship's angulins. The missile launcher was different. It fired a huge missile; the missile must have had angulins inside that provided the thrust for the warhead. Maybe that is the difference we are seeing – some of the new weapons are going to be guns, and some will be missile launchers."

"If that is the difference, we are getting two or three of the guns, and about four missile launchers", Susan stated.

"If the guns get all their momentum from the ship at one time, they couldn't go as far as the missiles. Since the missile could keep accelerating towards the target after it was fired, it could build up a much greater speed. The guns would have to be for close range fighting," Stephen mused.

"Closing to close range to a ship that is trying to avoid contact would be really hard," countered Darron. "If the ships were approaching each other, they would flash past each other in an instant. Unless they both chose to match velocities and come together. You might get a single shot as you passed, but with the velocities involved, it is hard to believe you would be likely to hit anything."

"So they aren't for shooting at ships. What else are they for?" asked Susan.

"What about missiles?" asked Stephen after a moment. "Hitting a missile that is trying to stay pointed straight at you has to be a lot easier problem."

"So the missiles are for shooting at ships, and the guns are defensive weapons." Susan concluded.

"Even with a missile that can target itself as it closes on the target, hitting a ship in motion seems next to impossible," Darron stated. "If the ships were on different orbits, they would flash past each other in milliseconds. There would only be one chance to hit. And if the missile is going to have time to make a course connection, it will have to commit to its course change a ways away from the target. Even if the missile can make very fast course changes, it would take time for the missile to register the target's position and then make a course correction. In that time, the target will have moved a significant distance. Because of light-time delay, the missile would have no chance to know what the ship's last-minute course changes had been. How would the missile ever hit?"

"So at the last minute the ship could have changed course, and the missile wouldn't be able to tell?" Susan asked.

"The ship could be anywhere - well, anywhere within a circle around the last known position. How could the missile ever cover the whole circle – it would pass through a single point on the circle as it flew past." Daron continued.

"Sprayers!" Stephen exclaimed. Both of the others looked at him in confusion. "Some of the Suvain talked about their weapons when they weren't careful. Sometimes they referred to "sprayers". Stephen looked at the others and saw that they didn't understand. "The missile must spray out – the missile warhead must be made of a bunch of tiny warheads that all spray out around the target's expected location. Like a shotgun shell."

"The circle the ship could occupy would still be really big. Even if the missile blasts out like a shotgun, even with hundreds of shotgun pellets, the amount of area you could cover would be really small." Darron stated, still unconvinced.

"What if the little ones had angulins too," asked Susan.

Darron stared at her for a few seconds. "Then they could make small last-minute corrections, after the main correction had been made by the missile before its warhead fires." Darron slid his food to one side, and squeezed some of his water onto the table. He drew a large circle. "So the missile closes on the ship, and centers itself on the predicted position of the ship when the missile path and the ship path cross. Since the missile will have a limit to how fast it can change course, there will still be a significant distance to the ship when the missile makes its final course change. Then the warheads fire out. In the time it takes the warheads to reach the ship, the ship may have changed course. So it will be anywhere in this circle. So the warheads are set to spread out over the circle, and would have to have tracking devices and their own thrusters." Darron dropped a bunch of water droplets around the circle. "They each track the ship and make last minute corrections. They would have very little time to change course, so even if they can make a big acceleration, they aren't going to be able to change course that fast. But they will still be able to cover an area of the circle, not just a single point as they fly past." Darron smeared out the water droplets, leaving a large circle, most of whose area was covered in little water smears. Darron looked at the table and conceded, "With enough shots from the missile, if each could maneuver, most of the circle would be covered. I guess it would have a good chance to hit with at least one shot."

"Would the explosive from one small shot be enough to damage a ship?" asked Susan.

"It doesn't need an explosive," Stephen stated. "Unless the ship trajectories are very closely aligned, the closing speed will be tens of thousands of kilometers an hour. It will shatter whatever it hits; it will probably blast a hole through the entire ship."

"So if the area of the circle is completely covered, the ship will be hit for sure?" someone asked.

"The ship could make last-minute adjustments as well, but yeah, pretty much, that's true." Darron answered, looking at the circle. "Of course acceleration makes a huge difference. The bigger the acceleration the target ship can make, the bigger the initial circle will be. And maybe the ship could try to slide itself into areas of the incoming swarm that don't look as dense with warheads. The missile acceleration would be the other factor. The bigger the acceleration the warheads could make, the larger the area each one could cover."

"And our accelerations are low compared to what the Suvain, and probably the VolatarA, can achieve," said Susan in a quiet voice. "Our circle would be pretty small, and every VolatarA shot will cover a lot of area."

Darron looked up at Susan. "Yes," he answered. There wasn't much else to say. He realized that background noises he hadn't been paying attention to had all stopped. He looked around and found that a dozen other crewmen had gathered around their table. All were staring at the circle, and everyone was silent.

Finally someone said, "So every missile they fire will probably score a hit, and ours will be lucky to hit once in a dozen tries." Darron, Susan and the audience looked glumly at the circle.

Stephen shrugged. "So we just fire 50 missiles at each target," he stated in a matter-of-fact voice, and started eating again.

Stephen, Darron, and Susan watched the signing ceremony together. The signing ceremony was being broadcast across every Terran system and colony. About a third of the crew was gathered in the mess hall. As the agreement was signed, the room broke into cheers. After a moment, Darron had found that he had stopped clapping.

Susan touched him on the shoulder. He looked over and she asked, "What?"

Darron looked down. "I don't know. I guess, I guess I still hoped something would change. That somehow, we would be at the end of a war, not the beginning. But that's not going to happen. We are going to have to go back, and shooting will start all over. And even if we somehow get past the VolatarA, we will still have to deal with the Suvain. And even if we make it past that hurdle, there is a whole universe to deal with. Things really won't ever be the same."

"No," she answered. "But that has been true since we met the Suvain."

"True," answered Darron, without enthusiasm.

"The only difference is that today we have a chance. A chance that you have helped bring about." She saw Darron sort of shrug and snort and smile at the same time. "And look at the benefits you have already had. How else would you have gotten a computer implanted in your knee?" Both laughed, and Darron turned back to the display screen. They had watched for another five minutes when the Personnel Officer sat down next to Susan. All three stopped and looked at the newcomer.

"An officer steps in, and all conversation stops'" MacDonald stated. There was a little laughter. "You are correct," MacDonald continued. "My presence is a sign that more duties are coming. Now that the agreement is signed, meetings with the Suvain will begin in earnest. The high and mighty have decided that we will get the chance to participate. I think we are still considered among the experts on the Suvain."

Susan could see Darron freeze up and start to withdraw. She could also see Stephen sit up in excitement. She turned to MacDonald. "This means we still don't get leave, doesn't it."

MacDonald laughed. "No more than I do. When the *Persephone* swings around to the station, the crew will receive one full month's leave. Except for us. We will transfer to a transport headed back out towards Jupiter. There we will meet with the *ProfitTaker*. Once there, both sides will work on a common defense."

"And you really think that we can help?" asked Darron.

"You have spent more time with the Suvain than any other Terran alive," MacDonald answered. "If anyone can read Suvain body language, it is you three. And you have seen the Suvain in a number of different emotional states. You are probably our best shot at knowing if our allies of the moment have ulterior motives."

"So the future of the human race depends of the social skills of a physicist and a programmer? We might as well die now," Susan declared.

After the *Persephone* slid down past the Sun, she came back up to meet the Earth moving along the other side of the star. The Earth system was always crowded. There were a few construction facilities on the colonies, but almost every Terran ship was still built near Earth. Even though they had expected to see other ships, everyone was surprised to see other ships everywhere. Ahead and behind them were another seven ships, coming in on the same transfer orbit from the Beta Quadrant. On the transfer orbit from Loren Station were a total of 22 ships. 17 more were moving down from the Intersection that led to Alpha Quadrant – the first Intersection humans had discovered. There were seven orbiting stations around Earth, five owned by different Earth Fleets. Every station was the center of a cluster of ships. As they pulled up towards the planet, the number of ships constantly changed as ships launched up to the stations, and others dropped back down to the planet.

Most of the crew were from Earth; this wasn't surprising as over 99% of Terrans still lived on their first planet. The *Persephone* had left Earth two and a half years before, and had not been back since. Over half the crew had been with the ship the entire time. As the ship pulled closer to Earth, the atmosphere onboard started to alternate between excitement and nervousness sometimes bordering on panic. Darron would have been on the nervous side, but he was going the other direction. Since he wasn't getting leave, he felt completely justified in feeling like a martyr. As everyone else got the ship ready for its refit and the station, Darron gathered together his things for his new trip.

As the transport pulled alongside the *Persephone*, the four "Suvain experts" met by the airlock. There was no ceremony as they left – the Captain had everyone busy during their last days on duty. The airlock seal was set, the doors opened, and the time to leave the ship had come. Moving into the airlock, Darron looked back – leaving the ship was also leaving the home he known for most of the last two years. Then the interior doors closed, the outer hull doors opened, and the four left the familiar for the unknown. Their only reception was a crewmen assigned to open and close the airlock. Once they were aboard, they were informed of the location of their quarters, and directions to the mess hall. Then the crewman saluted and left, leaving the four standing in the corridor with their transport boxes in hand. They wandered around a little finding their rooms, then each moved in to a new tiny cubicle sort of like a hermit crab crawling into a new shell.

After they each emerged for dinner, the four went together to the mess hall. Once there, they all stopped, not sure what to do. The transport did not have the usual collection of prepared meals for each crewman. Instead, there was a large open room that had a number of tables scattered around, and a buffet line of food, in steaming trays. The steam was the first thing they automatically noticed; no attempt was being made to reclaim all the moisture that was drifting up from the trays. Then their eyes registered the open coffee cups. Focusing on the prepared, non-dehydrated food came next. Last was the realization that the entire room was filled with officers. They all stood for a moment, then MacDonald led them in saluting the room in general, and they headed over to the food. A steward told them where to find a tray and silverware. The next minutes were consumed by the delightful experience of walking down the line, filling their plates. The four then found a small table in the corner and clustered together for safety.

Very rapidly, they realized that the ship was occupied by three very distinct groups of Terrans. The first was the ship's crew. The crew ran everything; it was strange to realize that on this ship, the Persephones were not experienced crewmen, but instead were rather annoying cargo. The second group was comprised of the official delegates from the United Governments and each of the five regional governments. There were several high-ranking civilians from each government, and officers from each corresponding fleet. The officers started with Admirals, and went down in rank to Captain. As every regional government ran its own fleet, there were five of everything. Piled on top of the fleet representatives were the small corps of officers from the recently-formed United Defense Fleet. The Earth Space Command run by the United Governments had been transformed from an exploration organization into a corporate fleet tasked with the defense of the planet. The new United Defense Fleet officers were all members of one of the five regional fleets. This could lead to awkward moments when a UDF officer was trying to provide "instructions" to a higher-ranked officer from his own fleet. The third group consisted of all passengers below the rank of captain. That group consisted of the four crewmen from the *Persephone.*

Group 3 sat at their table, trying to avoid the attention of the room full of superiors. Their attempt at invisibility failed; a captain from the North American Defense Force walked over and introduced himself.

They all rose and saluted, then accepted the Captain's invitation to sit back down and continue their meal.

"Welcome aboard", he stated. "Captain Alan Sorenson." He waited as everyone introduced themselves. "Meetings have already started as we head to the conference with the Suvain. As preparation for the Fleet and Suvain meetings, each of you will find background materials on your terminals. Part of the reading is the background we currently have on the Suvain. A lot of this comes from your own observations. If you find that what you said is very different from what has been recorded, let me know. There are also descriptions of the various suggestions made by each fleet for fleet weapons and tactics. Pick up what you can in the time you have. The meetings will be held here. Space will be tight – expect to stand in back with the Captains", he said with a smile. "If something comes up during one of the meetings, you are free to speak up. Of course, if there is something you want to talk about in a less formal setting, you can always talk to me after the meeting." All four acknowledged the suggestion to stay quiet when the flag officers were speaking. "I will check in with you each morning," Captain Sorenson stated, and excused himself.

All four finished their meal, and started walking around, trying to find out where to put their trays. A crewman came and quietly informed them that they could just leave their trays, the crew would bus the table. Hoping that no one had noticed, they sheepishly set the trays down and fled the room. They found the way back to their shells and crawled back in.

Darron opened up the list of files on his terminal and looked through the list. There were a list of reports about the VolatarA, and a list of reports about the Suvain. It was odd to see his own name included on both lists.

There was another collection of files produced by every fleet that detailed suggestions of how to organize and use a fleet of ships in space combat. There were several informational documents that described the new relationship of the regional fleets and the new United Defense Force. A lot of the files were video captures of the Terran-Suvain and Terran-VolatarA interactions on the Persephone and at Loren Station.

Darron opened up one of the recordings, and saw himself talking with GoDai. After a few minutes of watching himself, he frantically turned off the recording, and never looked at one again.

When they met the next morning, they found that everyone had looked at something different. Darron had looked around at a few of the background recordings, but hadn't really focused on anything. Susan had spent most of her time looking through records from activities with the Suvain on Loren Station. MacDonald had spent all night reviewing the new Fleet descriptions, trying to find out if they made any difference, or if he should just keep saluting everything that moved. Stephen hadn't looked at anything except the tactics descriptions from the North American Defense Force. "Why would I look at the recordings?", he asked. "I was there."

"I looked at the recordings a little", Darron started, and then paused. "Horrible, isn't it", laughed Susan. "Seeing yourself on the screen can be really painful. I spent most of my time wondering if I really looked that stupid."

"Seeing myself on screen led to a later, even worse thought," Darron admitted. "Most of the people here have probably watched the recordings as well." Three of the four at the table shrunk self-consciously.

"Maybe they learned something," Stephen answered.

Captain Sorenson said he was giving the newcomers a couple of days to get up to speed before having them join the discussions. MacDonald announced after watching everyone eat breakfast on the first day that time would be split between studying the background material and physical exercises. The other three laughed at the comment, then realized this was in fact a serious order. Physical exercise turned out to be useful in counteracting the presence of lots of good food, and proved to be useful in getting people to actually work on the background materials. Studying was the only way to claim you were doing something really important, and so should delay heading to the gym.

Having a gym on board a ship seemed incredible to the Persephones, until someone realized and then pointed out that this was a ship that never compressed to go through an Intersection. There was space everywhere. There were also lots of things designed to entertain very important passengers. The very important passengers did not include the four at the table. The ship expected to carry roughly 30 passengers; there had been 43 on board before the last four additions had shown up. With a cloud of admirals and important politicians to take care of, the transport crew was less than enthused about dealing with four low-ranking latecomers.

There weren't requests for details about the fight with the VolatarA. Every report had been gone over enough times, and there wasn't much else that the Fleet representatives thought they needed to know. When they started attending the meetings, the Persephones just stood quietly in back. Most of the discussion was about whether each fleet should operate independently, or if they should try to form a completely integrated fleet. Alongside the argument over how to organize the ships was another argument over how the ships should be armed. There was general agreement that the ships should be armed with missiles and what were now being called "Point Defense Cannons", but every fleet had a different opinion as to exactly what the armament should be. For those lined up in the back with nothing to say, it was hard to stay focused. MacDonald found himself going back through everything he had heard Tavir say about the frustrations of dealing with a race as disordered as the Terrans.

After standing around in the meetings, the Persephones would eat together, then be sent back to study, and as their last assignment, show up for exercise. After their workout, they would head back for actual showers. Last, they usually headed over to all stand in MacDonald's room and talk about the day. They weren't responsible to get anything decided, so they were full of opinions of what should have been decided each day. The presence of an officer kept the other three from making too drastic comments about their superiors. There were also questions about why the four of them had been dragged all the way out to the transport if they weren't even needed. No one really had an answer for this, but there was hope that when the Suvain showed up, things would be different.

Six days later, the Suvain did show up, and things were different. Tavir, GoDai, and six other Suvain were brought aboard. The Suvain were polite to all assembled, and then greeted the four Terrans they now considered friends. There was a formal assembly welcoming the Suvain aboard, and the Tavir gave all the right official responses. As soon as the required duties were done, all the Suvain gathered around the Persephones and demanded a description of the fight with the VolatarA. Suddenly the four were the center of all attention. MacDonald started talking, after the other three sat saying nothing. He had spent the entire fight on the *Persephone*; most of his description was of Captain Adam's comments when the entire bridge was dark. It was the safest description to give, as it was the only story that was funny. The Suvain then asked if any Terrans had actually seen the VolatarA during the fight, and the others had to speak up. Stephen described how they had ended up training using a video game, then found that in real life, the lights and gravity were off, and everything was different. When asked if he had seen a VolatarA, he muttered, "Briefly." One of the Suvain asked if the VolatarA saw him. "No.

Well, not in time." Darron and Susan watched Stephen carefully. This was the only description they had ever heard Stephen give. Darron skipped over the whole grenade incident and described how they had almost shot the *Persephone*.

One of the Suvain looked like he was counting the Terrans. Then he asked, "Where's Joran?"

There was no response at first. Then MacDonald said, "Jon died early on. He led the first team in. There was a big exchange, and almost everyone on both sides died." The Suvain were silent, and Darron suddenly realized that every Terran was silent as well.

After a second, the Tavir stated, "He died bravely in combat, destroying his enemies? That is the second-best death a man can have."

Darron asked, "What is the first?"

"Dying of old age in the palace you have bought with the loot of a thousand worlds after all of your enemies have died bravely in battle," answered the Tavir, as all of the Suvain waggled their arms. The Terrans joined in the laughter, and the moment passed.

When the Suvain joined the meetings, all of the Terran arguments were put on hold. The Tavir requested permission to give his review of the situation.

"From what you have told us, you are converting merchant craft into combat vessels." Darron and Susan could tell from his posture that the Tavir was using the phrase "combat vessels" as a courtesy. None of the other Terrans seemed to have noticed the Tavir's hesitations about the Terran conversions. "We are moving the Tavir fleets to support you. One of our biggest questions has been where to move the supporting fleets to. There are a lot of different possible targets that the VolaratA could aim for. They could look to cut the Suvain and the Terrans apart by positioning a fleet between Terra and Suvain space. They could try to blockade the Terran system, in order to ensure that you cannot draw resources from any of your colonies.

The other VolatarA option is to move as fast as possible on Terra itself." "I believe the VolatarA will choose to move directly on the Terran system, rather than trying to wear us down through a lengthy war. The longer the war continues, the more time the Terrans will have to try and build a fleet. If a long war is going poorly, there is a greater chance that the Suvain will panic and give the Terrans technology. If things drag on, there will be more chance that the war will spread beyond a border skirmish between the Suvain and the VolatarA. The VolatarA goal will be to end the war quickly and cleanly. The way to ensure the quickest end to the war is for the VolatarA to move every ship that can reach the system to Terra. Once the Terrans are crushed, the war will be over. Since I expect the VolatarA to be headed here in force, I am recommending that you focus all of your ships in this system for defense of your home planet; I am also recommending that the Suvain force be moved to this system as well. The question that will decide the war is who can get the most strength to the Terra system first."

"The VolatarA have an Imperial Fleet for warfare with other sentient races, and a secondary fleet dedicated to exploration. The Exploration Fleet is broken into exploration squadrons. VolatarA ships operate in "Hands". Each "Hand" is a command ship leading five others. A VolatarA Exploration Squadron is a Hand of Hands. Three hands are made up of light exploration ships. These ships are usually focused on finding Intersections, and making quick surveys of any systems discovered. Two hands back up the front three. These two hands have larger ships, with heavier armament, and marines in case ground combat is needed to deal with primitive races. The command hand is made up of actual combat ships – they are some of the same ship designs that are used in the Imperial Fleet."

"The VolatarA have probably been moving ships in this direction from the time the fight occurred. It takes time to move ships from Intersection to Intersection, and it will take them time to find the Intersections to move through. Our estimate is that the VolatarA attack will come in about 9 – 12 months. The VolatarA are scattered widely in this star cluster. We expect that two of the exploration hands are close enough to reach the fight. One of the two support hands is on this side of the cluster and will be present. The other is on the far side of the cluster – unless the VolatarA delay the attack, we do not believe the second support hand will be here in time. The command hand was deployed near the middle of the exploration fleet, and will certainly be leading the VolatarA fleet when it arrives. Four hands consist of 24 ships.

Two ships from one exploration hand have already been dealt with, so we expect 22 VolatarA ships will be present."

"In that time, we should be able to bring 21 ships to aid in your defense. Although the numbers will be similar, the size and weaponry of their ships and ours will be very different. Our ships are smaller on average,

and are almost all light ships for exploration. While we have effective missiles and cannons, capable of dealing with primitives for instance, we are not designed to stand up against actual military vessels. If we have any hope of success, you are going to have to have produced a significant fleet in the next 9-12 months." Tavir looked out over the assembled group and asked, "So what will you have ready by the time they are here?"

The Terrans looked at each other for a few seconds, and then turned to a captain currently serving as part of the United Defense Fleet. The captain stood, and began a summary of Terran production. "Each Terran Fleet has a production facility in Earth orbit. Each facility has been set up to arm existing Terran ships with both missiles and point defense cannons. Each Fleet is converting its own transport ships; if there is a backlog at one station, ships will be transferred over to construction yards with a shorter waiting list of ships. The ships under conversion are having new control and sensor systems added, extra angulins to power the point defense cannons, and spaces cleared for missile launchers. We have agreed on a standard size for the missile launchers and point defense cannons, so a series of spaces of standard size are being cut out, so that prepared containers can be inserted. Each container is the same size, and holds either a point defense cannon or a missile launcher. The interior wall of the container has access points for cabling to attach the weapon to the bridge control systems and the ship power grid. The containers do not have to be manufactured in space – they are being manufactured on Earth, Terra, and shipped up when needed."

"Terrans agreed on standardized weapon systems?" asked Tavir. The Persephones started smiling, seeing his disbelief.

"Well, no," answered the spokesman. "There have been several disagreements about exactly how the point defense cannons and the missile launchers should be designed. So each Fleet is making the design they are most comfortable with. We have agreed on a standard size that the weapon systems have to fit in, and the connections to power and ship systems that each weapon system will be allowed to require, so the spaces for the weapons can be easily prepared. The containers are standardized. The details of what goes into each container is up to each Fleet."

"So the ships are being prepared in space to hold sets of weapons," he continued. "At the same time, the weapon systems are being prepared on Earth. In addition to building missile launchers, we have a separate effort to build the missiles to go in them. We have been studying the missiles that were onboard the VolatarA scout ship, and have been producing a number of prototypes to determine the optimal type of missile to mass produce."

"A fourth line of work is converting the ship communication systems to control all the new equipment, and to integrate with the best long-range sensors we have. These conversions and the angulin upgrades are going on in parallel with the hull modifications. When everything is set, the ships should be converted as fast as the spaces can be prepared in the hull for the weapons."

"That is all good to hear," answered the Tavir. "But you have not given any specifics on the time involved. How many ships will you have ready in 9 – 12 months?"

"As we have been setting the entire process up, things have been much slower than anticipated. The weapon kits are just starting full manufacture, and it took extra time to decide on the container specifics. We have spent two months, and we only have a total of six ships fully converted. As we gain greater practice in making the needed modifications, things are going quicker. At our current rate, each of the five construction yards will convert a ship in about a month. The conversion rate is increasing – we are expecting over the next few months to have a ship converted, from initial docking to launching from the yard, in 2 weeks. With 5 construction yards running, that will be a rate of 10 ship conversions a month. Not everything will be complete. There will still be work on board to integrate the new weapons, but all of that can be done internal to the vessel without slowing down the conversion of the next ship. We expect the average conversion rate, for all of the Fleets combined, to move from the current five per month to an average of 10 per month in the next 6 months. So 6 months, we will have a converted fleet of roughly 50 ships. By 9 months, we will have 80 ships ready for combat."

"With an average of 7 weapon systems per ship, we will need 560 containers and either missile launchers or point defense cannons. Every Fleet has multiple production facilities on Earth, so the weapon systems themselves are being produced much faster than we can prepare ships to take them. The missiles are much more difficult. Our angulins are not nearly as compact as yours, so our missiles are much larger. They take a lot more space, and I doubt if they will have the acceleration yours have. There have been hundreds of designs proposed. So our approach has been to set hundreds of manufacturing plants making prototypes and preparing for mass-production. Each design is being tested, and the more successful versions will be produced by dozens of factories at the same time. Although not all ships may have the latest and best versions, there will be far more missiles available than we can fit on the ships."

"How many can you fit on each ship?" asked one of the other Suvain. "With the size of our missiles, we think we can store about 6 for each launcher. Our goal is to have an average of 4 launchers on each ship," the captain answered. There was a pause as the Suvain considered the numbers.

"So you think you will be able to fire over 80 missiles at each VolatarA ship," the Tavir asked.

"If they bring 22 ships, yes. Of course, our missiles will be slow, compared to yours."

There was a bunch of muttering back and forth between the Suvain. Eventually the Tavir asked, "You have had some time to go over what you took from the VolatarA ship. Have you made any use of what you found?"

"Some," answered the spokesman. "We have been able to take the missiles apart, and get an idea of what parts go into one. Even with the damage to the ship, we could see that the cannons were powered by the ship angulins. It was an exploration vessel, so we also looked at the other ship sensors. To be honest, we didn't understand very much. One thing that was surprising was that the VolatarA had three smaller ships that look like they could be sent out to help with intersection searching. They were a lot bulkier than the little survey probes we use, so we assumed they must be able to operate independently." The Terrans were mostly watching the spokesman; the Suvain were standing in front, arms mostly still, with a few little arm jerks.

A lot of the Terrans turned to stare at the back wall as the Persephones started whispering, then laughing. They were looking at the Suvain, whose arms started waggling.

"So that is why they have you here," said GoDai.

"Yes," answered Susan. "It was interesting how you reacted to the discussion about the survey ships. When a Suvain gives a little arm flick like that, usually there is something that is not being said."

"Let's go over those small ships again." announced MacDonald. "So what are they really for?"

All the Suvain had their arms completely still as GoDai answered, "You are quite correct. They are for finding Intersections." The laughter and arm waggling started again, until the Tavir started to answer.

"When you meet the VolatarA, what you will really see is a cluster of radar targets. Not everything you see will be a ship. If there are 22 VolatarA ships present, you will probably see about 80 radar targets. Each ship will have set out decoys – small deployable ships with transmitters. These transmitters will be sending out signals that match those of a real ship as exactly as possible. They have to look and act like a ship; every ship will be checking every radar signal to try to pick out the false signals from the real targets. Even a slight variation can be enough for an experienced officer to spot the decoy. Once it is identified as a decoy, the decoy is useless. Its transmissions will be subtracted out from the incoming signals, and any missiles already launched will be updated with a new target list which does not include the decoy."

"The VolatarA decoys will have to be dealt with. We Suvain will have our own. I do not believe it will be of use to you to try and develop decoys to carry on board your own ships. Although the transmissions of a ship are not that hard to duplicate, the ship reactions to an incoming missile swarm are a different matter. Building a decoy that can mimic a ship's motion during combat is the most difficult part of building any fleet. You can try to build decoys, but unless your technology is far more advanced than we have discovered, they will be seen through in an instant. Your construction of missiles and cannons is impressive, and should bring results. I would recommend you continue as planned, without being distracted by shifting efforts over to attempts at decoy development."

"Even if you can get the transmissions right, and can have the decoy making course changes along with the fleet, the first missiles fired at a decoy will usually indicate it is not a real ship. Of course, any hit on a decoy will destroy it. But missing a decoy usually destroys its usefulness. If a missile warhead fires near a ship, usually the target will be hit, or have had to make visible maneuvers or defensive fire. If a warhead fires near a decoy, and the decoy doesn't blink out of existence, but also has not had to take any defensive action, it will be identified. And an identified decoy is no more useful than one which has been destroyed."

There was a buzzing all around the room. Finally someone asked, "If you can tell which are the decoys, are you going to tell the Terrans?"

"Of course. You will know after the first wave of missiles reach their target. From what you have said, the Terran fleet is expected to fire almost 2000 missiles. If you fired at all 80 targets at once, you would fire about 25 missiles at each one. If you had missiles that had decent acceleration, 25 missiles would be more than enough for little ships like ours. For slow missiles like yours, how many hit, if any, will probably depend on the angle you are firing at. So you don't fire all the missiles in a single wave. The first salvo is designed to flush out the decoys. The main salvo follows afterwards, far enough back that you can see the effects of the first salvo. You fire about 250 missiles in the first salvo – this will be about three per target. Between defensive fire and maneuvering, you probably won't hit a single ship. But almost the decoys will either be hit, or be identified. So the number of targets will drop to some number closer to 25 or 30. The new target list is sent to the second wave, which will re-target to the new list. So when the second salvo of 1750 missiles reaches the target fleet, there will be around 60-70 going after each target. Even with slow missiles, you should score a good number of hits."

The meeting degenerated into lots of conversations as the set of officers from each fleet started talking with each other about the new information.

After the conversations had congealed back into a single stream, the Terrans had lots of questions about decoys. At last, as the meeting ground to a close, someone asked the Terran spokesman for a summary. An admiral with the uniform of the European Consolidated SpaceFleet and the insignia of the new United Defense Fleet answered. "Our attempts to produce armed warships with missiles and point defense cannons are progressing, and are considered reasonable by the Suvain. We have learned about a weapon system we were completely unaware of – the decoy. I think I can say that we have general agreement with the Suvain that attempting to produce credible decoys is a less useful approach than continuing our current focus on manufacturing missiles and point defense cannons. Both the Suvain and Terran fleets will be concentrated in the Terra system. Current estimates are that the VolatarA attack will come in around 10 months, with a force expected to be 22 ships. At that time, we will have 21 Suvain allies present, and should have a fleet of 80 Terran ships deployed. With a 5 to 1 advantage in numbers, I think our prospects are good, even given the more advanced technology of the VolatarA."

Everyone turned to the Tavir as he stood up. "I agree with your assessment. And if you can produce the fleet you are promising, I think our chances are very good."

Of the four Persephones, Stephen enjoyed his new assignments the most. Once the Suvain had arrived, a joint team was set up to plan how the fleet would operate. The Suvain had various computer models that were used to simulate ship combat, but they were not willing to share them with the Terrans. The Terrans wanted to develop their own simulation programs anyway, and so made no protest. The Persephones were all assigned to help with the simulation development – the Terrans thought that the four of them might have the best chance of getting information out of the Suvain. It was hard for Stephen to imagine that he was actually being ordered to write the same software that he was spending all of his spare time developing for fun.

The simulation started with a model of a single missile flying from a starting position to a target, and blasting off its shotgun warhead. That was a simple process of tracking the path of the missile, and the path of each warhead it shot out. Once missiles could be modelled, the simulation was extended to add a starting speed to the missile, and motion to the target. As the target could maneuver, it became clear that even though each missile blasted out nearly 20 warheads, hitting a fast-moving target that could change course rapidly was rare. The Suvain were willing to share the information they had about the VolatarA capabilities. As soon as the Terran set the targets in the simulation to change course as rapidly as the VolatarA did, and the missiles were set to the acceleration rates that Terran missiles were expected to reach, the Terrans began to understand why 80 of their ships would be hard-pressed to fight one quarter their number of VolatarA.

Once the simulation had reached the point that it could be handed out to the Fleet representatives, each Fleet started running tests of proposed formations and tactics. Each Fleet gave a report back to the combined group. The Suvain sat in on the group reviews, occasionally making comments or suggestions. As Tavir had mentioned, the effectiveness of the Terran missiles was strongly dependent on the original position and velocity of the firing ship and the target ship. If the VolatarA was flying directly towards the Terran ship, the Terran missile had a reasonable chance of catching the target. Even though the VolatarA ship could change course in all three directions, the missile only had to adjust for the target's course changes. If the VolatarA ship was flying across the path of the Terran from right to left, the missile had almost no chance of catching it. The missile had to adjust for the initial velocity of the target, and then try to adjust for course changes in any of three directions as well.

The Persephones met with the Suvain almost every day, and stretching their orders, showed them each stage of the simulation. Not long into the development, the Suvain were showing them the Suvain combat models.

Soon afterwards, the Terran simulator rapidly changed to look just like the Suvain. When the simulator was complete, each ship location was marked, along with every target. With each ship were cones stretching out in front and behind each ship. The cones indicated the region in which a target ship could be hit by the firing ship's missiles. The size and width of the cone was based on the firing ship's speed and course, the missile's acceleration rate, and the target's speed, direction, and maneuverability. After the model was finished, small clusters of people could be found all over the ship, leaning over mobile displays, trying out different approaches to group ships for combat.

While the four Suvain experts were playing computer games, the rest of the *Persephone's* crew had actual time off. When the ship reached the North American Defense Force station, the ship was officially turned over to the conversion corps. This was exciting for everyone but Captain Adams, who found the act of turning over her ship to someone else excruciating. Crew members scattered across the planet, heading for friends or family. Most found themselves temporary celebrities. Everyone wanted to hear about encountering the Suvain, or about the fight with the VolatarA. This interest lasted for about five tellings of the story, and then the crewmen's 15 minutes of fame were mostly over. The crewmen were left trying to find a way to fit back into a world most of them hadn't seen for nearly two years.

Emptying the ship left the question of what to do with the VolatarA prisoners. Acting Chaplain Soong suggested that he be allowed to escort the VolatarA to different places of interest on Earth. There wasn't any way for the parolees to send messages back to their fellow VolatarA, so they weren't seen as a security threat. An agreement was reached that a set of escorts would be provided – to protect the Terrans from the VolatarA, and to protect the VolatarA from the Terrans. Soong's family was on New Chicago, so he did not mind taking the time to show the visitors around. Eventually the sightseer glob grew to include two VolatarA, six bodyguards, Soong, and eight other Persephones who found sticking together to be a lot more comfortable than trying to find somewhere to be for a full month.

As Soong and company took their expenses-paid trip around the planet, Captain Adams headed to Fleet Headquarters to report to her superiors.

There wasn't that much to say that had not already been reported, but she found a way to extend the debriefing for three weeks. On the last week, she had no more excuse not to see her son. For her last week, she flew to Los Angeles, and was picked up at the airport by the son she had not seen for four years. Things were awkward and silent for the first several hours, as they returned to her son's home and family. Still a Captain, it was hard for her to interact with other humans without giving orders. She stumbled through the first couple of days, slowly learning to relax around the grandkids she had almost never seen. By Day 4, she could sit and listen to her grandchildren fighting imaginary VolatarA fleets with their *Persephone* models, and not feel desperate to jump in and instruct them how to fly the ship properly. On Day 5, she had a long, relaxed talk with her daughter-in-law while her son checked back in at the office; she realized for the first time how fortunate her son was to have such a spouse. On Day 6, she and the entire family went to a "theme park". On Day 7, not long before she was scheduled to leave, she sat on the back porch with her son, and watched the grandkids play in the backyard. The two were silent for a long time.

"Thank you for having me," Rose Adams finally said. They sat side by side for a few more minutes.

"I am sorry that I have never been the mother you deserved", she continued. Her son did not agree with or contest the statement.

"I am heading out today," she continued, in the firm voice that her son was more familiar with. "There is a lot of trouble ahead. Everyone thinks things will go well, and I would tend to agree. But even if things do go well, a lot of people aren't coming back." She turned back to look at her grandchildren. "I am afraid this could be my last visit. It is frustrating to think that I may well have spent my entire life not realizing what was truly important, only to find out when it was too late."

Her son reached over and took her hand for the first time in many years. "You are here now," he said quietly.

After a long while, it was time to go. Rose watched as her son stood up and called in her grandkids – the whole family was taking her back to the airport. Once the airport was reached, she got out, awkwardly kissed her son, embraced her daughter-in-law, and turned to her grandkids. Both were standing at attention outside the car. They all saluted each other, then she hugged them both, and waved to all four. Finally the car started to fill behind her as Captain Adams picked up her bag and started alone on the first leg of her trip back to her ship and profession.

As the Persephones started to return to a very different ship rumors spread out to meet them. The Fleets learned first that a ship of unknown design was moving towards the Intersection to Loren Station. As the news was released to the public that another alien race had been contacted, the news spread to fleet personnel that the new race was the Nemi-Vemzl. Everyone raced to the logs to see what had been learned about the new race. They found the descriptions given by the Suvain – the "NV"s were usually a bit taller than Terrans, and thin. They came from a planet with about 5% lower gravity than Terra, and occasionally used power-assisted chairs to move around on other worlds. The NVs were considered the most voracious traders in the galaxy.

When they weren't passing along rumors, the Persephones were learning their way around a very different ship. Much of the sensor equipment was gone, replaced by banks of angulins. The entire starboard side was a collection of weapon parts. They were supposed to have been installed, but actually had just been loaded onto the ship and left scattered everywhere. The starboard hull had been rebuilt, and weapon loading had begun. Once the disassembled weapons were inside the hull, the *Persephone* had been declared "Upgraded", and sent off to join the other "Upgraded" ships. Most of the ship was a mass of parts, cables, and angulins lying around.

Captain Adams had been the first to re-board the ship. She had looked at the chaos, complained bitterly, and shooed the upgrade crew off her property. She refused to admit, even to herself, that she was glad things were such a mess. There were plenty of tasks to keep everyone busy. Since she was in charge of putting everything in its place, everything was going to end up exactly where she wanted it. Having to put everything together also meant that she would learn exactly what it was that now made up the *Persephone*. After reasserting her authority, Captain Adams changed her mind and insisted that six of the upgrade team be reassigned right back to the ship they had just been kicked off of. As her officers reported for duty, each was given a set of assignments, and told to pick out teams from the crewmen as they reported back. Each of the six re-loaded upgraders was put on a different team; each was assigned to incorporate one of the new weapon systems.

As crewmembers trickled back onboard, the complaining began. It was hard to get back into the habit of working after so long off. With the ship in chaos, the hours of work were much greater than usual.

Then the crew found that all of their extra hours included taking apart their own cabins. Extra racks of angulins were being put in to power the PDCs, and so the space for the crew cabins was being cut to a third of its previous size. As if removing the only non-public space on the ship wasn't bad enough, the next task involved removing the mess hall. Missiles were going to be loaded, and they needed somewhere to live. So the entire dining area was cleared out, and storage racks were put in. By the time the new material was packed into the newly- created locations, the only open space left on the ship that more than four people could congregate was the forward loading bay. Congregating would be possible once the forward loading bay did not have loose stuff lying all over.

The VolatarA escorts were among the last to re-board. After they had finished their planetary tour, the VolatarA had been deposited on a Fleet station in Hawaii, to await the results of the expected combat. Duleka and his one remaining charge had finally decided that the Terrans were not going to suddenly change their minds and try to torture them for information. The Terrans understood that the two VolatarA did not have information directly useful to the upcoming fight; the Terrans were also too excited to get to talk to actual aliens to spoil things with torture and vivisection.

Soong and company came aboard, and did not know that most of the rest of the crew was watching them head to the places their cabins used to be. Everyone enjoyed watching the confusion as the group headed in circles; the corridors that used to exist were now replaced by corridors that started in the same place, but now led to completely different parts of the ship. Strangely enough, they saw no one as they wandered around lost. Everyone was watching the internal monitors, laughing as their hapless crewmates looked around in confusion at rooms they had never before seen. Eventually all nine were standing around among scattered parts in the forward loading bay. "There are nearly 90 people on this ship", Soong stated. "Why have we not met a single one of them?" They all looked around at the disorder, until someone looked suspiciously at one of the room monitors. A crewman on the bridge flipped a switch and broadcast the bridge noise back through the monitors. Laughter filled the ship. Then there was the voice of the captain ordering everyone to get back to work, and for someone to rescue the newcomers. Not many really went back to work – most kept watching to see the responses as a helpful guide led the group to their new tiny cubby holes. Finally there was an order from the captain for Soong and the rest to stow their gear and report to the bridge for assignments in five minutes.

In the downtime between tasks, Soong was filled in with the latest rumors coming from Loren Station. The reports published of the new interactions were positive –the Nemi-Vemzl were not issuing threats or demanding the Terrans surrender. From the reports being broadcast, the Nemi-Vemzl were more interested in peaceful cooperation with the Terrans that the Terrans were themselves. The officers on the *Persephone* were also hearing stories that weren't being broadcast. These were not nearly so comforting. The "NV"s were not just friendly, but also always wanted to trade. But what the NVs usually were giving up were trinkets and little toys that Terrans had never seen, and what the Terrans were usually giving back was either useful information or things of real value, such as all the power needed to recharge the NV ship. It sounded like any time the NV wanted or needed something, by the time the negotiations finished, the Terrans were paying the NVs for the privilege of providing the NVs service.

The NVs were very encouraging about the possibility of mutual trade, but the Terrans were non-committal. The NVs weren't making any specific promises, and no one wanted to spoil the hopes of cooperation with the Suvain. Listening to the NVs carefully, there were also suggestions that the "mutual trade" would be run by the NVs. All of the discussions about how trade could grow involved more and more NV presence and control throughout the Terran territories. With the NVs exerting more and more control, most of the Terrans suspected that the NV would end up just taking over the Terran possessions, and ruling the Terrans just as fully as the Suvain were intending. At Loren Station, orders had been given that no one was to make any deals or agreements, no matter how trivial, with any NV without the specific approval of the official Terran representatives.

Just as Soong started to get settled in, Captain Adams was called across to a meeting for captains on the Fleet station. When she came back, all time for exchanging rumors was gone; Captain Adams announced that she wanted all the new equipment in place in half of the previous schedule.

About the time the wanderers had returned to the *Persephone*, the NV sideshow had already been overshadowed in the strategy meetings with the Suvain. A brief message had been received from the *DoorFinder* – VolatarA ships had reentered the Kansu Transfer. The *DoorFinder* was running in a long race-track shaped path. She would build up a large speed, and then run with as little acceleration and energy use as possible to try to be less visible. After about a week, she would make the fastest deceleration she could manage, and then head back. The Suvain had taken a page out of the *Persephone*'s book, and left a string of Intersection detectors along their track to add to their chances of seeing the VolatarA ships when they came.

The transmission chain leading to Loren Station forwarded a brief message that four VolatarA ships had been detected. This was sent along to the Terran system. The *DoorFinder* was moving away from the VolatarA when the four ships were sighted; the captain kept on the current track until he was well away from the VolatarA scouts before starting to turn back to shadow the newcomers. The VolatarA were fanning out across the empty space. One was headed straight for the site of the fight with the *Persephone*. The other three ships were angling over towards the direction the *Persephone* was heading when she was first spotted by the VolatarA. The *DoorFinder* was needlessly ordered to stay out of the way. The Terrans sent a message to New Chicago to cease all transmissions, and the transmission line to New Chicago was turned off.

When the Terrans first established a communication line to their new colony, it was seen as a milestone in human civilization – the first permanent line between worlds. To ensure the new line was equal to the occasion, a backup system was established. The backup system was designed to monitor the primary line, and take over should transmissions fail. The backup line had never been used, and as maintenance cost money, the system was dropped from maintenance contracts. Over the decades it was dropped from memory as well. There were 12 transmitters in the line, all of which were expected to have an effective service life of 30 years. The transmitters had been built to last, and all had well exceeded the design life-span. Most had died long ago, but STS-4 still had just enough battery power to detect the lack of signals from the main line, fire up the transmitter, and start trying to notify New Chicago that the main transmission line was down. For the three days before the battery finally was drained, a signal was broadcast directly toward the Intersection to New Chicago. The signal was not picked up by the next relay transmitter; it had been dead for 20 years. The signal was picked up by a VolatarA scout ship, who immediately notified its neighbors, and started to determine the direction of the signal.

The VolatarA had been expected to return to the Kansu Transfer, so the news of the four ships did not cause that much distress. The first shock came a week later, when six more VolatarA arrived, sooner than the Suvain had expected them to. The Suvain had expected the Support hand to arrive after two more months of travel. The next week came the larger shock, when every VolatarA ship suddenly changed course. When the VolatarA locations and courses were relayed to the Terrans, the Terrans confirmed that the VolatarA were headed to the Intersection to New Chicago.

Four more Suvain ships had reached Loren Station; Tavir and the others had headed back to meet them. They had started to the Intersection when the news came that the VolatarA had somehow discovered the Intersection location. At an enormous cost in energy, they slowed, giving up all of the speed they had built up. Then they started back to the Terrans. The four Persephones were about to be picked up and taken back to Earth; they were going to get leave before they reported back to their ship. When the news came in of the VolatarA course change, leave was cancelled.

When the Suvain returned, the meeting room was again filled with both sides as they reassessed the new situation. The mood had changed from excited to grim. The Suvain and the United Defense Fleet representatives were in front, the other Fleet officers were in the middle, and the assistants and Persephones at the back. After brief greetings, Tavir asked, "How many Terrans are on New Chicago?"

"About four million", someone answered. The Persephones could see several of the Suvain tucking in their spikes for a moment.

"Do you have any idea how they found the Intersection so quickly?" asked a Suvain. When none of the Terrans answered, the Suvain asked, "Was there any possibility that someone may have been less than careful around the NVs?"

"From everything we have heard, contact with the Nemi-Vemzl is pretty tightly controlled now," a UDF officer responded. "We lost so much with every negotiation with the NVs, that no one is allowed an independent conversation with them now."

"If you are sure that there is no ongoing leak, I guess it does not matter", stated Tavir. "The relevant thing is that the VolatarA will find the Intersection to New Chicago very soon. I do not believe that even Terrans will kill four million of their own in time to prevent the VolatarA from finding the Intersection locations that lead to Terra. We had expected that it would take at least two to three months for the VolatarA to find each Intersection. As it is, they will know the path to Terra within two months at the latest. Two months shorter preparation time – that will mean 20 less Terran ships will be ready."

"Will the Suvain still be here in time?" someone asked. The Persephones recognized the Suvain embarrassment.

"Most of us", answered the Tavir. "My fleet, my brother's fleet, and several others. We should still have 18 ships present."

"So instead of 22 Suvain and 80 Terran ships, if the VolatarA are here as fast as you expect, we will have more like 60 Terrans and 18 Suvain."

"There is another point that is disturbing", Tavir continued. "We did not expect the support hand to be here for another 3 months. Either they were much closer than expected, or they have moved much faster than expected. We have been trying to get any information we can about the location of the VolatarA ships. Everything has suggested that the VolatarA support hand was not very close when contact was made. The commander of the Exploration Fleet must have called in resupply ships from the local VolatarA Imperial Fleet elements. All fleets have support ships which hold huge rows of angulins. The warships run their angulins almost dry as they race to a rendezvous with the supply ships. The supply ships then recharge them back up to full momentum. This allows ships to run at much higher accelerations as they go from Intersection to Intersection. Overall, fleets that resupply can travel about twice as fast as those that have to be careful to conserve their angulin momentum. If they can resupply, they may be able to get the second support hand into the fight. In that case, there will be another 6 ships available for a fight at Terra. So instead of facing 22 ships, we may be facing 28."

The room was silent. Darron was thinking back to the Tavir's statement that both sides were in a race to concentrate strength at Terra. From the reports coming in, it looked clear that the VolatarA were winning the race by a large margin. Eventually the question was raised, "If the Exploration Fleet is getting help from the Imperial Fleet, does that mean Imperial Fleet ships will also be in the attack?"

"No", Tavir answered. "This is not a major confrontation between the Suvain and the VolatarA. It is a skirmish between two exploration fleets. If the VolatarA commit their Imperial Fleet, the Tavir Clan could call for protection from the Emperor. This would be a major escalation. Neither empire will want such an increase in tensions. Borrowing a few resources gives the VolatarA an advantage, but it isn't really enough to make a big deal over diplomatically. The Exploration Fleet commander probably called in a few favors, or maybe the local Imperial Fleet commander is one of his classmates."

"We have been assuming that we could rely on having a big enough advantage in numbers to just overwhelm the VolatarA," stated a Terran. "With things as they are now, it sounds like we are going to have to start planning all over again."

"Yes," answered Tavir.

The conversation turned to discussions of the rate of Terran ship conversion, missile accelerations, and the difficulty of making realistic decoys. It slowed down, without any real change in anyone's view of the new situation. The meeting broke for lunch; the Suvain took out the food they had brought with them and sat down next to their Terran friends.

After a few moments, Stephen stated, "If we have to outsmart the VolatarA, it will be hard. In intelligence, they are a ways ahead of us, of Terrans at least."

"They pick up on things quickly", Darron commented. "I usually didn't have more than half the question out before Duleka was answering."

"They do cycle through a conversation a lot faster than we do." Susan stated. "They recognize the question, answer it, and have moved on to the next topic about as fast as I had the original question completed."

"So if we want the VolatarA to respond in a way we want them to, we need to give them something they recognize," suggested GoDai. "What do they expect to see?"

"Well, they expect to see Terrans try to fight back, and fail," answered Tavir.

"So we just have to try and then fail?" answered Stephen. "This will be easy."

A second Suvain fleet arrived after another month, led by TavirDai.

The *DoorFinder* was still alive, coasting by the VolatarA, then flying back to report the enemy's movements. As soon as the Intersection was found, ten VolatarA ships had moved into the New Chicago system. TavirDai brought the unwelcome news that the other six VolatarA ships in the Kansu Transfer had begun heading straight to the Intersection leading to the Beta Quadrant. There were a last series of meetings to bring TavirDai up to speed on the current planning. Then transports began taking the Terrans back to their fleets, and the Suvain fleets moved down to Terra.

IX

Four months after they had left, the four wanderers returned to the new *Persephone*. By the time they were there the new weapons had been installed. Captain Adams did not let them get sent on a long journey through the ship. Instead, she had them guided to their quarters, and then to a reception in the aft loading bay. There they were met by about 40 of the crew, the Captain, the Information Officer, and two new additions to the officer corps. There was now an "Executive Officer". This was a position which had been dropped long before in the North American Defense Force, and had now been reinstalled. As far as Darron could understand, the new Executive Officer was another pair of hands for the Captain. He was also in charge of the bridge crew and the auxiliary controls. This made him the new superior of both Susan and Darron. In addition to the Executive Officer, there was now a "Weapons Officer". He was in charge of all of the new weapon systems.

After greeting her returning crewmen and introducing them to their new superiors, Captain Adams gave a brief mention of all the work which had been required to get the *Persephone* back from the Kansu Transfer, and then gave a quick mention of the drastic transformations required to convert the exploration vessel into a warship. She then stated that one single crewman had a unique record of service during all of this exhausting work. During the first recovery, Darron had managed to miss all of the work by making some claim that his leg hurt. During the second transformation, Darron had missed everything by claiming he had some reason he had to go off to Jupiter. This made him the only person in the entire crew to have done absolutely nothing either time. There was appreciative clapping from around the room. Darron's embarrassment turned to concern when the Captain concluded by mentioning that since Darron was so well rested, if anyone had work to be done, they knew who was available. As everyone left, Captain Adams motioned for the four to stay behind. When just the five of them were together, the Captain ordered in a low voice, "You can talk to me, but to no one else." She looked at the four of them again and quietly stated, "The *Persephone* will lead in the Terran Fleet."

None of the four answered at first, then MacDonald stated, "We expected nothing less."

Darron found everything different from what he had seen before - The ship was rebuilt, his quarters were gone, he reported to someone he had never met, and his old assignments had been replaced by the new work in Auxiliary Controls. The losses to the Science Division had not been replaced. There were still three Physicists, but they were usually assigned to different tasks. Darron realized that Susan was now all alone – all of the other Chemists were dead or had been transferred off ship because of their injuries. The time in Auxiliary Controls was mostly spent trying to learn how to turn off or on various pieces of equipment all around the ship. Darron had no success remembering any of this, and started to make notes for each set of controls.

After he was reminded that in combat the computer might not be accessible, Darron started writing the controls on pieces of paper and sticking them to the front of each bank of controls. At the first review by the Executive Officer, Darron was very firmly informed that this was not appropriate. He was to remember the controls, and no room on the ship should be covered in scraps of paper. So Darron took them down before every inspection, and put them up again afterwards. Very occasionally, there was a drill in which Darron had to calculate the ship's orbit and determine which angulins to trigger to make course changes. These few moments were the joy he hoped for during every drill.

Drills occupied almost all the time on the ship. There were drills in which the ship practiced charging and firing the guns, and loading up the missiles for launch. There were drills in which the *Persephone* practiced flying in formation with other Fleet ships. There were drills in which different parts of the ship were assumed to have been hit, and had to be repaired with a random selection of equipment. There were even several drills in which the crew manned the new lifeboats that had been attached to the hull of the ship. Some of the drills involved ship maneuvers run from the bridge, and a few in which the crew in Auxiliary Controls had to issue ship commands. Darron was generally useless during these drills. As long as there was anyone else in Auxiliary Controls, they knew what to do, and did it. He could hear Susan over the intercom at times, relaying bridge commands to the ship. For several of the damage control drills Stephen came into Auxiliary Controls and went through the motions of repairing the backup computer systems.

Susan had almost never been on the bridge before her new assignment.

When she first reported, she had no idea where her position was located. She was shown to a small table near the door, which had a display with every compartment in the ship. For each there was a control for communications, and a status indicator showing where the systems in the compartment were still functional. From her new workstation, Susan could see the rest of the bridge. Along with everyone sitting at displays, a new large clear panel had been set up on the left side of the bridge. It contained a massive tree of the power distribution grid and angulins aboard the ship. Each was color coded with the current spin level and power flow. After registering, an operator could adjust the power flow by touching the angulins, and moving his or her finger along the desired path to the destination system. The right side of the bridge now had displays showing the current charging levels for each of the Point Defense Cannons and missile launcher status. Displays showed the environment around the ship, and marked the location of all friendly vessels. During the combat drills, it also showed the locations of hostile ships and incoming missiles. A 3-D display that Susan recognized as coming from Stephen's combat simulator sat to the side of the larger display. It showed the Persephone's location, and an operator could select other ships on the display. A cone extended from the Persephone, which changed based on the course and speed of both the *Persephone* and the target. When the target ship was within the cone far enough that the *Persephone*'s missiles could reach the ship no matter how it changed direction, the cone turned from red to green. Susan provided status as ordered, and watched as the *Persephone* was destroyed in most of the drills.

Stephen was bored during almost everything except the repair drills. He had the repair packs complete within a few weeks of returning to the ship.

During most of the drills, the damage control teams had to be in position, but did not have any role in the simulation. During the repair drills, he had to move from room to room on the ship. Since the ship layout had changed, he built a map of the *Persephone*, with directions from wherever he was to whatever it was he was supposed to repair. As he sat with nothing to do, he kept adding to the map; eventually it was about as complete a status of the ship and the ship's systems as the real controls on the bridge.

When the drills were over, there was even less to do than usual. During exploration flights there had been movies shown in the mess hall, but now there was no mess hall. There was the aft loading bay, but as the missile reloads were brought on board, they started to fill up the small space left for the crew; now all of the male crew members slept in the aft loading bay.

Without anywhere to gather, the crew scattered around the ship to find a place to eat their heated food. Darron, Stephen, and Susan occasionally collected in Auxiliary Controls – after the drills, the room was usually unoccupied. The day the VolatarA fleet drove through the Intersections into the Terra System, the three were together finishing up dinner. The *Persephone* was notified, and the notification was broadcast in the backup communication system in Auxiliary Controls. The three stopped and looked at the talking machine, then each other. "It's about time," said Stephen, and left to try to get more information. Both of the others watched him leave, and stayed sitting where they were.

"I guess that takes away any last chance for leave", stated Susan after a while. Darron gave a short laugh. "It is strange to think that I have travelled through three sectors, then all the way down to Earth, just to be stuck a couple of hundred thousand miles away from seeing my family one last, one more, time."

Darron had no idea what to say, so he asked, "Your family is in Albakee, right? Or something like that?"

"Albuquerque," answered Susan. "Albuquerque, New Mexico, Sonora."

"Sonora is desert?", asked Darron slowly. He seemed to be trying to remember long-lost geography lessons from school.

"A lot of it is, but not all." Susan turned to a display, and brought up several pictures from home.

Darron looked at the pictures, and remarked positively at what he hoped were the proper times. Then Susan brought up a picture of the Painted Desert and Darron sat forward. He said, "That looks a lot like home, except for all the trees, growing outside like that."

Susan looked at the pictures, up to Darron, and back to the picture. She had never seen someone look at the Painted Desert and focus on the specks of green before. She then looked again and Darron and stated, "We have known each other for about a year, and you have never once mentioned your family, or where you are from."

"It has never been relevant", answered Darron.

Susan just looked at Darron. He started to suspect that he had said something wrong, or that he was supposed to say the next sentence, even though under the normal rules of alternation, it was Susan's turn. "So, where are you from?" asked Susan.

"Oh", said Darron. "I am from Andy-B." Susan didn't respond for a second, so Darron translated, "Anderson Mining Company Station B. About 20 degrees South and 60 degrees West of Olympus Mons."

"You mean, on Mars?" asked Susan in shock.

"It is not that unusual," countered Darron. "The Martian Assembly has about 1 million people. That's a quarter the size of New Chicago. Isn't that about the same size as Albuquerque?"

"How big is Andy-B?" Susan was visualizing a tiny metal box. "About 10 square kilometers now," answered Darron. "It is almost 150 years old."

"How many people live there?"

"About 2,000. Anderson still owns the place – most are Anderson employees."

"But you are on a North American Defense Fleet ship," Susan pointed out.

"Sure. It is a North American colony. And a fairly high percentage of colonials spend time in Fleet service. There are three colonials on the *Persephone*."

Susan paused, then asked slowly, "Are you planning on living on Mars after you finish your tour with the Fleet?"

"No – there isn't much need for a Physicist in Andy-B. Of course, I will go back and see people, but beyond that, I haven't really thought about it."

Susan exhaled, then hoped that Darron hadn't noticed. "It is too bad we are having this conversation now; it would have been nice to take you outside and see what happens."

"I have been outside before", Darron protested, laughing. Then he stopped laughing, and stated, "It may not be too late. We might still survive this."

"Maybe", Susan said slowly. "Even if we Terrans win, your and my chances are not good."

Darron started to laugh, and failed. "We might live through this. If we do, and if we ever get leave, maybe we will get a chance to go down to the planet after all."

"If we do, I can take you to the Painted Desert, and you will be the only person who misses the mountains and sees the trees," Susan pointed out.

Darron did manage to laugh, and as they left the room, Darron suddenly really, really wanted to survive the next month.

Leave was cancelled, as everyone expected. The *Persephone* began a slow movement to the rendezvous with the rest of the Terran fleet at the Fleets' space stations.

There had been discussions about whether to try and defend at the Intersection Field. The VolatarA ships would not come through the Intersections all together. Because it was random whether a ship passed through an Intersection or stayed in its original region, if all the VolatarA ships moved through at once, about half would come through on the first try; the others would have to move back into the Intersection to try again. With the Terran and Suvain fleets on the other side, it was possible that they could flood the oncoming VolatarA ships with missiles before they could get organized on the other side. In addition to the fleets, mines could be placed near the entrance. There were lots of extra missiles that could not be fit on any of the available warships. With sensors added, the missiles could be set to fire at any target detected. Many simulations had been run in which mines were placed around the Intersections, backed by both fleets.

The attempts to guard the Intersection field were abandoned because the Intersection field was too large. There were 38 Intersections, spread over several tens of thousands of miles. Mines could be placed around each, but if the fleets were spread out enough to cover all the Intersections, there would be very few ships in any one place. The VolatarA fleet, concentrated in one part of the field, would tear through the nearby ships, and then have an advantage over the rest of the defenders as they tried to concentrate.

The Fleets were deployed near Earth. There were spare missiles anyway, so mines were placed around the Intersections. The missiles were set to accelerate no faster than $2.5Gs$ – it couldn't hurt to make the VolatarA think the Terran missiles were less capable than they really were. The communication trail back to Earth reported the VolatarA crossing. The first crossings were made by unmanned sensors that checked the Terra side of the Intersections. Next through were nuclear missiles that detonated once they had crossed, clearing out any adjacent Terran defenses. Once the other side was clear, VolatarA ships came through, with decoys deployed. Once through, they accelerated faster than the Terran missiles could catch and shot past. The missiles fired, and hit nothing. The VolatarA cleared out the obstacles near the handful of Intersections they came through, and ignored the others. Once through, the VolatarA fleet recovered the decoys, formed up in Hands, and started down to Earth. The Intersection defenses had cost the VolatarA eight nuclear missiles and three point-defense warheads used to clear out Terran missiles that looked like they might get close.

Once the VolatarA were across, the lines of communication beacons relayed their movements back to the Fleets near Earth. Warnings were sent back up the communications line to outputs further out in the solar system. The VolatarA fleet aligned itself on the plane of the solar system. The Command Hand established a long, elliptical orbit down towards the Sun. The orbit would take the VolatarA fleet on past Earth's orbit on the far side of the system. The fleet would then slide to the far side of the Sun, and then circle back up towards Earth. If the fleet began thrusting back against the pull of the Sun it would lose enough energy to be brought to a smooth approach to the planet.

Viewed from the perspective of the VolatarA command ship, the rest of the Command Hand was drawn up on a rough line to the right and left. The Right Support Hand was on the right of the Command Hand, on a line running parallel to the path of the fleet, spaced from slightly ahead and above the Command Hand to slightly below and behind. The Left Support Hand was deployed similarly on the other side. The Center Searching Hand was fanned out above and ahead of the main body; the four remaining ships of the Right Searching Hand were a screen below and behind.

There were no permanent Terran settlements beyond Saturn, only a couple of small research stations. The VolatarA course would pass the Uranus station without being too far away. As the VolatarA fleet approached, the station personnel got on their only ship and headed to the far side of the planet. As predicted by the Suvain, the VolatarA ignored the small station as they passed. There was no use blowing up something they could use in the future, and the station was certainly not worth the use of a missile.

The VolatarA progress was watched carefully at Earth. There had been two possibilities considered for the VolatarA approach. The VolatarA could slow down as they approached, so that they would match velocities with Earth and stay near the planet. If they chose not to slow down, they could hook around the Sun, shoot past the Earth at very high speed, and then fly on past back towards the Intersection field. This would be a useful approach if they intended to shower the planet with missiles, and then pull off until they could get missile reloads. A separate set of positions had been planned for the Terran and Suvain fleets, one set for each possible VolatarA approach. As the VolatarA fleet approached, every measurement of their progress was captured and new orbits calculated. If the VolatarA had established a simple orbit and stopped thrusting, determining their course would have been trivial. The VolatarA wanted a faster transfer to Earth, so they were accelerating down towards the Sun. Whether they would fly past Earth or meet its orbit would depend on when they started to decelerate.

As the VolatarA fleet crossed the orbit of Saturn the Suvain and Terran fleets began to assemble a million miles out from Earth. There were 65 ships present; one Suvain ship had not arrived, leaving TavirAyan and TavirDai with 17. The Terran projections had been optimistic – 48 ships had been converted. On the 17 ships, the Suvain carried 39 decoys. Moving out from Fleet stations were 50 decoys that the Terrans had built from Fleet facilities on Earth that had finished making missiles. The Suvain described the Terran decoys as "Pretty Good", which was equivalent to "Not quite good enough to be of any use." There were no long meetings about strategy. Everything had already been decided. Orders had been sent to every ship, with one set for a VolatarA fly-by, and the other if the VolatarA pulled up to the planet.

The Suvain were organized into three groups, two of 6 ships, and one of five. TavirAyan was in overall command, with his own ships in his group. TavirDai commanded his squadron, and the other ships which had reached Terra had been formed into their own collection, under one of TavirDai's subordinate officers. The Terrans were initially divided into the five Fleets the ships came from. Then there had been battle after battle over how they should be subdivided afterwards. The more subdivisions there were, the more opportunities for squadron commanders there would be, but the more confused things could get in combat. Most of the fleets ended up dividing the ships they had into groups of about 4 ships, each of which had its own commander, answering to its own Fleet commander. Who the Fleet commanders answered to had been the cause of the other long series of discussions.

While there was no question that TavirAyan commanded the Suvain Fleet, there was no obvious choice for the Terran Fleet. Eventually, a Terran Fleet commander had been named, with authority over all ships in the Terran Fleet, regardless of which regional fleet they came from. In theory, the Suvain and Terran Fleet commanders were at the same level, but as soon as he was appointed, the Terran Fleet commander had announced his intention to act in accordance with the guidance of TavirAyan.

TavirI had been gathering every possible scrap of information about the Exploration Fleet from his contacts with the NVs. The Nemi-Vemzl could be expected to have bought any knowledge of value about both sides, and were always willing to sell that knowledge for the right price. As information was determined, it was forwarded on to Loren Station, and then on to the Suvain at Terra. The last information received from Loren Station was handed out as the combined fleets waited for their last orders. The VolatarA fleet consisted of 28 ships, just as predicted. The size and type of each ship had been identified and sent along. As the ship classes of the VolatarA were very standard, this gave a good estimate of what weapons the fleets would be facing. Given the number and type of ships approaching, the VolatarA could be expected to have about 70 decoys on their fleet, as well as 800 missiles. If there was anything left of the Terrans and Suvain after the missile exchange, the VolatarA were bringing close to 70 of the close range PDCs. As the Combined Fleet was much smaller than expected, this was not good news.

The Suvain ships carried 336 missiles, and less than half the PDCs of the VolatarA. Even with only 48 ships, the Terrans had a full 1100 missiles to fire; the missiles were slow, but might get some hits, depending on what direction the targets were going.

When the VolatarA were around the orbit of Mars, they began pushing back against the pull of the Sun. As soon as the VolatarA actions were identified, the message went out to the Combined Fleet that the VolatarA path was set to pull up to match Earth's orbit around the Sun, not to shoot past the planet. After the VolatarA maneuvers were confirmed, the command went out to every ship that Orders Set 2 was to be executed. Crews were transferred back and forth between the Terran ships, trying to finish up the weapon installations aboard the last ships to be converted. On Earth, there were hundreds of additional missiles that had been made. These were either earlier prototypes that were even slower than the later versions, or extras that hadn't fit on the ships. The missiles were being gathered up at placed at a dozen locations scattered around the globe. Launchers were being built for the ground sites, since the ship conversions had stopped. Last-minute efforts were underway to send up missiles and control systems to the Fleet stations, so that they would have some sort of defense. The Suvain watched all of the Terran activity without much enthusiasm or concern. When asked, TavirAyan had replied that building the ground defenses would make people feel better, and give them something to do. Unconverted ships that could be bought down from Earth orbit were lowered to the planet's surface, and all construction machinery was being offloaded from the orbiting stations back down to the ground. A number of the simulations had ended with all of the starships in every fleet dead or crippled. Everything possible was being done to ensure that if the fleets destroyed each other, the Terrans could continue to build ships to take control of Terran space from any crippled VolatarA that might be still be present. Several people pointed out that the simulations where everyone died had been the ones with nearly 100 friendly ships, and only 22 hostile; now the VolatarA had gotten 28 ships to the system, and the Combined Fleet was much smaller.

As the VolatarA crossed the Earth's orbit on the far side of the system, crews from the Suvain and Terran fleets met one last time before moving off into their assigned locations. The *ProfitTaker* pulled up alongside the *Persephone*, and invited everyone over for a "deployment celebration". The Persephones brought a huge supply of Dark Cola, which TavirAyan promptly confiscated. With three-quarters of the Persephones, all of the ProfitTakers, and half of TavirDai's crew, the entire ship was packed. As captains, TavirAyan, TavirDai, and Captain Adams claimed actual seats in the off-duty area; despite the crowd, people managed to give them a little open space.

Even with more space it was difficult to hear, as the Persephones and ProfitTakers were busy demonstrating the songs of each race. After a few minutes the captains gave up and headed to the bridge, collecting GoDai and MacDonald on the way. All five crammed themselves into the Captain's Annex, but couldn't quite shut the door.

Listening to the tumult outside, TavirDai stated, "Your crews seem to have gotten to know each other quite well."

"Yes, they have," answered TavirAyan. "They have spent quite a bit of time together, especially on the Terran Station."

"It is sort of hard to tell which are the primitives," mentioned TavirDai. "We have been saying that for a year now," answered MacDonald.

TavirDai gave a slight flash of irritation as the others laughed.

"Usually you can look at which side is learning from which," stated GoDai. "But in this case, we have sort of learned from each other."

"What could we possibly have learned from Terrans?" asked TavirDai. "Do you remember the old joke about the best way to die?" answered GoDai. "That is something they have learned from us. What we have learned from them is the best way to live." Even the Terrans could see that TavirDai looked skeptical. "I would still like to die rich, old, and comfortable. But until then, things have changed. I usually think about me. The leftover thoughts are what I give to the Tavir Clan and to the Empire. What I learned from the Terrans, or really from the Terran religion, is that the best way to live is to realize that I am not the center of the galaxy – that others deserve as much of my attention as I do."

"So the proper life is to think of others as much as yourself?" questioned TavirDai. There were gestures of agreement from around the cramped room. "Is that how you motivate your crew to lead in the Terran fleet?" TavirDai asked Captain Adams.

"That is how I motivate myself," Rose Adams answered. "I don't motivate my crew – I order them." The three captains laughed.

"And you think the Tavir should negotiate with the Terrans because we should be thinking of the Terrans, instead of ourselves?" Tavir Dai asked the Terrans.

"We think the Tavir should negotiate with the Terrans because it is best for both sides," answered MacDonald.

"And you really agree with this?" TavirDai asked his brother. Every eye turned to TavirAyan. "Yes", he answered.

TavirDai managed to turn slightly in the crowded room to consider his brother. "If the shooting starts with the Terrans, which side are you going to be on?"

TavirAyan could see GoDai sit back a bit and flick his spikes out. "No matter what starts, I will be on whatever side our father tells me to be." TavirDai still looked dubious. "Being committed to whatever course the Tavir Clan sets does not preclude having an opinion as to which course is the most profitable."

"But this new religious clan is important to you. That is why people always stick to just one clan – to avoid divided loyalties."

"The new religious clan is not a clan like the Tavir. And the new religious clan tells me that I need to love God, but also to love my neighbors. And who is my neighbor, if not my brothers in the Tavir? It is the new religion that finally made me realize that I had not been committed to the Tavir, I had been committed to myself." TavirAyan looked at TavirDai, who was clearly avoiding saying something. He flicked his spikes and said "Go ahead, say it."

"The Terrans have a brain-damaging drink – Krola?" asked TavirDai. There were nods of agreement from the Terrans, and TavirAyan and GoDai's arm started waggling. "Have you been having a lot of it?" TavirDai asked, mostly seriously.

"Any is too much," answered TavirAyan.

"Not nearly enough," answered GoDai at the same time.

"So Krola-damage isn't why you are saying this nonsense," concluded TavirDai.

"I am saying this for the same reason I joined the Terran religion," answered TavirAyan. "I think it is true."

"How could you possibly believe some primitive religion is actually true?" asked his brother.

TavirAyan thought about describing the statement of the dead Terran chaplain, but the conversation seemed a bit awkward to have with the brother he had reconciled with. He moved to a different topic. "For one thing, perhaps not the most important, the Terran religion was the only answer to a very difficult question – How could a race like the Terrans ever reach space?' There was laughter all around the room.

"We are right here," mentioned MacDonald. "You do realize we can hear you." The others laughed again as TavirDai looked thoughtfully at the two Terrans.

"And they reached space three times faster than the Suvain," GoDai said quietly. TavirDai looked at him in shock, back at the Terrans, and then back to GoDai.

"Impossible," he stated.

"Miraculous," answered GoDai. "The Terrans went from animal-drawn carriages to space flight in 2,000 years."

"So that is why you were calling for the PE?", asked TavirDai. "The what?", asked MacDonald. TavirAyan started laughing, and GoDai just flicked his arms.

"The 'Preventive Extermination'", answered TavirAyan. "GoDai came in all flustered and said we should call for the Suvain Empire to support us in exterminating every Terran because you were dangerous." Both the Terrans turned to GoDai, as he flashed his spikes briefly at TavirAyan.

"Flustered?" he demanded. "I wasn't flustered, it was a completely rational response. The Terrans got to space quickly, with no apparent help. It was completely reasonable to fear what they might do in the next 1000 years." Several people answered at once.

"So you were talking calmly with our crewmen while plotting to exterminate our species? I will have to remember that in the future", answered Captain Adams with mock seriousness.

"You really thought the *Terrans* were a threat?", answered TavirDai. "The way you talked", TavirAyan protested, "we should all have been watching out for Terrans appearing under our beds." There was more laughter from around the room.

"So have you changed your mind?", asked TavirDai.

"It is too late. The special thing the Terrans had that allowed them to move forward was their contact with God. That has spread to us already. So even getting rid of the Terrans won't change the future of the Suvain. Of course, now I think the future of the Suvain is good, and I wouldn't change a thing."

"You really think God cares about these people", asked TavirDai.

Seeing GoDai dip his head in agreement, Tavir Dai asked, "So if God cares about them so much, why didn't he protect them from this fleet of VolatarA that is coming to end them once and for all?'

"God did send them help", GoDai answered seriously. "He sent them us."

"So if God really cares about these people", TavirAyan asked, "and sent them us, why didn't he send them a lot of heavily-armed help instead?" As several people laughed Captain Adams frowned at TavirAyan and pointed out, "You have claimed that you are a lot of heavily-armed help - is there something you haven't told us?"

"Of course we are heavily-armed help", TavirAyan corrected. "Very heavily-armed. And very capable of wiping out all the VolatarA and then dealing with the Terrans."

Captain Adams started to answer, then stopped to check the volume of sound coming through the open door.

"I think I need to collect my crew and get them safely back aboard their own ship", she stated. She stood up, and everyone else followed. She stood and looked at TavirAyan. "Thank you for your kind invitation", she said. "And however this ends, it has been good to know you, and an honor to stand beside you. God bless you and keep you and yours safe."

TavirAyan dipped his head in agreement.

"When this fight is done," Adams said to TavirAyan, "assuming we win, you are going to have to be the one to make everyone see the way forward."

TavirAyan looked at her for a second, then dipped his head in agreement again. He extended his hand, Terran-style. "Until our next meeting", he said quietly. Captain Adams gave a tight smile and nod, and the group headed out to collect their crews.

There was one last task for the *Persephone* before she headed to her position at the front of the Terran Fleet. A collection of Terran ships were to make one last stop at the Fleet station, so they could be filmed getting on board to go fight the VolatarA.

There was grumbling on board at the pointless task until the Captain informed the crew that they did not mind being ordered to fly all the way to the station and back and that everyone now enjoyed being filmed. The grumbling went underground, and the *Persephone* headed over for her film assignment. Four other ships were meeting at the station; after everyone boarded, the five were to impressively fly out together. When the *Persephone* left, the Personnel Officer was not going to be on board. The Suvain had requested MacDonald fly on the *ProfitTaker* to be a liaison with the Terrans.

Film crews met the crew as they disembarked in order to re-board. Everyone was decorated for the shot, and then told to wait in one of the loading bays. When the camera crew signaled they were ready, Captain Adams walked up to a loading ramp in front of the group. As crewmen noticed her presence, they fell silent and waited for her to speak. After everyone had turned to listen, Captain Adams stated "Persephones. You all know what will be at stake. So does everyone else. Every crew will head out knowing they may not come back, and wondering if we have a chance. The *Persephone* is the only ship that has fought the VolatarA before. And we won. So every eye in the Fleet will be watching this ship." She paused for a second and concluded, "So don't screw up." There was nervous laughing and then cheering from the crew. When the room was silent, she quietly ordered everyone into the four-wide column they were to use to board the ship they had just left.

The signal was given to the camera crews, and the doors opened. The column marched out, led by Captain Adams and concluded by the ship's officers. Without pausing or motioning, the crew of the Persephone marched in calm order up to the ramp, and into the waiting vessel. Darron almost hesitated for a moment as he looked at the ship with the open hatch waiting before him. For a second, it looked like a mouth waiting to swallow him.

The momentum of everyone around him kept him moving smoothly forward. The crew completed boarding the ship, and took their positions for launch.

The order was given, and the *Persephone* disengaged and began moving slowly away from the station, and from the Earth. The

Washington and the *Fuego* disengaged and moved slowly to her right and left. The three moved out at a sedate pace, until the *Elizabeth* and the *Siegfried* pulled up above and below her. The five moved out together until the filming was done, and then headed back at normal speed to their positions. They met the other ships of the Terran Fleet, and took their place in the set formation. Everything was complete except to wait for the final VolatarA approach.

Exploration Squadron Admiral VolatarA Volasal Elosak Lenoma watched his fleet swing past the second planet in the Terran system. He had five hands present, thanks to a brief conversation with a classmate who had diverted resupply ships in time to get the Left Support Hand here for the conflict. He had determined the Suvain presence was limited to no more than 18 ships, and his contacts in the Empire had provided estimates of what type of ships were present. A properly-timed gift of a transport contract had convinced the NVs to happen to mention that the Terran ship building program was behind schedule. According to the NVs, the Terran fleet consisted of 50 ships. The Terran ship types were about the only information he had been able to obtain. Not enough was known of the Terran ships to have a firm knowledge of the Terran capabilities. It was hard for a VolatarA to believe the NVs' other claim that the Terrans didn't really have defined ship types. The NVs had been very insistent that there were at least five entire families of Terran ship designs. It was difficult to believe that any race that had reached space, even a primitive one, had not determined optimal ship designs and standardized production. Having gotten every possible ship into the fight, and learned everything possible about the opponents, there wasn't much left to do but to wait. It was still another 24 hours before the shooting would start.

There were lots of devices that could allow people to join a meeting without leaving their ships. Admiral Lenoma preferred to talk face to face. There was still nothing that could compare to looking directly into someone eyes as you gave them orders. A call went out for all captains to meet in six hours. A room was prepared with displays on the wall, and on the table.

Displays of the solar system, Terra and its surroundings, and the VolatarA fleet were brought up around the room. One by one, captains arrived, were shown to the meeting room, and took their seat. When everyone was assembled, Admiral Lenoma stood and everyone turned forward to listen.

"We will be engaging the combined enemy force in one day", he began. "I would ask if your ships are ready, but there is no need." He looked the five OverCaptains; each nodded that their Hand was prepared. "We will be engaging a force that outnumbers us, but is of low and uneven quality.

The Suvain have about 18 ships present – they will have 350 missiles, and probably a little over 40 decoys. The Terrans should have a fleet of about 50. Assuming they have about 20-25 missiles per ship, they will have a possible salvo of 1000–1250." He paused for a second, so everyone would think about those numbers. "If we were talking about a VolatarA fleet, or even entirely Suvain, we wouldn't even think of engaging against such numbers. But we are talking about a fleet made up of primitives, and a few Suvain, who are mostly primitive themselves. There will be floods of missiles, but they will be slow compared to ours. Still – if you are clumsy when the missiles come, they are dangerous. The Terrans must have learned of decoys – they will probably have been trying to build their own. Decoys are the most complicated part of any fleet. The Terran decoys will be no problem."

"You have all seen your orders. The Hands will come together in formation four hours from now. When we approach Terra, orders will be given based on the positon of the enemy fleets. If they are together, we will approach to firing range, clean out the decoys with the initial decoy salvo, then fire at both fleets together. Once our missiles are in flight, we will break off and accelerate away. Breaking away after launch should minimize the chance of impact by the Terran missiles, and reduce the casualties suffered from the Suvain. After the missile exchange, we will circle back around to finish off whatever is left with short range cannons. If the two enemy fleets are separate, we will focus on whichever can be isolated and destroyed."

"Once we have removed the enemy fleets, suppression of the planet can begin. The Terrans will have plenty of time to have built more missiles than they can carry on their fleet. We have to expect that the others will be ready to launch when we approach the planet. Both Support Hands will operate against ground targets with the support of the Command Hand. Both Searching Hands will assist crippled ships as needed. Once all VolatarA have been assisted or retrieved, collect any Suvain survivors. Do not approach any Terran ship. We have no use for Terran prisoners. If a Terran ship still has power, finish it off. Are your orders clear?" He waited to see everyone agree.

"We have a superior fleet, superior weapons, and are a superior race.

But with this many opponents, they will still score some hits. Some of us may be together for the last time. But that is a risk we have all chosen when we joined the fleet. And we can know that the risks we are taking will have the reward of victory. Dismissed."

Darron woke up early after his last sleep shift. He tried to go back to sleep, but gave up after another half an hour. He tried to read up on any news, but he knew more about what was happening than had been released to the public. He tried to play a game to kill the time, but couldn't focus. He gave up a second time and made the short walk to the aft loading bay.

Stephen was already there. He was eating slowly, then fast, then slowly again. He saw Darron enter and waived him over. The room was already crowded – half the ship was up early. Darron sat down, realized that he hadn't actually gotten his food, got up and went over to the dispensary and started to select his Day 5 breakfast. Then he stopped and selected his Day 7 breakfast instead. No use in letting it go to waste. He brought it back over and sat back down in the same spot as before. He looked over at Stephen's plate. Stephen had his Day 5 breakfast. He looked over at Darron's omelet and asked, "Day 7? I should have thought of that. By Day 7, we won't be eating ship food, one way or the other."

Darron looked at Steven, and was again envious that he was not as unaffected as Stephen was. Darron looked down at his omelet, and suddenly lost his appetite. He played with his food for a second, and then put down his fork. Stephen laughed and finished off his cereal. Darron thought for a second of throwing the omelet at Steven, but instead picked up his fork and started eating. He wasn't sure what to say, but was saved by Susan sitting down next to him. Both greeted the newcomer, and then waited for her to start on her food. After she had started eating, she said with her mouth full, "It is finally the day. Good. I am so tired of the waiting."

"There is still waiting" pointed out Stephen. "At their current speed, we aren't going to actually get things going for another 8 hours. And after our last 4 hours we will have finished our last course change, and just be drifting. So there will be a lot of waiting still to come."

"How do you know the speed of the VolatarA fleet?" asked Darron suspiciously. His voice was low, hoping that no one else was hearing the conversation.

"I took one of my repair kits onto the bridge this morning to check that it was compatible with all of the bridge equipment."

"That has been checked a number of times before", Susan pointed out. "Perhaps. But you can never be too sure," Stephen declared.

"And while you were there, you just happened to notice the position of the VolatarA fleet, and our own." Darron accused.

"Of course. Not all of us get to see everything all the time, like you guys in the control rooms."

"I usually don't see more than a terminal with a map of the ship," Susan pointed out.

"I see walls full of blinking status lights," answered Darron. "They all mean something, or so they tell me."

"Aren't you supposed to know?" asked Stephen.

"Well, sort of. There are actually several other people there, so usually they know what to do."

"But you have to have a backup system for the control systems on the bridge," Stephen pointed out. You can see the displays, so at least you can see what is going on."

"We just track whether the bridge displays are working – we don't actually see them unless the bridge equipment fails." Darron explained. "But you have to have access to the displays in order to take over if needed. You could always log in and turn them on, if the bridge equipment is operational." Stephen tempted.

"It might be a good idea to have the big picture if you have to take over operations," Susan pointed out.

The three looked at each other, and then gobbled down the rest of their food and left to go give the backup controls access to the bridge displays.

All three sat in Auxiliary Controls and sat looking at the area map showing the Earth, the Moon, the Fleet stations, the Suvain and Terran Fleets, and the incoming VolatarA. The other two crewmen assigned to Auxiliary Controls had come by, seen the map, and stayed to watch. There weren't enough chairs, so a couple would sit while another couple of people would stand behind watching. There was a long discussion of how the fleets were positioned, and how things were going to develop during the day. This managed to burn nearly two hours; the group then broke up to get dressed to report to their stations. Exo-suits had been laid out in the aft loading bay for everyone. Darron picked his up and returned to his cot. He struggled into the suit, but didn't put on his gloves or helmet. He thought he should send some message back to his parents, but couldn't think of anything to say. He finally gave up, and started walking back to Auxiliary Controls. Halfway there, he stopped, and returned to his cot. He pulled his AGM out from under his cot and struggled to carry the awkward weapon, the gloves, and the helmet across the ship. He happened to pass near the bridge as he went. He found Susan, already in her suit, standing near the entrance. She saw him coming and waved. He started to wave back and dropped the gloves and helmet. She waited while he picked them up, and asked, "You are bringing the AGM? It doesn't seem very likely that we will need them."

"True. Still, it just seems comforting to have around", Darron answered. "Okay, it's not very rational", he admitted.

She laughed. "Not rational. Still comforting. I thought that this might be easier the second time."

"It is easier the second time, knowing what is coming", Darron answered. "And much, much worse the second time, knowing what is coming." Both laughed without much enthusiasm.

Susan stopped laughing and added, "Stay alive."

Darron wasn't sure what to say or do. "You too", he finally answered. Susan looked at him for a second, gave him arm a quick squeeze, and headed out to the bridge. Darron looked after her until she was out of sight, and then continued to his station at Auxiliary Controls. He set the AGM as far out of the way as he could, put on his gloves and set the helmet on the floor. There were still two hours to wait.

There were three assigned to the Auxiliary Controls. About an hour after everyone was at their station, Steven came by, claiming that he wanted to check the controls. As expected, everything was in order. Stephen still spent about 15 minutes "checking the equipment" while standing in front of the display talking with Darron and the others. Then he headed over to the old mess hall to join the missile reloading teams.

Darron and the others put on their helmets when the order to suit up came down from the bridge. The *Persephone* had already established her course, and was no longer firing any angulins except those necessary to generate a low level of gravity, and minimal life support. Everything possible was being shut down to lower the ship's energy signature as much as possible. Air pressure inside the ship was being dropped as well, so that if the hull was damaged, the outward pressure would not be as great.

After everyone was completely suited up, there was no action left but to watch the fleets close.

On the bridge, Susan suggested to Captain Adams that updates be given to the crew, since no one but the bridge crew and auxiliary controls could see what was happening. The Captain agreed, and started broadcasting a brief report of the situation each half-hour to the crew. Susan could see a map of the ship in front of her, with a color-coded status of each room. Touching any room would bring up a display of the room, with a list of all present crewmen and room equipment. Since the ship was completely intact, the screen was just a mass of green boxes. With nothing to do at the moment, Susan sat watching the large screen displaying the fleets. She could see the Suvain Fleet. The ships had carried 39 decoys; the Suvain fleet showed as a blob of 56 targets. Around the *Persephone* were the 47 other signals of the Terran Fleet. Moving towards the two fleets were a mass of signals. She knew that the VolatarA were expected to have 28 ships. There were a hundred targets displayed. All of them looked identical to Susan, and to the rest of the Terrans. It was hard to believe that 72 of the signals came from small decoys.

TavirAyan, official commander of the Suvain Fleet, and de facto commander of the Terran Fleet, watched the VolatarA approach. He was on the bridge of the *ProfitTaker*; TavirDai was with his squadron to TavirAyan's left. The crew was excited, but still functioning correctly. The Terran was quiet, watching the screen. TavirAyan could see MacDonald's head turn over to watch the Terran Fleet, where all of his friends were going into battle without him beside them. MacDonald's display was getting a feed from the Terran ships, showing dots with large cones projecting in front of them – at the extreme other end of the display were 100 dots. The VolatarA were still far out of range. There were no orders to give at the moment. The Suvain Fleet was moving slowly towards the oncoming VolatarA. The planet was behind and to the right, the moon was off to the right, and a little forward. The VolatarA had already matched Terra's orbit around its sun; now they were moving in straight towards the Suvain.

Admiral Lenoma stood on the extended bridge of the *WindLord*, the Command Ship of the Command Hand. The bridge had the usual ship equipment, and an extra semicircle of displays and communications stations. The bridge was a crowded place with the bridge crew and captain of the ship, the OverCaptain of the Command Hand with two adjutants, and the Admiral with his four. The Admiral stood facing the fleet displays, with the OverCaptain beside with him. The directions displayed had already been updated to show the center of the Suvain Fleet as "Forward". The fleet was moving along a path in the plane of the Earth's orbit around the Sun – "Up" was left as it was. With the new definition, the Suvain fleet was a blob right in the center of the display. The Suvain Fleet was smaller than expected.

With 18 ships, the Suvain should be carrying about 42 decoys. Instead of 60 targets, there were only 56. The Suvain fleet was moving forward, not that fast, and not making any course changes. The Terran fleet was not with them.

The Admiral turned to the OverCaptain and shook his head. "For now, we will continue on the prepared orders. For now. I still don't think the Suvain will just stand there and let us pick the time and direction of the missile salvos."

"To all Hands, original orders are in force. Left side Hands will target the Suvain, Right and Center the Terrans. Firing will take place at 120,000 km. First Decoy salvo will be 112 missiles, targeted at the Suvain fleet. Main Salvo will follow the Decoy salvo by 18 minutes. All Hands will stay on the same targets. Command Hand will join the Terran salvo with 180 missiles.

The Command Hand will fire remaining missiles afterwards at targets still firing. Each Hand will begin maximum acceleration to starboard after completing missile launch. All Hands are to be prepared for a change in orders before launch." Admiral Lenoma finished his orders for firing, and stood listening as it was repeated to every Hand commander. He could hear the Command Hand OverCaptain sending orders to his Captains describing how many missiles each was to fire during the Main Salvo, and which were to fire the final set of missiles.

Once the orders had been distributed, The Admiral and OverCaptain returned to watching the display. There was a set of targets of 56 Suvain, not maneuvering, just waiting. The Admiral shook his head. "This all looks too ordinary. If they had a much bigger fleet, and could expect to win a straight missile exchange, I can imagine they would stand in front and invite us to fly right into them. But if we are free to break away before the Terrans get a good shot, they will lose. And the Suvain, at least, must know that. Either the Terran ships are so poor they are afraid to even try to maneuver, or there is more here than we are seeing."

The Admiral turned to the Electronic Warfare Officer standing to his left. "Check all targets carefully. I want to know what else is going on." He turned back to the OverCaptain. "All Hands are to slow the approach – decelerate at 2 Gs. I want to take a little more time to make sure this is real."

Susan could see the VolatarA start to change their speed. She wanted to ask if that was good or bad, but she didn't want to disturb the captain.

MacDonald thought this was probably a good sign, but didn't want to ask TavirAyan what he thought – he felt embarrassed to be a Terran looking ignorant before a Suvain. Darron and the other two in Auxiliary Controls did ask, but since they were just asking each other, it did them no good.

The admiral looked at the lonely Suvain Fleet. "So if they aren't there", he asked, "where are the Terrans? The only place we can't see is behind that Moon. But if they are staying behind it, they won't have enough velocity to close and fire before we break up the Suvain. So they must be somewhere close. They must be staying on a steady course, and be as powered down as possible. Still, they can't be invisible. Find them."

It was less than 10 minutes later when the Terran fleet was located.

There were about 50 targets, not very bright. They were off to the left of the Suvain, and closer than the Suvain. They were moving in at an angle, and were set to pass just on the other side of the Moon. They were moving a lot faster than the Suvain, as well. There was about 60 minutes left before the Suvain were in range. Admiral Lenoma asked for the projected paths of each fleet. There were three possible courses shown, depending on how close the Terran Fleet was going to pass the moon. The moon had significantly less gravity than a planet, but could still be used to update the path of a ship. If the Terrans moved close to the surface it would adjust their course so that they would come up on the left and behind the VolatarA. Everyone looked at the Terran possibilities, and then stood back to give the Admiral a little space to decide.

"So they are planning to come up on the left and behind as we approach the Suvain. Then they will fire everything. The angle won't be good for their shots, but if we stay headed into the Suvain, the Terran missiles might well catch up. But if we break away from the Terran salvo, we will have a bad firing angle on the Suvain ourselves. I think their goal is to minimize losses from everyone's missile exchange. If the fleets exchange missile fire and do not cripple each other, then after we have passed, they will reload their ships with the extra missiles they must have on the planet. Without our own missile reloads, we will never get close enough to finish the job."

"So the Terran fleet is deployed to support the Suvain. But I don't see how the Suvain can support the Terrans. If we hold back on our approach, the Terran fleet will come around towards our fleet, not come up behind us. And the Suvain are going slow enough that they won't be able to accelerate fast enough to give the Terrans any help. The Terrans will be moving nearly straight towards us, and we will be crossing in front of them. Our missiles will catch the approaching Terran Fleet, but theirs will have a hard time catching us if we accelerate again after firing." The admiral picked one of the possible Terran trajectories, and then adjusted the VolatarA path to account for the fleet slowing down. "We brake as hard as possible here", he said, pointing to a spot not far ahead on their projected course. "When they come around into view, we fire at the Terrans here". He pointed a little farther down their path. "Once the missiles are on their way, we accelerate as hard as possible straight into the Suvain. We are not going to fire and turn away; we are going to close to maximize the effects of the salvo. If the Suvain want to exchange shots, fine. We will take some hits, but even after sending enough to clean out the Terrans, we will have plenty of missiles to cripple the Suvain. Instead of backing off, we are closing right on top of them and finishing them up with the PDCs." He turned to the others and stated, "The longer this drags on, the greater the chance of a more serious conflict with the Suvain Empire. So we are going to resolve things today." He turned to the OverCaptain. I want a Main salvo planned against the Terrans of a dozen missiles each. Cut the Suvain Decoy salvo to 56 shots. After the decoy salvo, remaining missiles are to be fired at the Suvain 14 minutes after the Decoy Salvo is launched." The Admiral turned back to the display as the OverCaptain began setting up the new targeting plans.

When the new orders were completed, OverCaptain VolatarA Volasal Dersev Arleus moved up beside the admiral. Lenoma looked, and gave a tiny nod. The OverCaptain asked, "They must know we can slow and turn on the Terrans?"

"At least the Suvain will," answered Lenoma. "But the Suvain have no more desire for an effective Terran fleet than we do. The best case for the Suvain is we and the Terran exterminate each other. If we aren't careful, that could happen. They may hope that we spend so much ammunition on the Terrans that we won't be able to fight them as well. If we fire off too much against the Terrans, and the Suvain start to break off, they may be able to just let us fire and get through our remaining shots without too much damage.

That would leave them loaded, and us empty. That is the one case we must avoid. So we will restrict the shots against the Terrans, and we aren't going to give the Suvain the chance to maneuver."

Darron had always imagined space combat would be exciting, with missiles going everywhere and frantic orders. Instead it was boring, with nothing to do in Auxiliary Controls. The ship was in perfect condition, so everything was controlled by the bridge. It was talking hours for the fleets to approach. Even though the ships were moving at a huge speed, on the display they seemed almost motionless. There were three people in the small room; after the first 15 minutes, no one had anything new to say. The room was cramped with people and equipment, so Darron didn't have the option to go into a corner and wait alone. Someone said that he wished he had something to do.

Darron reached over to the controls and typed in "Retnuh". Steel Commander suddenly appeared in place of the ship controls. Only one could play, but two more could watch.

Stephen was crammed in the mess hall with the missile reloads and the missile reloaders. Until the ship was hit, there was no need for a damage control team, so the damage control teams had been assigned to other tasking until the shots started coming in. There was even less room to pace than last time, and he had been immediately ordered to sit down. With nothing to do but sit on a missile and fidget he took out a hand display and started playing around with his space combat simulator. Someone looked over his shoulder and asked a question. Stephen answered and showed him the display, and more people squeezed around. Stephen starting placing ships and speeds in the rough location of the fleets, and a tight circle of exo-suits formed around the tiny glowing display.

Susan was looking at the real positions. There was no way to goof off or walk around — the room was infested with officers. She was supposed to be silent so she wouldn't disrupt the orders stream. She sat at the all-green display and listened to the orders and confirmations going back and forth between the bridge crew and everyone else. Susan found that she was muttering prayers under her breath. She thought she had been praying for some time, but she had no idea what she had been saying. Thinking back, it seemed like "God, have mercy" had been repeated over and over. The Moon was almost between the Terran Fleet and the VolatarA. The Terrans had not started their course change. As Susan watched, all of the velocity markers for the VolatarA changed. The VolatarA fleet was starting to slow down. The Captain waited for a few minutes, until the VolatarA speed change was confirmed. Then she ordered that the course projections for all fleets be updated. With the VolatarA fleet slowing down, the Terrans would come around the Moon directly into them. There was a bunch of nervous chatter in the bridge until the Captain snorted.

People were silent as the fleet headed behind the Moon. Once they were fully shielded from the enemy fleet, Captain Adams ordered the communications officer to clear all channels for the expected order. Within minutes, the order was received to change course; they were to drop towards the Moon's surface, and the VolatarA fleet. Upon receipt of the transmission from the fleet commander, Captain Adams repeated the order in a low voice to the navigator. Once the order was given, Captain Adams ordered that the ship's crew be informed that their final course change had been made. Susan looked back down to her all-green display. She thought back to the ruined VolatarA scout ship, torn apart by the released angulins. For a second, she imagined the display of the *Persephone* changing as rooms were shattered by incoming warheads and angulins ripped out of their moorings. Susan sat back and clasped her hands together to try and stop them from shaking. She looked at the walls, thinking of all of the angulins waiting to be released, so they could bring death throughout the ship. Susan looked down, then over to the power station on the left of the bridge. A bridge crewman stood before a large, thick glass display. It showed every angulin on the ship, and every transmission line for power to all ship systems. Each angulin and line was color coded to show the current level of power stored in each. Most were glowing red, to indicate that the angulins were fully spun up. Susan shut her eyes and looked down, trying to force herself to breathe calmly. When she thought she was returning to normal, she forced herself to look at her display and note that everything really was green.

Throughout the ship, people could feel the ship changing course and speeding up. The course change was a lot harder than normal; the ship hull was whining with the strain. Everyone aboard knew the significance of the maneuver, and knew that they would be passing around the Moon into the open in a matter of minutes. Captain Adams turned to the power station, and looked at all the red. "We don't need all that power", she said. She walked over to the display. "While we are covered, start reducing power in 111 and 121, 211 and 221, 212 and 222, 311 and 321, 313 and 323. Balance the output so they counter each other."

The crewman nodded at the order, and turned to the display. He set the controls on hold, and started clicking on the indicated angulins. He tapped on angulin 111 and a bar appeared beside its symbol. The bar was red 80% of the way to the top. He drew down the bar to 60%, and then drew his finger from the angulin along a transmission line to a battery reserve. He drew a line from the battery reserve to a driver next to Angulin 121 on the starboard side. He clicked the driver and set it to start pushing in reverse to slow the Angulin down. He set the speed to the greatest stress the hull could safely handle.

After setting the first pair, he moved down the outline of the ship, pairing off the angulins on each side. When all were set, he activated the commands.

The angulins started to activate, and as they started to pull against their anchors, the hull started to vibrate with the strain. The power was being drained much faster than normal, and the entire hull was groaning, and felt like small ripples were moving from side to side. The Captain felt the changes, and knew that the angulins were spinning down as ordered. Then she noticed a crewman nervously looking around at the unusual sounds and motions. Captain Adams looked around at the bridge crew, and looked back to Susan. Susan was sitting back in the seat, hands clasped tight together, head down, clearly trying not to hear the sounds coming from the hull.

Around the ship, people were looking at the walls, feeling the floors, and wondering if the ship was coming apart. The Captain snorted again and looked back to Susan. She saw the Captain look at her, point to the ceiling and turn her hand to indicate the whole room. She pressed the button for the ship-wide intercom.

"We are draining unneeded energy from the angulins. The hull is taking the strain from the energy transfer; everything is within safe tolerances. We are approaching the VolatarA fleet. As we come out from the cover of the Moon, energy transfers will stop." Captain Adams ended the broadcast, and turned back to the displays. Around the ship, the crew still looked at the walls. Just like her crew, the *Persephone* was shaking as she started to turn into the VolatarA fleet.

MacDonald sat on the *ProfitTaker* watching the display – the Terran fleet was disappearing from view. He was fidgeting, with nothing to do. "Some people say waiting for the firing to start is the worst part", GoDai said from beside him. MacDonald laughed nervously in agreement. "But they are wrong", continued GoDai. "Bleeding in a crippled ship with no air pressure is much worse. With no power or air pressure, blood goes everywhere, but it is too dark and cold to do more than feel yourself bleed."

"Being blown out is worse", said someone behind him. "If your suit is intact, but your ship is trying to get away, and you are left, drifting, watching your ship leave you, wondering if you should try to open the suit or just die slowly as your air runs out. That's worse."

MacDonald turned and saw all of the Suvain with arms waggling. He gave into temptation and punched GoDai in the shoulder. There were shouts and Suvain laughter from all around the room. "I told you the Terrans would turn on us", someone said.

"I tried to warn you all they were dangerous", answered GoDai, "but did you listen? No..."

"Stop baiting the primitives", the Tavir said in a parental tone. "Besides, one of the really bad parts is coming in a few minutes." MacDonald turned to Tavir. Tavir saw him look, and continued. "The VolatarA are using mostly passive sensors right now, along with their usual radars. They haven't turned on their targeting equipment, and really locked onto our ships in order to fire. When a ship is targeted, it will detect the higher-intensity signal and warn the bridge of the lock-on. Usually this is a combination of displays and audible alarms."

"The VolatarA have spent a lot of time on targeting radars. They can target every ship in the opposing fleet without getting confused which ship they are really shooting at. So when the VolatarA decide to lock on to a target to shoot, every VolatarA ship will activate their targeting radar at the same time. And every VolatarA ship will lock onto every enemy ship. So in a few minutes we will be cruising along, and will suddenly get a flood of warnings, all at the same time, that a VolatarA ship is about to kill us."

"Do all of the target lock-ons give them a better chance to hit?" asked MacDonald.

Tavir flicked his arms and answered, "No. Turning on all together isn't an attack on the target ship, it is an attack on the target crew. This really isn't a battle between three fleets. It is a battle between people, who happen to be riding in spaceships. And even if you are riding in a spaceship, you still have to make the decision to actually be shot at. Even after the missiles are fired, for a little while, there is still the chance to surrender. You can turn off all your own missiles, turn off your decoys, and stop maneuvering. You tell them you quit, and they take your ship instead of blowing you to oblivion.

Having all of the enemy ships target you at once brings home the fact that you are about to shot at by a lot of VolatarA. Especially if you feel outgunned at the start, watching and hearing all of those warnings at once can be the thing that pushes you over the edge – it makes you face what is about to happen. Sometimes opponents surrender when they are targeted, and often when they don't they are still rattled. Even if you know it is coming, it is a really bad moment."

Just before the Terran fleet turned into the clear, the order came from the fleet commander: "Bring them up." In the darkness around the *Persephone*, the lights started to come on.

Admiral Lenoma and OverCaptain Arleus stood watching the display. Given the expected Terran course change, the enemy fleet should be coming in view in a few moments. Admiral Lenoma thought of asking if everyone was ready, but decided he didn't need to ask. Beside him, OverCaptain Arleus was asking – demanding status from every ship in his Hand. Ship after ship was responding that they were ready to launch. Lenoma continued watching the display, knowing that every OverCaptain was making the final check of their Hand before firing started. All decoys had been launched, and were already active. Nothing was left to do but lock onto targets to fire.

As he watched, Lenoma saw the first targets appear from behind the moon. They had pulled down tight to the moon's surface, and had changed course as expected. He stood, watching the radar returns appear on the display as the first dozen Terran ships were registered. There was a sudden flurry of noise behind him from the Electronic Warfare station. The captain of the *WindLord* moved over, and OverCaptain Arleus turned to see what was happening. Admiral Lenoma choose to continue facing forward as if he wasn't listening to everything being said.

"Unidentified targets. New signatures, not recorded before." Lenoma continued to look calmly at the display. Half the Terran Fleet was now visible. OverCaptain Arleus officially asked for permission to report, and reported the news that Lenoma already knew.

"Are these more decoys? Arleus asked. "If so, where are the Terrans?" "The Terrans were already on an established course. There is no way the Terrans can be anywhere else than coming around that moon. The Admiral looked back at the display. Over forty targets were visible, with more appearing each moment.

"Unless the Terrans have some incredible acceleration, there is no way they could have been hiding behind the moon and been able to pick up enough speed fast enough to join the other ships. They must have turned on decoys," Arleus stated. More VolatarA were watching the screen – over a hundred targets were already visible.

The targets were coming faster now, filling the display. They were not just coming around from behind the moon. Targets were splitting, or appearing among the mob of others. "They must have had everyone on the planet making decoys," guessed Lenoma, correctly.

While the Fleets made the best decoys possible, the request had gone out to every production facility on Earth, asking for decoys for the fleet. For months, all around the planet, ship companies, private firms, individuals who could pay to build ships in their backyard, private teams with money accumulated from fund raising drives by schoolkids, everyone possible had been making small ships that could carry transmitters. The ships were all different sizes and shapes, and the transmitters were mostly sending signals that weren't very much like a starship. But there were a lot of them.

Admiral Lenoma gave up trying to keep count of how many targets were being tracked when the number went over 400. More were still appearing. Lenoma turned to Arleus. "Look at them all. This must be the hope of the Suvain. If we have to launch a decoy salvo to clean out decoys, we might end up without enough left to finish off the second fleet. That won't do the Terrans much good, but it isn't good for us either." He turned to his subordinates. "I want the decoys identified," he ordered. "We have much less knowledge of the Terran ships than usual, and the Terrans come in lots of shapes and sizes, so it could be easy to miss a real ship in that clutter. I want a computer identification, and a manual verification. Your time is limited, and we must get down to a reasonable number of targets before firing." He turned back to the display as the orders were relayed throughout the fleet.

Behind the fleet officers, the Electronic Warfare Officer stood before a large display showing a blow-up of the region around the edge of the Terran moon. There were 450 glowing dots. More were being displayed as he watched. He sent out a message for fleet-wide confirmations, and then tapped the display. Every target was outlined by a red circle. Red circles appeared around each new target displayed. The next button he pressed started the computer evaluation of the targets. As the computer ran through the signatures of the targets, any which it believed to be a decoy changed from a red circle to a yellow circle. At the same time, every other ship in the fleet began checking for decoys. The results of each check were broadcast to the *WindLord*. If 24 of the 27 ship computers sent a message indicating a target as a decoy, the circle changed from yellow to green. As each ship's electronic warfare officer made his or her determination that a target was a decoy, the update was sent to the *WindLord*. If 24 of the 27 officers identified a target as a decoy, the circle changed from green to blue. The *WindLord*'s officer looked at the display, and made his own estimate of which of the blue- circled targets were decoys. He indicated the blue targets that he also felt were decoys, and the blue circle went to purple. Every minute or so, he clicked for an update, and all purple-ringed targets disappeared.

The decoys kept appearing, even as they were identified and clicked off. Every officer was starting with the most obvious. The huge majority of the home-built Terran decoys were painfully obvious. The decoys were being dismissed as fast as the *WindLord*'s officer could click on blue targets. Even so, the number of targets was climbing, not dropping. The Electronic Warfare officer sent a message indicating that every Hand should evaluate targets independently, and authorized each Hand command ship to remove decoys from the list and broadcast the updated list to the fleet. He indicated 5 different regions for the Hands to focus on, and the removal process increased by a factor of five. The Admiral looked at the main display, and asked for the total number of registered and active targets to be displayed.

650 targets had been seen, and 410 were still active. Targets were still appearing almost as fast as they were being removed. Admiral Lenoma asked for the time to the launch point, and received the answer that firing was scheduled to start in 14 minutes. A few minutes later, the number of registered targets stabilized at 814. 320 were still active, and there was only 11 minutes before the Admiral wanted to launch.

"Should I plan for a decoy salvo?" asked OverCaptain Arleus.

"No", answered Admiral Lenoma. "We can't afford it. I want to fire a full dozen at each of the 50 ships, which will only give us about 200 missiles for the Suvain, after the decoy salvo. That is less than desired already. If we have to fire another 100 or so at the Terrans first to clear out the decoys, we won't have enough ammunition to finish the job. We may have to fire before the decoy identification is finished. Replan to fire 10 at each target, and to fire 8 at each target."

The active count on the screen started to drop rapidly, as there were no more Terran targets appearing, and there were 5 sets of VolatarA officers burning through the decoy signals. With 5 minutes to go, there were 94 targets. Most of these were not so easy to identify; several dozen of the decoys were a lot higher quality than most. Lenoma guessed, again correctly, that these were the decoys that had been manufactured by the Terran military forces. Even so, with each officer picking out about 2 targets a minute, the total was down to 53 by the time the firing point had been reached.

"That will have to do", stated the Admiral. Cut the salvo to 10 per target. Against primitives, that should be enough to render them harmless, even a few are not finished off." The OverCaptain indicated the prepared firing plan for 10 per target, and nodded to the Admiral.

The Admiral turned to the bridge; his communications officer activated the channel for the entire fleet. "Activate Target radars", he ordered.

The bridge of the *Persephone* was quiet – Captain Adams was saying nothing, and everyone else was following her example. The VolatarA were ahead of them, and a little to the right. They were getting close to the point where they expected to get the order to fire. The Suvain had activated their targeting radars, and were feeding location updates to a Fleet station; the station forwarded the information back to the Terran Fleet. The launch crews were at their stations, and the reload teams were waiting for the first set of missiles to be fired. There was nothing left to do but wait for the order.

The silence was broken by the sound of alarms filling the bridge with alerts. Around the bridge, monitors began frantically scrolling up red messages saying that a VolatarA ship had locked onto the *Persephone*.

People began reacting immediately. Half a dozen people starting reporting the contacts in raised voices. Everyone else looked around at the walls, as if the VolatarA missiles would hit any time.

"Turn that nonsense off!" thundered Captain Adams. "Now. Turn off those alarms. We already know they are targeting the ship."

One by one, people starting clicking on their displays, ordering the targeting warnings to stop. The sounds starting going away, and the powered- down room stopped flashing red. As things returned to normal, people moved from external demonstrations of fear and nervousness to internal feelings of fear and nervousness. The bridge had returned to order when, 100,000 km away, Admiral Lenoma stated "Fire Terran salvo."

The VolatarA Fleet had already moved into firing positions, with the right side hands pulling up above the Command Hand, and the left side hands dropping a bit below, so that the entire fleet was stacked like a staircase, with each hand having a clear view to the Terrans. From the WindLord's view, the Terran were a bit ahead and off to the left. The Terrans were moving towards the VolatarA, so the VolatarA missiles did not need to accelerate to the left to reach them – the Terran fleet would be flying into them anyway. The Terran fleet was not significantly above or below the VolatarA, so the VolatarA missiles didn't need to make a large acceleration up or down. The biggest problem for the VolatarA missiles would be the initial speed they inherited from the firing ships. The VolatarA fleet was still moving rapidly past the Terrans. If they did not change speed, the VolatarA missiles would shoot past the Terrans, long before the Terran fleet approached from the left. To target the Terran Fleet, the VolatarA missiles needed to launch straight backwards, in order to start slowing down as fast as possible. The weapon mounts on the VolatarA ships ran along both sides of the hull. With the other VolatarA, the *WindLord* dipped head down, so that it was flying angled down at almost 45 degrees to its course. This allowed the missile launchers to turn to the rear without pointing at the launcher behind them. Every missile launcher rotated around so that it was pointing backwards, facing directly away from the current course.

Inside the missile launcher, the launch commander stood by the command panel. Ahead were a row of crewmen, each sitting at a display with a light on the hull above it. The order to fire was repeated by the *WindLord*'s captain to the Weapons Officer; it was repeated by the Weapons Officer to all launchers. Within the launcher, everyone could hear the broadcast. The commander could see a row of purple lights from left to right. The launch commander called out, "Missile load".

"Confirmed" answered the crewman on the far left. "Missile status", asked the commander.

"Warhead confirmed. Angulins confirmed", answered the next man in line.

"Launcher status". "Launcher fully charged." "Target status."

"Target load confirmed."

"Orders confirmed. Firing missile 1 of 4." The launch commander flipped up the guard and pressed the button. The turret rocked back for a moment as the missile fired. All lights went from purple to red. In the magazine below and behind the turret a missile was rotated from storage into a reload tube. From there it was automatically slid forward into the missile launcher.

Each crewman started the checks on the next missile. As the checks progressed successfully, the lights moved from red to yellow to green to blue to purple. When every light was purple, the launch commander began the calls for status again. Across the fleet, the same sequence was being repeated over and over as missiles methodically launched out of the VolatarA ships.

On the bridge of the *Persephone*, tracking radars began registering incoming missiles. A second time, the bridge was flooded with alarms and crewmen's excited reports. A second time, Captain Adams demanded that the alarms be turned off, and shouting stop. After two long minutes she asked, "How many?"

"189, and still coming", responded the radar operator. "Time to impact?"

"About 16 minutes", answered one of crewmen at the navigation station.

"Very well", answered Captain Adams in an artificially calm voice. She waited another long two minutes and asked again, "Number fired?"

"354, still firing", came the answer.

"Ship –wide broadcast. Enemy missiles fired, expected in 14 minutes. All PDC crews activate targeting radar, all missile launchers prepare to fire." The captain started waiting again; asking too frequently for updates might worry the crew.

Before her next request, the radar operator announced "Missile number has stabilized at 528."

Susan sat looking down at her display of pristine green boxes. She found she had been praying again, but her prayers were alternating with the phrase "This is really it", over and over.

Someone asked, "Do you think they are still tracking any of our decoys?"

"No", Susan whispered to herself, having seen many simulations.

The Captain turned to the speaker and said, "Everyone will be wondering." She motioned to Susan to talk to the entire crew. "The VolatarA have fired 528 missiles at the Terran Fleet. They are starting to accelerate towards the Suvain. We are expecting the order to fire back any minute. The VolatarA did not divide their shots into a first and second wave in order to destroy any decoys they had not identified, so we have to assume that they have seen through the Terran decoy shield, and the missiles are targeted at us. From what I have seen so far, I think we have a very good chance of winning the fight, but it is going to get really busy here very soon." She paused, and then added. "You all know our chances aren't good. But we have done our duty, and when the sun shines tomorrow on a free Earth, it will have been worth it."

Around the ship, people cheered, or started to panic, or started talking, or all of the above at once. Then the message was followed a minute later by the order to open fire - the Terran Fleet was answering back. Every missile launcher was ready. The missiles were loaded, the targets had been uploaded, and the ship had been rolled over so that the launchers, all on the starboard side of the ship, now faced off to the left. The VolatarA were ahead and a little to the right. The Terrans didn't need to speed up towards the VolatarA, because the ships were already moving towards the target fleet.

The difficulty for the Terran missiles was that the VolatarA fleet was moving from right to left very fast, and might pass entirely by the missiles before they could angle to the left to catch up. So the *Persephone* was flipped over to allow the missiles to fire off to the left, and the nose of the ship angled over to the left, so that the initial push of the missiles would be mostly to the left and a little backwards. The backwards acceleration would slow down the missiles' forward motion to give more time for the missiles to build up speed to the left. When the order was received, every launch commander pressed the button, the missile fired, and the firing crew broke into cheers. A display showed the missiles flying towards the VolatarA; at different times, people remembered that they were supposed to be reloading for the next missile.

There had been no time to install fancy reloading tubes from the magazines to the launchers. There had been no time to install magazines either. There wasn't any way to get the missiles through the corridors from the mess hall to the launchers, so Captain Adams had cut holes through walls and bulkheads to make a path. Each missile had a set of straps running underneath; a team of crewmen raised it up and angulins were put underneath to compensate for the weight. The missile was then dragged to the launcher.

Once there, it was lined up with the firing tube, the angulins were removed and everyone shoved the missile forward until it locked into place. Once the missile was in place, a crewman slipped down a panel and plugged in a wire; the targeting information was downloaded. Once the crewmen nodded to the launch commander, the missile was disconnected, and declared ready to fire. There was no turning of the turret required – there were no turrets. All of the missile launch directions had been set by turning the ship.

An alert at the radar station informed the *WindLord* of the Terran launches. The operator informed the captain of the launches; he informed the higher- ranking officers, and placed the new radar returns on the display. Everyone watched the radar count slowly go up.

"Time to close approach?" asked the Admiral. The VolatarA fleet was already at full acceleration towards the Suvain. There was a larger pause than normal.

"Assuming that the Terran missiles have a maximum acceleration of 5Gs, 20 minutes", answered the weapons officer.

The Admiral looked at the display. The weapons officer had highlighted the location on the VolatarA path. The Terran missiles were expected to reach the VolatarA after the VolatarA have already fired at the Suvain; the Suvain were expected to fire back at about the same time the VolatarA shot. The Terran missiles were expected to arrive not long from the time the Suvain decoy salvo would probably be reaching the fleet. "This will give them a few more shots against our decoys", mused the Admiral. "But not many are going to lock onto actual ships."

"That far into their run, I doubt the Terran missiles will be able to change targets if they were locked onto a decoy and it gets destroyed by a Suvain missile", commented Arleus.

Lenoma looked at the smattering of missiles and did some rapid guessing. "There will probably be a few hits, but not enough to change the overall situation."

"Continue on our present course", ordered Admiral Lenoma. "No change to planned Suvain decoy salvo and Suvain main salvo."

"There are only – 48 – targets on track. They must have really slow launchers", pointed out Arleus. "If they are that slow, they should have started launching earlier. They probably won't even get off all the missiles they have on board."

"They must have needed to continue turning on their orbit before firing?" proposed Lenoma.

"Or maybe the launchers really are that slow? If so, why didn't the Suvain at least show them how to fire a missile?" Arleus asked.

"The Suvain probably don't care about the Terran fleet's attack, they just wanted us to either break off, or spend too much effort cleaning out the Terrans. From their perspective, us cleaning out the Terrans is the better option, and the last thing they want to see is a Terran fleet that can actually fight back." Admiral Lenoma looked at the display. A second set of Terran missiles was just showing up. Unless they were a lot faster than anything Terran that the VolatarA had ever seen, they were late enough they might not even catch the VolatarA at all. "We have decided things with the Terrans.

Let's see if we can end things with the Suvain before this skirmish becomes a war."

Steven was running back for the next reload. The reload team had moved the first reload missile through the corridors and opening to the door of the launcher. As soon as the missile fired, and people stopped cheering, they opened the door and moved in the next missile. The missile was set in position and the reload team left to pick up the next. They were hoping to hear the sound of the next launch behind them, but it was taking time to get the missile loaded and the launcher ready to fire the next shot. They got back to the missile storage in less than a minute, and moved to the next one available. Straps were already underneath the missile. The 10 crewmen hooked the straps to a crane and lifted the missile just enough for an eleventh to slide in three angulins underneath. He clicked them on and the weight of the missile was cancelled. The 10 then picked up the missile and started out the door.

MacDonald was sitting at his station, watching as the missile salvo headed towards his ship and his friends. There had been a little message traffic between the Terrans and the Suvain; the main reason for having MacDonald on the Suvain bridge was to explain if a message was unclear, or included Terran idioms that confused the translators. So far, there was very little to do but watch the missiles head towards the *Persephone*. "You are thinking that you would rather be over there with your friends," came GoDai's voice from behind him. GoDai came up and stood beside him. "No one is ever satisfied," said GoDai with the tiniest flick of his arms. "If you were over there, you would be wishing you were over here, with us." MacDonald gave a very quick but sad laugh and kept looking at the display. Cones were turning green, as the VolatarA came towards the Suvain fleet. Both turned as the Communications station reported a message from the VolatarA fleet.

Everyone stopped and looked to Tavir; he motioned for the message to be played. The voice coming from the machine was not that of a

VolatarA – it was the repetition from the translator, so the voice sounded like a Suvain. After MacDonald's headset captured the translation and re-translated it into English, it sounded to the Terran like two Suvain were talking to each other.

"Suvain commander. I am Exploration Squadron Admiral VolatarA Volasal Elosak Lenoma. Your fleet is targeted, and your primitives are about to die. This battle is decided. Turn off your targeting radars and leave; this conflict will be over before it starts. You may inflict minor damage on this fleet, but nothing that will change the fact that the VolatarA will own this planet in 30 minutes. This should end before there is any chance that the conflict will widen between our races."

Every eye on the bridge turned to the Tavir. He looked at the display for a moment, and then looked over to the communications officer. The communications officer pressed a single button on the monitor. "This is TavirAyan, commander of the Tavir fleet. You are correct that this conflict should not spread. You are trespassing on Suvain property. Leave now, and no other consequences will follow."

There was a general turn to the display, as if the next message really would be coming from the little glowing dots.

Aboard the *WindLord*, Admiral Lenoma shook his head. "Primitives", he muttered. "Your statements are pointless," he answered. "This is VolatarA property, as there will only be VolatarA ships present once our missiles erase your fleet and your lives. Your deaths will be pointless. Turn off your radars and leave. This is your last warning." There was a brief delay. As they waited for the Suvain response, the Admiral ordered the next missile salvoes to be readied. Everyone could see the display light up as a message was received, but the crewman hesitated before broadcasting it. Seeing the officers turning to stare at him, he went ahead and played the Suvain response- "At what age are the inflated egos inserted into VolatarA children?"

Admiral Lenoma commented, "Those idiots and the Terrans deserve each other. If they want to die together, fine." He looked at the display, where the proposed launch times were displayed. "Continue acceleration towards the Suvain. Tell all PDC crews to stand ready. Launch Suvain Decoy Salvo." The VolatarA fleet was moving straight towards the

Suvain, so the missile turrets had been rotated to fire straight forward along the path of the ships. From the fleet, 112 missiles began firing.

On the *Persephone*, Captain Adams had released the PDC crews to fire at the incoming missiles. The entire ship was giving tiny shudders as the PDCs started trying to damage the incoming warheads before they exploded out into a cloud of shots. The crew was still trying to fire off their own missiles in the last minutes before the VolatarA missiles started to hit; reloading had slowed down a little because all of the damage control crewmen had been ordered to report to their stations. Stephen was now standing in a small room holding two large cases filled with his repair packs. With nothing else to do, he was standing bumping them into each other. Darron was looking at the displays, and occasionally around at all the racks of glowing equipment, most of which were tagged with his notes that he had put back on after the latest review. Susan was looking down at her monitor that was still a uniform green and up at the display, which showed the massive VolatarA salvo spreading out to engulf all of the Terran targets.

Captain Adams was supposed to be sitting in her command chair, but she was really standing in front of the wall display. She authorized Navigation to maneuver as needed to evade the oncoming shots, and then stood, wishing there was something she could do other than stand and watch. Near the front of the approaching swarm there were about two dozen missiles headed in the general direction of the ship. As she watched, the missiles started to separate, heading for the *Persephone* and her two closest neighbors. There were eight missiles for each of the three targets – nine went for the target to the left, and only seven were coming for the ship. As they got closer and closer, the navigator started to slide the ship into the biggest empty space between the seven.

The PDC crews were firing as fast as the PDC angulins could be recharged from the ship power system. They had practiced during simulations, and already knew how hard it was to hit an incoming simulated target. They were rapidly finding out that hitting real targets was even harder. Even with all the shots, nothing had been hit until the crew of PDC2 lined up on incoming target number 3, fired, and saw a miracle happen. Target 3 was replaced by a tiny blob of returns, and then disappeared off of the screen. The screaming and shouting of PDC Crew 2 was somehow broadcast across the ship, along with the report that a missile had been hit. The entire crew joined in the cheering. With Missile Three gone there was a slighter larger hole in the incoming missiles for Navigation to aim for.

As the ship turned into the lower density region of the cloud, Missile 1 fired its spread of warheads. The missile payload cracked open and the cluster of 96 warheads were ejected. Each was a self-contained cartridge with a small solid shot and its own miniature set of angulins to provide thrust.

Each had a small forward-looking radar for viewing the target as soon before impact as possible to make last-minute course corrections. There was no explosive – the impact of the shot at tens of thousands of miles an hour provided all of the energy need to cripple a ship. The warheads had the initial velocity of the missile, and were shot out at all different angles so that the target ship would be enclosed by the sphere of shots. The *Persephone* shied away, and the warheads were too far out to hit. Missile 2 was off target as well- with three down, *Persephone's* luck was holding. Missile 7 was already past the ship when the warhead fired, and excitement went up on the bridge. Then Missiles 4, 5, and 6 detonated right in front of the *Persephone*, and shots slammed into the ship from three sides.

Captain Adams had sat back down by instinct when the missiles fired. She was not strapped in, and was knocked completely off the chair onto the floor as the shock from the multiple impacts sent shock waves through the entire hull. The sounds of shredding metal resounded throughout the ship like a roar of pain. As Susan recovered from the motion, she looked at her green display. Half the screen was dark, and half the rest was red. She looked up at the radar display – it was still working, and was filled with incoming targets. As Captain Adams started to get up, she looked up at the power status display. "Power - prioritize ship navigation over all other systems.

Navigation, continue evasive actions. "Damage report." She made it back to her chair and sat down. Susan's display was slowly refilling. The Damage Control Officer was trying to get information from everywhere on the ship; almost half the ship was not in contact. Susan started trying to make alternate connections to reach the cut off systems.

Darron could hear and feel an impact not far from Auxiliary Controls, and had a brief moment of terror. Then he could see that he was still alive, and that a bunch of the displays were blank. His coworkers were frantically pushing buttons. Darron went to the main display and tried to get some idea where the *Persephone* was now going. There had been at least 6 different impacts, and one of the main angulins had come loose from half its moorings. It was now firing, spinning the ship around, and pushing it off course. Darron checked the firing controls, and saw that the bridge controls for the power system were still working. He sent a notification about the firing angulin to the bridge, and waited to see if the bridge responded. On the other side of the ship, Susan saw a message from Auxiliary Controls about the firing angulin. The angulin was still dark on her monitor. She rerouted the controls through the backup lines to Auxiliary Controls, and the angulin suddenly appeared on the power system display. Once it was visible, the operator turned the misfiring angulin off with a tap of his finger.

The damage reports were finally getting through. The ship had been hit by seven different shots, five of which had blasted entirely through the ship. Two had hit bulkheads lengthwise and didn't go all way through. The shots passing through the hull had left fractures that loosed angulins and set the very air on fire. The entry and exit holes widened and heat, air, equipment, and crewmen were blasted out into space. Most of the shots that went through left holes in the bulkheads, but didn't destroy the integrity of the ship. One hit a bulkhead next to one of the holes that had been cut through to let the reload missiles through. The entire bulkhead tore apart, and the nearby structural supports collapsed around it. The lengthwise hits pulled apart the hull all along the joints with the bulkheads. Around the ruined joints, fractures spread out across the hull. Most of the rooms passed through by the shots caught on fire. Fire suppressors went off almost immediately, and the fires went out quickly. This was often because the fires were sucked out of the ship along with the air.

In the 80% of the ship that had not taken direct hits most power was off and most systems were off-line. As crewmen struggled to get things back together, Steven was finally released. He moved through the room, re-booting or replacing equipment as needed. As soon as he had finished the room he started in, he moved into the next. Medical teams were also moving almost as soon as the shock waves had finished washing through the ship.

One of the PDCs had been mostly charged when the strikes began. The crew had picked themselves up and started to line up the gun on one of the next wave of missiles. One missile launcher was loaded, but targeting was impossible because they had lost contact with the bridge. A second launcher still had communications, but did not have a missile to fire. A reload team had been on the way, and had survived the hits. Assuming they lived for another two minutes, the launcher would be reloaded. On the bridge, contact with the ship was being restored, the ship was moving forward without spinning to the left, and the damage control teams were starting to be told where to go. An incoming missile had been avoided. After less than four minutes after the ship was hit, Captain Adams looked around with a mixture of hope and satisfaction. Then she looked at the radar display, and saw the next set of incoming missiles.

Admiral Lenoma and OverCaptain Arleus stood watching the radar displays. The Terran fleet salvo had reached the Terran fleet as expected; the entire fleet had only hit a couple of the incoming missiles. The leading edge of the salvo had reached the Terrans, and targets were already starting to disappear. The Admiral looked over to the Suvain fleet, still drifting on waiting its turn. The VolatarA fleet was lined up on the Suvain and solidly in range. The Suvain's turn had come. "Fire the Suvain decoy salvo. Main salvo to begin five minutes after decoy launch."

OverCaptain Arleus was still watching the effect of the Terran salvo. "The Terrans are just falling apart", he pointed out. He and the Admiral watched as target after target disappeared as soon as the missiles started to land. "I hadn't expected the Terrans to be that fragile. They are dying like decoys."

Lenoma looked again at the Terran fleet. "They are dying like decoys", he repeated. "The Suvain have 56 targets", he said to no one in particular. "Which we think are only 17 ships, with only 39 decoys on board. And the Terrans fired so slow, and hit so few…" He trailed off and glanced at Arleus.

Arleus was watching his commander, then followed his gaze to the rapidly disappearing radar blips of the Terran fleet. He stiffened and turned to Lenoma.

Admiral Lenoma met his friend's gaze for a second then turned back to the display. The decoy salvo was well underway. He lowered his head for a moment, then took a deep breath and straightened up. "Communications – new orders. Searching Hands Center and Right. All forward acceleration is to stop immediately. Fire all missiles immediately. Do not wait to join the main salvo. Upon conclusion of missile launch, both hands are to put full acceleration in Z. Searching Hand Center OverCaptain is assigned temporary command of both Hands. Make for the Intersection." Everyone but Arleus turned to the Admiral in shock. The Communications Officer said nothing, thinking that he must have heard the order wrong. Admiral Lenoma demanded. "Send the orders. Now. Support and Command Hands continue on current orders." The confused officer repeated the orders to the fleet, and automatically asked for the orders to be confirmed. After a longer delay than normal, each Hand called back in. The Admiral saw the confused looks and relented. "I am sorry", he said quietly. "You are about to die because your commander was an idiot."

MacDonald was watching his screen as the Terran fleet was destroyed. He kept flipping back and forth between the green triangles pointing out from the Suvain fleet and the rapidly disappearing returns of the Terran fleet. Finally he couldn't stand it any longer, and turned to TavirAyan. "Now?" he asked.

"Wait. Wait a bit longer. We want them deep enough into the firing zone that they have no way to get out", The Tavir answered. Tavir looked back at the screen and saw the VolatarA rate of fire continue, even though they had already fired over 100 missiles. "On the other hand, maybe now is a good time. They aren't separating the decoy salvo from the main salvo. He must have figured it out already." He turned to face the bridge. MacDonald could see the Suvain all around the bridge stiffening with excitement. The Tavir turned to MacDonald and ordered, "Fire Decoy salvo." MacDonald turned to his display, pressed a single button, and watched as ship after ship began to fire.

Admiral Lenoma saw the entire bridge crew staring at him. "I saw what I was meant to see. We knew the Primitives would try to build decoys. We knew that building decoys on such a primitive planet would result in ships we could identify. So the Terrans built lots of decoys, and put a fleet behind them. And that is what we saw. We saw a fleet of 50 Terran ships hiding behind 800 Terran decoys. They made all those decoys so that we wouldn't have time to look carefully at all the ships we have been calling "The Terran Fleet". But while they couldn't build ships here, the Suvain could build transmitters. So the "Terran Fleet" I fired our missiles at was really about 10 Terran ships, and the 39 Suvain decoys - broadcasting Terran signals. The other 39 Terran ships are in front of us, with transmitters broadcasting Suvain signals. I have flown us right into the combined firepower of the two fleets." He listened as the reports of launches from the Suvain fleet began. In the first 30 seconds, nearly 150 missiles had been detected.

"Those missiles aren't as fast as the Suvain ought to be. They are using the Terrans to clear out the decoys, then the Suvain will be in the main salvo," OverCaptain Arleus mused. "And their firing rate is fine. They fired so slow before because there were only about 10 ships firing."

Admiral Lenoma straightened and spoke to the entire bridge. "Our goal now is to force the Suvain, and Terran, to focus on us. We are going to continue firing, and we are not going to attempt to break off. We will fly straight to the enemy, and give the light ships the chance to get away." The VolatarA were still firing – instead of a combined salvo, their missiles were coming out as more a series of clumps, because two Hands had already begun firing before the scheduled firing point. The "Suvain" decoy salvo was out, and the Terran and Suvain ships were getting set for the main salvo to follow.

On the *Persephone,* no one was paying attention to the VolatarA launches. The ship had been badly damaged by the impacts from the first set of missiles, but there had been hope of recovery in the few minutes before the next set came in. Not all missiles performed to the same level during their flight – some ended up a little slower than the others. Although everyone wanted their missile salvo to land at the same time, so that defensive fire and maneuvering would be minimized, all salvos tended to stretch out in flight. The missiles coming after the *Persephone* now were the missiles that were trailing behind the lead group, and who were retargeting onto the only target still existing in front of them. She had successfully dodged a lone missile when four more locked on, coming in from both sides. The wounded ship lurched upwards in an attempt to escape; the missiles adjusted easily and detonated at close range.

Darron was still focused on the *Persephone*'s path; watching the display, he could see the missiles coming in. The other two could hear him saying "Oh no", just before the room exploded. The shot did not strike the room directly – it blasted through the adjacent room as it passed straight through the ship. As it broke through the hull, it left fractures spreading out in all directions. The shock wave tore apart the wall between the rooms, and sent fragments flying like shrapnel through Auxiliary Controls. The entire room went dark. Darron had been the farthest from the door; he was thrown across the monitor onto the floor. He felt a blast of heat and rushing air; debris rained down around the room. His suit was leaking air through multiple tears, but it had kept him alive. He rose to his hands and knees, and thought at first that he was blind. After a moment, his head cleared and he reached up and turned on the light on his helmet. He crawled around the monitor to see the room. There was shattered equipment and wall fragments everywhere, and two dead bodies.

The other door to the Auxiliary Controls was intact. Darron crawled over to the door, and reached up to open it. He lay flat as air from the room rushed out. When the pressure dropped, Darron got in and shut the door. He found the room controls and turned up the air pressure. When the air pressure was restored, he pulled off his helmet and gloves and started trying to remove the metal shards from his arm, leg, and back.

Another five shots crossed through the *Persephone*, blasting holes straight through. Across the ship, the hull and walls whipped like a blanket and the sound of tearing metal echoed everywhere. The bridge was still intact but contact with nearly every part of the ship had been lost. After Susan gotten her bearings back after being shaken and blasted with noise, she saw that everything routed through the backup lines was gone; she told the Damage Control officer, and he added Auxiliary Control to his long list of places that needed to be checked.

Steven had already gone through three rooms when the second set of hits had occurred. He was sent flying by the blasts, then got back up in total darkness. He started to turn on his helmet light, then stopped. Stephen instead started feeling for the room controls in total darkness, until a sound distracted him, and without thinking he turned on his light and collected his repair kits.

Aboard the *ProfitTaker*, the agony of the *Persephone* was only visible as a series of converging radar returns. No one on the *ProfitTaker* was paying any attention to the "Terran" fleet. There were about 300 VolatarA missiles headed at the "Suvain" fleet —a set of 100, a cluster of about 50 more behind, and 150 behind that. There were also 300 Terran missiles headed out towards the VolatarA. The Terrans were about to start the main salvo against the VolatarA; as soon as they finished, the Suvain would fire as well. There was a little separation in the VolatarA fleet now – some of the ships were a little higher than the others. TavirAyan gave the order for the Terrans to fire, and then sat down watching the main display. After two long minutes, TavirAyan gave the order for the Suvain to fire as well. Tavir watched the missile salvos pass each other on the way to their target fleets. He tried to imagine anything that could go wrong at this point, and couldn't. "Prepare for a message to the VolatarA fleet", he ordered.

Admiral Lenoma was standing, staring at the display. With all missiles fired, and all orders given, there wasn't much to do at this point. Communications announced a message from the Suvain. "So now we hear the Suvain gloat", he muttered. "Report the message."

"To Exploration Squadron Admiral VolatarA Volasal Elosak Lenoma, from TavirAyan, commander of the Suvain fleet, speaking for the combined Suvain and Terran forces. Your desire to avoid useless bloodshed and to avoid an extension of this conflict is both wise and humane. I am in full agreement. I propose the following rules of engagement: all prisoners taken by either side will be offered parole, and given any needed medical treatment and lodgings until properly exchanged or the end of the conflict. Any ship taken by either side will be secured, its crew paroled, and left intact for return at the end of the conflict." Everyone on the bridge turned to the Admiral.

"Surprising tone", mentioned the Admiral. "Return the following", the admiral began. "The proposed rules of engagement with the Suvain are acceptable. The VolatarA make no agreements with primitives." The message was sent, and having nothing else to do, the Admiral waited for the response.

"TavirAyan of the Tavir Clan of the Suvain Empire will assume full responsibility for ensuring proper treatment of prisoners by Terrans."

The Admiral looked down briefly at the men he had probably doomed to death, then back at the display and answered, "The VolatarA agree to the proposed terms suggested by the Suvain."

MacDonald had listened to the whole exchange, and asked Tavir, "Do you really think the VolatarA will be taking prisoners?"

Tavir's arms waggled for a moment. "No. But he is a VolatarA commander, and they will be broadcasting a full record of the combat back to the Intersection. He could never have accepted an agreement that appeared to be unequal – as if he was receiving mercy from a victor. Framing the agreement as rules of engagement binding on both sides allows him to accept. The agreement itself lets the VolatarA know that if a crew is on a dying ship and there are lifeboats available, they can abandon ship without dooming themselves to future torture."

"And your agreement gives a chance for VolatarA and Suvain prisoners, but I was not so sure about Terrans", MacDonald pointed out.

Tavir waggled his arms again. "There isn't one. The Terrans are primitives, according to the VolatarA. He could never bring himself down to a treaty with you. So don't get captured", he suggested.

Tavir turned to GoDai. "I think that was all the talking there will be for a while. Go ahead to Auxiliary Controls. Make sure that the secondary lines to the fleet stay up at all times. If you lose contact with the bridge, go ahead and give the orders to the fleet as needed for the PDC exchange."

GoDai headed out and everyone turned back to the display.

MacDonald watched everyone sit down and strap themselves in. He looked back to his display. The Terrans were too excited to have messages going back and forth to the Suvain. The leading edge of the VolatarA decoy salvo was reaching the fleet. He checked that his straps were tight, and looked back at the display, just before everything started shaking as the PDCs started firing.

The *ProfitTaker* was an average target – two of the incoming missiles had selected her radar blip and were headed in. PDCs began blasting away at the two intruders, and the right-hand missile was removed from the radar display. The nimble Suvain ship slid right as the left-hand missile began its final course correction; the ProfitTaker also spun along its primary axis, and then to the left to minimize the view of the ship from the missile. The missile detonated in a cloud, missing the ship entirely. There were cheers from the bridge and the *ProfitTaker* slid back towards her station and orientation.

MacDonald was suddenly busy with ships reporting damage. One Suvain ship had taken a single hit. Most Terran ships had managed to evade the incoming shots, but a full third had taken damage. Most had been hit by one or two shots from a single warhead; a few had taken multiple hits. The incoming missiles did not divide evenly – by random chance some ships were ignored by all the incoming missiles, and the *Bolivar* attracted four. It had been hit by at least one warhead from each of the missiles, for a total of seven. The unlucky ship was sliding to the left and heat fluctuations showed the fires inside. If Tavir had thought that the battle would be close he would have been screaming orders to get the ship under control. As it was, he told MacDonald to get back in contact and tell the ship captain to concentrate on damage control and get the ship out of the firing line if possible.

MacDonald did a quick survey of the Suvain fleet, seeing that the first salvo had done little besides removing the *Bolivar*. The Terran salvo was just reaching the VolatarA. Radar returns were disappearing rapidly as the Terran missiles, three to a target, removed the VolatarA decoys. MacDonald had no way of knowing if the real ships were taking significant damage. As the decoys were destroyed or identified, the Suvain were updating the target lists, and forwarding the information in real-time to the Terrans and the missiles in flight. As decoys were removed, the missiles that made up the main salvoes re-targeted onto the real ships. MacDonald then glanced over to the "Terran" fleet. The Terran battle was almost over. Most radar returns had disappeared, or were now small, fuzzy blobs instead of distinct targets. A small handful of missiles were still moving towards the targets – the very tail end of the VolatarA salvo. MacDonald started to think about whether the *Persephone* still existed, then a set of alarms on the bridge snapped him back to his own fight.

As MacDonald looked away, Darron was giving up. He had taken out the three pieces of debris, and attached the nerve blockers on each. As the pain was dulled, his attention had shifted to his situation. He was in a small storage cabinet with a door at each end. There was air inside, but the only light was from his helmet lamp. The floor was covered with scattered spare parts and pieces of shelves. He slumped against the wall, and slid down with the other debris. The air was slowly leaking out, and his suit was torn. The room was getting colder – as the heat leaked out of the adjacent room, it was pulling replacement heat through the metal door. One door had to be blocked by something – it would not open. The other door would open, but it led to a decompressing room that would kill Darron in a few minutes at best.

The *Persephone* writhed and screamed as another three shots went through the ship. Darron was tossed back and forth across the room, along with all of the loose parts lying around. He ended up lying flat on the floor. A long-lost conversation suddenly reappeared in his memory – 'There were 86 on board, and 67 died during the initial explosion or afterward, in cold, dark, airless tombs'. Darron's room was clearly losing air and getting colder. There was one last source of light, but everything seemed to be getting darker anyway. Darron just lied on the floor for hours, waiting for the end. About two minutes after the latest hits, there was a sound from the blocked door.

Darron raised his head, and then saw a tunnel of light with a man-shaped shadow moving forward. For a moment, Darron wondered if he was dead. Then his eyes started to clear, and he could make out a sound, "Areyouokaydoyouhaveanyinjuries". Darron started to get up on all fours, and the damage control crewmen stepped in to help him up.

After the third repetition, Darron understood the question he was being asked. "Is Auxiliary Controls still up and running? Communications were lost."

Darron shook his head. "No. Everything is gone." "Other survivors?" "No, they died at the first hit."

The two crewman helped Darron out into the dark passage beyond. One took a plug off the door and handed it to Darron. "Power is out, so doors won't open. Plug this in, and it should open any intact door. If the door won't open, don't force it – the other side might be nothing but a hole into space." The two pointed Darron to the right-hand door. "Sick bay is that way." Both then left through the left-hand door, leaving Darron standing alone. He stood for a second, wondering where to go. He thought back to the displays he had seen before. The fusion reactor had been showing a slow growth in temperature. Darron wasn't familiar with the fusion reactor, but had read about fusion reactions many times. He had a mental image of two things that looked a bit like pool balls hitting each other and sort of sticking together, with little lines of energy leading away from the reaction. Armed with this mental image, the slightly concussed physicist with significant blood loss wandered off to fix the fusion reactor.

Steven had been going from room to room bringing up communications and room controls. Almost a quarter of the ship had some level of power; most of the repair kits had been used. After the second set of hits, Steven had looked around and decided that the ship was lost. He started focusing on getting power to the paths leading to the lifeboats, so the crew would at least be able to open the doors to escape.

The bridge had survived every shot. Captain Adams had been unable to stay seated and was stalking from station to station, looking at the damage done to her ship. Susan was frantically trying to get connected to something, anything on board. The Captain circled by and looked at the display. "What is the last time we had connection to the reactor room?' she demanded.

"Before the second set of hits," answered Susan.

Captain Adams growled at the red displays. "The last time we had connection, the reactor temperatures were climbing. I want to know what is going on. If you can't get the connections back on line, go down and find out yourself."

Captain Adams was pacing around, unable to keep her ship from disintegrating; Admiral Lenoma was standing still, unable to keep his fleet from disintegrating. The Terran decoy salvo had already cleared out the false returns, leaving only real VolatarA ships as targets. No ships had been hit by the decoy salvo – the VolatarA ships had enough defensive fire and maneuverability to avoid three slow missiles each. The main Terran salvo was just coming in. The main salvo was nearly 500 missiles strong, and there were now only 28 radar returns to choose between. Every ship had attracted at least 15 missiles, and an unlucky ship from the Left Support Hand was targeted by 23.

Ships were firing at the incoming missiles and dodging frantically, but there were too many missiles for everything to miss. The leading edge of the salvo was shot down or evaded, but there wasn't enough time to deal with the others as they came in. One by one, ships started to get hit. Admiral Lenoma sat down before the *WindLord* started to maneuver. There were no orders to give – every ship was acting on its own. The *WindLord*'s six PDCs were doing well against the slow Terran missiles – four of the first seven had been destroyed, which had given plenty of room to shift away from the others. But as the barrage thickened, the PDC fire started to fall behind. With fewer gaps in the incoming swarm, there was no way to avoid everything. The helmsman swung directly in front of one missile, in order to move far enough away from four others. Three warheads connected, digging through the ship.

Unlike the *Persephone*, the *WindLord* had been built to take such damage; paired rows of bulkheads took the initial shock and vented much of the momentum and heat out of the ship. One angulin did break free from its anchors and rip its way out of the ship through an unfortunate missile launcher, but after all three hits, the ship was operating at nearly full effectiveness.

Admiral Lenoma was tossed back and forth when the shots went through, but quickly went back to watching the main display. Half the Terran salvo had gone by, and only two ships were clearly out of action. The light ships from the Searching Hands were mostly still in existence. The heavier ships had avoided or absorbed the missile strikes and continued right through the teeth of the salvo.

TavirAyan was watching the same radar returns as Lenoma. He could see the separation building between parts of the Suvain Fleet. The 10 ships pulling up were behaving differently than the other 18 – the returns were fluctuating, as if the ships were changing perspective rapidly. The 18 that were coming straight in were showing as much more steady returns, and a larger number of missiles were disappearing in front of them. TavirAyan motioned for a channel to be opened to all Suvain ships. "All ships. Retarget everything onto the 18 targets directly approaching. Leave the other ten." He looked over and watched as the updates to the target list were prepared. He heard MacDonald relaying the new Suvain orders to the Terran ships, and turned to the Terran. "No changes to the Terran orders", TavirAyan stated. "It is probably too late to get the Terran missiles readjusted anyway. And keeping the Terran missiles after them will make sure the VolatarA light ships keep breaking off. How many of them live or die will not decide this war. But how many of the heavy ships make through the missile barrage will decide whether they get close enough to fire their PDCs one last time at our ships."

Admiral Lenoma was still watching the inevitable unfold. The Terran missiles continued to pour in; the Suvain salvo was starting to register as clusters of targets rather than an incoming blob. Most

VolatarA ships were still making active attempts to survive. Radar returns showed continuous variations, Terran missiles suddenly disappeared as they approached their targets, and almost all VolatarA ships were still providing high-level damage reports. VolatarA Volasal Elosak Lenoma alternated between feelings of complete personal failure and complete pride in the crews he had been given the honor to command. Everyone had to know how things were going to end, and that they probably weren't going to be there to see the very end when it finally came. The voices coming from the doomed ships were calm and concise. The only sign of stress was from the light ships, who had been ordered to try to evade the attack while their comrades died, hopefully in their place. Every heavy ship was boring straight into the oncoming storm, with no attempt to shy away from what felt like physical pressure. The admiral focused on the Suvain salvo. There was now a small separation in the radar returns, but the separation was to the right and left; there was no separation between missiles coming at the heavier Hands and others lifting up to go after the Searching Hands. If they could live through the Terran salvo, the light ships might get away.

TavirAyan had been watching the pleasing sight of his missile swarms closing on a fleet too small to stop them, or survive them. His attention was distracted away to the VolatarA missiles from their Searching Hands; they were just breaking out to target the 56 ships of the Suvain Fleet. Watching the missiles come in, Tavir realized that something had gone wrong after all.

There were 51 missiles in the second VolatarA salvo. With 17 Suvain and 39 Terran ships to shoot at, not that many ships should attract a pair of missiles – most should get only one, and few lucky crews should see no incoming target at all. Every Suvain ship had at least one incoming missile, nine had two, and one had three. Instead of facing about 17 missiles, the Suvain had been targeted by 28. While 20 might have been random chance, 28 was too large a number to ignore. TavirAyan looked at the Terran ships moving around as they readied to fire at the VolatarA missiles. The VolatarA targeting radars were very good. Now that the Terrans were changing position and using energy to change speeds they were adding their own signatures to the decoy transmissions being broadcast; they did not look like the Suvain ships any more. The VolatarA missiles were looking for Suvain targets and starting to register the Terran ships as decoys. As the Terrans were removed from the target list, more and more missiles were switching over to Suvain targets. The VolatarA had been holding back the first group of missiles from the Searching hands to try to let the missiles fired later to catch up. Behind the two or three missiles each Suvain ship was facing now was a salvo of 150 missiles. Making a quick guess, TavirAyan considered the prospect of another six to eight missiles headed for each Suvain ship.

Captain Rose Adams had almost no communication with any part of her ship. She considered ordering the crew to abandon ship, but had no way to broadcast the message. The external radar was still working and connected; she could see the scattered dim returns where the other ships of the Terran fleet used to be. Farther out, there were the changing returns from the beleaguered VolatarA fleet, and the swarms of closing missiles. There were also three bright returns from three poorly-performing missiles from the VolatarA salvo against the Terran fleet. The three sluggards had finally reached the Terran fleet; two of them were flying through the debris field without being able to change course in time to target the *Persephone*. The third was heading straight for the ship. If the *Persephone* had any maneuvering capability left at all, she would have easily have side-stepped the lumbering missile. Captain Adams had no way to order a course change, and the ship's hull was already so fractured that the stress of an angulin pulling against its anchors could tear the ship apart completely. The Captain stood in front of the display, straight-backed, silently watching as the missile detonated in front of her. Six warheads crossed through the ship; the first struck the bridge. The blast of superheated air and molten metal slammed into Rose Adams. Her body was instantly disintegrated and thrown back so hard that the separating fragments were imbedded into the steel wall behind her.

Around the Captain, everyone in the room died in a tiny fragment of a second.

The six final impacts finally broke the integrity of the *Persephone*. All passed completely through the ship, breaking through the weakened hull and bulkheads. Recently-restored lights and power went out again as the *Persephone* died.

Admiral Lenoma had long since stopped watching the death of Terran ships. He was busy watching the deaths of his own. As the Terran salvo completed its path into the VolatarA fleet the losses mounted. The second half of the salvo was scoring more heavily than the first. The VolatarA PDC crews were already busy and the ships had started to slow from the damage they had already taken. The light ships had varying amounts of damage. Three were thoroughly destroyed, and six others were more or less damaged. One had somehow hit three incoming missiles and danced through seven others without getting a scratch. All but two of the heavier ships were still fighting, but their fire was slackening as PDCs were knocked out of action. The faster Suvain missiles had caught up to the end of the Terran salvo, so the VolatarA ships were getting no break in between the salvos. The *Windlord* was the largest and most heavily-armed ship in the fight. She was attracting a lot of attention and had taken seven hits, but was still speeding up as she pressed on to close with the Suvain. Around her and behind her, the fast Suvain missiles were starting to tear into the weakened VolatarA ships.

Lenoma looked over to the Suvain – the first wave of missiles had reached their targets. There wasn't much information about how many were scoring hits, which suggested that not many were scoring hits. The main salvo was just closing. The missiles were starting to bunch up on about half the targets. Admiral Lenoma guessed that the Suvain ships were getting focused on – the missiles had originally been told to hunt down Suvain. He thought for a second about ordering his crews to update the missile target lists to try to do more damage to the Terrans. With all of the attention being given to surviving the incoming missiles, trying to update the target list might cause more harm than good. The admiral decided to just let the Suvain take it.

The admiral watched the display as the damaged heavy ships were swarmed by the Suvain salvo. The chair rocked again and again as warheads slammed home. He turned to the communications officer and asked, "Is everything being broadcast back to the Intersection? Including all of the radar signatures of the Terran ships?" After he was assured that all the information was being relayed, he sat down in his admiral's chair and silently watched the display. Ship after ship was crippled, as the *WindLord* pressed on.

He watched the ship's captain approach OverCaptain Arleus and state that the ship was lost. OverCaptain Arleus looked down, then nodded. He walked the two steps to the admiral, formally saluted, and stated "Admiral. It is my opinion that my Hand is no longer capable of inflicting damage on the enemy."

Admiral Lenoma looked at the display, and answered, "Agreed." He stood and turned to the Communications officer and ordered, "To be broadcast to all hands. Permission to take all necessary measures to save fleet personnel is granted."

Admiral Lenoma could hear the *WindLord*'s captain ordering that the ship be held with her bow to the Suvain, and for evacuation of all personnel, starting with the aft lifeboats. He looked over as OverCaptain Arleus ordered, "*WindLord*. Turn on everything." Everyone was quiet for a moment, then the captain nodded to his officers, and from every station, every ship system that still worked was brought up, broadcasting energy freely. Any incoming missile that had not already chosen a target saw dim returns from dying ships, and one huge, bright signal. The majority of the uncommitted missiles turned to the bright target, and turned away from crippled ships trying to disgorge their crews.

The radar display was still working as the last round of shots began to hit. The Admiral could see his last salvo tearing into the Suvain, and could see the radar signals flashing as the desperate ships tried to evade the VolatarA strike. That much motion would surely be accompanied by a good number of hits and damage. He could hear the bridge crew heading for the doors, but made no motion to follow them. The display was filled with half a dozen missiles at point blank range. Admiral Lenoma started to say the traditional dying oath of the VolatarA fleet – 'Victory to the Emperor', but the spray of warheads found the bridge as he said, "Victory".

TavirAyan had expected to see three or four missiles coming towards the *ProfitTaker*. He was now watching six approach, and was happy there weren't eight. The *ProfitTaker* had avoided the early shots, but with six coming in there wasn't much chance of staying intact. While the two PDCs had looked impressive to the Terrans, they weren't really much defense. Both were firing now, trying to open up a hole for the ship. One shot finally hit, and the helmsman adjusted course. Tavir could see that two missiles were far too close to miss. Just before the missiles exploded into showers of warheads, Tavir saw the other Suvain ships out of the corner of his eye. He lost all interest in the warheads about to hit his ship, and maybe him. There had to be at least 10 missiles homing in on TavirDai's ship.

He was shocked back into his own corner of reality when the *ProfitTaker* spun to the left, and then shuddered as a warhead passed straight through. TavirAyan breathed a sigh of relief at the relatively harmless hit; then another five warheads blasted in, through, and back out of the *ProfitTaker*. Metal twisted and screamed, alarms started and then cut off as they lost power, the bridge went dark. Some of the bridge crew had left their visors up as they sat at their stations; when the warheads hit, the visors automatically snapped down and closed. One warhead had struck only one room away from the bridge.

Tavir started to shout for the lights to come back on, but realized his voice was about to come out as a high-pitched squeak. Getting the lights back on was going to be someone's priority anyway, so he took several deep breaths instead. He found his hands were shaking, so he held them together. The backup lights came on after about 5 seconds. The crew blinked and tried to get their bearings. Everyone could see the Tavir, sitting calmly in his seat with his hands folded in front of him. The Tavir began giving orders in a matter-of-fact voice. "Get all tracking radars back on line. Helmsman, continue evasive maneuvers as needed. I want power restored to the PDCs as soon as tracking is resumed. Each section – damage reports." Tavir looked around and saw everyone at their work except for MacDonald. The fleet communications were down, so the Terran's screen was blank. The Terran was pushing the reset button, waiting for a few seconds while nothing happened, then pushing the reset button again. The Tavir decided that pushing the button was keeping the primitive happy, and looked up as the main display came back online.

The ship started to respond as one by one, backup systems began to come back to life. The Helmsman recovered control, and commanded for the ship to start a clockwise rotation to start moving away from a last incoming missile. Nothing happened at first, then ship lurched and took off as the angulins started to obey commands. The ship started to shoot forward, then the angulins reversed and the ship slewed back counter-clockwise and stood on its tail. The missile, tracking the first thrust, blasted out in front of the ship. The warhead spray went past without doing any more damage. There were cheers around the bridge. Damage reports were coming in, and the bridge controls were almost entirely operational.

"That was fast", stated the Tavir. "Good work, everyone."

The fleet communications finally came back on, and the reset button finally worked. "I am getting acknowledgements coming in from the ships of the Fleet – like they have just received orders," reported MacDonald. "You ordered the Terrans to stay back from the Suvain ships."

TavirAyan looked to him for a second, then said, "That had to be GoDai, giving orders while the bridge was down."

With the bridge controls restored, it was becoming clear that the *ProfitTaker* had taken severe punishment. Casualty reports were coming in from around the ship. Both PDCs were out of action, and over half the angulins were broken completely out of the ship or had been disengaged because the anchors were too weak to hold them. Tavir looked around and saw that repairs were already underway. He looked back up to the main display to see how his fleet was doing under the Suvain attack. Most of the Suvain ships were showing signs of trouble. TavirDai's ship was still showing a single target rather than debris. The Terran ships were over twice the number of the Suvain, and had been targeted by only a third of the missiles. They had still managed to take a number of hits. About half the Terran ships were far closer to the Suvain ships than they should have been; they had been trying to close up to shoot at the missiles coming towards Suvain ships. This had gotten them close enough that several had been hit by the same warhead spray that was targeting a Suvain.

Tavir shifted his focus over to the VolatarA. The VolatarA fleet was coming apart, figuratively and literally. Unless a chunk of VolatarA metal managed to run into someone, they were no longer any threat. Three of the Suvain ships looked like they were undamaged, along with a full third of the Terrans.

Tavir looked around to make sure that his own ship was under control, then turned back to the display. Becoming the Fleet commander again, he ordered the unhit Suvain ships and six of the Terrans to move to the Fleet stations and reload with Terran missiles. Then they were to head out to collect any of the fleeing VolatarA light ships that they could catch. The other intact Terrans were divided up and told to start matching the paths of the VolatarA wreckage so that any survivors could be recovered. Another third of the Terran fleet were in good shape; they were sent to try to pick up anyone left alive from the nine ships that had made up the "Terran Fleet".

TavirAyan ordered a signal to be sent to TavirDai, hoping there was still someone alive onboard to answer. After a couple of seconds, TavirDai's voice came over the comm system. "Tell the VolatarA to target us with everything. Nice Try."

Cheering broke out on the bridge. Arms waggling, TavirAyan loudly announced to the bridge, "He's still alive. Cancel my promotion celebration." After more cheering and a shout of outrage from TavirDai, TavirAyan asked, "Do you have need assistance? There are three ships in range if needed."

"Send one – we can use the power. How are the VolatarA?"

"They are finished. We are heading out to collect any survivors now."

Aboard the corpse of the *Persephone*, the battle against the VolatarA was over; the battle against the cold vacuum around the ship had just begun. No one on board had any way to know if help was coming, but no one had time to think about anything other than staying alive for the moment. In all rooms but one, anyone still functional was trying to get any local angulin connected to heat up the room. If power could be restored, then the next step was trying to find anywhere air was leaking.

If power could be restored and some level of an air seal achieved, people starting thinking about trying to find other survivors. Any hope of communication was long since gone – several parts of the ship wreckage were only held together by a few twisted cords of metal.

Steven found himself alive and uninjured, all alone in a room with the controls for one of the lifeboats. There was still power and air, but the door was jammed – it felt like something had been bent right up against the back of the door. Steven had been trying to fix the computer console, but all of his repair packs were gone, and the console wasn't actually connected to the ship computer. He looked around for a few minutes, and said to no one in particular, "Not really anywhere to go now." Then he looked over at the lifeboat. "I guess there is somewhere else a crewman could go", he continued to himself. He walked over to the lifeboat, opened up the safety panel and flipped down the manual release lever. Then he walked inside, shut the door, and launched himself out into space.

Darron walked slowly into the reactor room. There was no danger from the cold. The entire room was hotter than Darron had ever felt aboard ship.

Darron stopped and stared. There was nothing that looked like pool balls slamming into each other. There were lots of big metal panels covered with dials, with people going back and forth in a hurry. Darron noticed that a lot of the panels that used to form a nice clean wall were now twisted out of shape and lying around the room. From behind a tear in the wall, a head emerged, looked around, and fixed on Darron standing there. "You. Come here."

Darron moved over as a body followed the head out and moved to a bunch of tools piled together on the floor. It reached down, grabbed a drill, and motioned to Darron. The two headed back over the shattered wall of the reactor. "They are getting backup coolant system on line. But we can't have all this extra heat keep moving around the reactor. We have to get the shielding back in place, or it all goes," the man shouted. He motioned to a bent plate leaning next to the hole. "Hold it in place." Darron moved over, and helped pick up the plate and move it over into the gap. The metal was almost too hot to hold; Darron nearly dropped the whole panel as soon as his hands touched it. They moved it over, and Darron held it in place as the man took out a bunch of long screws in one glove, and attached the first to the drill. Then he started fixing the plate back in place, driving the screws into the upright supports behind the plate. When they were done, Darron was ready to collapse, but the man was already moving to the next. Darron looked at the reactor, thought about it exploding, and followed. One by one, they put any plate that was not so twisted as to be worthless back together. The room was a gray blur to Darron by the time they were halfway done, but things were starting to get cooler. People started to help before they were done – from the shouting, it sounded like the coolant systems were back on line, and the radiation leaks were almost sealed. Once someone else was available, Darron gave up and just slumped down against the wall. He sat there for several minutes, and then the door opened and the Chief Engineer came into the room. The Chief Engineer looked around, asked for status, was told the crisis had passed, and started to congratulate the reactor crew. Then he stopped, pointed to Darron and asked, "Why is that man not in protective gear?"

Darron looked at his unprotected body, thought of his torn suit lying back near Auxiliary Controls, said "Oh yeah", and passed out.

✕

Darron had woken up in the hospital three days after the death of the *Persephone.* He had dim memories of a ship arriving and taking people aboard. He had drifted in and out of consciousness as the ship took them back to the Fleet Station. He had no more tasks, and just staying asleep was a convenient way to deal with the slow release of the tension of the fight. After three days, he couldn't stay asleep any longer. After he was checked in to the hospital, he had been placed on lots of drugs. Every once in a while, he was wheeled out and placed in some strange tube-like machine for several hours.

He lay in the hospital bed, waiting to die from radiation poisoning. He was exhausted, and could feel his body starting to shut down. He saw a doctor come in to the room, and approach his bed. He croaked out, "How long?"

She smiled encouragingly. "Only a few more days." Darron stiffened in the bed. "Decontamination always leaves you exhausted", the doctor continued. "But soon it will be over, and after a little rest, you will be ready to get out of bed and start physical therapy. You won't have to lay there much longer."

"But the radiation", protested Darron.

"Yes, you did get a moderate dose of radiation", agreed the doctor. "We have been cleaning that out. The scans look for any concentration of radiation, and then the heavily contaminated regions are removed. If an organ was affected, regrowth is begun to replace the damaged tissue. But still, you should avoid radiation in the future. Even with decontamination, there are still residual effects. If you keep hanging around large radiation sources, the cumulative effects will start to catch up with you", the doctor continued.

It was slowly sinking for Darron that he was going to live. This brought fear at first, rather than comfort –living was a lot more work than giving up. Now that he had a future, there were all sorts of things to worry about. If he lived, he might be crippled. If he lived, there was a long recovery process that had to be endured. If he lived … Darron tried to sit up, and just managed to hurt instead. "Susan – did Susan make it?"

The doctor saw Darron's heartbeat and blood pressure go crazy for a second. She motioned for him to lie still and said, "I will check. What is her last name?" The doctor checked several other things that Darron didn't understand and headed out.

Darron woke up; he didn't remember falling asleep. As soon as he was awake, he knew he was going to live. He remembered some conversation with someone – they had said that Susan was fine, Stephen was fine, and Jon was fine. He just laid there for a long while, just enjoying being alive. It occurred to him that he couldn't remember the details of the conversation he had had. And something seemed wrong about everyone being fine, but Darron couldn't put his finger on it. He was still thinking about it when someone came in and started getting him ready for his last radiation treatment.

Darron awoke the next morning knowing that he was alive, and Jon was not. He had a real appetite at breakfast, for the first time since he was admitted. As he was finishing his meal, the doctor visited again. Before the doctor could speak, Darron asked, "Is Susan Underwood alive?"

"Yes", his doctor answered. "But she is still in critical condition. She is stable now, and will be sent down to the planet in a few days. You can visit her tomorrow, if you can walk that far. That will be your reward for exercising your leg." Darron sat back as the doctor kept talking. Darron looked toward the doctor, nodded, and didn't hear a thing.

Darron's first visitor came a few hours later. The Chief Engineer walked in and looked down at Darron in the bed. He waited until Darron remembered that he was supposed to salute. "I see that you are recovering", the Chief Engineer stated. "Good. Because you are to report back for duty in four days." Darron started to protest, then remembered that he wasn't allowed to protest against orders. "We are leaving for Loren Station. There is a move afoot to try to get this war over before the VolatarA deploy real ships. You are going to come as part of the Terran contingent."

"What am I supposed to do?" Darron managed.

"Absolutely nothing. Your job is to stand in back, or in another room, and do nothing, say nothing. You are officially along as a Suvain expert. If you think that the Suvain are holding back on us, let us know."

Darron relaxed for a moment. Being an alien lie-detector was now sort of a familiar task. He looked for a second at himself lying in a hospital bed. Before he could comment, the Chief Engineer continued, "By the time we leave, you will be able to walk on board. By the time we get there, you will be fine."

Darron sat back for a second, then stiffened. "Why are you taking me, not Susan or Stephen?"

"Susan will not be available for duty for quite a while. She was found in what was left of a corridor leading to the fusion reactor. Flying debris did a lot of damage. She was barely alive, and had suffered considerable organ damage. But none of the organs are completely gone, so the regeneration procedures have already begun. She has been in an induced coma since she was admitted. They are going to be taking her out of the coma tomorrow."

The Chief Engineer continued, "Steven Hunter will be arriving in time to join us. His lifeboat landed on a lunar station."

"Lifeboat?"

"Hunter took out a lifeboat and picked up 12 crewmen who had been blown out of the ship, but whose suits were still intact."

"He wasn't injured?"

"He was not injured. And he has been put up for a medal for saving the lives of the 12."

Darron sat back, happy that his friends were alive, and that he was as well. "Captain Adams?" he asked.

The Chief Engineer shook his head. "The Captain will never leave her ship. There is going to be a funeral service for all who were lost the day after tomorrow. You can attend from here."

Darron sat by Susan' bedside. She had been brought out of the coma, but was asleep. Darron had been told that she had woken up for a few minutes already, but would be waking and sleeping off and on for some time. Darron had managed to walk all the way to Intensive Care. He was supposed to walk back within a half an hour.

He sat quietly, and then saw Susan's eyes open. She saw him sitting there and smiled. She tried to move her hand, and Darron, without thinking, took it. The two sat together for several minutes without speaking, then Susan fell back asleep. Darron sat holding her hand until it was time to get back up, hold onto his walker, and slowly shamble back to his room.

Darron found he didn't mind exercise when it meant getting to see Susan again. When he visited the next morning, Susan was awake and alert. He staggered in, and sat down. She turned her head a little to watch as he sat down. She was white as a sheet, was missing half her hair, and her face was lined and drawn. She tried to sit up, and couldn't. Darron started to say Susan shouldn't bother to try to move, but he was still out of breath. They sat there for a second, until Darron managed to say, "We are a wreck."

"But we are alive", answered Susan. Neither spoke for a second. "They said I woke up a few times, but I don't remember. They told me that you came by earlier. Did I miss anything?"

Darron started to say something, then suddenly remembered taking Susan's hand. When he stopped, Susan worked to turn her head far enough to look at him directly.

Darron parried by changing the subject. "How are you doing?" he asked.

Susan tried to smile for a second, but failed. "They say I will make nearly a full recovery. Everything you can't live without is being rebuilt. It is going to be a long time until things are back to normal."

"It may be a long time, but you will be okay." Darron said. It was the only thing he could think of off the top of his head. He tried to think of something to say. "I heard that you were found in a corridor?" he asked.

"I don't remember much", she answered in a thin voice. "The Captain told me to get back in touch with the fusion reactor. All connection had been lost, so I was going down to check first hand. I don't remember much after that." They talked back and forth for a while, but Darron was still wondering about the "nearly full recovery".

"You mentioned a 'nearly full recovery'", Darron asked cautiously.

Susan was silent for a second. "Well, some things are past regeneration", she said quietly. "I wasn't really planning on children at the moment. But I guess that is out of the question now." She stopped talking.

She looked so depressed that Darron spoke without thinking. "We could adopt." He stopped, horrified at what he had just said. Susan tried to look over in shock, but had to settle for just shock. She could not suppress a brief smile as Darron squirmed, unable to decide what to do or say. He couldn't go back, so the only way was forward.

He was still a physicist, still unable to jump to the end. "You have brown hair. You have brown eyes. You are from Albuquerque. You are 5' 9". Your favorite character in *The Distant Soul* is Maria."

Susan managed to look straight at Darron. She started to speak, then stopped.

"I know all these things", Darron continued. "I remember everything about you. It just sort of happens. I don't know what color the walls are, but I remember you saying that you owned a dog in college."

"I only remember things that I realize are important", continued Darron. "And everything I hear about you I remember."

Susan smiled, and tried to reach for his hand. "What does that show you?" she asked.

He saw her hand move, hesitated, then reached out and took it. "That you are more important to me than anything."

She looked at him for a moment, then answered, "Not 'I love you', but I'll take it." They both laughed, stared at each other, and did not notice the time until the nurse walked in and informed Darron it was time to leave so Susan could get some rest.

Darron got up and started to leave. Then he stopped, and stopped smiling for the first time in twenty minutes. He turned back to Susan. "The funeral is tonight, in a couple of hours."

"Not for you", the nurse said to Susan. "It is time for you to rest. You can watch it later." She turned to Darron and pointed at his walker. Darron looked back at Susan for a second, then slowly turned to his walker. Then he shuffled back to his room without noticing any pain or tiredness. He laid back down on his bed, and was too happy to sleep.

The funeral was being held at the Fleet cemetery on-planet. A handful of *Persephones* were present –the other survivors from the crew were watching from orbit. There was a sizeable crowd assembled along with the Persephones. Family members had assembled from several continents; media had been held at a distance. TavirAyan and GoDai were present with a group of Suvain.

About half of the bodies of the 42 lost had been brought for burial. The others were represented with whatever had been recovered. Captain Adams was only present in the form of an inscribed memorial six foot high, and four foot wide. It was made of marble, and had been donated through hastily- raised private funds. The other graves and markers were arranged in precise rows behind the Captain. The crowd stood in a large semi-circle around the minister, listening or not listening to the standard commitment of the lost to God. The service was short, but seemed like an eternity to many of the crowd. When the service was coming to a close, but before people had been dismissed, TavirAyan suddenly walked forward towards the Captain's memorial. There was a pause – no one had expected him to be interrupting the service, but no one really wanted to jump up and stop him. TavirAyan came to a halt beside Rose Adams' grave, and laid his hand on the marble. He paused for a moment, then spoke in a voice loud enough for most to hear without the sound systems.

"Rest in victory", he declared, "Tavir Esurvith Adams Rothe." There were immediate movements and arm jerks from the assembled Suvain. Tavir paused again and continued in a lower voice. "Until our next meeting." He stayed by the memorial for another few moments, then returned to his place with the other Suvain.

As the service concluded, MacDonald leaned over to GoDai and whispered, "What just happened?"

"He named your captain, Rothe Adams, to be Tavir Esurvith. She has been formally adopted as Tavir for services to the Clan. It is unusual for anyone to be adopted in; almost never has a non-Suvain been adopted into a Suvain Clan and the service of the Emperor."

"So she is, was, a Suvain now?"

"She is a Suvain of our clan, her children and grandchildren are members of the clan, and full citizens of the Empire."

TavirAyan walked back to the other Suvain. When the service was over, GoDai led MacDonald and TavirAyan to where James Adams was standing with his family. GoDai gave the family a brief introduction to their new status.

"You are a lawyer", demanded TavirAyan. "You will accompany us to Loren Station. We will need to know if the Terrans are lying. If the negotiations with the VolatarA are a success, we will need to come to a solution that maximizes the Suvain profit, and preferably, leaves the Terrans alive. You are now a citizen of the Empire, and a Terran. Should we get to the point that the talks begin – you will be in a position to speak to both sides." James Adams was finding everything moving a little fast, especially when his mind was on his mother's funeral. He nodded. Tavir turned to where the rest of the family was standing. There was a daughter who was leaning back against her mother, and a son who was standing up looking at him. The Suvain looked down at the small Terran and asked, "Are you going to be a lawyer like your father?"

The small Terran looked up at the tall Suvain and answered, "I am going to be an explorer captain, like my grandmother", he declared.

TavirAyan gave a short arm flick as he watched the small Terran stare at him defiantly. "I knew long ago that Captain Adams' clan would have a distinguished future," he answered.

Duleka, Soong, and three other Persephones had watched the funeral from the European Consolidated SpaceFleet Station. The wounded VolatarA who had been recovered had all been taken to the ECS hospital station; the four Terrans had been rescued by an ECS ship. As Soong had the most experience around the VolatarA, he had been asked to stay to help deal with the aliens. Duleka had come up on the first transport to help the VolatarA deal with Terrans. Soong had seen the VolatarA funeral, and had invited Duleka to see the Terran funeral in return. When the service was over, Soong flipped off the monitor. The Terrans did not move for a while; they just looked at the blank screen or the floor. Duleka waited for the Terrans to do something. Finally he asked Soong, "Is that it?" When none of the Terrans responded, Duleka continued, "A VolatarA funeral is about the future. The dead are assured that they have not died in vain – that the cause they have died for will have victory."

"A Terran funeral is about the future as well," Soong said in a low voice. "But it is about the future of those who died. And it is about the past – a celebration of the lives of those who died, and of the fact that we were able to share those lives."

"How do you speak to the future? At the end of your funeral, the dead are buried, and there is no commitment that those who killed them will not triumph."

"The dead are committed to God. After all, He is the only one who can help them now. If I go out and shoot a VolatarA, it will not do my dead friends any good. And continuing the cause they died for is something we who are alive must do – the dead have done their part."

"So your own dead you discard to a god, and those who have tried to kill you you take to a hospital to help them back to life. How do your people even survive?"

"Placing someone in the hands of the only one who can help them is not abandonment. And a VolatarA who is unable to leave a hospital bed is not much of a threat."

"But the VolatarA in the bed did try to kill you."

"So what?" answered Soong. Duleka did not answer – he just stood looking suspiciously at Soong. "Would murdering a helpless VolatarA do any good? Would it bring the dead Terrans we just buried back to life? Would it encourage the VolatarA to stop your attack, or just be one more reason for the two races to exterminate each other?"

Duleka kept staring at Soong for a second, then said, "Your family was on New Chicago." Soong did not answer, but his face tightened. "You do realize that the Terran population of New Chicago was probably disciplined?" Duleka could see that the other Terrans in the room were watching Soong now as well. "You are helping the very people who may have been the ones who killed your family?"

"I am remember that every day", Soong answered in controlled voice. "But you still want to help them, not take vengeance?" probed the alien.

"Sometimes", answered Soong. "Sometimes I want to beat them to death with a club. Sometimes I have to remind myself every few minutes that Jesus has given us a simple command – love your enemies. And if anyone qualifies as an enemy, they do."

"So it is a religious taboo that causes you to help them?"

"It is a religious belief. It is a belief that God's love extends to a helpless VolatarA murderer as much as it does to me. And in my better moments, however few they might be, I realize just how dark the road of vengeance really is. Should I kill a VolatarA because he murdered four million innocent Terrans? Yes? But what if one Terran lived? If four million murders is bad enough to say that someone is beyond God's love, surely missing one by accident wouldn't matter. Surely just 3,999,999 murders is bad enough too. But if 3,999,999 is too many, then one less is still too many. And so on. That line of thought – 'how many can God forgive' – leads to only two places. Either God can forgive any number of crimes, or any number is too many. Any if any number is too many, who is there that I wouldn't feel justified in killing, or at least despising? Certainly not myself. God's statement to love my neighbor is not just a religious taboo. It is the only way to avoid a path that leads to you hating even yourself."

Duleka stood and considered Soong the way one might consider a bizarre insect. Finally he asked, "So if the VolatarA was made well, and wanted to just walk away, you would let him?"

"If he wasn't going to start killing people again, yes." Duleka still looked suspicious. "Look, what is done is done. If my family is dead, they aren't coming back. We can't change the past, but we can change the future. Ruining the future because you don't like the past feels good, but is really pretty stupid."

"I have read quite a bit of your history", countered Duleka. "You people are very good at ruining your future, and taking vengeance, and acting out of spite, and out of a simple joy of doing harm."

"Yes", answered Soong. "We aren't good, God is. For us, there is a best a constant struggle not to choose the wrong we like, but to choose the right that brings life."

"So you think the future should be shaped by what people choose to do in the future, not what people have chosen in the past."

"As God gives strength, yes."

Soong and Duleka stared at each other for a few minutes, then Duleka straightened up and said, "There are rumors that you and the Suvain are going to try to talk to the VolatarA to end the war."

"I think so", answered Soong.

"I would like to request to accompany your negotiation team. Having someone more familiar with Terrans might be of use."

Soong and the other Terrans looked at each other for a moment. "It is not my call", Soong said. "But I will see who I can ask."

Darron's recovery was much faster than the doctor thought possible. He woke up early, and wanted to exercise before breakfast. He and Susan talked for hours, Darron holding Susan's hand. Susan would not be up and about for days, the lower half of her body felt empty, she couldn't eat real food, she had been told to rest her voice entirely, and she felt like a princess in a fairy tale.

That evening, on Darron's fourth visit, he lost his dreamy expression.

Darron said, "I have to go – we are off to Loren Station."

"I know", said Susan in the small voice that was all she could manage. Darron looked nervous for a moment, opened his mouth, then closed it again. He started to lower himself to one knee. He was still too wobbly for this, and ended in a heap on the floor. As Susan started to speak, he sorted himself out, and got up to both knees. His head was about level with the bed. Susan watched, concerned, then suspicious. "I have to leave, and I have not been able to leave the hospital", Darron said. "So I haven't been able to shop for anything. I would like to transfer my back pay to your account. So when you recovered, you could choose a ring." Susan smiled, and squeezed his hand. "Susan Underwood, will you marry me?" he managed.

"Yes", she croaked, then lay back with a smile. She gathered her strength for one last statement. "I think I have wanted you to ask for some time now." They held hands for a moment, then Susan lay back and closed her eyes.

Darron disengaged himself, then found he couldn't get back up. His weakened leg wouldn't respond. He managed to get stretched out on the floor, worked on his leg for a moment, and made it back to his feet. He learned against the wall for a second to catch his breath, looked at his nearly- dead fiancé, and laughed for a moment. "This will be the first time in history where the groom is in a wheelchair and the bride is wheeled in connected to an IV."

Eyes closed, Susan smiled. "From what they are telling me we will both be up and about by the time you are back."

The trip to Loren Station was the fastest Darron had ever made. The ship had taken on 30 Terran diplomats, if the term 'diplomat' was extended so far as to include Stephen and Darron. The embryonic VolatarA diplomat had been allowed to come as well. Stephen had been on board when Darron hobbled on. Darron was still bent over from the work of walking. He looked up at Stephen, who hadn't gotten a scratch.

"You're as beat up as always," Stephen pointed out to Darron. "And you are strutting around in one piece", Darron accused. "Don't tell me you jumped around a door again", Stephen mused.

"No, this time I was just in the wrong place, and then got radiated while fixing the fusion reactor", Darron explained.

Stephen stopped teasing Darron and asked seriously, "You were fixing the fusion reactor? You? How?"

"Well, I didn't actually do anything to the reactor itself. I just held some metal plates that someone was reattaching. Did you know that fusion reactors are really complicated?"

"Yes", agreed Stephen. "Yes they are."

They both laughed for a moment, and then Darron sagged into a chair. "I hear you are up for a medal for saving a bunch of people", Darron commented.

"Yes", answered Stephen. "So I leave the ship in its time of need, and you rush into an over-heating fusion reactor and save the ship – probably singlehandedly. And I get a medal for bravery, and you just get radiation sickness. Funny how the world works."

"At least we are both still alive", answered Darron. Both were silent for a moment.

"There are rumors that Susan is in really bad shape", Stephen said. Stephen looked suspiciously at Darron. "And that you visit her every day."

Darron looked embarrassed for a moment, then stated, "Well, there is some news, I guess."

"About time", answered Stephen.

There weren't many assignments for Darron or Stephen on the way to the station; this left lots of time for talking, gaming, and generally goofing off. It also left time for Darron to go over and over what to say to Susan in the 8 second transmission he was allocated every third day, and to re-read her responses over and over.

They did get to watch a small fleet of ships that were crawling away from the Beta Quadrant Intersection. A group of ten Suvain and Terran ships were escorting four limping VolatarA. The four most damaged VolatarA ships had formed up and slowed behind the others. When the pursing ships caught up, the four turned to buy time for the three ships who still had enough working angulins to have a chance to reach the Intersection in time to get away. The pursuers had pulled up towards the four cripples and heard the VolatarA commander suggest negotiations. The Suvain and Terrans had a quick conversation about whether to flood the four with missiles and go on past after the other three, or slow down to talk. There was a general feeling that whether the three got away wasn't that critical to the war, and more prisoners might be useful. They answered back, and let themselves get roped into a 20-hour conversation about surrender terms. After the VolatarA had agreed to parole, the approaching fleet slowed down to match velocities and moved in to connect up their power grids and provide relief supplies to the wounded. The entire group then began a slow speed change to arc back to the Terran station near Saturn.

TavirAyan was accompanying them with a collection of Suvain for the meetings. He had transferred his flag to the least-damaged Suvain ship.

TavirAyan had not invited any full Terrans aboard for the trip, only the pair of new hybrids. James Adams and his son Brendan were travelling to the proposed conference with their new relatives. James spent most of his time trying to come up to speed on what Suvain society and the Tavir clan were really like. He had heard stories of Suvain emotions but he was still mostly at a loss to understand what was going on around him. Brendan Adams had no such concerns. The story had come out immediately that he was intending to be a ship captain and explore the furthest reaches of the universe. He had been immediately informed that as a Suvain, he started at the bottom, and had to earn his way to the top. He was put to work on boring and menial tasks; when he performed them without complaining, he was taken in by the crew as a cross between a ship's boy and a mascot. Each crewman would grab him for a few days and put him to work on whatever ship system the Suvain was running at the time. Every once in a while, his father would track him down and put him back to work on his schoolwork, but that never lasted long. By the time they reached the Intersection, Brendan Adams was probably the Terrans' leading expert on Suvain technology.

Duleka had warned the Terrans that the VolatarA might have no interest in coming – negotiation with primitives would be pointless. Just before they started to cross over, the news was received that the VolatarA would be present. While the VolatarA might not want to waste time with primitives, others apparently had no such scruples. The Suvain had invited any race that might be involved with exploration of the sector; the Zatheur, the Nemi-Vemzl, and a new race to the Terrans, the Jumanj, were all showing up. With the other important races coming, the VolatarA had decided it was better to be present than away.

When the Terran ship came through the Intersection, there were all sorts of radar returns from the station. Less than half the returns were from Terran ships. As they closed over the next few days, the radar returns resolved into the usual Terran menagerie, and ships of half a dozen other shapes. TavirAyan had pulled up alongside the Terrans, and the two ships were approaching the station exactly side by side. There were two VolatarA ships present – one was an unarmed transport about the size of the *Winged Vision*. The other was a very armed ship as big as the *WindLord*. As the Terran and Suvain ships closed, one radar return resolved itself into the characteristic caterpillar shape of the Nemi-Vemzl. Another clarified itself into a large, square block. That is the Zatheur, the Terrans were informed. The Terrans had been told that the Jumanj were one of the first races to discover the Intersections, and controlled the largest empire in the galaxy. In addition to being the most powerful race, they were also the most advanced. The Terrans kept looking for some giant, really advanced ship, but couldn't see one.

By the time the Terrans and Suvain reached the station, everyone else was present. The VolatarA and Suvain had agreed to a local truce for 12 VolatarA days. The VolatarA day was a little over 26 hours, so the meeting had just over 13 Terran days to complete, one way or the other. There was a formal reception to welcome the Terran and Suvain delegates, led by CE Aguilera and the Tavir. The hall was filled with Terrans and Suvain; no VolatarA were present. There was a deliberately restrained congratulation to the Terran and Suvain fleet, followed by a formal welcome to the arriving delegates, and then dinner was served. During the post-meal mingling, CE Aguilera made his way to Stephen and Darron. "I am glad to see you alive", he stated. "We were out of touch for a while, but heard about the loss of the *Persephone* when communications were restored. We were very sorry to hear about the death of Captain Adams." Both Stephen and Darron had no idea how to respond to this statement, so they both nodded and mumbled. "You have done your job", he continued. "Now it is time for us to do ours."

The formal meeting began the day after they arrived. Even the Terrans had realized that a meeting with half a dozen VolatarA on one side and 50 Terrans on the other would be cumbersome, so a list had been drawn up at Loren Station of the six Terrans who would actually be part of the conference. The rest would be watching, and free to talk with the formal delegates after, but not during, any meetings. Four VolatarA would be attending, along with six Suvain, two Zatheur, and one NV. There were three Jumanj at Loren Station; they had declined to participate, and stated they were only here as observers.

The only room at Loren Station with the desired size and shape for the meetings was an audience hall in Disney Virtual World - Loren Station.

When Darron and Stephen filed in the next morning, they were given seats on the third balcony overlooking a long table with twenty seats. There were two rows of more important people arcing along below them, and at the other end of the room, a huge display screen. Darron realized that all of the walls were really display screens as well; they had been changed from the usual decorations to a calm light brown. The table was laid out as a short, upside- down letter T. Along the stubby table in front were the four VolatarA, sitting across from The Tavir, TavirAyan, CE Aguilera, and a representative of the African Union. At the elongated crossbar were GoDai and three other Suvain, the other four Terrans, the Zatheur and the NV. The three Jumanj were not at the table at all – they were sitting with the bottom tier of observers.

This was the first look that Stephen and Darron had had of the new races. Stephen was very interested, and making quick sketches of the new- comers; Darron suspected that three new races were about to join the still-in- progress exploration game. The VolatarA looked a lot like tall and athletic Terrans, across from the bulky Suvain with their odd-shaped limbs. The NVs were even taller than the VolatarA, and much thinner. The NV representative was the captain of the NV ship which had now been at Loren Station for months. He sat in a power-assisted chair, which compensated for the Terran- strength gravity at the station. Stephen could get a much closer look at an NV by looking at the one sitting next to him. This NV was younger, and was sitting in a normal chair. They had greeted each other Terran-style; it took Stephen and Darron several hours to notice that the NV did not wear a headset – he was speaking English. The Zatheur was almost as thick as wide. It head was almost round, rather than the oblong of most races. The alien's skin looked like a cross between rhinoceros hide and snake scales.

It took a while for them to find the Jumanj. The giant display was currently showing the main table, and a bit of the lower tier of spectators was visible. Three Junamj were sitting in the best seats in the house. Each stood nearly 7 foot tall, and weighed close to 400 pounds. They were wide, with powerful arms and chests, and large, overflowing stomachs. If they were Terrans, Darron would describe their facial expressions as bored. Darron was watching the Jumanj when Stephen asked, "What are they doing?" People at the front table were talking at the same time, and the VolatarA were refusing to sit down. There seemed to be some disagreement about who was in charge of the meeting, and what the meeting was called – a "Discussion", or a "Negotiation".

The deadlock continued long enough for all the observers to start to lose interest. Finally, the NV suggested that a neutral observer be appointed as a moderator. Lots of people looked at the Jumanj, and the largest Jumanj got up, and walked to the head of the table. A seat was found that was large enough for the Jumanj, and he sat down in front of everyone. As soon as he sat down, the VolatarA did as well. The Jumanj turned to the Suvain, and asked for the Suvain to describe how the current conflict had begun, and what the Suvain thought should happen in the future. After a long description by the Suvain, the Jumanj turned to the VolatarA and asked them how the current conflict had begun, and what the VolatarA thought should happen in the future. The VolatarA description of the future included a full squadron of Imperial Fleet ships arriving to end the war with the primitives and the Suvain. Long before the VolatarA finished, Stephen and Darron had lost interest in the proceedings. They re-focused when CE Aguilera began to speak. The VolatarA statement had been completed, and the Jumanj had looked to the Suvain. CE Aguilera stood, said "If I may", with a bow to the Jumanj, and continued with a brief description of the location of the restrooms, and the directions to where a buffet had been assembled with what the Terrans had been informed were traditional foods of each race. He ended by thanking the Jumanj for his generosity in volunteering to moderate, and asked the moderator when he would prefer the group to reassemble to hear the continuation of the background descriptions. There was some muttering from the VolatarA and the audience, and all eyes turned to the Jumanj.

The moderator looked at the Terran for a moment and then answered, "We will reassemble in 2.98 hours." Everyone started to rise and head for relief or food. Groups began to form immediately, talking about the morning's statements. Darron and Stephen rose with the others, and waited for all the important people to go first. Their NV neighbor asked for their names, and then asked if they were the members of the *Persephone* crew. When they said they were, the NV asked if he could accompany them to lunch; he had been trying Terran foods, and wondered if they could suggest items for him to experience. As they waited for the buffet, they discovered that their new acquaintance was Jir-Sur-Radol, part of the communications personnel on board the *Kar-le-nu*; he was present because he was responsible for the NV headsets, and had to be present in case any new interfaces or re- programming were required.

During lunch, CE Aguilera came by their table, and looked at Stephen and the NV, who had been talking through the whole meal. "They seem to be having a good time", he commented to Darron.

"They are both programmers, and they are not being told to cooperate with each other, or give information to a non-programmer, or understand a set of rules that they didn't write themselves. So they will be having a very good time." Both programmers continued with their conversation.

"I believe you are here to warn us if the Suvain are less than open with us?" CE Aguilera asked.

"From everything I have seen, they have not been. They probably feel that a combined front is much more effective than trying to make a deal", answered Darron.

"For this conference, it will be", answered the diplomat. "Assuming we survive the first, it the next conference we have with them that will be their main opportunity for deception."

Two Jumanj hours later, the group reassembled. Even Darron and Stephen could see that every eye was fixed on the Jumanj.

"Now perhaps it would be useful to hear from the Terrans how the current conflict had begun, and what the Terrans think should happen in the future." There was a ripple through all the non-Terrans in the crowd, and the VolatarA looked mutinous. CE Aguilera rose, and gave a very brief description of the attack on the *Persephone*, and then the Terran worlds. His main effort was spent in describing a future in which present unfortunate conflicts were resolved without the introduction of Imperial Fleet elements into the region. He pointed out that the introduction by one race of combat vessels would lead to every race with an interest in exploration of the Intersections in this unclaimed part of the galaxy having to deploy combat vessels as well. This would lead to an increased chance of serious hostilities, rather than ensuring the current squabble did not lead to more significant bloodshed. He concluded by admitting that the Terrans clearly had interests in seeing a quick end to the current dispute, but pointed out that every race present would benefit from a move away from the costs and risks of militarization of the region – even the VolatarA.

With the background over, the "talks" (on one side of the table), or "negotiations" (on the other side of the table) began. The VolatarA talked to the Suvain. Then the Suvain talked to the VolatarA. Then the Terrans talked to the VolatarA and the VolatarA made it clear they weren't listening. The VolatarA talked at everyone. By then, most of the audience wasn't really listening. People listened less and less on the second day and the third.

A lot of the real talking occurred after the meetings. CE Aguilera made a point of talking with everyone who was willing; this included most everyone except the Jumanj, the VolatarA, and the official representatives of the NVs and the Zatheur. A lot of the questions dealt with the size of the Terran fleet, and the current relationship between the Suvain and the Terrans. Before the fourth day, CE Aguilera asked to meet with the Suvain before the formal talks.

"We have always talked about trying to end the war with the VolatarA first, and then decide our differences later. I now believe we need to resolve our own disagreements first, in order to end the war with the VolatarA."

"Why?" asked the Tavir.

"Every other race wants to see this end, so they can get on with their own expansion. But if they think that we might work together against them if the VolatarA leave, then they might as well let the VolatarA deal with us."

"And if they know that we are not, then there is much more incentive for them to press the VolatarA for an agreement", agreed The Tavir. He waited for the supporting nods from the Terrans. Then he continued. "But if we both just agree to go our own way, then the Tavir have lost everything, and gotten nothing in return. So we are better off going on against the VolatarA than just giving up."

The room was silent for a few moments. Then James Adams stood up. "As the only member of both sides, I have a vested interest in both sides surviving the VolatarA, and surviving each other. To survive the VolatarA, the Terran and the Suvain must be clearly separate when the war ends. For the Tavir to survive the conflict, the Tavir must profit. So we need to reach an agreement by which the Tavir profit by letting the Terrans go their way." We Suvain have a lawyer present", James Adams said. "So the Terrans should pick a lawyer to represent the Terran race, and we should sit down and come to an arrangement that will benefit both sides."

There were mutterings from all sides. "Do you think your new Suvain is trustworthy?" The Tavir asked TavirAyan.

TavirAyan looked at James Adams, who answered, "From what I understand, I am a Suvain now, as well as a Terran. And I am sure I am a lawyer, and that you are my client."

A champion for the Terrans was selected, and the two sat down to the strange legal combination of competition and cooperation. The lawyers were still fencing when the time came for everyone else to join the formal meeting.

The talks continued, but it was clear to everyone that something had changed. The Suvain and Terrans weren't really trying to make progress, they were just dragging out the discussions. By the end of the first break, the rumors had caught on that the Terrans would not be allied with the Suvain should the war end.

At lunch, the lead Zatheur representative, for the first time, approached CE Aguilera and suggested they discuss what the Terran intentions were should the war with the VolatarA end. They had a civil conversation in view of everyone. Most people ate a little, and watched a lot as the sentient Zatheur officially acknowledged the existence of the Terrans. Darron and the programmers were sitting in their usual seat on the top tier as the Zatheur- Terran conversation was occurring below. Stephen and Jir-Sur-Radol were about the only two who weren't paying attention. Their conversation had moved from the extension of the NV role in Stephen's new space exploration game to a discussion of whether it would be possible to keep players linked while in transit so people could play the space exploration game as they were actually exploring space. Neither noticed as Duleka came up to the three of them. Darron turned and greeted the VolatarA.

The other two looked up when Duleka began talking. He pointed down to CE Aguilera for a moment. "Would you trust that man?" he asked Darron.

"Yes", answered Darron. Darron looked down at CE Aguilera, wondering if there was some reason he shouldn't.

"If that man claimed we would be at peace, he would not really still be working against the VolatarA?" questioned Duleka.

"No", answered Darron.

Duleka looked at Darron for a second, then back down to CE Aguilera. "Why are you asking this Terran if that Terran is reliable?" asked Jir-Sur- Radol. "That would only be reasonable if you had reason to believe that this Terran is reliable."

"I do believe this Terran is reliable", answered Duleka. Darron was embarrassed and gratified at the same time. He was starting to mumble something when Duleka continued, "From what I have observed, these two Terrans lack the necessary social skills and social awareness to construct and maintain a believable false pretense."

"If the war did end, and we are once again exploring this cluster, would he be arranging to work with the other races to keep us out?" continued Duleka.

The suddenly-deflated physicist answered, "Not if we said we wouldn't. I think that the councilor wants to end a war, not to keep it going."

"If we did, it would just hurt you and us, while everyone else would expand around us", pointed out Stephen.

"So you would not be trying to undercut us, even though we are enemies?" Duleka said.

"Even though we *were* enemies", corrected Darron. "Whether we *are* enemies is up to you."

"You really believe that people can ever really stop being enemies?" Everyone turned to look behind Duleka as an arm-flick caught their attention.

GoDai was standing behind Duleka. He moved over a little so that everyone was in view.

"We asked very similar questions when we first stated dealing with the Terrans." GoDai stated. "Yes, I do believe that. It was one of the really strange things about the Terrans, and about their religion. The Terran religion, or really more than just Terran now, claims that God will cause, or enable, people to change. That people who were enemies can now be friends." Unlike the Terrans, GoDai could recognize Duleka's dubious look. "Part of this belief is that what is important today is not what someone did yesterday, or who they were yesterday – it is what you are going to choose to do today, what you are going to choose to be today."

"So even if the person lying in the hospital bed killed your family yesterday, today he is a person in need, and you should decide to help him?" suggested Duleka.

"I would never want to face that particular challenge, but yes, that is the basic idea."

"And this belief is what guides all your actions?" asked Duleka. There was general laughter.

"This belief is what is supposed to guide all our actions, and sometimes does," answered GoDai. "But our source of decision making is often the desire to be above everyone else, and revenge, and to put off difficult tasks, or to make everyone like us. Only God is perfect. That is why I referred to the situation where what is right is completely opposed to our usual desires to be a challenge."

"And 'God' is connected to this process of change?"

"Of course", stated Darron. "The center of mass of any self-contained system will continue in a straight line unless there is action by an outside unbalanced force."

Stephen looked at Darron, and slid off the conversation to the analogy. "What if the system went through an Intersection?" he asked.

"The momentum would be unchanged, there would just be a discontinuity in the position of the center of mass", answered Darron.

As Stephen started to ask about angulin use in the self-contained system, GoDai interrupted. "Yes", he summarized to Duleka.

"And you accept all this?" Duleka asked GoDai.

"I do now. After I first spent time with the Terrans, I suggested Preventative Extermination. Now I suggest we live in peace, to mutual benefit. I would suppose that I have changed."

When the afternoon session began, the VolatarA said they were going to discuss matters, and would be back to meet the next morning. They all then got up and left. People milled around for a bit, and then someone finally asked the moderator what the Jumanj thought would be good for the future.

The bored expression did not change. "Where one Fleet goes, many follow. We Jumanj would not recommend such a course." The Jumanj continued in the same calm voice. "When one, or two, races believe they can take too big a share of what is available, envy follows. We Jumanj would not recommend such a course." The moderator then got up, walked with his companions to the Jumanj portion of the dining hall, and helped themselves to a second lunch.

The meeting room with the VolatarA delegation was not a happy place.

The Pro-Fleet side thought the only way out of the current mess was to call the Fleet as soon as possible, and force the other races to accept the results. The No-Fleet side countered that calling in the Fleet could lead to war with the Suvain which was far more costly than this little backwater was worth.

And even in the best case, every other race in the area would be hostile. The Pro-Fleet side had no counter to this, but pointed out that a humiliating withdrawal before a group of primitives would lose them this cluster anyway, and would be unworthy of the Emperor. The No-Fleet side had no counter to this; both sides ended up sitting in varying combinations of anger and depression.

Duleka waited until the arguments burned down to ashes, and then asked to speak. "Frustration aside", he began, "we have to base our decision on the real situation. And I think if we review everything that is going on, we can see that the real situation is this – either we call the Fleet now and exterminate the Terrans, or the Terrans will be an independent and growing race in this cluster. If we back off, the Suvain will not try to remove the Terran presence. The Suvain are too disorderly to do so; the Tavir Clan is the primary group involved, and it will look to its own profit, not the glory of its Emperor. If we call the Fleet, nothing good will result. The Terrans will be destroyed, but the Emperor will have gained nothing. A radioactive rock is a poor return for the investment we have already lost, much less the cost of deploying one, or more, squadrons of Fleet ships. There is a realistic risk of war, and an inevitable build up in the cluster that will do nothing but make the rest of our exploration here risky and slow. So I would recommend we make our decisions based on the second possibility – the Terrans will be an independent and growing race in the region."

"If a ship of one of the other races attacked a VolatarA ship, we would be furious. We would demand an apology and compensation. So we should demand from the Terrans an apology and compensation. They can claim that everything is our fault if they want, but I think they will know better than to argue. So we demand that they formally and publically apologize for the affront to the dignity of the Emperor, and pay for all costs we have suffered in the war. We treat them just like we would treat the Suvain, or any of the other lesser races. This ends, the honor of the Emperor is upheld, everyone sees that we can attack someone's home world and make them pay us damages, and we can get back to exploring this cluster for planets that will be of profit to the Empire."

There was silence, until a Fleet side spokesman responded, "That would leave the Terrans intact to work against us everywhere in the cluster."

"I don't think they will", answered Duleka. "At least, no more than we all do. We will make it very clear to everyone that if they harass the VolatarA again, the truce is over, and our Fleet will obliterate them. If they are breaking parole, the other races will be much less likely to jump in. And I think the Terrans care more about their own future than they care about trying to punish us for the past. The Terrans need to grow into a race that must be taken seriously. Wasting time following us around to tweak our nose doesn't move them forward."

The room was silent again, until the Formal Representative stated, "So you are suggesting that we demand the Terrans give an apology and compensation."

"I am suggesting you summon the lead Terran Councilor and make your statement. He will understand, and agree."

"I do not like your suggestion, or the implicit recognition of the Terrans. But it is an option. Does anyone one see another path that could lead to the benefit and honor of the Emperor?" He waited, but no one spoke. The Formal Representative started to speak to Duleka, then stopped, then started again. "No. You stay put." He turned to the captain of the Fleet warship sitting at Loren Station. "You. You are to tell the Terran Councilor that I will address him here in 12 minutes. No other Terran is needed." The indicated VolatarA rose and left. Duleka found a chair to place at the end of the table. The others sat in silence.

CE Aguilera was in the main hall when the summons arrived. When the VolatarA was seen purposefully striding into the room, Aguilera managed to position himself so that he happened to be standing in front of the lead delegates of both the NVs and the Zatheur, with Suvain and Terrans spreading out behind them. All turned to watch as the VolatarA approached; from above, the observers could see the Terran negotiator standing as if in front of the united delegations of every other race, with the VolatarA standing alone facing them all. The VolatarA captain approached, and delivered his message.

CE Aguilera did not move. "If this is a declaration that the truce we have offered is now refused, and you intend to escalate the conflict, it will affect everyone here. It would be more appropriate if your delegation came here and spoke to all present." There were signs of agreement from behind him. "Or if the VolatarA instead wish to address a private matter, I would be glad to attend."

The captain growled, but answered, "The Emperor's spokesman will be available to speak to you in 6 minutes." He then turned and left.

As soon as he was gone, the entire room began buzzing with questions, rumors, and in the case of two Suvain, a bet. Each race began to converge in on itself as CE Aguilera waited two minutes, then headed out to talk to the VolatarA.

James Adams stepped up to the Tavir and the other Suvain. "Either the war is on, or it is off," he stated. "If it is on, agreements don't matter. If it is off, we need to sign an agreement with the Terrans right now. Our negotiating position will just get weaker and weaker as the threat of the VolatarA goes away."

The Tavir nodded, and TavirAyan asked all of the other Terran representatives to a nearby conference room. The two lawyers made a few final muttered comments, then called up a proposed treaty on a display. They started to explain the agreement when TavirAyan cut them off. "Just give us the general details", he commanded.

"The Suvain and Terrans agree to be at peace and independent of outside political control. Both are free to explore and colonize in any area not already claimed by the other. All international trade of the Terran race will be conducted by the Tavir Clan of the Suvain Empire. All international service agreements will be registered with the Tavir Clan. For its services, the Tavir Clan will receive 50% of all profits earned for the next 50 years. At the end of 50 years, the Tavir fee will drop by 2% each year. At the conclusion of the contract, the Terran Empire is free to trade as it chooses. There are lots of details and statements of good wishes, but that is the agreement in a nutshell."

Predictably, neither side was happy with everything they heard.

Predictably, the Suvain decided to be happy first. TavirAyan pointed out that the Terrans would outgrow the agreement someday, so putting an end date just encouraged the Terrans to live with the taxes, not grow too powerful and then throw the whole thing away. And he pointed out that 50% of the trade of a growing race was more gain than the Tavir could ever have imagined when they purchased the concession for this cluster. The Suvain were starting to head back out into the main hall when CE Aguilera returned. He gave a small nod to TavirAyan, who recognized good news.

The last race which still had to be convinced to let the Terran race survive was the Terrans. The agreement with the Suvain was immediately described as paying a 100-year mortgage on a house you already owned. When CE Aguilera got their attention and stated that the VolatarA were going to insist that the Terrans issue a formal apology and provide payment for all VolatarA expenses, there were immediately protests that the Terrans had nothing to apologize for, and that the VolatarA should be paying the Terrans, not the other way around. Finally CE Aguilera got them quiet.

"Arguing over who is in the right will not get us anywhere. I will personally make the apology. And if what I hear about a potential treaty with the Suvain is true, we can add any payment to the VolatarA to what we will pay the Suvain already, and let them forward it on. The dead fleet will be paid for and the payments will stop, and the Terran race will not. We need to remember why we are here."

"Maybe they should be paying us, not us paying them. But victory for the Terrans in this war will not be shown by how many planets we conquer. Victory in this war means that when everyone sits around carving up this cluster, we are sitting at the table with the others, not lying on the table as the main course."

"I am hearing statements from regional representatives that they do not have the authority to bind their governments to such financial costs. Neither do I. But we are going to walk out there and sign both treaties right now anyway. It could take months to try and decide who pays what and to who. And none of the other races would understand the delay. In two days, everything could have changed, and every alien out there could have decided they like the VolatarA now. So we are signing this treaty, today. If we wait, the human race might survive. If we sign now, the human race will survive. So we sign now."

After frantic preparations, the conference hall had been prepared for a dual signing ceremony. The audience was filing into the three rows of seats; on the platform in front of them a triangle of tables were waiting. Four Suvain were approaching the tables on the right, four VolatarA were approaching the tables on the left, and seven Terrans were walking up to the tables along the base of the triangle. Six sat down; CE Aguilera shepherded the others to their seats, and then walked past the table to the elevated podium beyond the tables. The Terran Councilor Extraordinaire walked up to where a holographic humanoid mouse usually invited people into the "galaxy's happiest place". When everyone was seated and paying attention, CE Aguilera started what he was hoping would be the Terrans' invitation into the galaxy's sentient community. He thanked everyone for attending, and then stated that the Terran wished to formally apologize to the Emperor of the VolatarA. He apologized for any offense that might have been given and assured everyone of the deep respect the Terrans felt for the Emperor. He expressed the deep regret of the Terrans at the loss of life the VolatarA had suffered due to the recent misunderstandings. He assured everyone of the Terran's willingness to pay for any damages that the VolatarA may have suffered, and for any cost the VolatarA might have incurred. He specifically mentioned that the costs of the VolatarA occupation of New Chicago would be reimbursed, and all costs associated with the return of the VolatarA garrison to VolatarA space. There was a bit of muttering from the VolatarA, as the future of New Chicago was described to the world before the VolatarA had fully adjusted to the idea of giving the planet back. Without interrupting the apology, the

VolatarA had little choice but to watch as the assembled races chose to consider the VolatarA silence as agreement. CE Aguilera admitted that as a young race, the Terrans might be unable to determine the true costs of the recent conflicts; he asked if the Zatheur, the NVs and the Jumanj might be willing to assist the Terrans in setting the size of the repayment to the VolatarA. There was a pause to look at the neutral powers; the VolatarA jumped in to assure the other three races that they would assist them in this task.

When the apology was over and the terms of the agreements had been described, the formal signing began. When the signing was over, the cheering began. Stephen and Darron were shouting with the rest, as Darron looked around at all of the crowd. Stephen saw Darron go silent for a minute. He looked at Darron, wondering what was wrong.

"Jon should have been here", Darron said. "He was the one who led us in and made all of this possible."

Stephen was silent as well, then gave a snort. "I would say the same about Captain Adams, but she sort of is." He pointed down to where James Adams was standing straight and still between the celebrating Suvain and the celebrating Terrans. Stephen then looked suspiciously at Darron. "Aren't you supposed to be thinking about Susan being here?"

Darron laughed, and the moment passed. "Always. But she will be seeing this soon. This broadcast will go up today, and be shown everywhere there is a Terran."

Darron never would have believed that the trip back was no longer than the trip to Loren Station. During the trip out, there had been the fate of humanity to consider. On the way back, there was an upcoming wedding to wait for.

Steven had no wedding to anticipate; he was having a great time meeting with Suvain, NVs, and even VolatarA, going over how each race wanted to be portrayed in his new imaginary world. His imaginary world was a lot closer to becoming real, as Jir-Sur-Radol had bought into the entire concept both figuratively and literally. The NV was about to become the very first non-Terran investor into a Terran company.

Steven could contact each race so easily because the ship was returning to Terra as part of a collection of nine ships from four different races. Two Suvain were returning; TavirAyan was going to be installed as the first Suvain ambassador to the United Governments. One VolatarA ship was coming to Terra to oversee the removal of the VolatarA wounded and prisoners. The VolatarA ships which had struck their colors had received emergency repairs, and were slowly moving out to join the returning multinational fleet. The NVs were heading to Terra as well. Their official purpose was to pay their respects to the Terran Government; many people suspected that the real purpose was to convince the Terrans to trade the entire planet for a handful of NV trinkets. Almost everyone who had met them were worried that the NVs might succeed.

In between preparing for compressed 8-second bursts to Susan, Darron spent the time playtesting Stephen's new game. This continued until their superiors noticed and returned both of them to physical training. Darron would have complained to Susan, but she was far enough along in recovery that she was busier than Darron.

As the days crawled by, Darron was informed that leave was delayed.

He was panicked at first, but was informed that he would be deposited in Albuquerque in plenty of time. The ships cruised past Mars without stopping; Darron pointed out Andy-B to Steve and MacDonald as they went by. MacDonald mentioned that perhaps Darron should spend a second or two of his message time sending a note to his family.

When the ships finally reached the Fleet Stations around Terra, there were a mob of 35 ships of all sizes and shapes converging on the stations to arrange for transport down to the planet. There had been a debate about whether to have a memorial for the lost or a celebration of the end of the war. Celebration won, with a concession to have a prayer for the dead somewhere near the beginning. The news of the conversion of a number of the Suvain had spread to Earth, so the celebration was planned as part of a service of thanksgiving at St. Paul's Cathedral in London. There were lines of people waiting to get down; the delegation was shipped straight to the front. The dropships landed and the passengers were unloaded into an underground station for a train to going the heart of the city. Steven was heading off to show

Jir-Sur-Radol the sights of the city. Darron was going to follow, but then he saw Susan Underwood waiting for them on the stairs to the exit.

Darron wasn't sure if he was supposed to walk or run forward and embrace his fiancé, so he just sort of awkwardly shambled forward. She waited for him to arrive, standing with the help of a cane. When he reached Susan, Darron realized that Soong and a dozen others were there as well. He stopped to greet them, and everyone laughed. Both groups globbed together, and slowly headed up the stairs to the outside. Darron was helping Susan up the stairs. Her recovery had progressed far enough that she could walk for short distanced unassisted, but did not seem to mind needing the help. There was a crowd moving up the stairs towards the outside, and a wind had picked up and was blowing down the stairs. When they were halfway up the tunnel, the colonial panicked. Darron nearly fell down the stairs, frantically grabbing for an imaginary air hose. Such a strong airflow could only mean there was a crack or even a breach in the station wall. Darron's eyes were wide, head turning frantically as he looked for some internal bulkhead that could be sealed. Everyone turned to look at him for a second, then Stephen realized what was wrong. He started laughing, and shouted "Breach", while waving his hands in the air. Darron looked around at everyone then stood still, holding onto the railing.

"It is called 'Wind'", pointed out Stephen.

"Wait – you have never felt the wind before?" asked Susan.

Darron was beyond embarrassment. Everyone was staring at him, and there was no hole to crawl into. "I thought that you said you had been outside before? On New Chicago?" Susan asked.

"I was outside", Darron protested.

"We took the undersea trip from the spaceport." Soong said. "You do realize that we were inside a closed ship the entire time?"

"We were still outside", Darron mumbled.

"Come with me", Susan commanded. She still had one of Darron's arms, and led him up the stairs. The entire group followed them as Darron slowly edged towards the glowing empty hole where the airlock should be. The entire group emerged into the sunlight, watching Darron slowly edge out of the tunnel and into the open city street. Slowly the colonial started breathing normally. There were laughs and cheers from the assembled crowd.

Darron looked around at the endless sky, the buildings receding off into the distance, and all of the people walking around, outside, without any exo- suit. On Mars, and on the *Persephone*, "Outside" had always been associated with death. He had seen movies where people had walked around in the open, but they had never felt quite real, until this moment. He spent the rest of the day walking the streets of the city with Susan. These were actually short walks ending in long rests, while Darron constantly turned to look at everything. Darron was standing in awe, looking at a flight of pigeons when a taxi drove up. Stephen and Jir-Sur-Radol got out. The taxi waited.

"We are here to pick you up for dinner", announced Stephen. "And then, you are wanted back in the hospital", he said to Susan.

"They fly so high", Darron said.

"Yes, they do. However, they are not edible, and dinner is." Stephen indicated the cab. All four got in, and the cab headed to an Indian restaurant. Jir-Sur-Radol had mentioned that most Terran food was a bit bland, and Stephen was looking for something he might like. Dinner turned into another adventure for Darron, who had been eating bland food for years. Dinner was paid for by Jir-Sur-Radol out of the credits he had made from the taxi ride.

He had attracted a number of taxis and pointed out how interesting it would be for future passengers to know that they were in the very same cab that was the first to ever carry a non-Terran customer. After the bidding war was over, the NV had pocketed 40 credits in return for using the taxi all day.

Susan was dropped off, and the other three headed to a Fleet dormitory for the night. It was a long night for Darron, who swore off spicy food forever. The next day everyone was gathered for the formal parade to St. Paul's. Terran and Suvain crews were on a formal march through the streets to the cathedral. They were joined by the paroled VolatarA, who were going to be formally released as part of the ceremony. There had been a lot of discussion on both sides about having the VolatarA participate in the events. On both sides, there had been worry that the VolatarA might be harassed or mocked. The Terrans finally had decided that if the VolatarA were mixed in with the others, things would probably be okay. Duleka had suggested to the VolatarA that they go ahead with the proposal. This would be a way to find out if the Terrans really intended to treat the war was over. The procession was also an opportunity - if the Terrans harmed or humiliated the VolatarA, it would give the VolatarA an excuse to break the treaty that the other races would probably accept.

The path chosen wound for two miles through the streets before reaching the cathedral. Each crew marched as a group, with Terran, Suvain, and VolatarA crews alternating or marching side by side. The full news of the VolatarA actions in New Chicago had not been widely reported, and most of the population of London were not personally connected to anyone on the colony. To the cheering crowd, the presence of the VolatarA marching to be formally exchanged was just another sign that the war was over. Nearly 40 Persephones had been gathered, following the Chief Engineer. He was the highest ranking Persephone left alive. Darron and Stephen marched in the parade; Susan had been taken to the cathedral to meet them there, as the walk was still too much for her.

The miles wound by, and then everyone came to a halt in front of the building. Steven and Darron were motioned forward to join the rest of the Terran delegation inside. The hall was filled with Terrans and Suvain and VolatarA, with a sprinkling of NV scattered through the room. There was a brief message declaring the end of the war, and a prayer of thanksgiving for the new peace. The VolatarA parolees were asked to stand. The current Chief of Admirals of the Combined Fleet, with the head of the VolatarA delegation standing by his side, declared all VolatarA prisoners to be formally exchanged, and now welcome guests of the Terran people. With the announcement, cheers broke out inside and outside.

After a semblance of order was restored, a group of representatives of the United Governments announced that formal invitations had been made to each of the other races to provide an ambassador in residence, to ensure that the new peace would be maintained, and to ensure that all races would have fair representation in their dealings with the Terrans. They were pleased to announce that the Suvain, the VolatarA, the Nemi-Vemzl, the Jumanj, and the Zatheur had accepted the Terran offer. TavirAyan was asked to stand, and The Tavir stood as well, stating that TavirAyan had expressed his willingness to represent the Tavir clan and the Empire. A formal statement of friendship form the Emperor's court was on its way, carried by an Imperial representative who would also take up residence as the Empire's ambassador. When the cheering had died down, the head of the VolatarA delegation was again introduced; he announced that VolatarA Borasal Kallim Duleka would be representing the Emperor. The commander of the NV trading ship that had first pulled up to Loren Station was now lifted into the position of ambassador to a newly-discovered race; he was already well on the way to becoming a very rich man.

The celebrations continued deep into the night, but for the Persephones they were briefly delayed. The Chief Engineer called everyone together, and announced that they would be receiving another notice asking them if they wished to volunteer for duty in space. At the statement, the survivors looked around, seeing again how few people were present, and how many were not just away, but gone. "Every Fleet is expanding as fast as they can build ships and train crewmen", the Chief Engineer stated. "Some of us are being promoted and reassigned", he continued, pointing to Soong. "Our beloved chaplain will be in command of one of the relief ships headed to New Chicago." There was cheering, and the Chief Engineer joined in the clapping. "Most of the rest of us are without a ship. However, I have been informed that I am to collect a crew to serve in a new ship scheduled for completion in one month. If any of you want to stay, I have arranged for either retirement from the Fleet, or good assignments planet-side. No one can say that you have not done more than your share already. If any of you wish to come, out of every Terran on every planet, I wish to offer you the opportunity first." There was more cheering, and caught up in the moment, lots of volunteering. "Take some time to think about it", the Chief Engineer stated. "Then let me know. If you are coming, you have a month's leave, and then don't be late.

Most of the rest of the crew will be brand new, and will need you to set an example."

Darron and Stephen were part of the delegation that had been at Loren Station, and might have been welcome targets for attention and the media,

but both wanted nothing less than attention and the media. Stephen found his way home, logged into his online game, and traded messages with scattered friends all around the planet until he finally was able to collapse and get some sleep. Darron met with Susan and they sat with MacDonald, GoDai, and several other Suvain. MacDonald had heard of Darron's outdoor adventure, and found a place to eat that had seats outside. Halfway through dinner, Susan mentioned how exciting it was to finally meet your fiancé after months apart, and have him spend his entire time watching pigeons. Everyone laughed, including Darron, who joined in while watching how the sunlight filed the bottom of a set of clouds as the sun sank. He looked around to see what people were laughing about and saw everyone looking at him. He wondered what he had done wrong, but Susan put a hand on his shoulder, and he wondered if he had done something right. This led to a discussion about Terran wedding customs, and GoDai mentioning that he had never seen one. GoDai was immediately invited, and before the meal was over, GoDai had changed his schedule, and was headed to Albuquerque in the morning.

Stephen, Darron, and GoDai travelled together on the sub-orbital shuttle the next day. After they had reached the North American southwest, no one they met had seen an alien before. Everyone stopped to stare as the Suvain marched by. Once they had arrived at the hotel, Darron immediately went back outside to look at the outdoors. He came back in in a few moments overheated and sweating; this was the first time he realized that the wonderful outside had no temperature controls.

There was a rehearsal that evening. The three found the location, and Darron started the uncomfortable process of meeting all of the bride's family. Stephen was setting up a video feed so that the service could be broadcast back to Mars. Darron's family was gathering for a celebration at Andy-B. The time delay was high enough that there was no way to have both groups really participate, but this way, at least the Masons could see what had happened.

When Darron, Stephen, and GoDai walked in, Soong was standing behind the podium, with Susan standing in front of him. She was talking with her family about what to do about the empty Maid-of-honor position. Susan hadn't lived in Albuquerque in years, and didn't have a convenient sister to dragoon into service. Darron walked up and was motioned by Soong to Soong's left. Stephen had failed in every effort to avoid being the best man; he walked up and stood behind Darron.

GoDai walked up and looked at the imbalanced group in front of him. He asked, "Why are there two on the right and one on the left?" Stephen is the best man who stands behind the groom, and they were still looking for the Maid-of-honor for Susan, GoDai was told.

GoDai stood, considering the empty space behind the unsupported Susan, and considering the statement that had come through his translation device – Susan should be supported by the "Made-of-Honor". He looked at Susan, straightened up and stated, "While TavirAyan is a true noble, and so has a more honest claim to be made of honor, I am a ranking member of the Tavir, and if you are need of a representative or ally, I would be glad to assist you."

There was a moment of confusion and buzzing as people considered this statement. Susan started to laugh, then recognized the translation mistake and stopped. She stepped up to GoDai and answered, "Thank you. I would be honored to have your assistance. You stand here", she said, pointing beside her.

In the morning, the group came together for the wedding. As the guests watched, the wedding party entered and stood before Soong. For the first time in Terran history, the Maid of Honor was wearing flexible composite armor, with a plasma gun at his belt, holding his bouquet of flowers at attention.

28 days later, Darron and Susan Mason met with Stephen Hunter the night before they reported for duty. There were other familiar faces

filtering into the Fleet station; Soong was not one of them. His new command had left 2 weeks previously for New Chicago. The VolatarA were leaving as expected, but much of what they were leaving behind was a wasteland. The colony had a little under 2 million survivors, and most were still at risk of starvation. The news had already spread that Soong had received an update from home. His father was dead, killed by the VolatarA when they shot every male in his town to ensure obedience from the women left alive. His mother had survived, and was awaiting her son's arrival. Steven had happier news – he had completed his prototype exploration game, and had turned it over to his newly-founded game company, where others would do all the tedious work of turning the prototype into a sellable product.

They all went outside one last time before bed. The next day, they were to report for transport to their new home, the *Phoenix*. The hull of the *Phoenix* had been constructed just before the first contact with the Suvain, and the frantic ship conversions that began soon afterwards. After the VolatarA defeat, building and conversion had not slowed down; the Combined Fleet had replaced the lost ships, and added 6 more to Terra's defenses. The *Phoenix* had was one of the first 8 Fleet ships that were not converted from a previous design, but had been built from the start to carry weapons. She had a larger arsenal than the *Persephone* had carried, and lots of internal strengthening. Salvage crews had also been at work going through the floating Terran wrecks and pulling out anything still useable. The captain of the *Phoenix* had requested that the salvage from the *Persephone* be assigned to his ship when possible. Much of the newly-added internal bulkheads had come from the metal recovered from the wreck, as well as miles of cabling, several large angulins, and the only undamaged wall section of the old bridge, which had been placed as the back wall of the bridge of the *Phoenix*.

As the salvage crews dissected the remains of the ship, they also had recovered personal items, and sometimes crewmen. Unclaimed items had been placed on display for any returning Persephone to identify. Susan and Darron had wandered through before dinner, and after a long month of joys, Darron had one more. An unfired AGM2 was lying on a table, marked as Owner: Unknown, Recovery Location: Auxiliary Controls. Darron snapped up his gun, and declared he was never going to space without it.

The next morning, Stephen Hunter, Susan Mason, and Darron Mason stood with 34 other ex-Persephones in front of their former chief engineer, now Captain Peter Washington. The 34 stood among 62 new crewmembers who were leaving the Terran system for the first time. They had already received their introductory briefing. The *Phoenix* was going with two other warships and five exploration ships to look for Intersections in a new region of space discovered by the Tavir, which the Tavir did not have the resources to search themselves. They were about to begin the first exploration performed by the Terrans since the war had begun. All searching operations were now to be performed in groups, with escort, now that the galaxy was a crowded place.

Captain Washington was standing on a podium to the left of the ramp leading into the transport that would take the crew to the waiting ship in orbit. The officers of the ship were standing by him; Stephen had wandered forward to look at the transport ship. Darron and Susan had come with him, and now all three were standing at the bottom of the entry ramp. The Captain was saying something, and as usual, Darron had lost the conversation. He was looking up at the open hatch in front of him. It did not look like a mouth to swallow him. It looked like a door to the outside. Not an outside that was a place of cold, emptiness, and death; an outside that was full of light, and opportunity, and nebulae, and dramatic singularities, and worlds for mining colonies, and worlds with outsides with air where birds flew, and possibly worlds with races of people no one had ever met. A long-lost statement from the old Chaplain Eisen to the young crew suddenly returned: "My time has already become the past, and a new day is soon coming – your time, the time when humanity takes its place among God's wider creation." Darron looked up when the sounds from the Captain stopped. The Captain was looking at him.

"Board", commanded Captain Washington.

Darron shifted his security gun to his right shoulder, took Susan's right hand with his left, looked across to Stephen next to her and nodded. They all stepped out together, heading up the ramp into the transport - the Lunatic Brigade leading the Terrans into the future.

445